The Ninao

Incident

The Ninao Incident

Renee Nielsen

Callaei Books

Published in New Zealand by Callaei Books (independent publisher)
callaeibooks.com

First published 2022

A catalogue record for this book is available from the National Library of
New Zealand.

The Ninao Incident (Kindall K series, Book 0)

ISBN-13 (paperback): 978 0 473 60911 5
ISBN-13 (hardcover): 978 0 473 60912 2
ISBN-13 (ePUB): 978 0 473 60913 9
ISBN-13 (Kindle): 978 0 473 60914 6

First printed in Australia and the United States of America

For Fatima

Author's note & content warning

The *12-Tau Ninao Kidnapping case* and the story revolving around it is entirely fictional, and any relation to actual events, persons and places mentioned herein is purely coincidental.

This story, as well as the *Kindall K* series as a whole, explores themes of realistically depicted or described experiences of trauma and PTSD (Post-Traumatic Stress Disorder). Of course, the personal experience of trauma varies from person to person, and one person's PTSD may look quite different from another person's PTSD. Nevertheless, the topic can understandably be a heavy one.

I write Yuuki's experiences of trauma and PTSD through my own experiences with trauma and Complex PTSD. While Yuuki's traumatic experiences are different from mine, I've tried my best to capture what sort of things Yuuki might be experiencing in terms of the psychological, emotional, mental, spiritual and physical sides of trauma as appropriate for this story, for Yuuki's experiences and for Yuuki's character. This is the same for the experiences of the Harrison family, too.

Although it is a fictional story, it is still a story describing a traumatic incident. Because of this, and primarily due to the nature of the story in general, this story may be a bit of a heavy read for some readers at times.

This story still deals with a lot of emotions and reactions that come with the human experience of trauma. It may be unsettling for some people to read. On the other hand, I hope that it can be even in the least bit cathartic for other readers who may have experienced, or be experiencing, similar things (with or without the presence of trauma in their lives). I've written this story wanting to describe the nature of trauma honestly, because I believe it is a topic that should be able to be discussed more openly – and of course, with the respect, seriousness, sensitivity and patience it is due.

In addition to a content warning for central themes of experiences of trauma and the constellation of symptoms that make up PTSD, I also want to warn for the passing of the Harrison family's old dog Ginger. Though this is not focused on, and happens in the passing of time during a time skip, I understand that such content may be upsetting for some (hence why I have mentioned it here).

This book was a somewhat difficult to write. But I'm really happy with how it has turned out. Reader, I hope you enjoy the book!

KINGDOM of ARKALA

Key: ▨▨▨ Native forest
Urbanisation

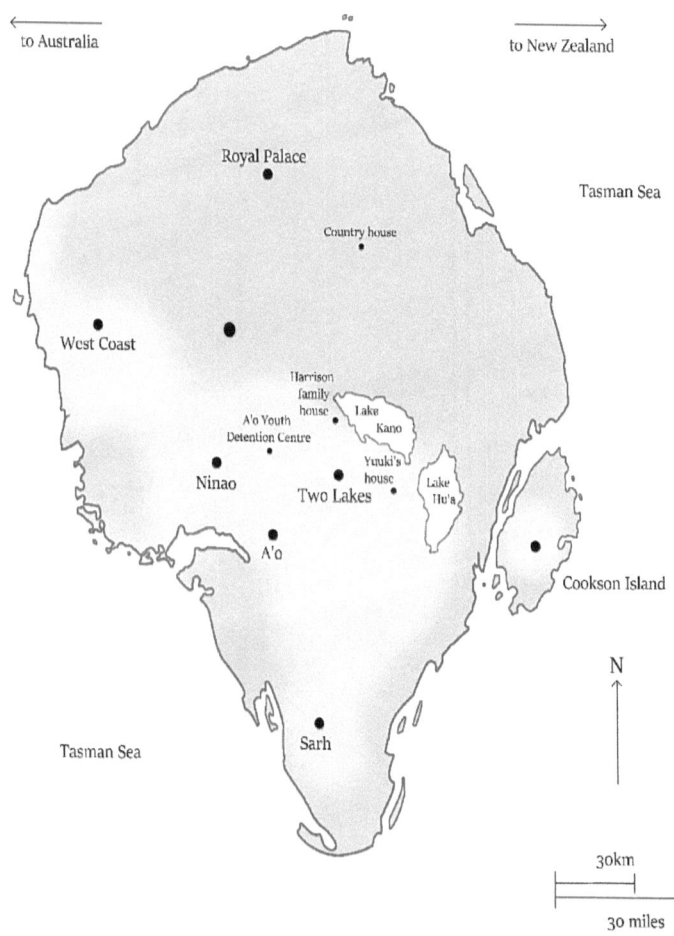

to Australia

to New Zealand

Royal Palace

Country house

Tasman Sea

West Coast

Harrison
family
house   Lake
A'o Youth   Kano
Detention Centre

Yuuki's
house   Lake
Ninao   Hu'a
Two Lakes

A'o

Cookson Island

N

Tasman Sea

Sarh

30km

30 miles

12-Tau Ninao Kidnapping:
The Incident

1

Yuuki could have noticed it, perhaps, had he been paying more attention: the subtle signs of danger, of something amiss, sitting in the carpark outside Ninao District Law Office. He'd noticed the newly planted native *amelia* flowers, in the roadside garden beneath the bare trees. He'd noticed that his tension headache – likely from stress, dehydration, and lack of sleep – hasn't been getting any better.

He ought to have paid more attention the cars without number plates sitting inside the north entrance.

Walking into the building, mind full of legal phrases and body exhausted from lack of rest, Yuuki isn't as wary as he should be, though. There is nothing concerning enough about the environment he's entered to warrant any cause of alarm, anyways. No sign of immediate danger. No hint at the upcoming kidnapping. No hint that Yuuki himself would be a target – if not *the* target of that kidnapping. The only suggestion that something isn't quite right, other than the cars, is how quiet the building is. The hallways are silent, bar the hum of the heating system against the winter temperatures outside. They're never usually this quiet during the

1

daytime.

People must be busy, is Yuuki's only thought towards it. If he's honest, he's relieved. It means not having to cross paths with anyone. Even though he's a judiciary officer himself – a security warden at a youth detention centre – and in uniform ready for work later on, it still makes him feel nervous entering a building full of authorities. He's done nothing wrong, not that he can think of. But still…

It doesn't shake the feeling of impending doom.

At the end of the hall is the office of lawyer and judge Timothy Harrison. Yuuki's friend, and the man with sufficient experience and expertise in legalities to help him set up the Youth Rehabilitation Trust – a public trust fund for incriminated youth caught up in the snares of Arkala's messed up national justice system. Alone, Yuuki's inexperience as a 24 year old security officer would not have been enough to see it through to this day. He has Timothy's 49 years of life experience and over 25 years in the justice field of work as both a lawyer and a judge to thank for it. Without him, the Youth Rehabilitation Trust would just be an idea that would only ever be something that Yuuki wished for.

Maybe he shouldn't have wished for it like he did.

Yuuki knocks on the doorframe. "I'm here."

Two people in the room glance in his direction. Timothy stands behind his desk, in the middle of taking a drink of coffee. He waves with his free hand. Timothy's son, Joshua, is here, too, sitting on the couch.

"Hi, Yuuki," Joshua says for both of them.

Timothy sets down the cup. "You made it."

Yuuki enters, and twists his satchel bag around to pull out the signed document in his bag. "Sorry, I'm later than I said I'd be. I missed the train I was intending to catch. But yes, I am here now." He nods at Joshua. "And you're here, too. Off on semester break?"

Joshua nods back. "Study leave. Final exams are in a couple of weeks."

"He got here yesterday," Timothy comments.

"Ah, I see," Yuuki says. "How's university going?"

"Well, I'm passing – so that's a good thing." Joshua leans back into the couch. "But the stuff's a lot more theory-heavy there than I thought it was going to be. So here's to hoping life throws no curveballs between now and exam week because I really need to cram."

Yuuki slips out the documents he's looking for. He offers a friendly, sarcastic smirk. "Looks like you're super keen on it."

Joshua grunts. "Gotta take study breaks to prevent burnout."

"I'm not arguing with that one."

Looking at the two versions of the same document in hand, Yuuki hands the one with pen inked signature on it over to Timothy. He keeps the photocopy.

"Thanks," Timothy says. "Your senior officer at your work was fine with signing it as a witness for you?"

"Yeah, it was no trouble."

"Cool."

Yuuki notices a pile of papers on Timothy's desk. All of them are related to the 8-Tau A'o Fire case. "You still working on that?"

Timothy glances in the direction that Yuuki is looking. His expression is tight. "Yeah... revisiting it. I'm not sure I'm happy with the verdict it was given back then."

The A'o Fire case of four years ago, on a night towards the end of May. Arkala lost an entire firefighting crew fighting a blaze sprung from a gas leak in a pipe. That incident was one of Timothy's first cases as a judge.

Yuuki considers the pile of papers. "You're still thinking it might've actually been arson, then."

Timothy frowns. "Hmm. Though that might be just a gut feeling. Even with reopening the case, I haven't found anything solid to follow that up – which is another problem, if my gut feeling is correct." He sighs. "But that's that, and this is this. For now, let's finish setting up something we can do."

Yuuki studies the copy of the Youth Rehabilitation Trust framework in his hands. It's essentially all set up and ready to go. But for some reason, he has a gut feeling that something isn't quite right.

It makes him nervous.

Scanning over the lines, he reviews the words he stayed up all night reviewing, tweaking typos and reconsidering wording where ambiguity could cause misinterpretation...

Like I haven't reviewed it so many times already.

Yuuki adjusts his coat to distract himself. The coat feels like an extra layer of protection against the nervousness he can't shake. It's a little warm in the office with the heater on. But he also can't be bothered taking his coat off. He'd only need to put it back on soon again anyways.

"Looks good to me," Timothy remarks from his office chair.

Yuuki wants to believe the same. They've put a lot of work into preparing for this – it has taken *months* to get all the legalities of this prepared. The last thing he wants for this is to see the potential of it go to waste – especially when he's not the only one who's worked so hard to set it up, and when he's not the only one who will be at a loss if it fails.

Timothy's mouth quirks. "You can relax, Yuuki. It's already been approved and all."

Yuuki grimaces. "I know, I know. But today's the official establishment day, so…"

All going well, from today onward, youth caught up in the snares of the current Arkala judicial law will have the option to seek rehabilitation as an alternative to extended lengths of imprisonment time. Currently, there's no such option in Arkala. There's also no support in place for youth in post-release. Both Yuuki and Timothy have seen the consequences of these things – it's what moved them to create the Youth Rehabilitation Trust that will finally – officially – come into existence as of today.

But they've taken a risk in setting this up. While it might be intended for good, Arkala's current usurper leader, Taularh, may view it as something else. A threat, for instance, in the form of allowing a loosening of punishments served in the name of justice. A stance of disagreement with Taularh's rules. An expression of retaliation, or uprising.

With a glance at Timothy, he wonders if his older friend is feeling the same. It's not hard to tell he's also been staying up poring over the details like Yuuki has. Last night was probably the worst of the overthinking things for Yuuki. Timothy surely hasn't had it easy with the overthinking things either. Between Timothy's work background as a lawyer-turned-judge and Yuuki's new career as a security officer, they're both more worried about not having thought over things *enough* than having thought about it too much.

Still, it's better to be prepared for what could go wrong in the first place than not be prepared at all. Even though they can't predict everything that might go wrong, the last thing they want right now is to run in trouble because they didn't explain things correctly. They especially don't want to get in trouble with higher authorities over misinterpreted wording when all they're trying to do is help the incarcerated youth that Timothy sees in court that Yuuki often ends up meeting later on his shifts as a warden at the youth detention centre.

They're trying to reduce trouble with the Youth Rehabilitation Trust, not incite in.

But Timothy is right – The Youth Rehabilitation Trust proposal passed all the legal checks, and today's simply the designated day they'll make it official. It's done. Approved. Signed, albeit with Timothy's messy scrawl of a signature and Yuuki's scribbled 高橋悠希 meant to read 'Takahashi Yuuki' in Japanese.

Timothy smiles wearily. "You can get some proper rest tonight, Yuuki."

Yuuki hadn't realised he'd been staring intensely, yet spaced out, at the copy of the paperwork that Timothy is holding. "Can I, though? It'll get busy from here on out."

"You can at least try to catch up on all the hours of sleep you've been missing," Timothy says, getting up to scan the documents. "If you can try not to let that background anxiety get to you."

Yuuki laughs dryly. "That would be ideal."

He doesn't need to look in the mirror to realise the tiredness settling in. As if to further the point about needing rest, his stomach grumbles.

Joshua, Timothy's son, takes one look at Yuuki's face from where he's perched on the arm of the office's couch and laughs. "Seriously," Joshua says, grinning. "If there were an apocalypse or something to happen right now, you'd be screwed."

Yuuki grunts. "Well, let's hope an apocalypse *doesn't* happen."

For everyone's sake here. If an apocalypse or something did happen, that mind render their efforts all for naught.

Joshua gets up and stretches. "How long are you guys going to be with the finishing up?"

The scanner whirs. "Just printing another paper copy to keep in the office," Timothy says. "Other than that, I just want to check that the files uploaded alright and then I think we're pretty much done here."

"Didn't you say you had to submit it to Taularh's administration?"

"The confirmation of establishment?"

"Yeah. Or whatever it was."

"Ah, I can do that later on. They already know from the proposal that today's when it's officially done and ready. The confirmation thing is just to, well, confirm that we are going ahead with it as per the plan."

Yuuki nods in agreement.

"So yeah, we're about done here," Timothy concludes.

Joshua gives a thumbs up. "Okay. In that case, I'm gonna quickly go to the bathroom. I'll be right back."

Timothy snorts. "Nice to know."

On his way out, Joshua waves his hand. "Any time."

In spite of the light-hearted joking, Yuuki can't help but feel off.

It almost feels like the air is holding its breath, if that makes any sense. Nothing might be happening, but it feels like that – like Arkala as a nation itself is holding its breath, waiting for something to happen. Whether that something is good or bad, or an uncertain mix of both, Yuuki isn't sure.

It just feels like there's a certain tension in the air.

Yuuki lets out a sigh. Maybe he's just stressed. *Yes, it's most likely stress.*

From here on, the Youth Rehabilitation Trust is something they'll both be responsible for managing. While Timothy's agreed to help him with the accounting and legal side of things, it'll still be a lot of additional stress to the job he's already got.

Still…realistically, it goes hand in hand with the job he's got. Working at a youth detention centre isn't easy. Seeing those youth struggle with getting out of the entangling snares of the justice system with little support is even less easy.

And that's why I'm doing this.

Timothy, once a lawyer and now a judge, also has his reasons: he's often now a judge of many youth court cases. As someone with two children, Joshua, who's 20, only a few years younger than Yuuki, and Samantha, who's 16, it's hard for Timothy to take those trials and not think, sometimes, that the youth being trialled are sometimes the same age as his daughter.

The Youth Rehabilitation Trust matters to them because of such things – and because they know the restricting nature of the current

Arkala justice system, and it frustrates them when they haven't been able to do anything about it.

Until now. They've been able to create something that might help with that. And not only does that matter to them, but it may matter a lot more than they truly realise to future recipients of the Trust.

"You're deep in thought."

Yuuki blinks himself back to the here and now. Timothy is standing over his office desk, frowning at the computer screen as he moves the mouse. Yuuki sees the moment Timothy gives a small self-satisfied nod and his gaze flicks to the wall beside them.

"There's a clock on the computer," Yuuki says, amused. He glances at the clock on the wall himself.

It's 12.34pm.

Timothy huffs. "The one on the wall is bigger, and I get tired of reading electronic words and numbers."

"Fair enough."

Outside the room, the hallway is very quiet. The door rests ajar.

"Once Joshua gets back," Timothy says, "how about we go out and get some food or something?"

Yuuki tilts his head. "Uh, yeah? I have work later on, though. So I won't be able to stay for –"

The door bangs wide open.

Yuuki flinches. Unknown people storm in. Two, three, four of them, dressed with their identity obscured. Wearing masks, but not the kind worn in cold and flu season.

Timothy watches them warily, alarmed. Frozen behind his desk.

9

A cold weight sinks into Yuuki's body.

Two of them head for Timothy. The other two have their eyes locked on Yuuki.

Timothy glances between the divided groups. "Hey, what are you –?"

Yuuki's on his feet and backing away before his mind can catch up with him. In his peripheral, he sees the other two advancing on Timothy. They don't answer Timothy's unfinished question.

If it were two-on-one, I might be able to help him. But as it is...

The first engagement in interaction is Timothy tearing a heavy old dictionary off the bookshelf behind him and launching it at the two approaching him. The two step sideways. The book collides with the wall with a thud, and the floor.

The two step forward undeterred.

While Yuuki's distracted, a fist swings towards his face. Yuuki sucks in a breath, dodges.

Noise. Timothy shouts. Two seconds later, it's turned into a muffled yell.

Adrenaline spikes in Yuuki's blood. He catches the next punch, grabs the person's wrist and yanks them to the side. The momentum has him stumbling sideways along with them – causing him to step right in front of the other person of the pair.

Oh shoot.

Before Yuuki can react, he's pulled into a chokehold from behind by the first guy. He staggers, thrown off balance. Caught off guard. He scrabbles at the guy's arm but it's useless. His face strains. The pressure on around his neck won't ease. Yuuki whimpers.

Think!

He drops his weight so that his attacker is forced to drop or bend or let him go. It works. Barely, because the guy is strong and clearly trained, and doesn't want to let him go. But it works – allowing Yuuki a brief second to tear himself out of the chokehold with a desperate gasp.

He doesn't get far. As he stands, a hand snatches up his wrist and *twists* it. Yuuki cries out. His legs are kicked out from under him and he falls. Before his knees hit the ground, however, he's tugged back upright by his arm. Yuuki's arm is twisted behind his back, then, and then his clothing is grabbed at the collar, and then he's yanked backwards. Off balance again, his knees buckle. Pain lurches through his twisted arm. He grits his teeth against a cry. He struggles to regain some footing and remain upright.

Yuuki makes the mistake then of looking past his own assailants. In front of him, he can only watch as Timothy's shoved into a bookcase. Timothy's grabbed, and a second later, is pulled forward. He's cut down with a hand to the back of his neck.

Yuuki chokes on a breath.

Timothy drops. He doesn't move. Knocked out. Collapsed on the floor.

The first guy who attacked Yuuki saunters up to Yuuki again, blocking his view. Yuuki's mind is frozen. He's too fixated on what's happening behind.

The other two assailants approach Timothy where he's lying helpless on the ground. Yuuki's eyes widen.

Ti –

11

Pain erupts in Yuuki's temple. Black explodes in his vision, and he meets the same fate as Timothy.

2

Joshua pauses as he exits the bathroom. He stays still for a couple of moments, but whatever he thought he heard somewhere else in the building has gone quiet.

Someone must be moving furniture or boxes of paperwork around.

Dismissing the concern, he makes his way back to his father's office. The bathroom is further down the hallway than he thought. Joshua has been here before, once or twice, and yet he still almost managed to get lost. Fortunately – or not so fortunately – he doesn't need to worry about getting lost on the way back.

People are coming out of Timothy's office as he nears. A whole group, dressed in casual black, navy and dark green clothing. At a glance, they could be mistaken for a group of clients – and at first, that's what Joshua automatically assumes.

That is, until he realises that their identities have been purposefully disguised, and that Yuuki and Timothy are being dragged out along with them.

Joshua stares. Before he can mentally make the call, his feet come to a halt. Fear rushes over him, adrenaline. He stands stock still, in the hallway where he is.

They haven't seen him. *They haven't seen me. I should stay out of sight, right?*

Both Yuuki and Timothy are slumped in the hold of their captors. Neither of them are fighting back. They're just…being dragged off, both of them flanked on both sides with their arms locked in a firm grip and their feet trailing on the ground behind them…

Call the police, let the Peace Forces handle it. I'm not the PF, I can't –

But something tells him that if he doesn't do something, he might never see his father and Yuuki again.

That scares him more than doing something stupid does.

Joshua hears that word 'stupid' playing in his own voice over and over in his head. He screams it at himself internally but runs in the direction of his father's receding figure anyways. Yuuki's shoes have already disappeared around the corner. He picks up the pace, runs with his knees high to gain more speed.

Then he's at them. He charges into the nearest group – the two who have Timothy. Really, it's Timothy who he charges at, hoping that his momentum will be enough to shove himself between the two masked people and pull his father from their grip.

He barrels into them. The impact hurts. Hissed exclamations follow him to the ground. Joshua twists around, and looks up. He finds the attempt half worked – one of the people lost their grip on Timothy's left arm. But that's as far as his luck goes.

Up ahead, one of the men holding Yuuki curses.

"Go on ahead!" The one of the two still grasping Timothy's arm yells out. "We'll deal with this one."

The two pairs of footsteps further down the hallway start up again.

Joshua scrambles to his feet in time to see them moving again, Yuuki firmly in their grasp.

A hand clamps down on Joshua's shoulder. He lets out a shout of alarm as he's shoved backward. His back hits the wall.

Before him, Timothy's hauled up over the shoulder of the stockier person here. Joshua lets out a breath and narrowly dodges a fist to the head.

"Is anyone here?!" Joshua shouts. "Someone help!"

There's no time to figure out an action plan. It doesn't take much for him to get himself caught, backed against the wall as he is. He knew this might happen – would probably happen – and yet it alarms him nonetheless. Joshua struggles, but he's not as strong as the person he's wrestling with. He's not as skilled – at all. He tries all sorts of tricks, but his play fights with Sam and or Timothy never prepared him for this. He kicks at the person's knees, but it has little effect. His own legs are swept out from under him then. And then the hands descend on his jacket, jerk him upright, and start tugging him forward.

Towards the door down the hallway – the one that his father's currently being carried to, and the one that Yuuki was last seen being pulled out of a minute ago.

There's two cars. Neither have number plates. The one closest is the one that Joshua and Timothy are being forced towards. A door slams shut. Joshua's attention snaps in that direction. The other car, the one parked in front, is now already pulling away from them.

Outside, the sunlight is bright and warm. The day's atmosphere is almost happy. But Joshua only feels sharp contrasting terror.

Not minding the other car leaving, the person holding Timothy grunts with the effort of keeping Timothy upright. Awkwardly, he opens the back door. Joshua's pulled away, around to behind the car. In front of him, he watches as Timothy's manhandled into the backseat. Essentially just thrown in. The boot is then opened, blocking Joshua's view, and Joshua himself is thrown into the car.

He barely has time to tuck his legs in before the arm extended up to the raised boot lid is the last thing he sees before he's slammed into darkness.

Joshua's heartbeat is rapid. He can feel the vibrations of the boot shutting still. There's more slamming – of car doors. He feels the vibrations throughout his whole body. The car shifts – presumably with whoever shifting around inside, moving Timothy around. Muffled exclamations reach his ears. He can't distinguish the words but they're from voices he doesn't recognise.

The engine revs.

And then the car starts moving.

Joshua's eyes are slowly adjusting to the dimness. His other senses hone in on everything around him. The petrol fumes. The vibrations. The sounds of the unknown voices, and the car *vroon*-ing and the road speeding away beneath the tyres.

His hands are clammy. His arms are stiff, too tense. Held in front of him like he's ready to cradle his head, braced for impact.

The car swerves left and right.

Abruptly stops, maybe for traffic lights. The sounds of other vehicles around get louder. The smell of gasoline gets stronger.

Joshua swallows. He should call for help, but he can't get himself to. All he can do is stare at the shut lid of the boot in front of him, and mentally prepare himself for when his body's going to get jolted in its direction when the car moves again.

If he screamed right now, would anyone hear him? What about Timothy – can anyone see him in the back of the car right now? Maybe, for the first. Probably not, for the latter.

Then I should try the first.

He knows that if he does, the other people in the car will hear him. That might end badly. But they won't want to stop to get him to shut up, will they?

Okay, I'll just do it –

By the time he opens his mouth to shout, the car starts forward again.

What do I do? Is there really nothing I can do? If I can't do anything – I can't do anything! – then there's nothing, and we're screwed. All of us are screwed. They've got Dad, and Yuuki, and now me, and I should've called the darn PF instead of trying to solve things on my own like that.

It's a terrifying kind of fear that overwhelms him. It's filled with adrenaline and helplessness like Joshua's never been acquainted with before.

He'd had the opportunity to do something – but it had failed. Even now, perhaps he's the only one who can do something since both Timothy and Yuuki have those people right with them.

But Joshua left his phone in his coat, and he's not wearing that coat right now. He'd taken it off in Timothy's office. Had he thought about it, he could've run in to get it before attempting to stop the kidnapping.

17

He hadn't thought, though. And now he's been kidnapped himself.

Somehow, it's that thought – that realisation in words that he's been kidnapped – that leads him to the one idea that could save them.

The tail-lights. This car has taillights that can be kicked out.

In the boot somewhere, there's likely to be an emergency release cable. If Joshua were desperate enough, he'd look for it right away. But judging by the pitch and timbre of the road, the car is travelling far too fast to escape out of – safely – that way. Even just opening the boot could be a costly mistake. All it would take is for the car to abruptly brake or turn and Joshua could be sent flying out onto the road, and tumbling straight into road burns and oncoming traffic.

Yeah, no. Definitely no. Let's not do that.

And so he crawls. Half-crawls, half-shifts around in the limited space of the boot to angle himself in the right direction. The interior carpet is coarse on his hands. He realises soon enough that kicking forward or straight down isn't going to work well. Not when he's stuck lying on his side like this.

Which means, in that case, he's going to have to kick backwards.

Joshua turns onto his other side. Now facing the back of the rear seat makes the space he's got feel even smaller. *Don't think about it. Just focus on kicking.*

He shifts backward, to the side. Aiming for the right taillight, with his right leg. Anchoring himself with his left leg against the carpet, he pulls his right knee forward and then *kicks*.

It takes a few goes. It takes putting his whole body into the motion. But on the fifth attempt, his foot goes through.

The taillight has successfully been kicked out.

Joshua inhales sharply. *The next one. Do the next one.*

He shuffles around, repositioning himself for the left taillight. He hits his head on the top of the boot in the process and grits his teeth against the pain. He's shaking slightly now, and the feeling of panic is rising with the fear that this might be the last real chance of escape they get. Because of it, it takes seven kicks this time.

But with five kicks and seven, both taillights are kicked out.

Joshua doesn't delay any longer. He crawls around so that he can reach the hole with his hand. He presses up against the front of the boot and shoves his arm through the hole. And waves.

He doesn't know if anyone's even following. He's tempted to yell, but that'll only alert his own captors or annoy them. He doesn't know what they'll do – maybe they'll pull over on the side of the road and threaten him with harming Timothy. Maybe they won't, maybe they'll just drive until they get wherever they're going. But Joshua doesn't want to risk it.

He withdraws his hand and peers through hole. *Well, there's people at least.* He puts his hand back out, waves. Tries to keep his desperation under control. He feels sick. Dizzy. On the verge of panicking – *really* panicking. He's never known this kind of panic. It's scary.

For a while – for what is a hopeless while – nothing changes. There's no change in the speed of the car. No swerving or loud curses from inside.

Then the car speeds up.

Joshua's thrown backwards as the car swerves around a sharp bend in the road. His wrist bangs into the frame of the car. He lets out a yelp.

And then he hears it – sirens.

In the distance, they sound.

There's a loud curse from inside the car, accompanied by a lot of frustrated yelling. Joshua picks up the words *'how the hell did they get onto us?'* The nervous excitement that spreads through him – a strange mix of adrenaline and triumph – is greatly welcomed.

And then all of a sudden the car slows and jolts to a stop.

Car doors slam. Footsteps crunch on roadside gravel, and there's shouting. Joshua braces himself for the boot to open, to be hauled out, but no noise even comes near the boot. In fact, aside from the car still running and the incoming PF vehicle, there's no noise at all.

Joshua wonders about the car being left running. *Did they really just abandon it?* The sirens sound louder, and louder. There's the sound of a vehicle pulling up behind them.

Through the hole of the missing taillight, Joshua can see flashes of blue and red. He breathes quickly, sinks down on his forearms.

A door opens. Footsteps approach, crunching over roadside gravel.

Joshua holds his breath. *It looks like the PF, it sounds like the PF, but –*

A knock on the boot startles him. "Arkala Peace Forces. Stay calm. We're here to rescue you."

Joshua's not sure whether he feels relieved or not. The way his heartbeat is… and the way he's not sure whether he should believe this to be a rescue or a 'kidnapping: part 2'…

The boot lid clicks, and is opened. Joshua flinches. Light floods in.

Joshua squints. He reactively tenses at the silhouette of a person blotting out a decent portion of the view outside. But it's not one of the men who kidnapped him. It's a person in uniform, wearing a vest and a concerned expression.

"It's okay," the person says. "I'm with the PF."

A Peace Force officer is standing there.

"Are you able to get out okay?" they ask. With one gloved hand braced against the side of the boot, they extend their other non-gloved hand out to Joshua.

At a loss for words, Joshua simply accepts the hand – or rather, lets them grasp his hand and pull him forward. The open surroundings of *outside the boot* greet him. Joshua lets the PFO help him out of the boot. It's awkward, and he's not feeling right. But being able to sit upright and straighten his legs out again is such a good thing. The open space around him is so much better than the cramped box-like space of the boot.

When his feet touch the ground, Joshua realises he's shakier than he'd like to admit. He looks around. They're pulled over on the shoulder of a highway. Joshua doesn't recognise where they are straight away. But then he realises, if the nearby city buildings are anything to go by, that they're still in the Ninao district. The sight of the road makes sense now.

They haven't travelled far. *We weren't taken far.*

A relief, but the two people who took them are nowhere to be seen.

Glancing at the front of the car, the engine still running but no one sitting in the driver's seat, it's not hard to tell that they fled – likely into the bush growing on this side of the road. It's the only real direction to run and hide in.

From there, though...? That's as far as Joshua's thoughts will go.

"There's another person in the vehicle."

Someone else's voice sounds from behind. Joshua turns to see PFO's

21

partner peering into the window of the back of the car.

Joshua swallows. *Dad. Oh, thank God they didn't take him with them.* The though hadn't occurred to him until now – that when the kidnappers fled, they might have grabbed Timothy out of the car and taken him with them.

A radio bleeps. The PFO describes the situation, though Joshua misses most of what is said. He's distracted by the PFO putting on a pair of disposable gloves. It occurs to him why both PF officers are wearing them when the PFO in front of him opens the back door and scans the rest of the interior.

Joshua tries to remember if the kidnappers themselves had been wearing gloves. He thinks they were. It makes sense that they had been – surely they wouldn't have been so stupid as to get their fingerprints all over stuff after going to such an effort to successfully pull of a kidnapping at a law office.

A groan brings Joshua back to awareness of what's happening in front of him. His father is being carefully helped out of the car, the PFO's hands on Timothy's upper arms to support and guide him out. Joshua sees why. There's rope around his wrists, tying them together behind his back. And when he stands and turns to face the scene around him, he looks dazed.

Timothy sees Joshua then, and the confusion and alarm on his face turns into something more like the beginning of emotional shock settling in.

"What's going on?" Timothy asks, uncertain. His face is pale.

The PF officer who pulled him out of the car keeps an eye on Timothy's expression. "Kidnapping, by the looks of it."

They're both walked over to the PF vehicles. Away from the abandoned car that's still running, and whatever threat it may contain. The doors are left wide open.

"How many people were there in that vehicle besides yourselves?" the PFO asks. "Friendly or otherwise?"

Joshua shivers. It's colder outside than in the office. "Um…two, I think." *I didn't see anyone else.* "Not friendly."

An army knife appears in the PFO's hand. Joshua didn't even see them grab it. The knife is used quickly, and Timothy's hands are cut free of the rope. Slowly, like a delayed reaction, Timothy brings his arms around in front of him.

"So there's no one missing from this vehicle, is that correct? Besides the two people?"

Timothy's frowns and blinks hard. "Yes…"

The PFO nods. They continue, their eyes flicking between Timothy and Joshua but lingering on Timothy's face as though noting something. "Are you able to describe the two people for us? What they were wearing, their build, any distinguishable features…?"

"…they were wearing black," Joshua offers. "And masks." *I think one sounded female, but I'm not sure.* He voices this thought of his, just in case.

Timothy raises his hand to his face, dazed. His fingers find a place on the back of his neck that makes him wince. "They were prepared – and I think trained in some kind of combat skills. They subdued us pretty quick."

"Were you knocked out?" the PFO asks.

Both Joshua and Timothy nod. Joshua inclines his head in Timothy's

23

direction. "He was. They didn't do that to me. I…they already had their hands full, I guess."

The PFO nods after them. They turn to their radio to report the few details they've gained. Among the words spoken, 'possible concussion' catches Joshua's attention. *Ah.* Joshua realises now why the PFO has been glancing at Timothy's face, monitoring his expression.

That's not to say they're neglectful of Joshua's outward appearance and behaviour, though. The PFO steps away, scanning their surroundings and still talking on the radio as they go, and then return with a blue blanket. It's Joshua who receives it. The look in the PFO's eyes when they give it to him suggests that the blanket is a necessary precaution and not a mere offer of comfort. Still, Joshua doesn't know what to do with it. He just stares at it blankly for a few seconds, before the PFO grimaces then eases it from his grasp to wrap it around his shoulders.

Even without a concussion, Joshua's in a similar shaken up state as his father – whether he's able to admit that or not.

"Am I right in presuming you're family, you two?" the PFO asks.

Timothy looks at Joshua. Like he's forgetting something – not about being Joshua's father, but about something else. "Yeah."

"Well, your son here kicked out the taillight, and flagged us," the PFO says, taking Timothy's concussed delayed reaction and response times in stride. They fish another blanket out of the car, unfold it and drape it over Timothy's shoulders in the same way as they'd done for Joshua. "Highway patrol. We were on lookout in regard to another case. We weren't exactly expecting this sort of thing out on duty today, that's for sure."

Not that it *should* be something expected, but that's beside the point.

Since the fumes from the exhaust of the idling kidnapper's car are becoming an environmental and human health risk, the PFO carefully approaches, does a quick check and turns it off. Nothing explosive happens. The humming of the car shuts off.

Timothy frowns at the red lines wrapped around his wrists. He pulls the cuffs of his sleeves up so that he can rub them a little.

"We've called an ambulance. They're on their way. In the meantime, we'll stay here with you. Can I have your names, please?"

"Timothy Harrison. And Joshua Harrison. But, uh…what about…" Timothy trails off, casting a nervous glance out at the bush on this side of the road.

"My partner is calling for backup," the PFO says. "Once they arrive, we'll scour the area and see if we can find the people who took you. Since there's no one missing, we can wait until then. Do you know if they were armed?"

Beneath his breath, Timothy mumbles, *"Missing…"*

Joshua looks uncertainly at his father. "I'm not sure."

Timothy looks up. "'m not sure, either. They attacked us without weapons."

The other PF officer looks over Timothy and Joshua, and then glances at his partner before addressing whoever he's on the phone with again. Both PFOs exchange information, and Timothy and Joshua's names get passed on along with what information they've currently been able to give.

As he's listening to it, Joshua's starting to feel colder. Displaced. He wraps the blanket around his shoulders a little more.

Why do I feel like we're forgetting to tell them something important?

"Okay." The PFO nods. "Do you have any idea who it was who took you, or where they might have been taking you to?"

Timothy shakes his head. He winces. "No idea."

"They just – " Joshua starts. He swallows. "We were just at the office. Dad's office."

"I'm a judge at Ninao District Court," Timothy explains.

"There were four of them. I don't know what they were doing. I went to the bathroom, then when I came back, I saw them being taken away."

The PFO notes this. "When you say 'them'…was there someone else in the office besides you?"

Timothy's lips part. But instead he turns to Joshua, horror creeping into his eyes. He looks around. Runs a hand through his hair. "What happened to…? Is he not here?"

Realisation dawns. Joshua gets what they've been missing. For all their talk of 'us' getting attacked or 'them' getting taken, they've been forgetting to mention one very important thing: the name of a third person, unaccounted for.

Timothy's eyes are wide. He glances around, as though his anxious thought will be answered, and quelled, by a sight or sign around them. It is not.

Joshua hadn't wanted to think about it.

"Where's Yuuki?"

3

"*Where… you guys at?*"

"…pulled over… highway. Why, what's up?"

"*Urgh, we have a problem…away.*"

"What?"

"*…out…light…call the PF.*"

"…we've still got Taka…"

"*It…we wanted,…operation is already…*" A sigh. The phone speaker crackles. "*…vehicle will have been identified by now. Are you…pursued?*"

"…wouldn't count on it lasting. Do you want us to – oh, hang on, I think he's waking up."

A noise of a glovebox opening. A rustle of clothing. Yuuki's too dazed to interpret what it means. Pain pulses in his head. Throbs.

"Don't breathe it in. Keep it over his face."

Something – *cloth* – is pressed over his nose and mouth. The normal air morphs into something chemically pungent. Through the pain and confusion in his head, Yuuki registers that he needs to get away.

But he can't get himself to move, and the cloth is held firmly in place.

"*Do you want us…drop…somewhere?*"

Yuuki's thoughts grow foggy. Foggier. Overwhelmed.

"...*it...we...back...*"

"Wait, there's..."

"..."

Yuuki groans. Too much fog and... confusion and....feeling ill to fight through.

"...there."

"..."

"..."

4

Joshua watches his father sitting on the edge of the floor at the back of an ambulance that's arrived, a blanket over his shoulders. How Timothy's fingers keep finding the reddened indents wrapped around his wrists. The tries not to think about the fact that his father was nearly – was just – kidnapped in broad daylight in front of him.

And I nearly missed it. I nearly missed the opportunity to try to save them.

After a moment, Timothy senses himself being watched and meets Joshua's eyes. There's an unsettling blankness to that gaze.

"Yuuki is the other person who was with you?" asks the PFO with them. "Or who you saw being taken?"

"Yuuki," Joshua says, distracted. He belatedly nods. "Uh, Yuuki Takahashi. H-he was with us. But they took him. They…I saw them taking him out the door. Ahead of Dad. I think they put him in a car, too, like us. I heard one leave when they were taking us out to this one."

The information really settles in then – and the scene replays in his mind with that additional knowledge. How had it not crossed his mind back at the carpark outside the office?

The car that left before them – that's the one that had Yuuki in it.

And now we have no idea where he is.

Perhaps the scarier thought is the one that is subsequent. *Or if we'll ever see him again, in the same state, or if at all.*

Could Joshua have tried to save them both? He barely managed to save his father – and himself. And even then, it was realistically the highway patrol who saw them who saved them.

But Yuuki doesn't have anyone to kick out the taillights for him.

Joshua's stomach churns. *We got free. But what's happened to Yuuki?*

"Okay," the PFO continues. "And what were the three of you doing at the time and place of the incident? You said you were at your father's office?"

"The Youth Rehabilitation Trust."

It's the first lot of coherent words Timothy has spoken in a while.

The PFO turns, and patiently waits.

Timothy rubs at one wrist with his thumb. "We were finishing setting up the Youth Rehabilitation Trust. Well…officially setting it up."

"And this was all authorised, and the process went okay?"

"Yeah, it has been. It did. Uh…until now."

Joshua is starting to feel cold.

"Were you also involved in the process?" the PFO asks.

It takes Joshua a moment before realising the question is directed at him. "No? I was just…"

"He's on his break from uni," Timothy says. "He came along because he could, and Yuuki's a family friend, and he's over from West Coast for the break. Joshua, I mean. Will be going back afterwards."

The PFO jots down notes.

"My son has no reason to be a part of instigating the kidnapping.

Please…don't consider him as a suspect."

Joshua stares numbly. "…what?"

Timothy stares back at him. "You went out to the bathroom right before they came."

"…why the hell would I…?"

"I know it wasn't you. I know you weren't involved."

The PFO's hand hesitates on the paper. Timothy sees this, and the blankness in his expression is replaced by a firm confidence. Joshua, standing by, realises a fear he hadn't known.

"Dad, you can't mean…"

But he does mean that. Timothy's a lawyer and judge. More of a judge nowadays, formally, but he still carries out lawyer work where necessary. In any case, it means that he knows how Joshua's timing of leaving for the bathroom right before the attack might be presented at a case trial.

It means that, unless there's reason to doubt it, Joshua could be pinned as a suspect for the kidnapping.

"It's okay," the PFO says, seeing Joshua's expression. "We're not concluding anything here."

"But you yourself are thinking it," Timothy observes, "aren't you?"

To that, the PFO is unable to answer.

Joshua wraps his arms around himself. He's now keenly aware that anything he says or does could be used as evidence against him. "I get it. You have to consider the possibilities…but I p-promise…" His cheek twitches. "I promise I didn't want that to happen at all. No way, I…Dad…and Yuuki…I wouldn't…"

He wants to cry, suddenly. It feels like crying. His jaw wobbles.

There's a pain behind his eyes, but the tears won't come. He leans forward and covers his mouth with one hand.

Why is it this *that makes me suddenly so anxious and emotional, but the actual being almost kidnapped and seeing Yuuki and Dad get dragged away didn't?*

Timothy gets up. One of the ambulance staff notice straight away and step in, try to get him to sit down again, but he ignores them. Joshua looks up, wide-eyed and unsure as his father approaches. But then Timothy's arms are coming around him, and the blanket is falling off his shoulders –

Joshua hastily catches the blanket and grips it in his free hand.

Timothy's arms hold Joshua steady in a similar way.

"They came for us," Timothy murmurs. Something in his own voice sounds unsteady. "Me and Yuuki. Because of the Trust. I don't know why, when it was fine before."

"It wasn't me," Joshua forces out. "I wasn't a part of it."

"Yeah, I know it wasn't you. I'm sorry. I wasn't suggesting it was – I just wanted to address any potential suspicion that it could be. You're not a suspect. I just want to make sure they don't start thinking of you as one and questioning you as one." One of his hands clasp Joshua's shoulder. It's a reassuring support. "It's enough...shock as it is, this. We don't need extra stress happening, or playing in the back of our minds, after this. Especially with Yuuki...when we don't know what's happened to Yuuki. Where he's been taken."

Joshua's not sure if it's himself shaking or Timothy. Or both of them. "Then why did you bring it up? They're not...what if they start thinking it's me because you brought it up and, I don't know, maybe you're just defending me because I'm family and – "

"It's okay. That's not going to happen."

"And what if it does?"

"You have no reason to have attacked me and Yuuki like that."

Joshua's throat constricts. This *feeling* is awful. He still hasn't processed the fact he almost got kidnapped, and that Yuuki's missing, and that all of this has really happened just now.

They're here – him and Timothy – they're fine, they escaped, they got away from that event going south any further.

But Yuuki?

Timothy hugs him, still. Perhaps it's as much for his own sake that he won't let go. Nearby, the PFOs and the ambulance crew stand by. Phone calls are being made, and decisions are being made on how best to proceed from here. For Timothy and Joshua, it's too much to think even thirty seconds ahead of now. The words spoken around them filter in and out.

It hasn't even crossed their minds yet, how they're going to break it to the rest of the family.

Susan Harrison comes to pick them up from the hospital. She marches in like she's on guard duty for them post-surgery. It's only an additional check-up that Timothy and Joshua were sent here for, but that doesn't take much weight off the reality of the situation.

There's more to be concerned about than only physical injuries.

So when Susan lays eyes on the two of them, the sight of them – sitting a seat apart in the waiting area, bandage-less, no blood staining their skin or their clothes, and no conspicuous bruising – the stress creasing her brow doesn't ease.

"The PF called me," she says sharply. "And then the hospital."

Timothy locks eyes with her, wordless.

"Are you guys okay?"

The nurse that checked them over approaches. He observes the interacting of the three, then turns to Susan and asks, "Are you Susan Harrison?"

Susan's body language turns defensive. "I am." Joshua doesn't miss the way she takes a cautionary protective step into the space between the nurse she doesn't know and her near abducted family members.

The nurse appears resilient to her nervousness-induced anger. "If you like," he says, "I'll give you an overview of their condition. As for what happened, I'll leave that to them, or the PF, to tell you."

"Could you please give me the detailed full version, please?"

The nurse blinks.

"I'm trained in field and first response. I'd like to hear it in detail."

"I see. Alright then…"

Joshua doesn't take in the technical words like his mother does, but understands the general gist of what they're saying. It's not anything different from what they've already been told: aside from a minor concussion and the psychological shock that Timothy's dealing with, the most they have to worry about are bruises from their individual scuffles.

As a trained field doctor, though, Susan takes all this in and yet still observes them closely for any signs of anything missed. Perhaps, Joshua wonders, she's not looking for what is present now, but what could be present later.

If how she's responded to our family's previous first aid needs is anything to go by.

"We're fine, Mum," Joshua says after the nurse has left.

Apparently his tone is unconvincing, because the response he gets is a harder frown and then a raised eyebrow.

Joshua studies the entry-exit door within view across the foyer.

"I don't even need physical signs of injury to know you're not," Susan says tightly. "For all our sakes, let yourself be honest about how you're actually feeling."

Timothy's hands twist to rub at his wrists, but then he consciously changes the motion to pull the cuffs of his sleeves down a little more.

Susan notices the motion. "How bad is it?"

Timothy looks up, but doesn't answer.

After a moment, Susan crouches down in front of them both we're they're seated. She gently takes a hold of one of Timothy's hands, her actions careful and slow. Then she raises the cuff of the sleeve and pulls it back up further.

The marks the rope left have mostly faded now, all but for a barely visible dull line. Susan's mouth is pressed in a hard line as she rotates the wrist. She checks the other one, too, with one of her hands cupped beneath it supporting.

"I'm not going to believe either of you," she says, "if you try to tell me you're fine. You said…everyone's saying that Yuuki's still missing?"

Timothy nods.

Susan moves her husband's forearm to rest sideways across his knee, then takes his hand and interlocks their fingers with one hand and covers the back of his hand with the other. She looks at Joshua. "You can let me know if I'm being too much. But if you're feeling something, even if it be that you're frustrated because I start getting overprotective or whatever…you can voice that, or express that, okay?"

I don't know if I want to, Joshua thinks. *I don't know if I can.*

"It's okay if it's hard to. If you don't want to speak about it much, that's fine. I get that. But keeping quiet about it is going to cause more hurt. For yourselves, and for me and Samantha. If not right away, perhaps in the long run, when those pent-up feelings finally start having a chance to be free."

"We don't want you having to experience a secondary version of what we went through," Timothy murmurs.

"You don't have to protect us."

Timothy's 'calm' façade wavers. "We should try to protect *someone.*"

Susan's silence is sharp.

"Our trauma is ours to bear," Timothy says.

"Is this about Yuuki?"

Joshua studies a loose thread on his sleeve that he's just noticed.

Timothy clears his throat. "I know…there's realistically nothing we could've done to…not let him get taken. Not when we both were also taken ourselves. But…there's at least something we can try to do to prevent you and Samantha from having a share in this too."

Joshua agrees. Regardless of the old social role of the men in the family protecting the women, and in Joshua's case, the older sibling protecting the younger sibling, he also feels that his mother and younger sister shouldn't have to get fully involved in something that happened to him and his Dad, and Yuuki. Yes, they're a family, the Harrisons are, and an unusually close-knit one at that, but still…

Susan takes a deep, controlled breath. "No matter how much you try, the four of us are immediate family; we're also inevitably going to be dealt a hand in the aftermath of it. It won't necessarily be the same as what the two of you will have to deal with, but it's not like we can escape it. On top of that, this wasn't just some random event that you two happened to be at the wrong place at the wrong time in, either – it was a targeted attack, and one of you was a main target by the sounds. Even if it was a random event, and not a premeditated one, there would still be the prospect of trauma to deal with."

"Couldn't you let us help minimise it?" Timothy murmurs.

"The only way we're going to be able to do that is if we're there for each other properly. Sure, we'll each have our own emotional load to bear, but whatever it comes to, there's also a collective trauma element to it that we'd be kinda foolish to not acknowledge."

Timothy nods.

Joshua isn't sure whether he should stay alert or start zoning out.

"I get it with Samantha – I think it would be a good idea to try minimise what exposure she has to any of…this. This reaction to the thing that just happened. But the reality is, she's going to be exposed to it second-hand one way or another. So –"

"Does Sam know?" Joshua interrupts. "Has she been told? About what happened?"

Susan nods. "She's been excused from school and has been briefly told about what's happened."

"She's not in any danger, is she?"

Timothy's brow furrows. "I wouldn't say *none*, but...since they didn't specifically target either of you, I'd say she'll be left alone."

"There's a Peace Force officer with her at the moment," Susan adds. "They'll meet us at home in a bit."

"Is she okay, though?" Joshua asks. "Relatively?"

"I don't know. It's not my place to say for her."

Timothy nods slowly in understanding.

"What I will say for her," Susan says, "is that her processing this, as well as whatever comes, may look different from what we expect. Each of us are going to have different ways of processing it. What we see of each other's reactions may not be a full description of what whoever is actually feeling. And our experiences of this are different, of course. As for Samantha, when she comes home – and in the next few days, weeks or even months from now – she's going to be exposed to the aftermath of the experience you guys just had. I will be also, but don't worry about me – this is about Samantha. She's going to have her own experience of dealing with this."

"About Sam." Joshua hesitates, eyes flicking up to the door and back again. "You said she's got someone with her, and maybe she isn't likely to be targeted – but I guess that could change, if... if... I mean, I'm just meaning, what if she... what if someone..."

"What happens if she gets taken as a hostage," Timothy finishes. He says it in a flat voice like it's a statement, not a question.

There's a stiff silence between them. Susan's shoulders are tense.

"It has to be said."

"Any of us could get taken, yes," Susan says tightly. "Samantha, me, or either of you again. But let's not assume something *will* happen again, or we'll get paranoid. We're going to have PF officers hanging around us for a little while. That's probably going to start getting us as it is and making us feel on edge as it is."

She's not wrong. It might not have settled in yet, but sooner or later that anxiety and uncertainty and irritation awaiting them is bound to snatch up their feelings.

"And I haven't even mentioned Yuuki."

Timothy stares at the floor, not really looking at it.

"He still hasn't been found, has he?" Susan asks.

Joshua glances at his father. "Not that we've heard."

Susan nods.

"Is there anything we can we do, while we wait?"

"First thing we'll do is go home. Other than that, we can be careful. We can do what we can to prevent putting ourselves at greater risk of such a situation happening – and in your guys' case, of happening again. But there's only so much we can do to keep each other safe. But there's more than just physical safety to watch out for. Let's try to minimise what psychological emotional harm this... experience... poses."

Her voice softens. "That way, when it's over, it has less of a chance to haunt us."

5

Yuuki's aware that he's been drugged: it's the only explanation for why he could be feeling this awful. And why there is no in between memory he can recall of what happened in the time that passed between what he'd been doing before...and *this*. Given the way his head *throbs*, he'd been knocked out with something else too.

There'd been a fight,...right? An attack? And then he...?

He groans. The sound is muffled, and the vibrations feel weird in his mouth. Distorted. Wrong. But Yuuki can't tell whether it's his perception and state of feeling that makes it feel like that or something else. His mouth is dry. It tastes like cotton. He wants cold water to wash away the sick sensation of it on his tongue. That, and help with the tingling burning in his mouth and throat.

With effort, Yuuki shifts uncomfortably. It's hard to move. His left wrist throbs. The movement, what little he can manage, also makes him feel worse. He's already feeling, extremely disorientated and groggy. He's shivering. There's an awful nausea in his gut that swirls and won't stop swirling. He has a terrible headache, and his arm hurts from lying on it. He processes the sensations, trying to overcome the drugged disorientation and ignore the pounding in his head. Maybe he has a concussion, or it could just be the having being drugged. Or maybe it could be both.

His mind is going around in circles, he realises. He can't think straight.

Where even am I right now?

While he's dealing with all that, he's also coming to terms with the fact that he's tied up in an unfamiliar place. Coming around has been slow, and the gradual regaining of a better sense of awareness has been awful, but in the very least it's kept the panic at bay. His arms are pulled behind him, his wrists bound with something coarse and fibrous he can only presume is rope. It's tied securely, with no give, and knotted out of reach of his fingers. He tries to pull his arms sideways, or twist his wrists, but it's tied firmly. It won't budge. The most he can do is rotate his hands a little.

His ankles are tied in a similar way. He can't pull his feet apart. The insides of his shoes press hard against each other. If he moves, it makes it worse, and his ankle bones feel like they're scraping against each other. The way they're tied makes it feel exactly the same as how his wrists are – presumably with rope. If Yuuki were to look, he'd be able to see, but right now he doesn't have the energy to haul his upper body off the ground and twist around to check.

He's also been gagged. There's tape sealing his mouth shut. His mouth is dry with the cloth that's been stuffed in his mouth behind the tape. It tastes like it had been soaked in chemicals. It's worn off now, but Yuuki wonders if this is the reason why it took him so long to wake up properly. At least that explains why his mouth feels weird.

He hasn't been blindfolded at least. Because of that, he's allowed to

41

try and understand what kind of place he's in - or rather, where he's been moved to. The space he's in is small, and the atmosphere, size and material tells him it's some kind of old shed. He hates the sound of his muffled voice so keeps quiet.

When he feels alert enough to understand what kind of situation he's in, that's when he finally musters the will to try to do something about it.

He struggles. Puts energy into wriggling and wrestling and fighting the restriction of the rope in an attempt to loosen it, even if by a fraction. Stress soon sets in, though, when he realises he can't get free of the bindings in spite of his struggle. The nausea and dizziness renew.

Yuuki struggles more. Needing to try to do something, if only to relieve the sense of helplessness that overcomes him. He focuses his energy on it. He can't twist his hands free of the rope binding his wrists behind his back, and the rope around his ankles is secure too. He can't reach either knot with his fingers – at least, not without dislocating a joint and risking limiting his movement even further.

Would it be easier without my shoes on? Yuuki contemplates it. But kicking off his shoes might not be enough, and he also knows he won't be able to get them back on in this state if he does. He doesn't know how long he'll be here. It's winter; it'll get cold tonight. It's already cold. Yuuki has enough energy at present to think rationally about it: he'll need the insulation of his shoes.

As he takes a moment to rethink what else he could do, while waiting for his mind to stop being so foggy with the lingering effects of the drug, he tries his best to keep calm. *But given this situation, how could anyone stay calm?* All the physical sensations of discomfort only serve to make it harder to keep his emotions in check. He feels sick. With hunger, with nausea, with dehydration. With dread.

If he's honest with himself, he's afraid of losing his calm. He doesn't know what awaits on the other side losing it. He doesn't want to find out. Once he's lost his calm, there's likely to be little he can do to regain it. The most he can do is fight for a grip on his composure, and keep fighting... over and over...

Yuuki can't stop the muffled whimper that escapes him. Surely it shouldn't be too hard, right? He's keenly aware of the tightness wrapped around his wrists. The rope trapping his legs, and the gag –

No, it should be difficult. Because whoever restrained him knew what they were doing, and they've obviously kept him here like this because they don't want him having any chance of escaping - not before they come back to deal with him.

But really, all that means is that Yuuki should try all the more harder to get free, before they come back, before they come and Yuuki has no choice but to let them do whatever the hell they want with him. In other words, if he wants any chance of getting out of this situation before things turn bad - before he has to face whatever situation may await him in the other side of that door - then he needs to minimise the amount of disadvantages he has.

The rope won't give yet. After resting a bit, and regaining his breath as best he can through his nose, Yuuki reasseses the situation.

He tries getting the gag off first, but only succeeds in straining his neck against his shoulder. The tape is pressed flat against his face. And it's duct tape, he guessed, giving the colour of it, and how adhesive it is to the skin on his face and lips. It's stuck, and he can't see anything in the shed he could use to scrape it slowly off with. If he could just have his hands free...

He wrestles again with the rope around his wrists, and writhes on the floor, testing to see if he'd be able to pull his feet free, but it doesn't seem like he'd be able to, so he aborts. He gives up with a stressed huff, and lies his head back down on the floor.

So that's... not happening... anytime soon...

If he can't escape what's restraining him, then he could try seeing if he can at least escape the room instead.

With that thought, Yuuki shifts across the floor towards the door. It's not that great of a distance, but bound with hands behind his back and feet tied together, it takes a while. Shuffling awkwardly, he continues until his feet touch the door. He inches a little closer, pulls his knees up and then gives it a kick. It seems locked.

With a grunt, he wriggles into a sitting position leaning against the door. He gives himself a moment to breathe. He then shifts his bound legs beneath himself and, leaning his shoulder against the door for support, braces himself and stands up. If the door isn't locked, and he falls straight through, then... Here's hoping there's no one outside to watch him fall to the ground in this humiliating state. Or at least, no one who find the escape attempt amusing. If the getting out of this room, this shed, were to result in someone seeing him who might be able to help, however...maybe being seen would be worth the humiliation.

He plants his feet, narrows his eyes, stands up straight and then shoves his weight against the door. Definitely locked. Yuuki does it again but all it does is hurt his shoulder. He almost loses his balance. Tears prick his eyes. He lets out a muffled whimper. He tries again, but the door is locked and he falls in a heap on the floor. He lands heavily on his shoulder, chest slamming into the floor and his cheek following.

With a groan, he shifts uncomfortably. He tries yanking on the bindings around his wrists. Wrestling with them and the rope around his ankles.

Defeated, Yuuki stills, breathing fast, the air not fresh and full enough to get a deep breath.

It's too dusty in here.

Too confining.

Too confusing.

And Yuuki has no idea what's going to happen to him. No idea what's happening to him, aside from the fact that he's been kidnapped by who knows who and has been tied up and dumped who knows where. It places a desperate confused edge to the panic.

Did they put me to come back for later? Or did they decide they couldn't be bothered coming back for me at all, but just didn't want me being found...or...

There is a chance that no one might come at all.

But just in case, he shuffles away from the door. Rolls over onto his right side so that he's facing the door. Whether someone comes or not, Yuuki would rather be as ready as he can be. Not that he can do much to change what happens to him when he's bound up like this. It may, however, help to minimise the psychological and emotional impact whatever may come may have.

In the meantime, it seems like it's a waiting game. Yuuki is conscious

45

of the chill in the air deepening. It's cooling down outside now, approaching sunset probably if the dimming light is anything to go by. Or maybe he's just dealing with the symptoms of being drugged. And trapped. And –

Don't think about it.

Deep breaths – aren't possible, really, but –

Don't think about it!

Yuuki's glad he's still wearing his coat. That he didn't end up shedding it in Timothy's office. It's the only extra layer he brought for over his work uniform. Now he's subconsciously regretting not having worn something a little warmer still.

It makes him worry for Timothy, the more he thinks about it. What had he been wearing? Just a long-sleeved work shirt and trousers? He hadn't been wearing any jerseys, or extra winter layers. If he's in any similar situation to what Yuuki is right now, he'll undoubtedly be cold.

Yuuki is too scared to think about what might actually, *physically,* be happening to Timothy right now. He doesn't want to let his imagination run wild yet.

And Joshua – is Joshua okay? He hadn't been in the room when those guys has come in. Maybe he is okay. Maybe he was sensible and stayed hidden. Called the Peace Forces, or security.

And didn't end up in this mess.

6

Back at the house that the Harrisons call home, the familiarity and usual connotations of being here ought to be comforting. It isn't.

Timothy hopes to have had his mind rest a little, maybe – to be able to breathe a little more and calm down a bit by returning here. But there's Peace Force officers outside, and a PF car sitting on the road, garnering the attention of one of their neighbours who is standing outside.

Right now, the house offers no such depth of reprieve.

Susan has her eyes narrowed in an almost-glare as they pull up. A *'where do I park the car if all these officers are here?'* questioning face. If Timothy didn't know any better, he'd mistake her expression as pure frustration rather than understanding it for what it is: alert, concentrating and calculating.

The officers see them and stand aside, so Susan drives up the driveway and parks in front of the house as she would usually do. The only difference to now and that usual is that there is a PF vehicle parked where Timothy would usually park his car, and a couple of officers standing outside talking right in front of the door. Timothy recognises them as the two officers from before – the ones on patrol who Timothy and Joshua met earlier.

Susan parks the car. There's a moment where her, Timothy and Joshua stay sitting in the car doing nothing. Gathering themselves. Procrastinating. Then Susan sighs, and the three of them take that as their cue to move on out.

"They didn't let the dog out, did they?" Susan wonders aloud as she unbuckles her seatbelt.

Timothy belatedly realises they might be an issue.

Joshua gets out of the back of the car. "I'll go look for her."

"Hang on," Timothy says, getting out of the car, too. "Joshua." He glances over at Susan, also doing the same. "Let's make sure everything's okay around here first. We don't know if anything has happened here while we've been out." *While we were getting kidnapped, and at the hospital, and…*

"The PFOs might be have her somewhere, anyways," Susan adds.

Joshua hesitates. He glances at the wide open front door, concerned.

The Harrison family's old golden retriever, Ginger, has taken to wandering off on her own and not finding her way back lately. If they leave the house door open without keeping an eye on her, it's all too easy for Ginger to see that as an invitation to head out on a stroll when she feels like it.

"We can go look for her right after," Timothy reassures.

Seeing the dilemma happening, the partner of the officer Timothy and Joshua spoke to most on the highway comes over. "Hi. Is something the matter?"

"Our dog," Susan puts flatly. "You haven't seen her have you? She's getting old and likes to wander. We were wondering where she is."

The officer raises their eyebrows. "Ah, the goldie? Deb's looking after her around the back. I'm Conrad Johnson by the way. I don't believe I introduced myself earlier. I'm the PF partner of Marina Tu'u, who was talking with you earlier. She's just on the phone with another on our team. She'll be over in a moment."

Joshua shifts on his feet. Timothy and Susan stand there, unsure of what they should do. What they're allowed to do, what with PFOs standing between them and their house.

"Can I go get our dog?" Joshua asks.

The officer nods. "We've just finished checking the place, making sure there haven't been any unwelcome visitors come by. All looks good, though, so yes, of course."

Joshua takes the opportunity to leave and heads inside.

"So, are there any other concerns we need to know about," Timothy asks. "I'm taking it that there *are*, given that you're still here."

The officer grimaces. "There's just some things we need to double check before we leave, and we wanted to check in with the whole family first. I'll give you an update while we wait," Conrad Johnson says. "Like I mentioned just now, we've finished checking the house and surroundings. It appears this place was not a focus for them, based on our observations. For your safety, though, we will have a team stationed in the vicinity. Should any situation arise following the kidnapping earlier today, there will be people nearby to respond immediately."

Susan murmurs, "Okay, thanks."

Timothy wonders about that. He envisions the situation as happening quite similar to what the attack at the Ninao District Law Office did –

49

prepared, organised, *quick*... If they were able to pull off a kidnapping in a law office in broad daylight with lots of people around, then they could most likely do it again even in a neighbourhood with PF officers nearby.

Hang on......there were lots of people around at the office, right? Surely someone would've witnessed those four people entering like that. It wasn't only Joshua who was around to witness or attempt to apprehend the attack, right?

Timothy feels cold all of a sudden. Uncomfortable. Something unsettling settles in his gut. He decides not to concentrate on it. *I don't know if I want to follow this train of thought right now...*

The officer Conrad Johnson is saying something else, but it all sounds like standard formalities and information about investigation proceedings that Timothy as a lawyer and judge is already familiar with. Still, he nods vaguely like he is listening. He's been zoning out, if he's honest, but he's not missing anything – he thinks – and so continues to do so.

Until Susan notices his inability to really focus – his distantness, which isn't usually something he has an issue unless there's something wrong. She rests a supporting hand on his upper arm, and brings the topic of conversation back to what Timothy is really more concerned about.

A pause. Susan asks, "And what of Yuuki?"

The officer hesitates. That's all the information Timothy needs for a summary. *They haven't found anything.*

Marina Tu'u walks over to them. "Samantha is on her way here," she reports.

"And Yuuki?" Susan repeats.

"We've got teams looking for him," Marina says. "But as of our last update, we have yet to discover any clues to his whereabouts." Her partner takes a slight step back as though to indicate letting her lead this part of the talk. "The vehicle presumed to have taken him was last seen in northern Ninao district. At the moment, we're looking into any clues that might be found at the site of attack, and any potential correlation between the two vehicles and any places nearby. But I cannot confirm anything yet. Our own unit is involved in the tracing and tracking, so we'll be the first to hear about. If we find any conclusive evidence we can tell you, we'll inform you when we can."

Neither Timothy nor Susan are surprised that they won't hear any more than what the PF choose to tell them. They know how it goes – Timothy's in a similar line of work too. Even amongst family, there's only so much that Timothy can divulge of cases he's working on before it crosses the line of confidentiality and caution.

Marina quickly responds to a text message that pops up on her phone. She then looks at Timothy and Susan, and then Joshua respectively. "I understand that your daughter – your sister – is a student at A'o High School?"

Timothy hums. "Yeah, she is."

Susan frowns. "Do you think it's not safe for her to attend classes?"

Marina tilts her head. "I'm going to leave that up to her. She has friends at school?"

"She does. They regularly hang out, both at school and in their free time."

"I see. That's good. She'll need that support. Moreover, they'll be like surveillance for her... security. I would prefer to place an officer from my unit near her, just in case, but I understand that too much will only stress

51

her out and may result in the situation turning out worse. We've had that happen in the past, where people we're protecting have felt too watched and thus deliberately left the security bubble we tried setting up for them. Fortunately nothing came out of that situation, but nevertheless, we don't want that happening again.

"I would advise though, that your daughter not spend too much time out alone at this stage. Until further investigation is done, it would be best if she has someone with her or nearby at all times."

"And not stay out after dark, that sort of thing?" Susan asks.

"Well, considering that the incident happened in broad daylight, at noon…"

Susan nods. "Right."

Beside Susan, Timothy barely reacts to conversation.

Catching the underlying sentiment of the action, Marina nods. "Alright, well. That's essentially all I have to tell you right now. You have my number. If anything suspicious or concerning happens, call me right away. We'll have someone monitoring the area – they'll most likely be patrolling around, to ensure that the house is being watched from all sides for you. I know that this is a nerve-racking time for you, and that the security presence will not help you very much with resting, but…try to get as much rest as you can. Leave the investigation to us, and just remember to make sensible and careful decisions about where you go and when. Keep your phone charged and on you at all times, just in case."

Susan grimaces. "Thank you. And…please update us as soon as you can if you find anything about where Yuuki is."

"Will do the best I am able."

Footsteps crunch on the gravel. Samantha, with her roman sandals providing little purchase on the driveway. She's wide-eyed as she takes in the scene before her: a seemingly normal return home from school, except she's earlier than usual and there's a PFO standing outside their house.

Samantha sees the way Timothy and Susan are standing. Her own expression doesn't change from one of disbelief.

Marina glances at the others, and ushers Samantha a few steps away from the door where she repeats what she just told the rest of the family. It gives Samantha some privacy to process what's going on.

Joshua reappears with the Harrisons' family dog. Ginger wags her tail briefly before reading the atmosphere. She slowly walks up to Samantha and stands beside her. She glances at the rest of the family, back at Marina.

After Marina inclines her head and answers a call on her cell phone, turning to walk a little away, Samantha hugs the dog and sinks into a crouch.

Usually, at this time on a Thursday afternoon, they'd be starting to think about what they feel like for their once-a-week takeaway dinner night. No one has mentioned anything of their preference. Timothy hasn't any appetite to even want to think about it. He's not sure Samantha, Susan or Joshua do either.

Timothy and Joshua were nearly kidnapped today, Yuuki's still missing and they have no idea whether this was a one-off attack or if the Harrison family should prepare for another. The Youth Rehabilitation Trust still hasn't been fully officiated yet, either – Timothy was supposed to send those documents. But right now, he doesn't even want to think about. He doesn't have the emotional capacity to.

Later. Truthfully, he doesn't know if he'll be feeling any better later either.

Susan lets out a shaky breath. "Alright. I'll go make coffee."

Darkness is unyielding.

So is the rope.

The tape.

The cold.

Yuuki knows he shouldn't let his imagination go wild, but it's hard for it not to. He's got nothing else to do but think. He's got no distractions available to prevent him from getting lost in his thoughts.

Still no one has come, and there's no sound of anyone coming either.

Is Timothy locked in a place like this, or is it just me? Have they got Timothy right now – dealing to him in whatever way they see fit – and are coming for me afterwards? Did… or did they somehow not manage to get Timothy, or Joshua, and I'm the only one they caught?

If it's the latter, then the reason for this kidnapping is most likely the Youth Rehabilitation Trust.

Yuuki's stomach sinks. Dread washes over him. Guilt. He feels sick. He should've known. No matter how careful they were, they were bound to get on Taularh's bad side for trying.

And as it's already dawning, it seems unlikely they'll be able to escape this mess of a situation.

Not unless the Peace Forces care enough to find him.

If they can, of course, find him at all.

Yuuki fights to keep himself calm, lest he start panicking and breathing too quickly and ending up desperate for air that the gag will not allow him. But it's hard not to fall into a state of reaction, when there's one stressful and dreaded question he has no idea of the answer to:

What's going to happen to us?

The fifth of June was supposed to be a day of achievement for them. Now it's only become something of horror.

7

Samantha goes to school the next day. There's no security officer accompanying her or following her as she goes, and she's glad. It's enough to have PF presence surrounding the house and nearby streets. She'd like to have a break from the supervision, even if it is 'for her own safety'.

Am I nervous? She's not sure. There's people all around – morning traffic, cyclists and kids on their way to school. Adults on their way to work. If anyone wanted to kidnap her, they'd have to do so in front of all these people. What of when she gets to school, and on the way home? What about then? *But even there, there's people around. There's bound to be some PF officer monitoring the area, if just because my family was involved in the incident and I'm one of my family.*

Even without PFO presence, there's plenty of teachers and students around, and Sam's already certain that her friends aren't going to readily leave her alone in a hurry once she gets there. She's just glad it's Friday. There's only so much socialising she can handle when the attention's on her.

56

That's…not something Sam's looking forward to. As much as she's grateful, and even feels safer, having the assurance she's got people looking out for her, this level of being watched out for is…somewhat too much.

At least she was allowed to go to school.

Fortunately, it didn't take much to convince her mother of it. Susan's only condition was that she be near other people as much as possible, and have her phone ready at all times. Timothy tried insisting Sam stay behind – stay at the house, where it was better protected – until he also realised that trying to keep Sam in some 'protected zone' would just end in something worse happening. She and Joshua might start an in-house uprising if they're not given the space and freedom they need. Were they in imminent danger, or their going out was highly likely to put other people at risk, then they would consider staying back to be a necessity indeed.

But there isn't a plague or a civil war happening outside. This isn't even an attack on the Harrison family, to be specific. By the looks of it, Yuuki was the main target, Timothy the second target, and that's it.

'And that's it'… Sam frowns at the wording of her own thoughts.

From what it seems, anyways, the attackers haven't seemed to have any real interest in going to the extent of targeting the rest of the Harrison family to get to them. If they'd wanted to, they could've kidnapped Sam and Susan when they went to kidnap Yuuki and Timothy.

But that wasn't on the agenda. At least, not from what Joshua has concluded from what he observed.

Sam exhales sharply and glares tiredly at the path ahead of her. *This is making my mind run in circles.*

"We don't know exactly what we're dealing with," Timothy had argued. Which is true – Sam can't find fault in her father's worrying about that, especially when he was a victim of the kidnapping attempt himself.

But driving themselves crazy with paranoia and anxiety isn't going to help the situation either. It's not going to help them stay calm and let the PF handle it. It's not going to help them not do anything stupid.

So long as they're careful of where they go in the meantime, and so long as their going out isn't putting anyone else at risk, they won't be harming anyone.

There's no homeroom class that morning, for which Sam is glad. She'd have avoided it anyways.

It's biology, first period, where the first wave of concerned classmates greets her. Her classmates know about the attempted kidnapping of her father and brother. Of course they do: it was on the news, and word gets around. There's a mix of mild shock and concern. They ask Sam if she's okay, and greet her with questions and with sympathies. It makes Sam uncomfortable. She's too tired to fend them all off politely, but she tries her best to not be rude about it.

The classmate she shares a desk with in biology is quiet, watching her with non-intrusive understanding regard. Sam half expects Kyle to offer sympathies too, but he doesn't. Just sits silently beside her. The aura emanating from him is respectful, and offering an air of emotional comfort. It helps, even minimally. Sam knows that the reason why it *does* help, when all the sympathies only make her bristle, is that Kyle genuinely gets the kind of thing Sam is experiencing – she remembers, a few years ago, how his own father was in an incident and perished in it. No one offered him any sympathies then, though. That's another reason perhaps why Sam feels sickened by the sympathies offered to her – they're not fake per se, but they're not born of deep concern for Sam's wellbeing. All it is, from her perspective, is a mild passive concern that will only last a short while, then people will forget about feeling like they cared.

She hears Kyle mutter under his breath as their classmates are murmuring behind them about if the Peace Forces have found Takahashi yet, "Pretty sure it's *Tah-kah-hah-shi,* not *Tah-kah-HASH-i.*"

On a different day, Sam might have laughed. *Kyle says to himself exactly what I want to say out loud so often.* She wonders, briefly, to what extent Yuuki finds himself bothered by such mispronunciation.

In the wake of the kidnapping, the thought feels empty and pointless.

It's a relief when the teacher arrives – and finally moves on from expressing their own concern – to start the class. The attention of the room is pulled away from Sam, and Sam's own attention has something else to focus on besides the Ninao kidnapping. And Yuuki still being missing.

The study is not as much a distraction as she'd like it to be.

At lunch break, Sam doesn't want a break. She doesn't want to pass time socialising. With no patience or appetite, she just wants her physics class last period to be over and done with so she can just leave.

Maybe I could skip class. It's a tempting thought. But she'd then need to have a conversation with several people explaining her absence, bearing

RENEE NIELSEN

with further sympathies in regard to the Ninao kidnapping impacting her, and she'd also have to catch up on a lesson that would be much easier to study and note take for in class. For what it's worth, it's probably better just to wait.

It's also probably much safer.

She finds her friends group in their usual place outside the music building. Laura, Avi and Logan tend to always beat her there when they have separate classes. Sam attempts a fake smile as she approaches. It fails. No one questions her about it when she plonks herself down on the ground beside them to join the loose circle they've created.

An uncertain silence stretches between them. Sam's mood is eminent when she doesn't even pull any food out of her bag.

Avi clears his throat, glancing up from peeling the mandarin in his hands. "So,…how have classes been since we last saw you this morning? I mean, y'know…"

Sam gives up a half-hearted thumbs-up. "Fine."

Avi doesn't look the least bit convinced. In fact, none of them do. Given the circumstances, though, it's hard to pull off a convincing lie.

"Did you forget your lunch?" Logan asks. "I got a spare sandwich. You can have it if you want."

Sam raises an eyebrow. "You know I don't like jam."

Logan shrugs. "It's food if you want it."

Irritation sparks beneath Sam's skin. She mentally shoves it back down, suppressing it.

"You're welcome to have one of these," Avi says, gesturing to the paper bag of fruit.

The offer is kind, like Logan's, but Sam can't muster the energy to do anything but stare.

Avi glances at the others. He clears his throat. "You guys can have some too, if you want."

Laura frowns. "It's okay," she says, exchanging an awkward look with Logan. "You'll end up with none for yourself if you share between us as well."

"It's fine, really." Avi's tone is genuine. "We've got a huge mandarin tree. I can get myself some more later. And I've already had other stuff for lunch. So go ahead."

Hearing this, Laura murmurs a thanks and takes one. Logan is too busy munching on his sandwich to do the same.

Sam feels less guilty about the offers, however the shame – and disappointment in herself – of not being up to accepting them lingers. The mandarins look nice. If only she had enough appetite to actually eat, then she'd have some too.

Avi reaches for another mandarin. "Something up, Laura? You've been really quiet, too."

Laura cringes. "Oh, it's just…Charlie's been overprotective again. You could say it's been putting me on edge as well."

"Ah." Avi nods, offering her an understanding wince.

"Yeah, he tends to get…anxious when things like this happen. Not that things like these happen all the time, fortunately, it's just…"

"He's in the same work field as Sam's dad and Yuuki, right?"

Laura nods. "He's a youth advocate."

"An in-between of them, almost," Logan muses. "In that Timothy's a judge slash lawyer, and Yuuki works at the juvie."

"Pretty much."

"So how much does it affect him?" Avi asks.

Laura wrings her hands. "As in?"

"Well, in terms of work….and I guess personal life, as well. I don't mean to pry, but I remember you've said that Charlie's had a bad experience in the past that makes him anxious when these things come up. It must be affecting you as well."

"Yeah. I don't know. It doesn't really affect his line of work, except for wondering if the Youth Rehabilitation Trust will go ahead. Otherwise, I think the anxiety is worse than the situation, since the kidnapping doesn't…doesn't affect as directly, so to speak. And then Charlie's anxiousness makes *me* nervous…because of course, I've had some things happen to me too, before Charlie took me in. I guess it's just on my mind, or I'm feeling it emotionally. But…of course it doesn't impact me as much as it does Sam."

And with that, the topic of conversation re-centres itself directly on Sam.

Sam feels the back of her neck prickle. She narrows her eyes. "Sorry, guys. I just…want to be alone right now."

Maybe some other time, being with friends would help her process stuff or distract her from it. But right now she just wants to *not be around people* who seem to have a better time processing the whole idea of what happened yesterday, especially when Sam herself has yet to get a grip on any sort of processing. For her, it doesn't seem real. For her, it's not clear on how she should feel about it all.

All she really knows is that she needs a quiet, still place to be alone and let her confusion settle.

She goes to the library with the aim of finding a senior room study desk to hide in. Away from the natural response sympathies that just make her feel worse. Away from people, in general.

At the top of the staircase to the study room, she halts. The study room isn't empty. It almost is, but for the one person sitting hidden away near the corner: Kyle, in his usual library haunt. It's only Kyle, mind, which normally wouldn't bother her. He's never really bothered her and she's never seemed to bother him. Outside of class activities, their only interaction is introverting alone together in a shared space such as this.

In other words, it should be fine.

But Sam is in a mood, and needs some time alone – *actually alone.*

Kyle regards her carefully, eyes keeping track of her expression and body language as she moves around the block of desks. Sam regrets the way she glares at him when she glances in his direction. This is only a venting expression of what she's feeling internally. Kyle of all people doesn't deserve to receive the brunt of it.

Sam redirects her gaze at a desk in the far corner. Mentally, she sends an apology his way, but it never makes it into vocalised words. With a sigh, she decides to at least try a half-hearted attempt to keep her venting in check, for Kyle's sake.

But there's so much unprocessed stress pent up in her muscles. When she arrives at her desired desk space and pulls the seat back to sit down, it's with a yank. She drops her school bag on the floor straight afterwards. Carelessly. It makes a *whump*.

In her peripheral, she thinks she sees Kyle flinch.

Sam mutters a frustrated noise beneath her breath. She thinks about apologising – again – for her stress, for Kyle's sake, but considering the fact that even that would come out in a tight, stressed tone, it's probably better just to keep it to herself.

She can express her apology by not bothering him with her issues, in the least.

She feels Kyle's attention shift to her, but he gives her space. She's conscious of the fact that he stays. Sam is expecting him to leave out of her making him uncomfortable.

Why am I expecting him to be the one to leave? If anyone should leave, it's me – I'm the one crying here like this.

Sam cries silently, stressed. She questions why on earth she's crying like this. Her father and brother are safe. She and her mother seem to be being left alone, too. For now, at least, the whole family is relatively 'safe'.

But Yuuki isn't. They don't know where Yuuki is, or what's happening to him.

Sam hasn't known Yuuki for long, but he's come around to their house several times since becoming friends with her Dad. Yuuki's a good guy, and Sam likes having him around. He's like another older brother, another member of the family the way he fits in. The way he enjoys their company, and the way they enjoy his.

But Yuuki's gone. Missing. For how long until they find him, they don't know. Maybe they'll never get him back. It's not a thought that's good to dwell on, but it's a possibility.

This…this is what Sam's crying about.

THE NINAO INCIDENT

She's crying for Yuuki.

8

Yuuki sits slumped against the back wall. It's uncomfortable. His shoulders hurt. His legs, tied at his ankles, extend in front of him. He feels detached from them. From himself. His right foot twitches in his shoe. His lower back hurts, but he can't bring himself to move from the position – he *can't* exactly move much anyways.

He shifts, ever so slightly, and it provides him with a renewed reminder of all the sensations digging into his muscles – the rope, the uneven planks of wood beneath him, the growing awareness of pain. In addition to that, there's the sensations sticking to his skin. Namely the tape stuck across his lips and cheeks, and the dry taste of rag filling his mouth. The constant feeling of it stays there, taunting him with the knowledge that he can't do anything about it because his hands are tied behind his back.

I have no idea what time it is. I have no idea how long it's been.

Yuuki managed to sleep, if only for a brief while. Sometime near dawn. It had been dark, and then he'd woken up to light and a stiff neck. It's been a while since then. He'd estimate it to be afternoon now, but 2 o'clock sometimes feels like 4 o'clock, and 4pm sometimes only feels like 2pm; he doesn't trust himself for accuracy when daylight and dragging out of time are the only things he has to go by.

It's been long enough for physical stress and mental fatigue to start setting in, though. It pulls at his limbs and his sanity. And by this stage, Yuuki's inevitably wet himself. It's humiliating, uncomfortable and nauseating. The fact that he can only breathe through his nose at this point only makes the issue feel worse.

When he doesn't fixate on all those uncomfortable sensations, they're not so apparently bad. If he forces his mind to *go blank* as best as possible. But the psychological effort is draining, and the swing back into feeling his emotions again when the mind blanking effect isn't so strong is emotionally straining. No matter how much he tries to 'stay calm', there's only so much energy – sense of *sanity* – he has to spare. Were he not tied up and gagged and stuck in a shed like this, maybe he'd be able to get a better grasp on what he could call composure.

Yuuki tries to stay calm but it's an endless prison. The mental distress of nothing happening and not being able to do anything and not understanding *why* is getting to him. This, as well as the increasing assortment of physical pains, discomforts and irritations biting at him.

The situation won't change unless someone else arrives. That, or Yuuki somehow manages to do *something*. Otherwise, this is what it is: he's alone here, alone with his mind, unable to do anything but struggle against the restraints and hope someone comes soon.

Do I really want someone to come, though? Would I rather be taken elsewhere, to be beaten or tortured or used in exchange for information or something, than this?

The answer to that is something Yuuki isn't sure he wants to discover.

…maybe this is *the plan they had in mind for me – to leave me here to experience all the distress and discomfort of my mind and body deteriorating until I die in this shed?*

It would make sense, right? Why no one's come yet?

Something still doesn't add up: the why – *why* did they leave him here like this? If they were angry about him participating in establishing a trust acknowledging that Taularh's justice system is inadequate, then killing him and Timothy on the spot in Timothy's office would've been sufficient. Instead of going to the effort of kidnapping them, they could've just killed them – right?

And even then, after kidnapping them – or Yuuki at least, for them to just tie him up and leave him here…wherever here is…? Why? Why did they do that? To psychologically torture him? Pit him against himself in some kind of sickening mind game to see how long he'll last?

What if…what if they don't come back? Is the objective then to see me suffer the slow deterioration of my body and mind over the course of days until there's nothing left and I…?

Yuuki's arrived back at that conclusion all over again. Maybe that's it. He'll be left here, unless anyone decides to come back for him. The result of that happening is that he'll eventually die here.

And, of course, before that…he'll lose his mind first.

Just the fact that this situation is inescapable in so many different ways – the discomfort, the mental stress, the bindings, the tape on his mouth…the *shed* – is enough to make one frustrated thought spiral.

Is there anything he *can* do, but try and fail at keeping his head above the water in this psychological tug of war?

Dehydration makes him feel faint. Yuuki can feel a headache starting again in earnest. Clenching his jaw around the cloth stuck in his mouth probably isn't helping. Whatever they put on the cloth probably isn't helping either – they being those who kidnapped him and left him tied up like this, in which case…it's probably chloroform. Or something.

Something chemical I don't want to be tasting and breathing in every last fume of.

Yuuki realises, dimly, that at the moment he doesn't get much say in the matter. *The gag…I should try again to get it off…out….*

He looks around, searches for something to scrape off the tape with. This shed is empty – all but for himself, and all the insects and other creepy crawlies already occupying it. There's no tools he could use, though. He supposes it would have been stupid for his kidnappers to leave him here with anything, anyways. Unless Yuuki's being kept here was only temporary, and or someone was confident he, they wouldn't want to leave anything in there with him. Or maybe there wasn't anything eft in here to begin with. What with how dusty and decorated with webs of settled-in spiders this interior is, the latter is more likely to be true.

Yuuki just has to work with what there is, then. Any wooden edge that might work, or thing he can use without the use of his hands. There's enough of a ledge by the window – a small frame of wood set into the wall around it – that he could use, but in order to access it he'd need to stand. With how thin the frame is, and how high up it is, though, Yuuki's not sure he'd be able to successfully use it. Not with both his feet tied together. Not without risking using up a lot of energy for an attempt that may fail. He's already not feeling well and his energy reserves are limited and not likely to be replenished anytime soon. Yuuki needs to conserve what energy he can – to brace himself for what might be coming, to endure what might be coming, and to survive what already is. If he wants to get the tape off his face and the cloth out of his mouth, then he'll need to try to find a method that uses a minimal amount of energy and stress.

And the place in this shed where he'll be best able to find such a way...is the floor.

Yuuki stares at the floorboards around and underneath him. Due to the small size of the shed, there's not a lot of options. Down the centre of the floor, there's a crack snaking through the wood. It's hard to distinguish the edges of the wood from shadow and old wood discolouration in this light, but there is a hand-sized area of wood that's dented down. The broken edges of wood on either side of it appear rough. The outermost edges appear to be lifted up slightly.

It's not much, but...

It takes a while before he can muster up enough mental will to move. Sitting up against the wall isn't comfortable, but neither is lying down. Having his hands tied behind his back, it puts more strain on his neck and shoulders lying down. It's also harder to find a position to rest in that allows him to breathe alright without pain spreading through his muscles. The only things less comfortable about sitting up are the way the rope feels tighter around his ankles, the way his bottom grows numb, and the way he can feel the blood and hydration levels draining slowly from his face all the more keener.

So slowly, at first, he leans to the right and lets himself slide a little down the wall. He tries to steady the descent by moving his legs. The movement only propels the descent. Yuuki drops onto his side. The impact jars his shoulder. He groans. Tilting his head back, he weighs up the distance – bound, crawling distance – to the jutting out edge of broken wood.

Here goes.

It takes effort. It's awkward. It makes him feel like a half desiccated caterpillar, the way he shuffles across the floor with disjointed movements. Shifting forward by rolling back and forth off his chest and right shoulder takes his breath out of him. His heart beats hard. His pulse feels heavy, hammering, in his head. The lack of purchase he's able to get from the soles of his shoes, the rope preventing him from attaining a decent angle to place his feet down. He could raise his knees, put his feet flat on the floor and slide along his back – but his hands will only get pinned beneath his back that way. There is the option of raising his body off the floor and sliding along the backs of his arms, but he'd rather not that way. The action makes him feel exposed along his front in a way he doesn't want to feel or think about. It also sends blood rushing to his head with a sickening feeling.

Crawling, as he is, is the preferable option.

Reaching the split in the wood, Yuuki turns his face against the floor. He lies there until his heartbeat and breathing have steadied a bit more. Then he re-evaluates the edges of the wood before him. There's not much fibre sticking out of it within usable reach, and the edges don't jut out as much as he'd hoped. But there's enough of a solid edge there and coarse texture to it that it might prove useful – at least the most useful tool Yuuki has access to that might allow him to get the gag off. He grunts as he repositions himself, trying to press his body closer to the floor in order to be able to rub his face against the edge of the floorboard properly.

Please work. Eventually, he manages to get the top right corner of the tape to catch on the edge of wood on the opposite side of the crack. Determination flares in Yuuki's mind...but it's short-lived. The rough wood digs into his skin, scraping. The abrasion of it only seems to be slowly gouging out a defined cut on his cheek. It scrapes and digs into his skin more than it gets the tape off. Yuuki succeeds in getting the corner of the tape to peel slightly, but that's it.

He can't get the tape off any further.

His composure slips like a landslide. If even he could just...have the option of breathing through his mouth again, and not have to feel the cloth filling it or the tape sealing his lips together, the tape pulling at the skin on his cheeks every time he tries to relax his face. But his shoulder's sore, his neck is cramping, and he feels so utterly ridiculous and frustrated. Moreover, he's losing his sense of calm.

He closes his eyes and lies still, trying to ignore stress. It did work a little, right? The edge of the wood on the tape? It's not enough to unstick the tape from over his lips, but if he keeps trying then maybe he'll eventually be able to get it off completely. Maybe he'll be able to ungag himself and have some time to taste air on his tongue before the kidnappers come to get him.

If they come to get me.

Yuuki doesn't give that thought anymore thought. It'll come back to mess with his mind soon enough anyway.

9

Sam sits on the stairs, one step down from the top, not sure what she's doing. She feels like she's stepped into an alternate reality. Being in the shadows half between the light of the living room and the semi-darkness of the unlit upstairs where her room is seems to be the most consoling place she can find.

When her brother emerges from that semi-darkness, the fading light of the sunset making him nothing but a silhouette at first glance, she feels a bit better. Only a bit, though.

Joshua joins her, sitting down a step below her. "Hey, Sam."

It's somewhat a relief, hearing the shortened version of her name spoken. There's no newfound connotation of Peace Force officers, family troubles and people gone missing with that name – it's just a nickname used between herself and Joshua. She doesn't want to be, or become, 'Samantha Harrison, daughter and sister of two attempted kidnapping victims'. That's not how she wants to be looked at. That's not how she wants to think of her family – in particular the two people described as victims in the kidnapping event.

No, not two – three. There's three victims. She's still trying to process the reality of what apparently happened yesterday, but for some reason what disturbs her the most out of all the information is that Yuuki got kidnapped – *successfully kidnapped* – and is still out there, somewhere, missing…

Yuuki…has been kidnapped. Her brother, who is sitting beside her right now, was almost carried off into the same situation. Her Dad, too. And for what? *Why is this happening? All Yuuki was doing was something* good *for society. Dad, too. And Joshua was just…there. Sure, he tried to stop them, but couldn't they have just left him behind? Taken Yuuki and Dad, and left him alone…*

But the rising implication of that is that, had that happened – had Joshua *not* ended up taken himself – then it wouldn't just be Yuuki who's missing; Sam wouldn't be seeing her Dad, and hearing his voice, around the house if Joshua hadn't been in a position to rescue at least one of them.

So then what the hell are they doing with Yuuki? What the hell is the point in this whole kidnapping thing…?

"This whole atmosphere is a bit unsettling, huh…" Joshua murmurs.

"What do they want?" Sam mutters aloud. Broken out of her whirling thoughts, she pulls a face.

Joshua looks at her. "Who?"

"You know what I mean."

A sound like a grimace crossed with a sigh.

"It can't have been the Trust."

"What else could it have been? It's the only thing that makes sense."

"A *rehabilitation* Trust. How is that something to kidnap someone over?"

"I don't know."

"Did Yuuki and Dad actually do anything *wrong?*"

"It was perfectly legal, Sam. *Is* perfectly legal." Joshua softens his voice. "They wouldn't have gone ahead with it – they wouldn't have been allowed to go ahead with it – if it wasn't."

"Then why?"

"Don't forget, they were being kidnapped, not arrested. Someone wanted Dad and Yuuki because they must've done something that someone didn't like."

"Then they'll come back for Dad, won't they?"

"I'm not sure. We're not sure."

Sam is quiet.

"But they have Yuuki, presumably."

The unspoken after thought: *and we don't know what they're doing to him as we speak.*

"It might be," Joshua says carefully, "that they planned to take both Dad and Yuuki, but in the end having only one of them is enough. Having just Yuuki, and not Dad as well, suffices."

"Then what happens with him – with Yuuki?"

"That's not something I have the answer to."

Sam huffs out a breath. *I know.* She knows. Would she feel better if he did, though? If someone did – have an answer, that is?

"Sorry, Sam" Joshua murmurs. "I know this is confusing for you, too. It doesn't make sense to me either."

She attempts a mumbled acknowledgement back, but no sound comes out of her throat.

The remaining light of day fades.

Downstairs, their mother is in the kitchen. There's a lot of clamour of cutlery and plates from the dishwasher. Underneath that loudness, the coffee machine grinds and hums and whirs. There's the aroma of freshly made coffee filling the air. Those things aren't atypical for the Harrison's house at this hour: Susan typically unloads the dishwasher when she gets home from work around this time, and if Timothy's home then he's likely to be having coffee in preparation from a few hours of additional case work.

But there's an underlying tension cutting through the air and choking out the atmosphere like stagnant water or a stuffy room with lack of ventilation, or an incoming rainstorm heating up the air. It's coming from Sam, and Joshua, and Susan and Timothy – it's coming from all of them, and all of them sense it from each other.

It's only a matter of time before efforts to ignore it fall short.

As Susan turns away from the bench to put something away, her elbow connects with the nearest cup sitting on the bench. The cup and its freshly made coffee contents are sent to the floor. The smash resonates differently in this sort of silence.

Susan stands still. She stares at the cup like it might pick itself back up by itself and put itself back together. It doesn't. Her shoulders sag. With a frustrated mutter, she dumps the tea towel she's holding onto the bench and seeks out the reusable dish cloths.

Joshua quietly rises from his seat beside Sam on the stairs and descends. Susan steps over the broken cup and puddle of coffee, and goes to fetch the dustpan. Joshua carefully approaches the kitchen.

"Here, Mum," Joshua murmurs. He outstretches his hand, gesturing toward the dustpan. "I'll do it."

Usually, Susan would insist on doing it herself. Usually, Joshua and Sam and Timothy would let her. But this time, Susan is quiet. She relents, and hands over the responsibility of cleaning up after herself to the person offering to take over. When Timothy comes into the room and offers to take over the coffee making, she steps out of the kitchen.

Timothy takes over the coffee making.

Susan continues watching, though. "You two should be resting," she says like in a defeated attempt of a protest.

After finishing readying the coffee machine, Timothy pauses in the coffee making. He reaches out to where she's standing and carefully draws her into a one-armed hug. He turns his head and kisses her on the forehead. "I know. And we're shaken up by it. So are you. And Samantha."

Susan frowns hard. "We're less so."

Timothy presses a button on the coffee machine with his free hand. The machine whirs. "Then you can look out for me and Joshua, and we'll look out for you and Sam – that way we'll all be looking out for each other, making sure that no one's shaken up experience gets overlooked."

Susan hugs him.

"Remember at the hospital, how you said to us that we need to all be there for each other in order to minimise the impact this situation has on us all? That includes you, you know. That includes us being there for you, too."

"I know." A huff.

"I know you're worried about protecting Samantha and supporting us. But please don't neglect supporting yourself in sacrifice. Your wellbeing is equally important."

Joshua finishes sweeping and mopping up the coffee and cup from the kitchen tiles. He steps out to deal with it. Ginger rises from wherever she was napping in the lounge to follow him out.

Sam stays where she is on the stairs.

The coffee finishes. Timothy continues hugging Susan.

"So," Timothy says, "rather than keeping your own feelings yourself, try to be open about what you're feeling too. If you can."

Susan's brow is pinched. "The last thing I want is to cause extra stress from venting. You know what I can get like. I might be better at recognising it now, but I really don't want to risk me snapping. It's not a fun experience for me, and I don't want to do that to you – to any of you."

Timothy hums. "Think of it more as expressing your emotions instead of suppressing them. You can consider how much you're venting, sure, but don't keep a hundred percent quiet about what you're feeling. Wasn't it you who told me that internalising it can cause damage to one's physical health as well as mental health?"

Susan is quiet.

"Expressing emotions is something necessary and normal, is what you told me. The extent to which we do and how mindful we are of the impacts they have on others, sure, that's something we need to be careful of. But not expressing them can become unhealthy, too. Especially in these circumstances, where it's hard to find a de-stress outlet that works. And when it might not be safe, or feel safe, to try what you usually might."

A small mirthless laugh. "Yeah, I'm pretty sure an intense exercise workout isn't going to do much to quell the stress right now."

"Exactly," Timothy says gently. "And I get that talking might not do much either. But you're allowed to talk about it. You're allowed to express that you're hurting, too – I know you're not making light of ours, or exaggerating your own unnecessarily. And I know you're not about to vent without consideration for our health and wellbeing either. We know you're not like that. So vent. Give yourself space to, too. Express what you're feeling when you need to."

"And if it gets out of hand?"

"I think it's going to get out of hand at some point, anyway. We...I don't know about you, but I... I'm still trying to understand what's happening here. It's not sunk in yet. But when it does, I feel like it's not going to look pretty when it does. I'm sure holding it in will only make it all the more unpleasant of an experience, though."

Susan says something indistinguishable.

Timothy readjusts his hug. "Hmm, but you've got to allow yourself to let it out too. To feel stressed and unsure in all this, too. You're human too...right?"

"To the best of my knowledge."

"So, look – if you snap, you snap. If you unintentionally vent after unhealthily silencing yourself, then let yourself accept that as a normal reaction to such a situation as this."

"..."

"Didn't you say that the best way to get through this is if we can be there for each other properly? The best way we'll get through this, then, is if we're all able to share in the hurt and try seek shelter amidst it together. And by that I mean, creating an environment where we each of us – including you, no matter how much you try to exclude yourself subconsciously – can be open and plain honest with each other while we're coping with this."

"..."

"And I'm pretty sure you'd also say that it might hurt at times, to be honest with each other, but it'll be healthier for us all in the long run. And surely, it'll help us cope somewhat better in the coming days, when we don't know what's happening with Yuuki and we don't know what may or may not come for us."

"...you're sounding like me now."

"I had to learn this stuff from someone."

Sam exhales slowly, quietly, and stands. She creeps back up the stairs. She finds her way in the dark to her room. Once inside, she shuts the door and stands there, in the dark still, confused and feeling fuzzy. She leaves the light off and sits down heavily on her bed.

Experiencing this situation now, and looking at the scene before her, Sam feels like she's looking at a flipped piece of digital art. This all just feels so inherently *wrong*. No matter which way she looks at it, she struggles to adapt her mind to it: what Timothy and Susan have been saying, Sam can't bear to force herself to think the same. She can't handle taking it on board. She doesn't want to have to find some way to cope because she doesn't yet know what exactly she's trying to cope *with*.

She doesn't know where she stands in all this.

I'm the daughter and sister of two victims, and I guess others might say also a family friend of the other. I'm confused by how I should react. I'm worried about what might've happened to Yuuki, and I'm frustrated that other people seem to be making a bigger deal about this all than what I am able to fully feel myself.

Sam realises then that she's been doing what it seems her mother's been doing – trying hard not to vent. Trying hard to keep tabs on how wild and awful her emotions are allowed to get. But she's afraid of what might happen if she does. How will her friends react if she vents at them? What if it's too much for them, or what if it's too much for Sam? She doesn't want to make her friends worry about her or try too hard to make her feel better. She also doesn't want accidentally become akin to an irritated female dog at them.

Her mind churns. *This…it's similar to what Mum is apparently dealing with right now, isn't it?*

Sam doesn't know if she can be open about what she's feeling though, not when she can't articulate it. But maybe…maybe she could try. She could try answering a little more honestly the next time someone she trusts asks how she's handling the situation. Perhaps if she finds she doesn't want to do that with her friends just yet, she could try within the network of this family in this house. Or even just to herself. She could start being honest with herself, first.

And then maybe….maybe it could benefit more than just her – maybe it could her help Susan, too, if Sam has a go at being more open and honest, thereby indirectly encouraging her to do the same.

Perhaps it's idealistic, though. Who knows what's going to happen to us from here? And who knows how things are going to turn out once we find out what's happened to Yuuki. We might not even see Yuuki again. What'll happen to the idealistic coping together strategy then?

Sam doesn't know the answer. All she knows is 'now'.

Later that night

Timothy sits at the table, another emptied cup of coffee beside him. Illuminating his laptop screen n front of him, there's the blank white space of a yet-to-be-written reply to an email titled:

'Re: TAKAHASHI YOUTH REHABILITATION TRUST [Request for documentation of officiation]'

The email he's responding to is from Taularh's administration. Received 4.51pm. Timothy's only read the email now; he'd deliberately not looked at it when the notification showed up on his phone screen earlier. He hadn't been ready to.

The email mocks him. It's like some sick sort of taunting joke, written in fake oblivion as though the government officials haven't had adequate time to see the news of the kidnapping attack in Ninao yesterday. As though they're unaware that the reason why they have yet to receive the documentation confirming officiation of the Youth Rehabilitation Trust is because Timothy and Yuuki's submission of them was interrupted yesterday.

For Timothy, it feels like it carries the underlying question of *'you've seen what happens when you express disagreement with Taularh's established rules for the nation. Are you sure you wish to proceed?'*

There's still no report of having found Yuuki, or any trace of him. No update from Marina. No miraculous update from Yuuki himself either – though in this case, an update from Yuuki could very well mean an update from the kidnappers of him…and Timothy's not sure he'd prefer that over hearing nothing. The best update would be if Yuuki were to walk right in here, unharmed and not under any coercion such as a threat or forced to carry in an item rigged with a hidden explosive,…having escaped on his own and…

Timothy bows his head and puts presses his palms against his forehead. He takes off his reading glasses. *Then we could decide how to respond to this email together.*

Susan enters. Timothy turns his attention away from his laptop screen and tries to evaluate how she seems to be doing, after her earlier stressing. She acknowledges his concern with a softening of expression and a wave of her hand. *'I'm fine at the moment,'* it means. Susan notices Timothy's body language and expression, however, and raises her eyebrow at the blank email reply.

Timothy scrolls down so she can see the main body of the message he needs to respond to.

Susan's frown deepens with every line she reads. "They're seriously sending you this *now*? Have they not watched the news?"

"Hmm, I don't think it's out of ignorance," Timothy says carefully.

Yuuki's missing and they have no idea where he is. He was kidnapped on the day he and Timothy were to formally establish the Trust. And now

Timothy, who was actively involved in helping Yuuki set it up, and who nearly was kidnapped himself, gets sent this official notice asking them for their confirmation of establishment…

It feels like a sign screaming 'STOP' at them.

Timothy could submit the official files. He has the files – signed in pen by both Yuuki and himself. They're backed up on the cloud drive from when he scanned them in his office yesterday. He remembers the upload clearly because it finished at the precise moment those people came in. But he's not sure he wants to attach them to this email. Given the recent development of events, he's not sure he should.

"What are you thinking?" Susan asks.

Timothy hesitates. "I don't know. That's what I'm thinking – I honestly don't know what I should do with this."

"Hmm."

"What do you reckon?"

"Do we know for certain that they came for you and Yuuki because of the Trust?"

"Circumstantial evidence would suggest it so."

"And you can't think of anything else they might've attacked you for?"

Timothy tilts his head. "Not anything I can think of offhand. They didn't touch anything in my office."

"Except the three of you."

"Well…"

"They didn't leave anything in disarray?"

"Nothing. They didn't erase any of the digital files on my computer, or destroy the physical copies of the Trust documents. Even the paperwork of cases he'd been working on was as I left it, all bar the A'o Fire case that I'd considered revisiting, but I'm pretty sure that got knocked off the desk during the... the fight. I can't remember. But Marina said she didn't see anything out of place. It seems like what they came for, they took: me and Yuuki, that is. They probably would've left Joshua alone if he hadn't tried to stop them."

Susan directs the intensity of her stare at him. She is silent a moment, before reaching up to lay a hand on Timothy's shoulder. "As much as I don't want to think about Joshua putting himself at risk like that, I'm glad his efforts resulted in something good. I'm glad that you are here and not...wherever Yuuki is."

"Do you think they'll come back for me?" Timothy blurts out. He presses his lips together.

Susan ponders, then gestures at the laptop with a nod of her head. "If they are considering it, I would say it might depend on how you answer this email."

Timothy won't lie: he's also wondered about the possibility of his fate depending on his reply to this email, too.

Given this way of thinking, it could be said that Timothy's been given an ultimatum: the Youth Rehabilitation Trust or his (and presumably Yuuki's) safety. Timothy doesn't know if the rest of his family will get dragged into this by his decision. He also doesn't know if his answer will have any impact on Yuuki's fate. Unless the ultimatum becomes official – that is, Yuuki is offered in a hostage exchange for Timothy's executive decision to terminate the Youth Rehabilitation Trust – then Yuuki's fate might not be something that Timothy has the ability to determine. Whoever has him is able to do whatever the hell they like with him. They can choose not to let him go. They can choose to harm and injure him in any way they like while they have him.

Timothy is afraid to let those thoughts get carried away any further.

At the end of the day, though, he has to confront himself with what he's been ignoring: *if the kidnapping were instigated because of the Youth Rehabilitation Trust, what the hell are we supposed to do with it?*

Timothy tries to think clearly, reasonably, but can't form proper sentences in his head to do so. He's confused. Stressed. Forced to make a decision, one that makes his brain hurt like when he has to conclude a difficult case he's judging in court. He tries his best to appear collected on the outside, but Susan is watching him like a hawk. Timothy can't fool her with any façade. In his peripheral, he notices Sam and Joshua, returned to their perches on the staircase, watching him the same.

This affects the whole Harrison family in this house, this…this trauma. It's not just Timothy and Joshua's. It's not something Timothy and Susan should try protect Joshua and Samantha from. And it's not something that Timothy and Joshua can prevent Susan and Samantha from experiencing second-hand.

Even when the one still out there kidnapped and missing isn't biologically one of their Harrison family group, Yuuki's kidnapping is something that affects them all individually to whatever extent regardless.

Yuuki is a family friend, after all.

It's hard to know how best to proceed when they don't know what's happened to him. And who's responsible. It's not Yuuki's fault simply because Yuuki wanted to establish a trust for incriminated youth to find help. Can Timothy say it's not his fault, either? Timothy doesn't feel comfortable saying no. Timothy helped him make it official – so then, did Timothy screw something up in the documentation? Did they forget something when checking it over? And if so, then does that not make this partly Timothy's fault?

Would Yuuki have still been kidnapped if not for the Trust?

No. The answer is no – probably. But the Youth Rehabilitation Trust was not founded in anything morally contradictory or grey. So then…*why?* And what do they do with the Trust now? Should Timothy continue it, knowing what's happened, or discontinue it, in some hope of bringing Yuuki back safely?

Timothy doesn't know, and the uncertainty makes him feel so helpless.

If all this happened because he and Yuuki decided to establish the Youth Rehabilitation Trust…

…*then what do we do?*

10

Day…two. Outside the shed, time passes. Daylight shifts, slowly. The wind blows, occasionally picking up in strength. Birds sing and squawk at irregular intervals. The day goes by at a mentally exhaustingly slow pace. At some indiscernible time, 'day two' turns into the start of 'day three'. Still no one comes. Time continues passing as though it is not aware of the existence in the shed, and Yuuki has no choice but to endure it.

Yuuki's muscles cramp. They ache, painfully. His stomach is tight, cramping also. And his head spins in dizzying circles. Underneath that dizziness, nausea. A persistent headache.

And beneath all that…confusion.

How long are they going to keep me here? Yuuki is beginning to *want* someone to come, if it would mean that this nervous tension of not knowing what'll happen to him will ease. It's a mind game. It's having him alternate between forcing himself to stay alert, to stay mentally prepared, and the acceptance that maybe no one is coming, that there's nothing to anticipate and so he should get comfortable with this silence because he's not leaving it anytime soon.

He's not leaving this tied up situation any time soon, either. The rope around Yuuki's wrists and ankles remains tight. Secure. When he shifts, he feels the pain of bruises, of chafing and of the bindings. Throughout the course of his several attempts wrestling with it, his skin feels raw. The cuffs of his sleeves have slipped up, no longer acting as a thin barrier between his skin and the rope fibres. Yuuki had thought it might make the rope feel looser, but it hasn't. All it has done is make the chafing a whole lot worse every time he puts up a struggle.

The sheer defeat in all his failed attempts to free himself accumulates. It's yet another thing tempting him to lose a grip on his composure. It's another thing to add to his frustration, and also to his shame.

Yuuki doesn't want to imagine being rescued anymore. Even though he doesn't want to let go of hope for such a thing happening, he also doesn't want to think about being found in this pathetic state. If his kidnappers returned, that kind of 'being found' might be more preferable, because Yuuki would get the taunting remarks that he deserves. He doesn't want it, and he knows it would be awful to be humiliated in such a way. But at least it would take the humiliation and self-shaming out of his own head. At least he could give it a different voice, an external one, and direct his anger at someone else than himself.

He hates himself for even thinking that way.

Yuuki naps. He wakes to pain throbbing through his head. The headache, not getting any better. Only getting worse with dehydration. He stares at some dust motes floating about. He finds himself unconsciously clenching his teeth around the gag against the pain of the headache, in spite of knowing full well it won't help the situation at all. At least it gives him some sense of coping with it.

Has anything…changed?

It doesn't take long to catalogue what has changed, because nothing except his pain sensitivity and the aura of daylight has shifted. Still no one has come. *It's day three now*, Yuuki reminds himself. Maybe he should stop expecting anyone to come.

His legs ache from not being able to shift into a more comfortable position. The rope around his ankles doesn't allow for much repositioning. His shoes make his feet uncomfortable, and press hard against the insides of his ankles depending on how he lies. It's another impending hurt on top of another, something else for Yuuki to be troubled by. He contemplates wrestling them off, again, but last night was cold. Trading a little bit of comfort for less resistance to the cold isn't a good idea. Yuuki intrinsically knows that, and so he resists the idea and instead fixates on the discomfort rather than the idea of escaping it.

While he's still got some grasp left on sound decision making, he should adhere to what the wiser part of his brain is telling him.

His bladder gives way, again, even though he's had nothing to drink since…for the last…time he can't remember clearly. The rope chafes his wrists in his desperation to get free. He gets bitten by insects. His body is sore and achy, stiff and cramping and seizing up from being tied up and lying on the hard floor.

His mind is succumbing to the whole experience too. He thought maybe could stay sane, or stay psychologically or at least mentally sound, but…

Yuuki's not sure anymore. There's only so much one can do to protect their sanity in a seemingly never ending situation like this.

There's only so much he can from a psychological point of view.

The shadows in the room…he can't keep them from growing. Or maybe they're not growing at all, who knows. Is it a trick of the light or a trick of the mind? He isn't sure how far into the afternoon it is.

What day even is it…? If he's been counting the days right – of which there's only been two whole really long ones – then it must be Saturday afternoon. The day Yuuki and Timothy had settled on for officiating the Youth Rehabilitation Trust was a Thursday, so…

He's missing so many hours of work. Thursday he'd meant to work the afternoon-evening shift, possibly even with overtime through into morning. Friday was supposed to be a short shift, at night. Saturday…he was supposed to work today as well. For a moment, mental stress bears down on him – of wondering how he'll be able to afford to pay rent and everything else he needs, especially after having used up his savings to kick-start the YRT.

Then he reconsiders his situation. All that isn't exactly the highest priority of concerns right now. Besides, on this other side of this, it's likely he'll be given a little time for him to figure out how to deal with it all in the wake of this…kidnapping.

That's assuming there will be a rescue in the first place.

Yuuki daydreams about various possible things that might happen to him.

He imagines being hauled out of the shed, blinded by the light. Shoved in a car and taken somewhere else. He imagines Timothy there at the somewhere else, bound and beaten to various degrees depending on which version of this particular daydream Yuuki's mind gets lost in. He imagines himself being beaten to get Timothy to talk. About what, exactly, he's not sure. He imagines the opposite: Timothy being hurt further to get Yuuki to talk. He wonders what would happen to Joshua in that situation. Would he be the one subjected to harm, to torture, in order to get Timothy and Yuuki to talk?

Maybe it's not about being hurt in exchange for information, though; maybe it's just about punishment. *Punishment for what...?* For the Youth Rehabilitation Trust, probably. Maybe. Yuuki doesn't know. But it's the most likely reason. It's the only reason he can think of. He and Timothy, they don't know anything. Neither does Joshua, as far as he knows.

If the YRT is the reason, and it most likely is, then as long as Yuuki's the one receiving the most suffering, and not Timothy, and or Joshua, Yuuki's fine with this. He'll take it. If it means they'll leave Timothy and Joshua alone, he'll take it.

Still it scares him, that thinking – because right now, it could be that Yuuki's being left alone in this shed could mean that he's actually the one who's being spared of anything. In other words, what if, right now, somewhere Timothy and or Joshua are being subjected to a much harsher hour by hour? Joshua could be used against Timothy, just as Yuuki's absence could be used as a threat against them both.

If that's the case, then Yuuki might be being spared because Timothy is accepting the most harm. And so –

Stop. With a large amount of effort, Yuuki forces his thoughts to a halt. *Stop before you start thinking about everything too much. Need...need to preserve...conserve energy...not waste it on overthinking 'bout answers I can't find a conclusive conclusion to.*

But it's nice, in an exhausting way, letting his mind wander. It passes time. It distracts him from the array of bodily sensations that won't go away – the pain, the nausea, the draining feeling of hunger and dehydration and stress. Even if just a little bit, it helps him endure the psychological emotional strain of *waiting* like this. It's an alternative to stressing himself out with trying to free himself to no avail, and disturbing the shallow sense of 'calmed down' he's managed to find.

And so, Yuuki lets his mind drift.

Do I regret trying to establish the Youth Rehabilitation Trust?

Yuuki automatically denies regret. It speaks too much of defeat, and of contradiction to the motivation he possessed while working on creating it. He hopes, sincerely, that the Youth Rehabilitation Trust can, over time, help with financially assisting finding therapies that *help*. He hopes that it'll be worth this mess he's gotten himself into. If the Trust will be allowed to remain in existence at all.

A subsequent thought: *If* we'll *be allowed to remain in existence at all.*

While this Youth Rehabilitation Trust won't change the nation or be anything of such significance, really, he'd hoped that it could be at least *something.* That it could become something for someone. Working in a youth detention centre for the last few years, Yuuki's seen how the Arkala justice system is skewed against some of the young people in there. While for some of them, perhaps the time spent in detention *is* a necessary means of discipline. But for others, it's not a helpful 'correction' facility and can only make matters worse.

Some of these kids make one mistake and get themselves incarcerated. Others make many. But when all they receive are punishments as a result, what hope is there for them then? Discipline can only help so far. Discipline with the absence of healthy therapy will only reinforce the downward spiral they got themselves caught up in in the first place.

It leads to the question: how much at fault are they when society may have failed them first?

There's too much focus on the punishment side of things and not enough on helping the people recover after. Yuuki can understand the underlying rationale of Taularh's strict law: harsher punishments may discourage crime, adequately punish people who decide to partake in criminal activities, and ensure potential reoffenders get the warning not to act up again. But it's not necessarily going to help make a better society, going about it that way, unless there's some kind of healing element also involved in reform. A detention centre on its own isn't a rehabilitation facility.

And for the youth, it's more of an issue because many don't come from social or financial backgrounds where seeking rehabilitation or therapy is an option. While it might be an ideal option, that doesn't mean it's an accessible one for the people who need it.

For youth struggling to stay afloat between the weight of punishment and the costs of seeking help and rehabilitation…being incarcerated won't help them. It won't help them come away from bad habits. It won't help them avoid sinking back into the behaviours and mind-sets that landed them in court in the first place. Free counselling services are the bare minimum they're able to get, and even then it's not like there's never been anyone let down by a counsellor.

There's significance, importance – a necessity – for the Youth Rehabilitation Trust. There's worth in it. Given that they already have committed donors who have pledged financial support of it, others see worth in it too.

And yet here Yuuki is, bound and locked in a shed, presumably for it. He doesn't get it. *I don't get it.*

Do I regret trying to establish the Youth Rehabilitation Trust, if this is what it has earnt me? He's not sure. He can't answer 'yes' or 'no' with confidence.

The temperature outside is dropping. The shed doesn't offer much shelter from it. A cold draught sweeps in from the unsealed edges of the door.

Yuuki is lost in another rabbit warren of thoughts.

We were kidnapped from a law office – a law *office.*

Of all places, that building should've been one of the least likely to have a successful kidnapping take place. *How did the attack happen so easily, unhindered and quick? How'd those guys even get past security coming in like that?* It occurs to Yuuki that he hadn't seen any security guards at all. The entrance was left wide open, and no one was monitoring comings and goings from that end of the building. No one that cared, at least.

Were there not any potential witnesses for the assailants to be wary of? Where were all the staff?

Yuuki had presumed that it was just quiet because everyone was busy. Staff and visiting clients get busy. And the plateless cars outside might have been brought there in relation to some case being worked on or trialled in another part of the building. There was no one in them when he passed, or around them. Not that he saw, anyways.

Were the two things not a coincidence?

To anyone, surely, those factors alone aren't enough to become overly suspicious about. Not unless preluding circumstances suggested they were. But it's almost like attention was diverted *away* from the area for the kidnapping to happen, and in any case, Yuuki had no reason to anticipate the kidnapping coming.

For Yuuki and Timothy, the only possible prelude to the kidnapping he has his attempt to establish the Youth Rehabilitation Trust. It is the only thing that makes sense – that the Youth Rehabilitation Trust is the reason for this. Maybe it's not the reason, but Yuuki is willing to believe it is. He'll accept it. He has to, if he's to attempt to stay as psychologically grounded as possible. But...

After this is...over, if there is an over...how am I meant to face Timothy now?

They might have to drop their input into developing the Youth Rehabilitation Trust. They might have to cease it altogether. But even if, after all of this, they lose the Trust, Yuuki's not sure he's ready to lose one of the only closest friends he has.

Timothy is 24½ years older than him - twice Yuuki's own age – but treats him like a friend. Dare Yuuki say it, even extended family. It makes Yuuki grateful but uncomfortable, no displaced, in a way he can't word. He doesn't know how he should react to it. He has to refrain from using or tagging 'sir' after speaking Timothy's name, if just to show some of the respect Timothy Harrison ought to be given due to his older age and greater work experience.

It's something Yuuki is still adjusting to – this friendly familiarity between them. He'd had it drilled into him in Japan to respect power distance. *"It's different here to Arkala,"* his sister would tell him insistently. *"You need to make sure that you remember that, Yuuki. It's considered rude, otherwise."*

And then, lectures from his mother – *"Remember, here you need to verbally demonstrate social respect."* – and father – *"We're not in Arkala anymore."*

Yuuki spent so much energy schooling himself and being schooled in proper Japanese cultural etiquette that there's always a voice in the back of his head – one that sounds remarkably like his older sister's or his mother's – telling him he should correct his behaviour where it differs.

But no, here is Arkala. What is considered too personal over there is perfectly normal over here, though. Culturally appropriate, even. In Arkala, first names are used as a sign of respect, acknowledgement and familiarity. Even between friends and or couples, nicknames aren't necessarily favoured above a first name. Last names are used to demonstrate respect between people unfamiliar with each other, or in formal situations where a higher degree of respect is due. It's different from Japan, and different readjusting to Arkala culture that Yuuki once knew as a young kid. The naming system here shouldn't feel unfamiliar to him, but he got so used to being called Takahashi while living in Japan – another thing he'd had to adapt to – that he still finds it weird to be called by his first name here by those he knows.

Whether Timothy is okay, or he isn't – whether they both survive this ordeal or not – Yuuki wonders what might become of their friendship after this…or rather, what distance might wedge itself between them. Would it go back to feeling like they were strangers?

But Yuuki will give it up – he'll give up this friendship if it means that Timothy and his family can remain safe. This situation, this kidnapping, is most likely Yuuki's fault: he's the one who wanted to establish the Youth Rehabilitation Trust, after all. It's not Timothy's fault; it's Yuuki's. Timothy doesn't deserve to be harmed because of this.

Yuuki's throat constricts. There's enough water in his system to allow a few tears, but otherwise his eyes just burn. The stress, the frustration, the emotional toll that this whole *not knowing anything* is taking on him…

It's too much.

Yuuki can bargain all he wants, settle with himself that he's fine so long as Timothy doesn't have to suffer for his own mistake with pursuing the Youth Rehabilitation Trust creation, but…

No, don't acknowledge it!

It's too much.

Don't let it get to you!

Yuuki digs his fingernails into his palms, hard. A strained whimper escapes him. His jaw hurts. His muscles feel like lactic acid. He curls in on himself a little more, and turns his head to press his forehead against the rough shed floor.

Right now, it's like the rope wrapped around his wrists and his ankles is the only thing holding him together.

11

7th June, 12-Tau – evening

It rains a bit in the late afternoon, only a passing shower. Fortunately. The shed is old, and the roof might have leaks; if it were to rain heavily, the shed might not be much of a shelter. This time, at least, Yuuki doesn't have to find out if the shed roof has holes in it, or how much it leaks. He hopes he doesn't have to find out, because leaks mean dripping, and dripping means a sound he cannot escape from.

He shudders. He doesn't want to find out what that could do to his mind.

In last of the light, Yuuki decides to reattempt getting the tape off. He's almost too tired to try, but it'd be better to try while there's still just enough light to see by. Once it's dark, the process of trying to ungag himself will only become more frustrating. Yet the idea of not wasting energy stressing is… tempting. He doesn't want to subject himself to extra stress right now.

Yuuki is afraid to throw himself into those waters. Staying afloat emotionally, psychologically, is getting more and more difficult as it is. If he attempts and fails, he'll be stressed and distressed and have to expend yet more energy calming himself down to a neutral blank-minded non-reactiveness. But he's realising, and he can't deny, that his energy is failing, and it's getting harder to breathe and his mouth is dry. He can feel an irritation settling into his lungs as well, and a scratchiness at the back of his throat. Leaving the tape alone and letting the cloth stay in his mouth will not help this situation in the least.

He needs to get the gag off – and *out* – now.

Yuuki doesn't have to drag himself far to the spot he found earlier. Yesterday. The day before. He hasn't moved much from the general area of the shed since his last little crawling expedition. It's harder to find the uplifted edge of the split floorboard than in broad daylight, but he finds it and positions himself soon enough.

Closing his eyes, briefly, Yuuki steadies his breathing as much as possible. Tries to slow the nervousness hastening his rapidly beating heart. Tears prick and burn his eyes. His throat constricts. His breathing unsteadies.

He grits his teeth against the cloth and scrapes his face against the wood. Over. And over. Like an itch that cannot be traced. Frustration fills him. Fatigue. Desperation, to just *not have to feel so forcibly shut up and powerless and humiliated and restrained…!*

A whimper vibrates in his throat and through the fibres of the cloth. It chokes him. It snaps up the futile grasp on 'steadiness' that he had tried to maintain.

This is pointless.

No. No, I can't give up – at least not with this. I need -…need to breathe.

But I can't…I can't…

His energy is depleting. It won't be refreshed. He's likely not going to receive any water drink anytime soon. Sustenance is probably out of the question, even if his kidnappers did arrive to give him water. If he can't have either, could he at least be allowed to gulp down air?

The tape peels. Air meets to very corner of his mouth. Adrenaline – it makes him feel sick to the stomach, but it gives him the boost of energy he needs to wrestle with his mind and *not stop.*

Air. More of the tape peels away. It's lost it's adhesiveness. Saliva slips through a small gap made between the tape and his lips. Yuuki can't taste air through the gap because the cloth is barring the way. He's almost begging for it by the time the tape unpeels across halfway. His body registers the close proximity of a decent amount of air to his throat, to his airway, and his whole body convulses – wretches. Gags, but there's a gag in his mouth still and there's still sufficient amount of tape keeping it there, obstructing it.

Come on…!

By the time the tape tears to three-quarters of the way off his lips, Yuuki's stomach is churning terribly. His mouth is dry. Nausea swirls. The skin on his lips burns with the tearing of the tape – it had been numbed by the adrenaline slightly, but now that adrenaline is wearing off and giving way to sheer exhaustion. The cut engraved in his cheek, near the edge of his mouth, stings and throbs.

The shadows inside the shed grow deeper.

When he finally manages to get the tape off his lips, even right to the corner of his mouth, he finally lets the urge to throw up take hold. He can't be bothered straining his neck anymore to get the tape fully off. It stays stuck to his cheek. He doesn't care. He doesn't have the energy to truly care. He's trembling as he forces himself to unclench his jaw, work the muscles in his mouth that's been clamped up for the past two days, and shove the cloth out with his tongue. What follows is a relentless surge of nausea.

He's sick with relief, and with shaken-up nerves. He spends some time convulsing painfully on the floor with dry-retching. It's horrible. But he can breathe. He can breathe through his mouth again. Between the awful gagging on nothing but his own gag reflex and spit and remnant stagnant taste of cotton and dehydration… dusty air is being sucked into his lungs. Whole mouthfuls of air. The absence of cloth, of pressure and adhesive keeping his mouth shut and obstructed from breathing…

Yuuki doesn't know how long it takes before the sickness has settled down. It never truly fades. It just… lessens in degree of horridness. It becomes bearable enough to breathe around. He tries not to get hysterical about it – the fact that pressure is gone, although the memory of it is tauntingly fresh in a way that makes him feel like maybe he's just fooling himself that he ever freed himself in part in the first place.

But no… the saliva-dampened cloth spat onto the floor right in front of him is still there, and the tape doesn't reseal itself back across his lips. He can feel the dampness of the cloth touching the tip of his nose. He doesn't have the energy to move anymore. He just lets that feeling be, and serve as a physical reminder that he's no longer gagged and that he can breathe.

In the darkness that has now befallen wherever he is in Arkala, Yuuki crashes off adrenaline and slips into an exhausted sleep.

Sometime during the night, he stirs. It's dark; he can't see anything but the faint ambient light emitted from the window. Maybe the moon is out.

Yuuki raises a question at the darkness – it has no words, just a sound. The sound is no longer muffled, but carries just as much stress and uncertainty as when it was. The sound turns into a cry. He tries calling out – for help, or for some conclusion to this, he's not sure. But even when Yuuki waits or cries out in question, no one comes. His voice is hoarse and weak and he doesn't have energy to spare in shouting. It also brings him close to throwing up.

He closes his eyes and forces himself to breathe in and out, slowly. Nausea wells in his throat. With a stressed groan, he swallows it down. *Deep breathes.* His stomach swirls. He wants to cry but he can't. Even if he could, he can't afford to dehydrate himself further.

You can breathe.

Just breathe – focus on that.

When the nausea has finally quelled a little more, he lets himself open his eyes again. The same view of the shed walls and its dusty window greets him. Looking at it from this angle makes his head spin, with his head tilted and forehead resting against the floorboards.

Yuuki lets out a cough and closes his eyes again.

He shifts in discomfort, shoulders aching. He rotates his hands, but the rope tied around his wrists holds the same. It's useless, he's already established that. He gives the bindings around his ankles a kick out of spite. The action gets him nowhere. All it does is remind him that the

103

restraints aren't going anywhere any time soon.

And neither is he.

Why won't they just come for me already?

He's at the point now where he'd prefer getting beaten up than continuing... experiencing this. This waiting, but for what? If something – some physical kind of hurt – were happening to him right now, then at least there would be something for his mind to work with. The people who took him and brought him here... are they even coming back?

Yuuki can feel his willpower unravelling, thread by thread. He's been trying so hard to keep a grip on some sort of composure in spite of the situation. But he's tired. He's stressed. Scared.

It's become a psychological fight – against himself, and himself alone.

And it's undoing him.

12

8th June, 12-Tau – early hours of the morning, after midnight

Andy Park rests his chin in his hand, elbow propped up on his desk. The Peace Force uniform overcoat bunches in a weird way but he ignores it. The situation at hand is taking all of his necessary concentration.

He stares at the monitor in front of him and taps his finger against the side of his face. The updated digital report on the Ninao Kidnapping case progression sits in front of him. There's no progression. Inconclusive evidence. No leads. No witnesses.

"Hey, Jeff," Andy calls out. "What's the story with Takahashi? What're we doing with him?"

His commanding officer is busy pacing and back forth behind him. He stops, briefly, distracted. Andy watches his shadow in the reflection. "What?"

"Takahashi," Andy repeats. "The guy your group had kidnapped." He says '*your group*' like he's not also part of this inner circle of Peace Force officers conducting illegal activities under the radar, but Andy himself isn't an active member of the group and he hasn't been invited to be. What knowledge he has comes from his job position under Jeff's commandership. Even then, what he knows is already more than he perhaps should.

But I have no desire of assimilating myself into that group and partaking in their activities more than this.

A minute passes, and Jeff still hasn't answered his question – or won't, too busy searching for a lost phone.

Andy clears his throat and prompts, "He's been in that shed over two days. Two and a half, to be exact."

"He can't get out. Search and Rescue won't find him either."

"That's not the point. He won't last the week."

Jeff resumes his pacing – looking for something among the mess of papers scattered around his desk and the spare table sitting in the middle of the office.

"He'll be of no use to you dead."

"Alright, I'll...look, if he dies, he dies." Jeff lets out a frustrated sigh. "If you haven't realised yet, our group has got something else on our hands right now. And as you're aware – as we both know – 'Code PRINCESS' takes priority over one man's life. We have a lead on this case, *finally*. Let's not waste it."

Andy lowers his hand and pretends to scroll down the document displayed on the monitor. "The Ninao kidnapping is of high priority, isn't it? The officers in charge of the Ninao Kidnapping case investigation still haven't found anything. Are we really just going to do nothing?"

"The Ninao operation didn't work out as planned for us anyways."

"So what, are we just going to leave him?"

"Call it collateral damage or something."

Andy stops scrolling at that. "..."

"Look, we busted our chance to get it done smoothly. Timothy Harrison got away. We could try again to get him, but we'd risk exposing ourselves and screwing things up worse. Deborah made the call before that info on the other mission came in - we're leaving it for now."

Jeff rustles a plastic bag loudly and then heaves a sigh of exasperation. "There it is! Why the heck did I not see it there before?"

Andy swivels around in his chair. He raises an eyebrow. *For now? How long do you think Takahashi can stay alive waiting for you to recommence the mission?*

But his commanding officer is already off on his mission, cell phone in hand this time after misplacing it again. Jeff presses buttons as he goes. Nearly bumps into a support beam. The cell phone screen lights up with a call and he hastily answers it.

"Ah, Deborah. Any updates on the whereabouts of the –"

Jeff leaves the room with a slam of the door.

Andy sits there, doing nothing, but mind whirring. *Have fun following a lead that'll get you nowhere.* He hopes he hides his smirk well enough. The small amusement fades quickly, however. Andy is the one who gave them that info on the other mission, anonymously. It was a fake lead meant to distract them, since it is becoming increasingly apparent that

At this point in time, the ~~commander he's~~ assistant commander the perpetrators of the Ninao kidnapping ~~to~~ has have no true intention of retrieving Yuuki Takahashi from that shed. As far as he's aware, they've left him there to be 'missing' until he dies.

Andy stands and stretches, contemplating. The search and rescue teams aren't likely to find him in time. In fact, Commander Jeff is likely involved in diverting potential searches of that area to someplace else. It wouldn't surprise Andy if that were the case.

Andy now has a choice to make. At this point in time, the commander he's assistant commander doesn't suspect him. If Andy does what he should, and stays quiet, then he won't have any repercussions to worry Yuuki about. However, if he stays quiet, Yuuki Takahashi will die in that shed. A few more days, give or take one. If he doesn't do what he shouldn't, and finds a way to get the captive young man rescued without endangering himself and his family, then…

The Youth Rehabilitation Trust, if this is what that operation was about, isn't something that Takahashi should lose his life because of. It's not harming anyone – in fact, it aims to benefit society at both the collective and individual level. And it's not an active protest against Taularh's reign.

Yuuki Takahashi does not deserve to die because of it.

And so, so long as a rescue team can find him in time…

Andy frowns hard. He slips out his phone, and opens the photos app. With a quick glance toward the door, he taps the last photo he took. It's a photo of someone else's phone – or rather, it's a photo of an encrypted message sent to someone else's phone. Jeff's phone, to be exact. Andy took it a couple of days ago, shortly after Jeff received the message, a message consisting only of numbers and some symbols.

Co-ordinates. Co-ordinates to a place in rural Ninao.

Andy doesn't have to investigate further to know what those co-ordinates are for…or *whose* co-ordinates they are. He inwardly thanks his commanding officer for his tendency to leave his phone unattended and in easy to misplace places.

But having a copy of the co-ordinates suggesting Yuuki Takahashi's whereabouts isn't enough. Andy alone can't go and get him out of there – it'll draw far too much suspicion, and if things went wrong then he could easily be used as a scapegoat and get framed for the whole kidnapping. So then, if *he* can't pull Takahashi away from this impending – no, *apparent* – left-to-die fate, then Andy needs to find someone else who can, and who can do so swiftly.

The name of the lead investigator on the Ninao Kidnapping case report might be one idea. *Marina Tu'u*. But Andy isn't sure if prompting a Peace Force led rescue is a good idea – she could be in a similar position to himself, or could accidentally let the inner circle of corrupt PFOs know that their kidnapping operation could be about to be interfered with.

Andy closes the photos app on his phone, locks his screen and slips his phone back into his pocket.

He'll have to think, and he'll have to think fairly fast – both for Yuuki Takahashi's sake, and for the sake of allowing enough opportunity to plan and execute something to begin with.

Time to make some coffee.

.

13

Hunger hurts, pulls at his stomach. Dehydration has him nauseous and faint. He can't think clearly. His shoulders are constantly aching. The scratch near the side of his mouth itches. It hurts when his cheek twitches. Yuuki wonders if it's getting a little infected. The skin around his mouth feels irritated, too – probably from the gag.

Breathing properly isn't as easy as he'd thought it would be, with the gag gone – not with his throat dry and burning, and his stomach cramping, and his hands pulled behind his back like this. The air quality of the shed probably isn't helping.

Yuuki's mouth feels so dry. The thoughts in his head whirl. *Non-dusty air would be nice to taste, to drink, to inhale.*

His muscles ache, feel so faint. His nervous system feels like what too much lactic acid feels like in the muscles, except it's anxiety and cortisol and exhaustion and who knows what else. Yuuki turns his head against the floor again. The only thing he can really find grounding besides the restraining pressure around his wrists and ankles – although that isn't something truly grounding, just something that reminds him he can feel.

Still feel.

That's a good thing, right?

Although, at this point in time, Yuuki wishes he could just stop feeling at all. He can't last like this. Mentally, psychologically, emotionally… he's already gone. It's not that he's given in, it's that he's given it all already. He has no energy left. What little energy remaining is barely enough to sustain this disorienting, ever lowering level of alertness.

Yuuki's already come to the realisation that it's likely he might die here. If left like this, he inevitably will. If he does, there's nothing he can do about it. It's an appropriate conclusion, really. He's tried, but he's stuck here, like this. The most he can do is keep breathing… keep breathing….

…and try to stay alive as long as he is able, one breath by one breath… be it another hour or another day, or two, or three…

He just has to… survive.

14

Timothy stands outside the house, staring at the garden. There's some sunshine, but it's barely warm enough to find comfort in. And it gets choked out by all the clouds covering the sky soon enough anyways.

It rained a little yesterday. Maybe it'll rain again later, tonight.

3.37pm. Yuuki's been missing for over three full days. Longer than Timothy knows how to keep his emotions numb for. They still haven't heard anything about Yuuki's whereabouts. No one can find him. It makes Timothy think, is anyone in the PF actually searching for him at all, or do they have other priorities and all the security around the Harrison's is just some illusion to make them think Yuuki's being actively and intensively searched for.

At this rate, Timothy's tempted to stage his own rescue attempt if it came to it.

It's been 75 hours now – longer than the golden window of opportunity to find someone and rescue them in a survivable state. Time continues passing, and the likelihood of finding Yuuki unharmed and or alive decreases. Timothy waits for an update anxiously, but he's beginning

112

to accept that 5th June, 12.35pm was the last he'd ever see of Yuuki.

It makes him whether or not he did the right thing with the Trust, or rather, with the email he sent to Taularh's administration a couple of days ago regarding the officiating of it. He'd sent the documents. He'd sent them, in spite of his fears for his family's safety and for Yuuki's safety. He'd gone through with it with the rationale that, if whoever kidnapped Yuuki and tried to kidnap Timothy heard about Timothy's decision to go ahead with the Trust, then it should be Timothy specifically who they come after.

They left his family alone the first time, with the exception of when Joshua interfered. And there's security around them at the moment, and the kidnappers already have Yuuki…

There's a bleep on his phone. It's from Samantha, saying she'll be staying over at Avi's with her friends until later on.

Timothy sends back, 'OK'.

It doesn't come as any surprise: she said she needed to go somewhere else for a break, and one of friends' houses is a safer option in the meantime. Logan, one of her friends who happens to live round the corner by Village Park, came to pick her up for them to walk to the train station together, so Timothy has less worries about something happening. Still, he tries not to think about the fact that he and Yuuki were attacked in a law building…and that it doesn't necessarily make too much difference if someone is with Samantha and it's still broad daylight. Anything could happen at any time.

Or it could it not – and nothing happens, leaving them stressed out and excessively paranoid.

Timothy sighs and pockets his phone. His head feels like a chaotic mess. A tangle of thoughts. If Yuuki were here, they could talk about it. Maybe unravel some confusion about what on earth they should do with the Youth Rehabilitation Trust. He doesn't want to bother the rest of his family with it anymore – it's Timothy and Yuuki's responsibility to handle, not theirs. And even if he wanted to someone to talk to about, or even some company in this…silence…it's not something he wants to pressure any of them to have, even himself. Every one of the Harrison family is feeling the mental and social stress, and needing alone time. Or at least, a break from the accumulated stress of the Harrison family household: Samantha is out at her friends; Susan left a while ago with the excuse of needing to organise things at work; Joshua is out taking Ginger for a walk, possibly with some PFO tailing him for his own personal safety; and here's Timothy, with some alone time, too – just himself and the mirage of thoughts still plaguing him.

It's getting cold. Timothy's obsession with checking his emails pricks at his brain. He takes one more moment to blankly observe the sky before going back inside.

He makes coffee, and starts his laptop. Again, he debates with himself about the decision to go ahead with the Youth Rehabilitation Trust. He knows he'll go through the same argument with himself, and eventually arrive at the same resolution, but he needs to reaffirm it for himself. In the stretching out of time of Yuuki's absence, it's one of the only things he feels somewhat in control of.

If he gets a response regarding the Trust, it'll be one of two things: 'official' acceptance or backlash. In the end, though, he decided to send the official documents of confirmation based on the foundational principle of the Trust, and based on the thought, *what would Yuuki want me to do?* Both are answerable in an indirect way with the inference of what will happen to the present and future incarcerated youth of Arkala if this Youth Rehabilitation Trust never exists?

There's more than just Yuuki, Timothy, and the rest of the Harrison family's lives at stake here. Someone Sam's age could be convicted, sentenced and then later be dumped into a position post-trial or post-release from imprisonment where they have to try *crawl* their way out of their troubles on their own. Timothy's fortunate he himself came from a well off family, but Susan didn't, and he's well aware of the struggles she had to go through to cope. He's also well aware, from his job as a lawyer and a judge, of how much more difficult it is to manage in today's society, under Taularh's rule, than it was under the previous ruler King Fahlu's.

Timothy doesn't want to let all of Yuuki's, and his own, efforts go to waste. Not only because it would be a disappointment for themselves, but because they'd thought they had come up with something that genuinely could be of benefit to an overlooked part of society. Yuuki didn't pursue this idea for nothing.

But Yuuki's been missing for 75-going-on-76 hours now. Timothy and Yuuki were targeted specifically. Why were they attacked in the first place if not for the Trust, if not for someone having a personal reason to hate them for it? The Trust's cause is genuinely hoping for kids to have access to therapy – surely that's not something warranting an attack and a kidnapping for?

Timothy doesn't know. He doesn't know how much he cares about the reason anymore. There are times when cases get left unsolved, and if this is to be one of them – as he's so thought before – then so be it. If they could just have Yuuki back, alive, unharmed if possible, then…

Then…

Timothy isn't sure what they'll do. He isn't even sure getting him back is a real possibility anymore. For now, ensuring the Trust survives even if they don't is the only doable thing Timothy can manage. That way, if they never find Yuuki, or if they find him and he's dead, then at least Yuuki Takahashi would have left the legacy behind that he wanted to leave for the good of the community around him.

It's the truth I'm pre-emptively accepting, isn't it? That we're not going to see Yuuki again. That feeling isn't made any better when he pulls up his emails and finds nothing new in his inbox. The only change since he last looked is an increase by one to the number of emails in the junk folder.

Disappointment settles, again, in his chest. The coffee is ready but he can't be bothered getting up to get it. Out of an excuse for something else to do, he clicks on the junk folder, observes everything as useless and satisfied, habitually goes to exit his emails.

Some detail stops him.

That unread email in the junk folder. Recently received, at 2.49pm. Subject line: *YT.*

It looks like spam. Given the email address, which looks very much like a burner email account, it probably is spam. Even the automatic filtering thinks it is. But those are Yuuki's initials in the subject line. And in the small preview of text that appears beneath that line is a series of numbers – and that's it.

A series of numbers that look suspiciously like co-ordinates…

Co-ordinates.

By gut instinct, Timothy open the email. His body grows fuzzy. His muscles heat up, and a cold sweat envelops his skin. He's shaking slightly as he copies the numbers. He's not sure what he's expecting when he searches them up on the web maps. A warehouse. Some ominous location. But the co-ordinates show somewhere in the middle of nowhere. Rural Ninao, to be specific. But there's nothing there. Just a house, but the house itself doesn't seem to have a registered address.

Timothy stares at the screen.

The door opens and he startles. Joshua stands in the doorway, with Ginger padding in ahead of him. Ginger gives a shake, a yawn, then heads over to her bed in the corner of the lounge. She settles down as Joshua closes the door behind him.

"Dad?"

It doesn't take Joshua long to notice the strange expression Timothy probably has on his face.

"What is it?"

Wordlessly, Timothy gestures with his hand to the laptop screen. When his son comes around behind him, the best explanation Timothy can come up with in that short space of time is, "Someone sent me this."

The map is still on the screen. Timothy flicks back to the email.

Joshua reads it.

"I don't know who they are. I don't know how they got my address, but…" Timothy returns to the map. He leans back in the chair.

Joshua lets out a breath. "You don't think this is where they're holding Yuuki?"

"I'm not sure."

"There's no other emails. Just this."

"No threats?"

"Just this."

Timothy zooms out on the map. It's in Ninao district, out rural. He thinks about it – the likelihood that a group of people who kidnapped a person would be camped out here. It's not out of the question; there is a possibility that they could be.

But it seems weird that this email only has co-ordinates, and no threat or message or hostage video, or something beckoning me to come alone or something...

"Do you think this is where they are?" Joshua asks. "Where they have Yuuki?"

Timothy doesn't respond right away. His attention flicks back to the subject line with 'YT' written in it. "I'm not sure about them being there. But..." *But it seems like Yuuki might be.*

"Why wouldn't they be, though? If they gave you co-ordinates, it's most likely a trap. Why else would someone leak what we're presuming to be Yuuki's location to us?"

"It could be a whistle-blower," Timothy says. It's the first time that thought has actually entered his mind as a plausible explanation.

Joshua raises an eyebrow.

"I don't know. But if I were going to lure someone in quietly, I wouldn't give them material that could compromise the whole situation, aka that material getting handed over to the PF. You know what I mean? There's no threat or anything they sent along with it. No explicit incentive for us *not* to notify the PF. They haven't even cautioned us to not enter from a certain direction, or beware of the dog, or something. It's just this."

"So you're thinking that what this is *is* someone on the inside giving us an opportunity to rescue Yuuki?"

Timothy glances at Joshua with a questioning expression.

"Isn't that what you're thinking?"

Timothy grimaces.

"Yeah, see?"

Timothy lets out a long breath. He leans his elbows on the table. Clasps his hands in front of his face and leans on them. "I'm fifty-fifty."

Joshua grunts. "Between doing something stupid and not doing anything, right? Well, I don't know if it helps, but I'm opting for the first option. So…"

"We don't even know if Yuuki is even at this house."

"Dad, that's part of the reason why it's a stupid idea."

"Yes, I realise that."

"But you're still considering it anyway, am I wrong?"

Timothy can't argue. "Whether or not I'm considering it, we – "

"Hang on," Joshua interrupts.

Joshua takes the mouse scrolls in, zooming in further. The satellite imagery doesn't get any clearer. He zooms out. Moves the map around a little.

"It's not the house," Joshua says.

"What?"

"The co-ordinates are pointing here."

"Yes, they are."

"No, as in….specifically *here*. Look. Not at the house. They're pointing at the property, but not at the house on it – look at this thing here." On the screen is blur of a small rectangular blob. "This…I don't know, it looks like a garden shed or something?"

Timothy blinks.

Joshua's eyes are wide, brow creased. His tone becomes stressed with Timothy's lack of reaction. "Dad. The co-ordinates are pointing specifically at this. In other words, they're saying…"

The sentence doesn't get finished. Timothy doesn't want to finish it either. If the coordinates aren't wrong, the anonymous source has just given them Yuuki's exact location and that exact location is a garden shed in the middle of nowhere in rural Ninao.

Which means, in other words…

Timothy's skin is washed with a cold shiver. The zoomed in map image on the screen blends with his and Joshua's reflections.

…Yuuki is in that shed thing.

"I think we should go there, Dad."

Timothy's breath gets caught in his throat. Of all scenes he'd imagined of Yuuki's situation…being hidden away in the space of a garden shed on an abandoned property in rural Ninao was not one of them. He leans forward and put his head in his hands.

"Dad?"

"I think we should call the PF."

"And what are they going to do?"

Timothy straightens up. "We can call Marina. She's reliable."

"Yes, but..." Joshua lets out a stressed sigh. "Yeah, I think we should call her, too. I do. But, like...also..."

"What are you thinking?"

"That we shouldn't let this opportunity go to waste. If we call the PF now, who knows what'll happen to Yuuki. He might be gone before they get there. He might be moved. We don't know if there's someone on the inside of the PF who knows what's going here. There might be several people. If we let them know we know something, they might act before we get a chance to get Yuuki back."

The words strike a minor chord. Joshua's right. Before, Timothy had questioned the lack of incentive the anonymous person gave for them to *not* call the PF. But looking at it now, the lack of threats and whatever else may very well *be* the incentive.

Whoever this person is, they contacted Timothy directly. They only sent him co-ordinates. It might be a wild interpretation, but it's like they're asking Timothy to use his brain, interpret the situation correctly and go rescue Yuuki himself.

"I just think," Timothy says slowly, "that this isn't really something we can handle on our own, though."

"No, but...you know I mean, though, right?" Joshua tilts his head at the screen. "If this email really *is* from someone on the inside of whoever organised the kidnapping, and they decided to give you the information instead of sending it to the PF, even when they know we could call the PF...then they know that they...argh, I'm about to contradict myself. What am I saying...?"

"Then they know that the coordinates shouldn't be given to the PF,"

Timothy finishes. "Hence why they gave them to us. To avoid anyone on their team from realising that these details have been exposed. Specifically anyone from their team who might be in the PF, or otherwise soon have the information leaked to them from the PF directly."

"That. Exactly that."

With a heavy exhale, Timothy leans back and puts his hands on his head.

Joshua taps his foot against the floor. "So are we doing this? Please say yes."

The look Timothy shoots him is one that he *knows* says he's already made up his mind to do so, despite the rational voice inside his head otherwise saying no.

Joshua raises an eyebrow. He checks his phone to look at the time.

"My gut is telling me we should," Timothy confesses. "*But* I still think we should call Marina. We need to have someone on the line in case things go wrong. It…might be too late by then, if something does go wrong – which in all likelihood it might…but…"

"Okay, then let's go with that. Better safe than sorry. How much time do you think we have?"

"Depends on what you mean." *And is there any part of this that is actually safe?*

"Window of opportunity. To follow those co-ordinates."

Joshua doesn't really need to clarify. *Before we lose our last chance of saving Yuuki. Before we lose it – lose him – for good. Before it's too late.* For both their sakes, he starts with beating around the bush instead.

"…I think it's more a question of how much time does Yuuki have."

Until he's beyond saving. "...and I think the sender of this email realised that too."

It's already been over 72 hours. Past that time, the probability of a missing person's survival drops notably. They have no idea what kinds of things have happened to Yuuki in that time. Timothy feels sick imagining it.

Even if these co-ordinates lead us to Yuuki, what state will he be in when we find him? Will he...even still be alive? The sender of the email just as well could have sent them the co-ordinates to find Yuuki's dead body somewhere. Or maybe Yuuki isn't there at all, and it's all just some ploy to lure him out there, in which case Timothy and Joshua might end up getting themselves captured or killed...

Timothy frowns. *No. Why would they send co-ordinates so obviously suspicious manner like this, then, if that were the case? Rather, if the objective was to have another go at getting them, then a sort of hostage situation threat would have been the go to. Instead, this anonymous sender has given something that I would more likely take to the PF on receiving.*

"Dad...?"

But then...why not anonymously inform the PF directly themselves?

"Dad, are we going or not? I don't think we have time to have a court case discussion about this if we're trying to save Yuuki while we can."

Timothy's overthinking is taking him around in circles. He needs to think things through thoroughly in a situation like this, but...

...but hesitation can also kill.

"Let's do it," he says.

Joshua takes a moment to register Timothy's answer. "So what...we should leave now, right?"

Timothy nods, expression tight and grim. "Yeah." He closes down all the open applications on his laptop. Shuts it down. "Change into something suitable. Pack whatever you think we'll need. Fifteen minutes. I'll call Marina as we're leaving."

He closes the laptop. "We're leaving now."

15

Timothy and Joshua leave for the site. The drive out of the city is adrenaline, silence, and a filled with the pretence that they know what they're doing. They've successfully avoided any patrolling PF vehicles monitoring the area, and they weren't seen and followed by any stationed ones in Two Lakes.

The GPS on Timothy's phone, held in Joshua's hands, leads them out to rural Ninao. They're out of their own supposed safety bubble of PF protection now. Whatever happens now is their own responsibility to respond to. The risk is high. But still, Timothy can't help feeling relieved at the release of subconscious pressure of being monitored.

That relief sinks back into nervousness when they arrive at their destination.

Timothy pulls over on the side of the road, the driveway of the abandoned property now just 100m ahead. There's no one around. No other cars. No other people. Only birds, and the lonely weather-worn state of the old abandoned homestead sitting in a field full of wild grass and wildflowers. If the vibe weren't so eerie, and the mission weren't so dire, it might be a pretty sight to behold.

"This is it?" Joshua asks.

Timothy keeps the car running. They sit in the car, assessing the scene in front of them. Joshua double-checks the coordinates. Timothy tries to calm his nerves.

"Are we going to park here?"

Timothy thinks. "I don't want to risk going up the driveway. But then again, I don't think we should leave the car too far away from that shed. Can you see it from here – that shed?"

Joshua moves around in his seat, squinting. He pauses. "Ah, yeah, I see it. That tree by the driveway is in the way of our line of sight. And it blends in a bit with the trees in this kind of lighting, but it's there – it's got brown walls, I think."

Timothy finds it then. "Ah, yep. How's our time?"

"Four forty-one."

"We have less than an hour of daylight left."

Joshua hums. He hands Timothy's phone over. "And you might want this. You just got a message, by the way."

"Thanks."

Timothy takes the phone. Beside him, Joshua sends Susan and Samantha an 'in-case' last message. Looking at his own phone, Timothy finds a single message in reply from Marina displayed:

'Call me when you're there, if there is anything or nothing.'

They've messaged Marina. They've called no one. Timothy's rationale is that they don't want to have a long conversation with Marina about their insistence on going themselves, without waiting for backup. They haven't called Susan, or even messaged her yet, because they know she'll worry – Samantha too. In either case, they don't want to risk being talked out of this mission. They know it's stupid. But there's something about this whole situation that makes them *need* to follow their gut and go after this lead.

And they need to follow it without any distractions.

Timothy compromises: instead of calling Marina, he texts her. He sends her, '*Here*', along with the co-ordinates and a brief message to say they'll call her once they confirm if there is 'anything or nothing'. From what he understands of Marina's message, she just wants them to call her regardless of the presence or absence of friend and or foes. The smartest thing to do would be to keep Marina on call, but Timothy doesn't want to be distracted by an active phone call. All his and Joshua's attention needs to be on their surroundings up until they get the shed, and thereafter. Only once they confirm the contents of the shed and reassess their surroundings will they call Marina.

Timothy goes over the plans, make sure Joshua is on the same page.

"We good, then?" Timothy asks.

Joshua gives a thumbs up. He's staring at the shed, frowning, as he says it. "Ready as we can be, I guess."

"Okay. I think I'll drive up closer. It'll be easier to make a quick getaway if need be. Then let's go."

Driving further up the road, Timothy is able to see the shed better. They reach the driveway. Timothy drives them in. It feels like heading into a trap when he turns and starts driving up the dirt and gravel driveway. A fence made of wire and crooked wooden posts guides them towards the house. The path is bumpy with uneven ground and clumps of grass growing through the gravel. Timothy's already tense body tenses against the jolting motions even more.

There's an open space in front of the house. Timothy directs the car to the farthest side of it, as far away from the building as the wild grass and battered old fence will let him. Timothy brings the car to a stop. He reluctantly engages the handbrake, shifts out of gear and turns the car off.

Timothy's ears hum with the tense silence. He looks right at the shed, then left at Joshua sitting in the passenger seat. With a grim nod of acknowledgement, Joshua unbuckles his seatbelt, grabs his backpack of bare minimal emergency supplies and gets out of the car.

Leaving the car feels exposing. Timothy wishes he had protective gear on. He half anticipates bullets to whizz by or puncture his body. None of that happens. There's nothing but the wind and conjurings of Timothy's loud imagination. The immediate surroundings are still. There's no perceivable activity in the abandoned house. There's no sense of anything lurking in the long, wild grass. Timothy's expecting, at least, something or someone to come jumping out at them, but strangely, there's no one. Nothing.

Joshua echoes his thoughts. "There's no one out here…"

"Let's not speak too soon," Timothy warns. Internally, he desperately hopes the universe doesn't jinx them. But it's true. There's no one out here. No one except for the two of them, and…

Timothy's gaze falls on the shed. *And maybe one person in there.*

The fence leading up the driveway stops just before the open space in front of the house. Timothy scans the grass for any signs of wire. He tests the ground with the tip of his boot. After a few steps in with no apparent hazards underfoot, he looks ahead to the shed.

The grass is about knee height. Taller stalks reach up to Timothy's waist, but it's not too difficult to walk through. He starts navigating his way through it, watching out for unexpected dips in the ground, any puddles, or any booby traps. The ground isn't as boggy as he wondered if it might be. *Maybe it didn't rain as much out here last night,* he thinks. *Or otherwise, maybe it didn't rain enough to stay muddy long.*

Either way, it makes the wild grass tramping a little easier.

Joshua follows close behind him. "What if this is a trap?"

Timothy doesn't break pace. He keeps his voice low. "We've been over this."

The only way to confirm whether this is a trap or not is to scout the surrounding terrain, scope out the building and check the shed. Both the first two options are far too dangerous for them to do on their own, however, and it would only waste time. They're better off leaving that to the PF. For now, they'll stick to their plan of checking the shed only.

"If you see anything of concern, though," Timothy says, "yell out. Or maybe yell out, with a quiet voice. If that makes sense." When Joshua doesn't reply, he slows and turns around.

Joshua has his hands up in front of him, his phone held to his chest.

"You all good?" Timothy asks.

"Yeah," Joshua says flatly. "Sorry, I was getting the thing going."

"The thing?"

"Recording. Video recording. In case something happens."

Timothy nods. *We're likely going to need it as evidence* for *us, too – so that we have more than just our words, our testimonies, to go by.*

They resume walking. Joshua watches their backs as they walk with

129

regular glances thrown over his shoulder. Timothy focuses his attention on scanning their surroundings – their immediate surroundings, the overall environment, the ground beneath their feet, and the shed – for any signs of danger or circumstantial evidence to suggest anything they need to know.

The first thing Timothy notices is that this area does indeed seem abandoned. The grass is untouched. What mud there is seems mostly unchurned. Aside from himself and Joshua, he can imagine it being likely that there has only been one other instance of human presence lately; the only people that would have been here, besides Timothy and Joshua, are the people who came here with Yuuki. *Presuming we have the right spot, and Yuuki is, in fact, here.* If that is correct and the kidnappers were here, it doesn't seem like they stayed long: there's no pathways made for ease, no rubbish collections, no signs of anything having been organised or set up in recent years. It's like they came, did what they had to, and then left.

Left and never came back.

Whatever they left here besides footprints, they abandoned just like this property was left before.

None of it makes sense in Timothy's mind. Trying to make sense of this kidnapping only makes him more confused. If Yuuki is here, in that shed twenty – now ten – metres away, then doesn't that mean Yuuki was kidnapped only to be abandoned? Was the whole kidnapping thing supposed to just be a scare, or…was Yuuki abandoned for some reason – for instance, because he died on whoever had him?

Timothy shoves the theorising to the back of his mind. That's not what's of most importance right now. They can try figure out the *why* of everything later.

One thing that pulls Timothy's attention back is colour of the shed. The shed isn't brown, like Joshua perceived it to be from afar – it's a rusted corrugated iron. Another thing to note is also how small the shed is. It's not the size of a barn, or a garden house. It's a shed, built for storing a general assortment of gardening tools and equipment, and that's it. It's no larger than two and half metres across, two metres deep and two metres high.

Timothy's suppresses the emotions arising from the implications.

A quick walk around it reveals one dusty window filled with cobwebs on the west-facing side, and no holes in the walls big enough to peer through. He rejoins Joshua at the front of the shed where it faces south.

Joshua looks between shed and abandoned house, and back at shed again. "You think he's actually *in here*?"

Timothy feels sick just thinking of it. He wants not to think of it as true but...if it is true, then that means they'll find him. They can rescue him, if he's right there. *Provided this isn't a trap...*

Trap or not, he's not sure what he's hoping to find here. Yuuki, of course. But what about a dead Yuuki? Or a severely beaten up and mangled Yuuki? Would he rather find that, or an empty shed? What do they even do if the shed turns out to be empty after all? Presume Yuuki, if he was ever there in the first place, got moved somewhere else, and then simply high tail it out of there before anyone not friendly discovers they've arrived at this location?

Timothy's imagination stirs again, flitting sharply between an image of discovering a battered Yuuki-looking corpse and a different kind of jarring discover of finding nothing but an empty, typical old garden shed interior.

Both ideas send adrenaline coursing through his system afresh. He wants neither option to be true.

Joshua's holding his breath when they approach the door. Timothy is too. He notes how his son's face has paled slightly. He takes a deep breath, looking Joshua directly in the eye to suggest he do the same, then turns his attention to the door.

There's a rusty bolt lock across the door, locking it. Not a huge one, but it's apparently sturdy enough that it can still keep the door shut in spite of the weather. *And keep something inside from getting out.* Unless the shed had been locked at the time it was abandoned, then there should be no reason to lock it. Timothy's heart beats faster.

Timothy turns around and does a quick scan of the surrounding environment. It's just him and Joshua, the abandoned house and the open field of wildflowers and grass. No new arrivals. Nervousness pricks at him. *They could still be near, though – Yuuki's kidnappers. They could be hiding in that abandoned house. They could lurking behind the treeline past the fence on the far side of the field…*

"Dad?"

Timothy turns back around. Joshua has brought the phone camera up closer to the lock. He's peering at the lock, a spooked look on his face.

"What?" Timothy asks.

Joshua presses his lips together. He flashes his father a nervous glance. "Look at the lock. I-it's rusty, right? But…there's some bits of rust flaked off. Like this bolt got moved…and recently. When it hadn't been moved for…the entire duration it was becoming rusty. If that makes any sense?"

Timothy's mouth twitches, a smile that won't let itself be realised. "You're taking after me with your attention to detail."

That comment only serves to prolong the time it takes for the realisation to sink in – that detail Joshua pointed out, then, can only mean one thing.

…he's really in here, isn't he?

"Dad?"

"You still recording?"

Joshua nods.

Timothy clears his throat, hoping he can try keep how shaken he truly is out of his voice. "Okay."

Belatedly, he remembers about leaving evidence for the PF investigation teams. He forgot gloves – they both didn't think about gloves – so Timothy bunches up the end of his sleeve in his hand and shields the rusty metal bolt from his fingerprints with the material.

"I'm opening it, okay? Whatever we see in there…"

Timothy doesn't finish. He doesn't know how to.

The bolt is hard to move what with all the rust over both it and the metal brace, but giving it a few jolts and one sharp pull sideways does the trick. Timothy yanks the bolt the rest of the way off to the side. The door shifts open a little in response.

Timothy takes a deep breath. No terrible bloody or rotting smells cross his nose or his mind straight away, so that's one thing. There's another pungent smell that greets them, but he doesn't let himself think any longer before he entrusts Joshua to lookout duty and opens the door.

Light breaks into the semi-darkness within, and the person lying on the floor reactively squints. Timothy forgets about situational awareness in that instant, and in his peripheral, Joshua grips with both hands the phone he's recording the unveiling of the scene with.

The door squeaks on its hinges.

Timothy's voice comes out fractured. "Yuuki…"

16

Yuuki is lying on his right side on the ground. He doesn't react to Timothy and Joshua, and barely reacts to the door opening at all. He just watches, eyes glazed and half open.

Timothy moves, and his shadow blotting out the light moves off of Yuuki's face. Yuuki squints hard as the light falls over his face, eyes slipping shut at the brightness of it.

"Hey, it's just us," Timothy murmurs. The pungent tangy smell filling the air is overly apparent to him now. *Urine.* He clears his throat. "We're going to get you out of here."

The way his voice pitches at the end makes it sound like a question.

Yuuki's eyes stay shut.

"Joshua," Timothy says quietly, "if you've got this much, I think it's a good idea to call an ambulance. We need to get someone here, ASAP."

Behind him, Joshua murmurs an uncertain agreement. Timothy interprets it as most likely aimed at the part of stopping the recording.

Timothy cautiously approaches Yuuki. Careful not to startle. Keeping his voice volume low. "Hey, we're here. We're here now. I-I'm sorry, no one knew where you were. No one could find you. The PF, and Search and Rescue, they've been… but we only just…" He's not sure what he's trying to say. He hesitates. "Yuuki? Are you with us?"

Yuuki doesn't open his eyes in response.

Has he been drugged? Timothy can't tell. *We were both knocked out, from what Joshua said he saw. So he could have a concussion or something.* That's not even mentioning the fact that Yuuki's been missing for three days. He's likely exhausted, from whatever experience he was put through. Whatever they did to him. From however much effort he put into trying to free himself.

There's a piece of duct tape hanging off his cheek. Dried saliva tracks from the edge of his mouth, down his chin and across to the side of his face in the direction of the floor. There's a wad of cloth sitting on the floor near his face. An inflamed scratch on his cheek suggests how he must've managed to get the tape off…and presumably, the cloth out.

Kneeling down in front of Yuuki, Timothy gently lays his hand on Yuuki's shoulder. Beneath it, he feels the movement of Yuuki's chest rise and fall with every slow breath. Yuuki's arms and shoulders are forced to carry the motion of each breath, too, due how his arms are pulled behind him. Timothy shifts his hand, pressing the back of his hand against Yuuki's neck, the side of his face, and then his forehead. One of Yuuki's fingers twitch from where his hands are tied, pinned behind his back.

Timothy notes how the rope wrapped around Yuuki's wrists and ankles is the same as what was used to restrain himself. He doesn't remember it clearly, because he'd been knocked out. The only recollection he has of it is seeing it after he was rescued and cut free of it. He remembers it hurt, though. The tightness seemed to linger long after the rope itself was gone. His hands were only bound for not even twenty minutes, at most. But Yuuki…

…has he been tied up like this for three days?

As a lawyer, and officially a judge, this kind of scenario shouldn't be as horrifying as it is. He's seen worse pictures presented by the prosecution. More disturbing evidence shot by the PF. Heard more sickening narratives. If this scene before him were to appear in submission of evidence for a court trial, Timothy wouldn't normally find himself being overly sensitive to it. But this…

It's a whole lot different when the victim of a case is a close friend.

Timothy shakes himself back to the present, out of his thoughts.

"Right, ambulance." Joshua mutters. He lets out a tense breath and stops the recording. "Ambulance."

"Let them know I'm doing a first aid check when you get connected with them," Timothy says. He has to decide where to start first. "I'll let them know anything of concern as best I can when they ask for details."

"Okay." Joshua and lowers the phone. After a couple of seconds, he lifts his hand up again and focuses on the screen. "Wait… would it be a better idea to call Marina first?"

"Why?"

"It's just…if Marina's responding to us first, she's going to need info first. We need an ambulance, but Marina could send through a call for us, right?"

Timothy frowns. "True."

He's right. It's more imperative they let Marina know what the developing situation looks like. Timothy had told himself he would do so once they confirmed if Yuuki was here or not, and see if there seemed to be any indication of the kidnappers around, and they've been able to do both. Yuuki's not in such a life-threatening condition that the difference of a few minutes in ambulance arrival could be what determines his survival. But those minutes in terms of PF arrival could be what determines the safety of all three of them.

"You know what, let's go with that." Timothy fishes his phone out of his pocket. "Marina's number is on here."

"I have it too. I'll just use mine."

"Okay. Once you're done giving her all the information she needs," Timothy says, "for the PF and for the ambulance, go back to video recording if you're okay with it. Actually, no. Just take photos. You'll need to stay on the line with her. And I may need you to help with Yuuki, so you'll need your hands free."

Joshua nods. "Yeah. Yeah, okay."

After hearing the other end of the phone line connect, and the answering voice of Marina, Timothy redirects his attention to Yuuki. He only half listens to Joshua starting to give Marina, and the other subsequent emergency services, a rundown of the situation.

"Yuuki, can you hear me?" Timothy says lowly, so as not to distract Joshua or stress a likely hypersensitive Yuuki. As anticipated, there's no response from Yuuki to let him know. The most reaction Yuuki gives is a barely audible, feeble groan when Timothy taps him hard on the collarbone. He doesn't open his eyes or react otherwise.

His stomach churns. *Crap, this is bad.* "I'm going to check you over for injuries. Let me know if anywhere in particular hurts, okay?"

If you can hear me.

Careful not to move him, Timothy checks Yuuki over as he is. Untying him without checking for injury first might only hurt him further. Timothy would like to avoid that as much as possible.

"I'm just going to check your sight," he says, for Yuuki's sake.

Timothy gently places his right hand over Yuuki's cheek, half expecting him to flinch or react in some way to being touched on his face. But Yuuki doesn't even twitch. Timothy lays his palm down, ignoring the way his throat tightens at Yuuki's lack of reaction. He braces his free hand over Yuuki's eye and parts his eyelids with his thumb and forefinger. Yuuki's pupil seems dilated. The sclera on both his eyes have an irritated red tinge to them. Timothy lifts his right hand and waves it back and forth, the light on Yuuki's face shifting from daylight to shadow. The pupil constricts accordingly, even if only by a fraction, and slowly.

Timothy withdraws his hands.

He lets out a breath, as slow and controlled as he can manage.

He continues.

Timothy keeps his touching gentle and as non-intrusive as possible, being mindful also to take care not to move his fingers in such a way that might damage already torn muscle tissue or cause further injury to any bruising or broken skin or bones. He also checks Yuuki's skin for fever, infection and dehydration. Based on his earlier check of temperature, Yuuki has a fever. No bones seem to be broken, but there may be torn ligaments or sprained muscles, especially in the shoulders. Yuuki's dehydration is bad, his skin not returning to its usual position as soon as it should after being pinched. The scratch on Yuuki's cheek is reddened and yellowed with infection.

Beyond that, Timothy will have to untie the rope to check for the condition for Yuuki's wrists and ankles. And as for the rest – the areas of Yuuki's body not as easily checked without removing layers of clothing – that is something for the hospital staff to do.

And that's not even mentioning psychological stress.

Perhaps we should've gotten Susan to come with us. She's trained in this. She'd be doing a much better job at this whole thing than me. But Susan's not here. Timothy and Joshua are the first responders before the first responders get here. They chose to come alone, and the providing first aid if needed is, no matter the circumstances, just part of the package of responsibilities they need to accept.

As overwhelmed as Timothy might be, he has adrenaline and he needs to use that adrenaline, stay focused, and do what needs to be done. No matter how overwhelmed he and Joshua might be feeling, Yuuki must be feeling far more so.

"Dad," Joshua says.

Timothy turns to look over his shoulder.

Joshua holds the phone at his shoulder. "They're asking what his condition is. As in, the ambulance that Marina called."

Not a good one? "Uh…deteriorating. Dehydrated. He probably has a concussion," Timothy reports. The phone is on speaker, judging by the way Joshua holds the phone out to face him. "Since he was knocked out when he was kidnapped, I'm suspecting that might be the case. Otherwise, dehydration, stress…appear to be the major things of concern."

Marina's voice answers. *"Can you describe his state of awareness for me?"*

"He…"

"Not very responsive," Joshua supplies.

"Can he obey basic commands?"

"No," Joshua answers. "He saw us enter, but he hasn't said anything or reacted to us being here. He won't respond to any questions, verbally or physically."

"If you tap the collarbone hard, does he respond to that? Or any other pain?"

Timothy finally regains some words. "Yes, he did. But minimally. I'm not sure about other pain. I'm not sure how conscious he is."

"Would you define it as closer to stupor or unconsciousness, or going in and out between such states?"

Lying on the floor, face drained of colour, eyes closed, facial muscles slack, Yuuki might not be awake at all. Timothy has no way of really knowing if Yuuki's with them or not – or if Yuuki is even aware that there's other people actually here with him. He might've seen them come in, but the way Yuuki's responsiveness seems to be lessening, and he seems to be drifting further and further out of awareness...

"Maybe stupor at first," Joshua offers. His voice loses its projection. "But maybe closer to unconsciousness now. He... he seems pretty exhausted."

Marina relays that to the other line she has open.

"Is there any bruising on his torso? Any signs of internal bleeding?"

Timothy forgot to check that. "Hang on."

Fortunately, when he pulls the fabric of Yuuki's shirt to untuck it and raises the hem enough to check, there's no concerning swathes of discoloured skin. He checks Yuuki's back too, but it seems clear as far as he can see. With that, he resettles the clothing back down. "No sign of

141

bruising there or internal bleeding that I can see."

"Okay."

There are no questions asked immediately after – at least, none that Joshua can't answer himself – so Timothy shifts his attention to considering what else might need mentioning.

The wad of cloth lying on the ground in front of Yuuki's face is damp. Judging by the strip of tape hanging off his cheek, that cloth had been stuck in Yuuki's mouth for a while. Yuuki might have a lung infection, at this rate. Being inside that shed for presumably three days straight, in dusty air, and in a distressing situation, and gagged with a cloth stuck in his mouth for who knows how long before he managed to get it out...all these things would have only contributed.

After voicing his concerns to Marina, Timothy bites back a curse. *Why had they even bothered to gag him when all they were going to dump him out here, anyways? It's not like anyone can hear him out here.*

Unless Yuuki had enough energy to shout at the top of his lungs, that is, and someone with incredibly sensitive hearing happened to be passing by on the most near point of the West A'o trail. Even then, it's doubtful any of Yuuki's screams for help would've been heard.

Thinking about it makes Timothy anxious. *Has Yuuki truly just been left out here, in this shed, the whole entire time he's been missing? Or had they taken him somewhere else first, and done something else to him there before bringing him here and ditching him?* Either way, whatever Yuuki's experienced in these last three days must've been something horrible. Here, seeing Yuuki, lying between them, greying out, if even sometimes conscious at all...

Timothy and Joshua got off lightly with a concussion, bruises and a rescue from a near successful abduction.

"By the way, there's an ambulance dispatched," Marina says. *"They're on their way to you. I am too. The ambulance crew know the situation with you arriving at the scene before me, so don't worry. We'll need to have a talk about it, but don't concern yourselves too much. More importantly, are you in any particular danger right now?"*

Timothy exchanges a glance with Joshua. Joshua ducks his head out the door and surveys their surroundings.

"I don't think so," Joshua says.

"I would advise moving Takahashi out of the shed. You're more at risk staying in there."

Timothy clears his throat. "Is it safe to move him?"

"Staying in the shed limits your situational awareness and puts you at risk of all becoming trapped there. If you can, move him outside while you wait for the ambulance to arrive at your location."

"Okay. A-and…should we,…should we leave him…tied up, or is it safe enough to…?"

"Is he tied to *something?"*

"No."

"What is restraining him?"

"Rope."

"Do you believe you'll be able to remove the rope without resulting in further damage?"

"There's enough light to see by. I don't know if I'll be able to undo the knots by hand, but I have a pocket knife. I was planning on using that. I just…don't want to, like you say, risk hurting him any further."

"Use the pocket knife, make sure you can see what you're doing and try not to

jostle him whilst cutting the rope. It's up to your judgement whether you think it'll help you move him better. Just make sure that you don't manipulate his limbs too much afterwards, or you'll risk tearing tissues and causing further injury. Otherwise, if you're careful to keep in relatively the same position as you found him, more or less, then it should be fine."

"Okay. Thank you."

"I'll be staying on the line, so stay connected until the ambulance gets there. They've given an ETA of about 20 minutes. I'll be there in about ten."

Twenty minutes feels like a long wait. Then again, the drive out here felt long as well, though comparatively short in adrenaline-loaded hindsight. While they wait, Timothy sets his eyes on the bindings keeping Yuuki tied up. Joshua switches back to using the camera on his phone.

Timothy frees Yuuki, working on cutting the rope around his wrists first. He's careful to keep the sawing motion of the blade restricted to the rope, but there's a couple of times where he puts a little too much pressure on the last fibres and accidentally knocks Yuuki's fingers with his knuckles.

Yuuki doesn't so much as twitch.

One minute later, the last line of rope tethering Yuuki's wrists together breaks. The whole thing pulls away free. Timothy's overcome with an adrenalised wash of relief. It settles back down in an unsettling way – beneath the space where the rope has sat for three days, Yuuki's skin is rubbed red and bruised. Some of the skin is pulled and rubbed raw around the bonier edges of his wrists. There's still colour in his fingers, though, as Joshua reported to the ambulance crew earlier – which is, at least, a good sign.

The rope wasn't tight enough to cut off circulation, but it was tight and well-wrapped enough that no amount of struggling let him free.

It makes Timothy question just how well practiced Yuuki's kidnappers are in this. The manner in which they've done this to Yuuki seems too intentional to be a fluke, too much like a trained skill – an art – than a one-off 'we tied him up and this is how it went.'

"Dad," Joshua says. "Are you okay? Is something wrong?"

Timothy blinks. *Right, I'm not finished yet.* "No. It's okay. Sorry, I'm just having a moment."

Joshua nods, and reassures Marina and the ambulance crew correspondent.

Leaving Yuuki's arms how they are, though now simply resting in that position instead of being forced to stay like that, Timothy moves on his knees over to start working on the rope around Yuuki's feet.

As he does, Joshua fixes his eyes on Yuuki's face, frowning. He walks over, bends down and puts his phone between his head and shoulder. With both hands free, he braces both hands on Yuuki's face and then – swiftly yet gently as possible – tears the tape off Yuuki's cheek. Yuuki's head lolls against the floor a little.

"Thanks," Timothy murmurs. "Sorry, I should have done that earlier."

Joshua grimaces. "Where should I put this?"

"Maybe leave it on the floor, with the cloth, for now."

Timothy tries not to think about how silent – how defeated – Yuuki is right now. This isn't the Yuuki he's used to. It's hard not to feel additionally unnerved by it. Fortunately, since the rope around Yuuki's ankles is easier to cut through, there's not too much time to dwell on that thought.

He'll have to come back to it later, no doubt.

"Uh, Dad?" Joshua says suddenly. "It's got my finger prints on it. The tape. I didn't think, 'fore I touched it. Um, what do I…"

Timothy blinks. He unravels the rope from around Yuuki's ankles. It's not so bad with him having touched the rope, but the tape is an easy pick-up of fingerprints. And in Joshua's case, fingerprints not belonging to the true culprit but one's that could be used to frame a false one.

"Don't worry about that," Marina says. *"We know the situation. Like we said earlier, I don't see any reason for you to have participated in the organising and execution of the kidnapping. We're not about to pin you as a suspect without some explicit and reasonable evidence to suggest you were."*

Joshua nods. Marina can't see it, but his silence speaks for him.

"This is why I would've preferred if you'd notified us first, so the PF could handle it and avoid risk of contaminating evidence. But I'm sure you had some logical reason for putting yourselves in danger like you did, and we'll have time to talk about that in detail soon. For now, we focus on getting Yuuki help, if you don't mind me referring to him by first name. Get him help, get everyone out of there and then we'll discuss things."

"Okay," Timothy says.

"In the meantime, if you can get yourselves out of the shed as soon as possible to prevent keeping yourself in a position of danger, then please do so. Don't be sitting ducks. You don't want to end up all three of you trapped in that shed if anyone shows up before I do, or the ambulance does."

Marina's right. The thought of that door closing – and locking – on all three of them doesn't bode well at all.

Some talking ensues on the phone. Timothy realises Marina must be talking with the ambulance staff. Marina's voice them comes back to them more audibly, repeating a question the ambulance must've asked.

"How much light has he been exposed to in that shed? Or how little? The ambulance agree with getting the three of you out of that shed, but we need to take into consideration Yuuki's possible photophobia – that is, light sensitivity. You might need to find something to cover his eyes with if he's been kept in the dark."

Timothy's stomach churns. *I really don't think Yuuki would do well with us placing a temporary blindfold over him when he's been bound and gagged for the last…however long.*

"There's a window," Joshua says shortly. "The light in here is dim, without the door open, but it's enough to see by."

Marina relays the information. *"Okay. Use your judgement. It should be fine to leave his eyes uncovered, given the time of day, but provide him with shade if possible."*

"Okay."

"One last thing. When moving Yuuki, make sure to move him slowly and try to keep his body in approximately the same position as you found him. Any sign of further damage, leave it – we'll come to you. Only move him if it's safe to do so. If it weren't for the circumstances, I'd err on the side of caution and just stay as you, leave Yuuki as he is.

"But to reiterate, that shed is a danger. You've done a first aid check. It should be safe enough to move him and it will minimise the risk of danger catching you unawares if it comes. And we're still on the line if you need talking through anything. Do you feel confident enough to attempt safely moving him?"

Timothy glances at Joshua with an eyebrow raised. Joshua nods.

"I think so," Timothy says to Marina. "As in, I believe we'll be able to do so, if we're careful – which we will be."

"Alright, then I'd say go for it."

"We'll do that, then."

"I'm almost there. Stay on the line, and do what you can in the meantime."

The conversation finishes there. Before they decide how best to move him between them, Joshua takes the initiative of slipping his the phone into one of the chest pockets in his jacket. He's able to talk to Marina hands free this way, and without the awkwardness of trying not to drop his phone off his shoulder in the process. Timothy double checks that his phone is still in his own pocket. There's several missed calls and messages from Susan. He repockets the phone with a stab of guilt. He's nervous about checking those later.

Joshua clears his throat. "How are we going to…? How's best to do this?"

"I'm going to sit him up," Timothy says, thinking. He looks at Joshua. "Do you mind helping me?"

Joshua moves to crouch down in front of Yuuki. "…how do we…?"

Timothy has one hand on Yuuki's elevated shoulder. He positions his other hand on the nape of Yuuki's neck, fingers curled slightly around into the small open space between Yuuki's head, shoulders and the floor. "If you're even just able to support him from underneath as I lift him? Just to make sure that being moved doesn't hurt him."

"Would it be easier if I…" Joshua trails off. He shakes his head and frowns. Instead of attempting to finish the half worded sentence, Joshua shuffles around to kneel by Yuuki's head. He slips his left hand beneath Yuuki's face, cupping his cheek. Leaning forward, he then eases his hand further, creating a wedge between Yuuki and the floor with his arm. His forearm supports Yuuki's head, almost cradling it. Yuuki doesn't react. Timothy can see Joshua grow ever unsettled. "I-I'm going to hold him up. Are you ready?"

Timothy nods.

As Joshua raises Yuuki's head, neck and shoulders off the floor, one hand braced against the centre of his chest for support, Timothy pulls Yuuki up. They're careful to make sure that Yuuki's arms stay parallel or behind his body. Careful not to move him too fast. Timothy moves his hand supporting Yuuki's neck, now that Joshua's got it, and hooks his arm under Yuuki's shoulder and wraps it around Yuuki's chest. He's able to keep Yuuki's arm from moving by doing this.

It's safer this way. Yuuki may or may not be conscious, but either way he'll be able to feel pain. Timothy doesn't want to put Yuuki through the pain – and additional recovery time – of shoulder muscles tearing in his shoulder, which has been pressed hard against the ground for an unknown time, and in his arm, which has been pulled behind his back with barely any option for stretching.

If they were in a rush, and leaving right this very second was an absolute must, then they'd have no choice in moving Yuuki kindly. But as far as they know, there's no one out here. They still have to wait for Marina and the ambulance crew to get here. Moving Yuuki risks injuring him, and he's already likely experiencing a fair amount of stress already. It's best not to add to that if they can help it. It's best not to prolong

Yuuki's recovery time when there are ways to minimise doing so.

Joshua has Yuuki leaning against him until Yuuki is upright enough to tilt back against Timothy. Even with Joshua being careful to remove his arm from behind him, when he withdraws his hand Yuuki's head drops back against Timothy's chest. Yuuki groans weakly at the being manoeuvred. The scratchiness of the sound wrings Timothy's gut.

Grimacing, Timothy readjusts his hold. He slips his hands beneath Yuuki's armpits, pulls Yuuki up a little and then moves his arms around his chest in a secure hold. Yuuki's head lolls.

They pause – to recollect their thoughts, and to let Yuuki rest. Yuuki lies motionless in Timothy's arms. His legs are still lying awkwardly extending outward, but Timothy and Joshua will be picking him up soon to carry him anyway.

"Shall we move him outside then?" Timothy asks. *Fresh air. Yuuki really needs fresh air, and…space and light and out of this dang dust shed.*

Joshua presses his lips together. He stares at Yuuki's face for a moment before nodding. The lines beneath Joshua's eyes seem more prominent.

Joshua is ready at Yuuki's feet, crouched over the lower half of legs with his arms hooked around Yuuki's knees. He raises his eyebrows at Timothy.

Timothy takes a deep breath. The light and fresh air of outside beckons. "Alright, let's move him."

They stand. They haul Yuuki's body up off the floor, carefully without moving him around too much, and carefully without risking dropping him. Timothy shuffles around to the door. He checks backwards over his shoulder as he and Joshua slowly take those few steps out the door.

Yuuki is heavy, a dead weight between them. Not reacting, strengthless... too quiet. Yuuki's skin colour has lost its pallor. It appears to have even taken on a greyish tone. His hair is limp and dull. Messy. There's a bruise on his temple, half-hidden behind his hair. Small, slightly inflamed insect bites litter the sides of his face and neck.

Stomach clenching with angst, Timothy redirects his attention to the ground beneath their feet.

Finding a patch of grass that's not muddy or soggy, together Timothy and Joshua lower Yuuki to the ground and set him down. Timothy shrugs off his coat and lays it out over Yuuki's chest and torso as a short, makeshift blanket. Joshua has emergency blankets packed in his backpack, but Timothy's coat has warmth already in it.

Timothy lays a hand on his shoulder. Beneath his fingers, he can feel the slight rise and fall of Yuuki's chest. Timothy leans over to check his breathing. It's weak, but the rhythm is still there. Raspy, but somewhat fuller sounding than it had in the shed. Maybe it's the change in acoustics, or...

Maybe this is the first taste of fresh air Yuuki's had since...since he was put in there. Timothy wonders how that feels. If Yuuki feels it at all – the breeze washing over his face, the fresh air drawn into his lungs, the ground made of grass and dirt pressing against his back. The scratch on his face might sting a little bit. The light and open surroundings might drown out all awareness of everything else around him.

Yuuki doesn't seem to register any of it at all.

In the light, they see just how bruised and chafed Yuuki's wrists are.

His ankles aren't so bad, but there's still marks printed on them. Timothy remarks he doesn't think Yuuki would've been able to get his ankles free even if he had taken his shoes off. The people who carried him off here obviously didn't want him getting free easily. Besides, even if he had – even if Yuuki had managed to slip his feet free by taking off his shoes, he still wouldn't have been able to escape the shed.

Joshua comments, "At least they let him keep his hands and feet."

Timothy is silent and pale with the thought.

Needing something to distract himself with, Timothy narrows his eyes at the slightly off shade of colour of Yuuki's hands. He double checks them again, and the bruised and chafed skin around Yuuki's wrists. With a slow exhale, he considers giving each of Yuuki's hands a careful, brief massage, with the hope of encouraging a better circulation back into his fingers. But one careful brush of his thumb pulls also at the skin on his wrist, so Timothy immediately aborts the action. He doesn't want to damage the area any further.

No one mentions it, but in the back of their minds they all are aware of the fact that Yuuki's most likely been in that shed the whole three days. And with or without the gag that had been in and over his mouth, there had been no access to water in those three days. Three days without water. In the basic rules of survival, three days, maybe a little longer, is how long someone can survive without water. Organ failure and then death will set in. In other words, Yuuki, lying on the grass before them, could be considered to be in or near critical condition.

It's not something any of them are brave enough to speak out aloud. At least, not to each other. Not here, not now.

Timothy notices how Joshua won't look at Yuuki's face. Not for long periods, anyways. Glances, every now and then. But that's it. He won't look at Timothy's, either.

Just out. Around. Watching. Waiting.

Timothy catches his son's eye. Joshua looks at him then, eyes wide and staring. Whatever Joshua sees in his eyes, Timothy sees in Joshua's.

It's something neither of them are ready to put to words. The knowledge that the Yuuki they pulled out of the shed could've been lost to them for good.

Marina arrives. It's a relief when she does, but that relief quickly fades. The most Timothy can really call it is a reassurance. A little bit of extra safety. A slight raising in probability that Yuuki won't be taken from them just after they've found him.

"How's he holding out?" Marina asks. She's walked in from the driveway. "Any change to the situation?" Her eyes flick from the surroundings, to Yuuki, to Timothy and Joshua, and back to the surroundings. In particular the shed, as she gets closer, and at the front line of trees beyond the fence at the end of the field behind them.

"No, nothing's happened," Timothy reports. "No one's come, if that's what you mean. Otherwise, uh, Yuuki…"

Marina appraises Yuuki's condition. She grimaces. "…we've found you now, Takahashi. Whatever you experienced these last few days is over now. Hopefully. Though I'm not sure you're able to hear any of these words, let alone believe them."

153

"By the way, I've parked in front of you so that the ambulance can have more room to manoeuvre, when it gets here. I'm not blocking you from leaving."

Timothy glances at where their cars are parked. Marina's partner, who Timothy has already forgotten the name of, has also come along. He remains by the PF car, in deep discussion on the phone. He speaks in firm tones, voice carrying across the fifty metre stretch of open field between the shed and the driveway.

"Yeah," Timothy says belatedly, "that's fine." He can't think of how to respond to that.

They wait for the ambulance. Marina surveys the landscape around them with a frown. Her partner does the same from where he is. Marina looks inside the shed. Timothy adjusts his rain coat over Yuuki's body to distract himself from visualising what he knows Marina sees in there: the balled up damp cloth lying limp on the floor along with that strip of duct tape and an array of cut rope.

Marina emerges from the shed, her frown heavier. She narrows her eyes at Yuuki's wrists.

"What is it?" Timothy asks nervously.

"Some of the rope has blood on it. Just a little. It's barely noticeable."

Timothy hears Marina reporting an update on Yuuki's condition just then. She asks something about pressure sores. She's looking at Yuuki's chafed wrists when she says it. It draws Timothy's attention to the underlying implication of this: Yuuki struggled to get free, desperately, but couldn't no matter how much he tried. Timothy doesn't want to imagine how stressed Yuuki must've been because of it.

"They'll let one of you ride in the ambulance with him," Marina says after a while. She raises her voice and articulates more, so Timothy can distinguish between

"They'll let one of us ride with him?" Timothy repeats.

"Only one, and that's only if you want."

Timothy glances at Joshua. Seeing how his son is struggling to even look at Yuuki in this condition, it's obvious which one of them that'll be. "I'll go with Yuuki," Timothy says. "Joshua, are you able to drive the car back?"

Joshua blinks. "Uh…"

Marina covers the mouthpiece of the phone. "Can you come back with me to the station, actually?"

"…in the police car, or in our car?"

"Either all. If you don't think you're up to driving safely, I can take you back in mine." She pauses to tell the person on the other end of the line to wait a moment, then covers the mouthpiece again. "You're not in trouble. We just need your statement. The sooner we get it from one of you, the sooner we can get things moving with the investigation. It also means you'll have some down time afterwards as opposed to having more PFOs knocking on your door needing a statement you haven't given yet."

To Timothy, she says, "If you're going to be waiting at the hospital, I'll come by later or send someone around to collect your testimony later. But if Joshua comes now, it'll give you some breathing space."

"I'll go," Joshua says. "I-I have evidence…on my phone, of how we found him."

"It's highly *unlikely* you'll be pinned as a suspect," Marina says. "Either

155

of you. Don't worry. We've already been through that side of things on our side, too. Unless you actually instigated the kidnapping or partook it in its execution, you have nothing to worry about."

Joshua still looks nervous.

Timothy clears his throat. "There's not enough evidence to prove, beyond reasonable doubt, that you were involved in it, Joshua. You're still worried about the timing of you going to the bathroom, aren't you? But like they've discussed before and reassured you with, you have no reasonable motivation for being involved in what happened at my office. Okay?"

Joshua's brow furrows. He sets his mouth in a firm line and nods. "Hmm."

"If you follow me back to the station," Marina says, "we can go over all the evidence you gathered just now, and talk about what happened. Get the anxiety out of your system. You're a victim in this too, as much as your father and Yuuki."

Timothy can almost read Joshua's thoughts: *But I didn't end up like Yuuki did, and I wasn't a target like Dad also was.* Unfortunately, he can't think of adequate words to reassure Joshua. Survivor's guilt is something that both of them have to work through, but neither of them are yet ready to. They've saved Yuuki now, they've found him, and surely that's got to count for something. But the only thing that could mitigate this guilt is Yuuki's recovery, and even then Timothy doesn't think he'll so easily forgive himself for having escaped the experience Yuuki was subjected to on his own.

Timothy closes his eyes a moment. Imagines Susan's tone of voice.

Feels the rise and fall of Yuuki's chest beneath the thick raincoat material. He'll forgive himself for being less of a victim than Yuuki in his own time. Right now, there's only here and now. There's only getting Yuuki away from this shed, away from this experience and into hospital and recovery and care.

The ambulance arrives with no sirens or lights. It doesn't turn either on to announce its arrival, and it doesn't need to. The sound of a new set of wheels slowing down on the main road and then meeting the gravel on the driveway with a crunch is enough. The sight of the van is plenty of alert enough.

Timothy rubs Yuuki's shoulder lightly. Tears prick his eyes, but he won't let himself cry just yet. Later. Once Yuuki's safe, and they've dealt with all the initial PF and hospital talks. Timothy and Joshua still need to face the rest of their family after pulling such as an act as they did. Crying can wait.

The ambulance drives up and stops behind Timothy's car. The doors open, and two staff get out of the back, first aid bags held and slung over one of their shoulders, and a stretcher carried between them.

"This is Yuuki Takahashi?" one of them asks. They have 'paramedic' written on their uniform vest.

Timothy nods.

"And you are Timothy Harrison, is that correct?"

"Yes." He inclines his head towards Joshua. "And Joshua Harrison."

"Alright – Timothy," says the paramedic. "I'm going to call you by your first name, if that's alright, to ease confusion between the two of you. Thanks for your help with relaying information. Helps give us a heads up

157

of what we're going to be working with. We'll take it from here, so if you wouldn't mind standing back so we have more room to work, we'd appreciate it."

Timothy doesn't need to be asked twice.

They hand him back his raincoat and begin assessing Yuuki's condition. They have information from what Timothy and Joshua have been able to give through Marina, but there's likely things they've missed or aspects that they haven't been able to describe in the words necessary for medical evaluation. Timothy clutches the raincoat in his hands. He trusts them not to hurt Yuuki while they touch him, but it makes him nervousness. So while he stands back out of the way to let them do what they need to, he does, however, hover.

Timothy's afraid that if he stops watching – stops monitoring what people, who he doesn't know, are doing to Yuuki – something might happen to Yuuki. It's an irrational fear grounded in anxiety from what happened on June 5, in his own office, a place Yuuki should've been safe. Timothy knows that the ambulance staff aren't going to subject Yuuki to any harm, and trying to prevent them from doing what they need to will only hinder their ability to provide Yuuki with the care he needs. He knows that. He realises it enough to not interfere, to not act on that fear and anxiety pricking at his nervousness beneath his skin. But it's still there. And Timothy can only subdue it by being able to see what's happening to Yuuki and watching the ambulance crew like an unsettled hawk in the meantime.

The ambulance crew check Yuuki over thoroughly. Hands press down over Yuuki's body, clinical, methodological, checking for injury. Double checking. Yuuki's jacket is parted, his shirt collar loosened. They check Yuuki's pupil dilation with a pen light. Check his temperature, pulse, blood pressure, breathing…and this time with tools to read it all far better than Timothy and Joshua's approximate and general evaluating. Yuuki's breathing falters, but Timothy's not sure what it means.

It doesn't matter – what it means is for the ambulance crew to decide, not for Timothy to speculate about. Timothy's grateful not to be asked anymore questions, anyway. He's running out of capacity to talk. Fortunately, any additional information the ambulance crew would need to know has already been given either by Timothy or elaborated on by Marina. At this point of time, he's fine just to stand by and watch.

The paramedic raises her voice. "Takahashi. Yuuki. It's alright. We're just checking you for injuries. We're here to help. Relax. Deep breaths, okay?"

"What's happening?" Timothy asks.

There's talk of oxygen therapy. The scratch on Yuuki's cheek is cleaned, some kind of ointment rubbed into it and then a soft plaster is laid over it. While the fingers touch his face, Yuuki's breathing stutters and shallows.

The technician answers Timothy's question. "It seems that he's stressed by being touched," they say. "He's having trouble breathing properly."

Timothy can see it now. Yuuki's tense, like he's in the middle of having a nightmare. The touching won't stop – can't stop, because this is first aid and they need to assess him – and Yuuki is reacting to that, bracing himself against it by breathing less. By holding his breath,

159

unconsciously.

"It could be something to do with him having been kidnapped," Joshua suggests.

"Perhaps. Are you aware if he has any sensory issues that might be contributing?" asks the technician. "Or if he's touch adverse, in any way?"

Timothy stares at Yuuki uncertainly. "I – I'm not sure."

"Get the manual resuscitator ready," the paramedic cuts in.

The technician nods, and does so. They continue speaking as they do what they need to, "It's not just notes on physical health we need to pass on to the hospital – if possible, we should also account for any mental or psychological factors that might be contributing to his condition. Furthermore, it will be important to make note so that later on it is easier to recognise and then distinguish between what might be a pre-existing condition and what might be a symptom of trauma."

There's a silence at the word. Timothy feels cold. *Trauma.* A word he's used in appropriate and formal contexts many times, yet thinking of it applying to Yuuki, in the overwhelming psychological sense, is… something that Timothy's mind fails to grasp.

The technician places the silicon oxygen mask over Yuuki's nose and mouth. Yuuki's brow twitches. The technician holds the mask in place and begins pumping air.

The paramedic hums. "We had a kid reacting badly to the nurse giving him treatment recently. Actually, might've been last year. Teenager with a burn on his side. Touch-adverse, from what I gather. Made treating the injury difficult, that's for sure." She lets out a sharp exhale. "I can't say any more about it, but the point is, knowing this might've made it easier for everyone and less stressful of an experience for the kid."

Before them, the skin on Yuuki's face appears to drop yet another shade of colour. His breathing is ragged, shallow. Barely any breath can be seen fogging up the mask.

Exchanging a glance with the paramedic, the other technician finishes writing a note, then turns to Timothy. "Don't overthink it, but if you're aware of anything, let us know. Bear in mind this could be a reaction resulting from the kidnapping experience, like you said." The paramedic and first technician speak reassurances to Yuuki. The second technician frowns. "But if there's any other layer to it... preferably let us know as soon as possible, in case his consciousness levels change and we have something else to manage."

Timothy glances at Joshua. This is the first time anything like this has happened for Yuuki, though, as far as they're aware. He hasn't been physically messed with before. It's probably more a personal thing. But Timothy can't think, offhand. Except – "I'm not sure about it, but I think he's pretty selective about who he lets touch him, and when. He has to emotionally trust a person, I think. Otherwise, it's..."

It's what?

The paramedic radios in to whoever, reports an updated evaluation of Yuuki's condition and advises them to prepare a mild sedative. Timothy's blood runs cold at the idea of drugging Yuuki – especially right after he's just been through a kidnapping ordeal. But he understands the rationale, and he trusts their judgement. Yuuki needs rest, not more stress.

Once the other technician has finished their assessment, and reported in medical terminology what is necessary information to relay, the three start packing up gear.

"Alright," says the paramedic. "We're moving."

The second technician looks at Timothy. "Are you riding with us?"

Timothy glances with Joshua to check he's alright going back on his own, then nods. "If that's still okay."

"We can only allow one person to ride in the van with us. If it's just you, then that's fine."

Joshua gives the thumbs-up.

Timothy nods. "Yes."

"Okay," the second technician says, "then follow us."

The paramedics and technicians first move Yuuki onto the orange stretcher. They position themselves around Yuuki, hands firmly placed against his body. On a briefly spoken cue, they haul him up off the grass on a few centimetres, lowering back down again a few seconds later on the stretcher. An emergency blanket is laid out over him and tucked in around him. Yuuki's shoulders are slack, arms limp at his sides. The technician resumes pumping air.

They pick up the stretcher.

Yuuki is carried away, the paramedic at his feet and a technician holding the handle by his head. By his side, the other technician pumps the manual resuscitator. Ahead, one of the newly arrived Peace Force officers has a camera. They've already started taking shots of the surroundings, the house, the shed. The driveway. Yuuki, shielded by the paramedic.

Arrived at the ambulance, the stretcher is lifted up onto a gurney. With practised movements, the ambulance crew push the gurney up and into the van, its legs folding up under itself. With that, Yuuki is loaded safely into the ambulance. The technicians climb into the back after and ahead of him.

Timothy lays his hand on Joshua's shoulder. "I'm going ahead. What will you do?"

"Have you decided?" Marina asks.

"I'll meet you at the station," Joshua says to Marina. He turns. "Dad, I'll see you at the hospital, later?" He looks uncertain.

Timothy attempts a reassuring smile. It's far too grim an expression he pulls for it to be a smile. "You'll be fine. You're not in trouble, remember? Just answer as best as you can. Marina's not going to expect a perfect answer from you, so just…do the best you can to describe what you need to, but don't put too much pressure yourself. If you're unsure of anything, I'll be round at some point to give my own statement, and I can help fill in any blanks of vague areas or what have you."

Marina nods. "Just as your father said. Don't worry too much. Are you going to be okay to drive?"

"Yeah," Joshua replies. "I think I could do with some processing time, to be honest."

Timothy hums.

"Also Dad, do you want me to take your jacket?"

"Oh…if you wouldn't mind?"

The jacket has been lying over Yuuki's damped clothing as a shield, so Timothy doesn't think it's a good idea to put it on again until it's been washed.

Joshua takes the jacket, folding it in half, ensuring to hold it by the collar.

"We're just waiting for the investigative team to arrive," Marina says. "Once they're here, we'll go when you're ready. There's not much light left, so we want to do a quick scour of that house, the shed and the surrounding area before it gets completely dark. If you want to hang around with us while we do a quick check, that's fine too. Just if you're needing to leave, make sure you let me know. For your own safety, especially after this rescue mission, I need to make sure you have one of us with you on the way the back."

The ambulance crew call they're leaving. Timothy waves to Joshua and Marina, then makes his way back over to the van.

"When we do leave, just drive safely, okay?" Marina says to Joshua as Timothy's leaving. "I'll go ahead of you, but I'll be right ahead of you. So if you need to pull over, or you need to stop halfway and want to hop in for the rest of the way, then come back and get the car later, that's totally fine, too."

Timothy climbs up into the ambulance. The soles of Yuuki's shoes greet his face. In his peripheral vision, he sees Joshua gives a nod.

"Thanks."

However the rest of the conversation goes, Timothy doesn't hear it. No sooner are both his feet up onto the floor when the van doors are being shut behind him. He navigates the small space, sidling over to sit on the small bench.

Timothy sits. His heart pounds.

"You all good?" asks one of the technicians.

Timothy answers with a thumbs up.

Yuuki's skin tone looks even more drained of colour under the ambulance interior lighting. The technician is in the middle of swapping the manual resuscitator with an oxygen mask. Timothy wouldn't have thought it would have taken that long, but they could've been doing additional monitoring of Yuuki's respiratory system while they waited for Timothy.

The ambulance starts driving. They turn. The technician waits until they've cleared the bumpy gravel dirt driveway and the van hits the road before setting the oxygen mask in place.

Timothy gets the hesitation now. Yuuki's eyelids part. He 'wakes' briefly the moment the mask is pressed over his face. The technician doesn't pull the straps around Yuuki's head until they're sure of Yuuki's reaction. Timothy feels a tear slip down his cheek. Yuuki's eyes open, but his eyes are rolled back and he likely can't see anything. When Yuuki's startling settles down, and his eyes slip shut again, the technician deftly secures the straps around Yuuki's head to keep it in place hands-free.

He was gagged. At some point during the kidnapping, someone had their hands pressed against Yuuki's face. They put cloth in his mouth and taped his mouth shut with tape. Did they make him breathe in anything? If they drugged him...if they made him breathe in some chemical drug to subdue him, then who knows how long they kept their hands on his face for. Those kinds of drugs don't work like they do in movies; they would've had to keep their hands over Yuuki's nose and mouth for a while – for as long as it took for the drug to completely subdue him.

Timothy's skin feels cold. It's getting darker outside, and colder by the minute, but this is a different kind of cold. *No wonder he's reacting to the mask.* The technician has been talking to Yuuki, still is, reassuring him, telling him to breathe normally, that it's just oxygen. But whether or not Yuuki registers any of that, it's hard to tell. Yuuki might not trust the voice that's telling him this. He's being told to breathe in the air that the mask is filtering for him, but he might not want to.

Timothy reaches for Yuuki's hand. He stops himself, throwing a questioning glance at the paramedic. They don't tell him not to. Timothy can't forage for the words to ask.

"Yuuki," he says, his voice patchy. He takes Yuuki's hand, one hand beneath, supporting, and the other over the back of his hand, covering, protecting. He's careful of the pressure sores on Yuuki's wrist. "Yuuki, you're in safe hands now. Just hang in there, okay?"

Yuuki lies still. Eyes closed. Hair limp on the cushion supporting his head. His breath fogs up the mask, but perhaps not as much as it should.

"We found you. I promise we're all going to make sure that you feel more okay soon."

Timothy knows he can't promise that Yuuki *will* feel okay anytime soon. But he will try to help him to feel somewhat okay. He must try to. Because Timothy inherently knows that rescuing Yuuki doesn't stop here.

The kidnapping of the Ninao incident might be over, but the impact of it surely is far from it.

17

His body... disconnected to himself.

His mind is far away.

At some point, Yuuki's wrists are no longer bound together. But the rope has been tied around them so long, it doesn't feel like there's any difference. Yuuki barely registers he's been untied. The sensations of bruising, unrelenting tightness are still there. And he's been hearing things this last while, after all. Nothing has changed, and he's accepted already that it won't. There's no one coming for him, to rescue him or haul him off elsewhere or otherwise...

But he can hear voices drifting around in his mind.

They speak lowly, in tones of quiet questioning. They don't sound like imaginings of his own mind.

There's a pressure on his shoulder, keeping him tethered to the ground, keeping him from floating away. He continues hearing the voices, and a part of him wants to believe that it sounds like Timothy's voice in amongst them. Because it doesn't make sense for Timothy to be here.

Therefore, he is hallucinating.

He must be hallucinating, because the voices are still there. Somewhere. And there's another voice that sounds like Joshua's. It makes no sense for Timothy to be here alone, with Joshua. The other two who were with Yuuki at the office. Not unless…

…not unless they were also kidnapped, and have been brought here into the shed with him. But Yuuki doesn't want to entertain that thought any more, just in case it turns out to be real.

And he doesn't want to wake up any more to find out if it is.

..

…

More voices. And a siren.

Hands touching him. He doesn't like it. Foreign – unfamiliar – voices. He doesn't hear the words they're saying. But he can't react or respond enough to move away or tell them to *please stop touching* him.

Gravity shifts. Dizzying movement.

Noise alters.

…

Something is pressed over his nose and mouth. It scares him. It sends a spear of fear stabbing through the centre of his being. Voices talk. They talk like they're reassuring him. He doesn't have the energy to try understand why.

He realises that the mask held over his nose and mouth doesn't restrict his breathing like he half anticipated it to. It doesn't choke him with chemically potent air. Instead it is tasteless, clean, and makes it easier for him to breathe.

Yuuki relents.

Timothy's voice stays nearby.

That's the last thing Yuuki's aware of for a while.

18

The sun sets, and the sky starts to darken. Kyle is on his way out to Village Park when the game show his foster mother is watching is replaced by breaking news: Day 3 of the Ninao Kidnapping case – Takahashi found.

They've found Yuuki Takahashi, apparently. He's alive. In a bad condition, but alive. He was found in a garden shed on an abandoned property in rural Ninao. He's been taken to A'o Hospital. There's no more details to be given besides that – the update on the 06/05 Ninao Kidnapping is just a preview for the upcoming news channel at 6pm. Kyle isn't staying in the house for another twenty-five minutes to listen to though.

Arriving at Village Park, Kyle sits down on one of the swings. He grabs his phone out of pocket of his thin jacket. He searches up the news on the internet. The update illuminates the screen.

The most recent update is within the last ten minutes. He doesn't watch the livestream of the news because it would churn through what little mobile data he has. Instead, he's finds a written article.

The article only has the bare information necessary for the update. Peace Forces are conducting an investigation into the purpose and the perpetrators of the kidnapping, but they can't determine much until Takahashi has recovered and can tell them what happened. The major concern for Takahashi's health is dehydration and hunger. There appear to be no other significant complications. For whatever reason, Kyle feels an ominous "*yet*" looming over that statement.

Kyle thinks of his classmate Samantha Harrison, and the strangeness of knowing someone who's directly involved in such an incident. Sure, Sam herself isn't a direct victim of the case, but two of her family members are, and someone the family knows is. He saw her breaking out of her neutral emotional façade at the library the other day. This whole thing does impact her directly.

Vaguely, Kyle wonders what sort of person Yuuki Takahashi is. He has no idea. Besides the general information of age and work position and a portrait photo of him shown on the news, the only idea that Kyle has of Takahashi is that he's close with Harrison family. That, and something about some new youth recovery trust or something that he'd been finishing up with Sam's father when the kidnapping happened.

Yuuki Takahashi seems like a good person. None of it is my personal concern, though.

They're two separate lives. Kyle has no connection to this Yuuki, and neither does Takahashi to him. What kind of person Takahashi is and how he'll be doing in a week, a month, a year's time is none of his personal concern. Kyle can't see anyway that they'd ever become acquainted beyond formal introductions with last names. There's a weird churning in his chest, a kind of disappointment hollowing out something deep inside of him – like some potential connection by fate that he has to give up on, because it's not his business to mind and it's not his place to be.

Still, Kyle hopes that Takahashi is somewhat able to get his life back after such an experience. At least he's not alone in the aftermath of it. The Harrison family will likely be at the hospital with him over the next few days. The whole group have the support of each other.

Unlike me. Unlike Kyle, who was left alone to cope by himself in the aftermath of the 8-Tau A'o Fire that took his father – the only person Kyle had for family and the only person he could consider a friend – from him. The pain nips and gnaws at the centre of his chest. It stabs just below the sternum.

It's bittersweet to be relieved for a stranger's wellbeing to be cared for in the aching absence of such an experience for oneself. Kyle won't call it jealously or envy, because he's conscious of what different emotions feel like in himself and it's not that.

No, it's not jealousy. It's grief.

With a grimace and mixed emotions regarding the aftermath of kidnapping rescue, Kyle closes the app. He turns off his mobile data and put his phone back in his pocket. The wind blows, and Kyle's hair catches in it and flies about his face. He tugs the collar of his jacket closer around the back of his neck.

Whatever happens to Yuuki Takahashi and the Harrison family, happens. Right now, Kyle still has his own aftermath to worry about. The only thing he can hope is that Takahashi isn't left to grieve alone like Kyle has been.

19

The Ninao Peace Force station feels oddly not busy. Joshua's nervous system feels busier. He bounces a knee up and down, the seat he's sitting on quaking a little with it. It makes him nervous, sitting here alone.

Marina appears again soon enough, fortunately. "Sorry to keep you waiting," she says. She hands him back his and Timothy's phones. "We've copied all that we need. It's going to take a short while to officially process, but I won't keep you here while we do that. We just need your statement regarding what's happened – particularly in the last couple of hours. It'll help to verify some details for us."

Joshua nods. "Okay."

"Are you okay doing it here?" Marina asks, weighing up his expression. "Your giving your statement, I mean. Or do you want to go to a private room to talk about it?"

"Will a private room make me feel like I'm being investigated for conducting the whole thing myself?"

Marina stares at him a moment, expressionless. But there's a shift in her body language. Her demeanour isn't so rigid, and her stance not so explicitly ready for a fight. She's cautious, but not of Joshua. Instead, she's looking more cautious of herself.

"We're not investigating you as a culprit," she says calmly, and this time a little more gently than the tone she had been using before. She continues in that lower tone, "The only thing you're in trouble for is recklessly pursing a lead that could've gotten yourself and your father in danger."

Joshua pulls his jersey around himself. He wonders if other officers might see this action and consider the possibility of him concealing something. He swallows.

"Shall we start the recording of your statement here, then? We can move to another room if you feel you'd rather some privacy."

"Okay. Thanks."

Joshua zones out while Marina finishes getting set up. He tries to think of something, of *anything,* but can't. There's no words he can summon to mind in advance for the statement, no reassurances he can reassure himself with. He's not sure if he'd feel any better if his Dad were here – no, he would feel better, because Joshua's a university student studying security and monitoring technology and Timothy's an experienced lawyer-turned-judge who knows how things go down in the justice field of things.

"We're not investigating you as a culprit," she'd said. But what if I accidentally word things wrong and frame myself and make myself out to be one?

Marina appraises his body language, his expression. "After this, you're free to go. I can take you the hospital afterwards, if you would like – that's where Yuuki has been taken, and I believe the rest of your family will be there a little while."

"Okay."

175

The last Joshua checked his phone, there had been messages from both Susan and Sam saying they'd be meeting him and Timothy at the hospital. Sam's friends' parents were going to drop Sam off. Susan is probably already there. There's new messages again, on Joshua's phone and on Timothy's phone, but Joshua doesn't look at either lot of them.

Everything is still being processed in his head. Joshua doesn't have the spare mental energy to respond to those while trying to form good enough sentences in his head to report to the PF.

"I'm going to start the recording now," Marina says. "I'll keep it going, but if you need a break – if it gets too much – you just let me know, okay?"

'I'm worried I'm going to say something wrong,' Joshua wants to say, but all that comes out is another simple, "Okay."

A *bleep* and a red light on the voice recorder on the desk. Joshua stares at it like it's going to determine his fate. He notices Marina watching his expression, his body language…and he takes a deep breath. Marina isn't looking to condemn him. She's not the kind of person who would coerce him into giving a false statement. She's not the kind of person who will make him trip up over his own words just to find something to use to convict him with.

They talk through the happenings. It's more of a discussion than a questioning, and less of a 'describe everything in detail and in chronological order' than Joshua was expecting. Joshua starts with describing his and Timothy's reasoning – the concerns they had and debated with before they packed their things and left the house.

"We knew it was dangerous," Joshua says. "But we were worried

176

Yuuki might be gone by the time anyone got there if we called anyone. Or that maybe someone would overhear and shift him. O-or kill him."

"I'm sure you were both aware of the danger," Marina says, "otherwise you wouldn't have notified me and called me while you were there."

Joshua nods. His hands are clammy. "...I'm sorry we didn't call you sooner. I know we should've. And I know what we did was stupid. I...we just..."

"It was justified in your minds, and you've expressed what concerns you had with what you saw was at stake. And besides, your recklessness isn't an unexpected *stupid* behaviour given the circumstances." Marina grimaces. "It's part of the reason why we had security nearby for you all – not just because of the possible danger someone else might've posed to you, but also because of the potential danger you posed to yourselves."

"Still..." Joshua hesitates. He's aware of the camera recording and feels ashamed. "I'm aware that what we did was stupid. S-so please don't...I don't even know what I'm asking. I-I guess I'm just...- I mean, Dad's a lawyer and a judge, so I *know* he wouldn't go into something that could get us framed or something, or...but...it's just that there was no one else there, at the office, and then...I..."

Marina raises her hand to the camera. "Do you need to take a break?"

Joshua shakes his head. "No. I'm sorry."

"It's okay. Listen, you don't need to explicitly label your actions as wholly right or wrong. Cases such as these are personal, and the fear involved in such situations can make people do reckless things."

Joshua grips the two phones in his hands.

"You both may also have been dealing with survivor's guilt that you got free but Yuuki didn't. I get that you're greatly concerned about the possibility of being considered a culprit in all this, but even right here right now, where you're getting ahead of yourself, there is no evidence that we have that says – beyond any reasonable doubt – that you were involved in orchestrating the kidnapping. And I get that, in spite of that, you may still be feeling some kind of guilt and that guilt that you might be experiencing could very well be – is highly likely, in your case – to be survivor's guilt. What I'm trying to say here is, we're here for your witness statement, not an excuse to condemn you."

The reassurance is…reassuring. It doesn't stop Joshua from experiencing anxiety over the idea, though. The thought that, in another time and place, another officer – someone other than the understanding Marina – might think otherwise remains with him. For some reason, Joshua can't seem to rid this nervousness from his mind.

"We can neither say," Marina says, "that what you and your father did was right or wrong. Instead, the better description would be in terms of risk: it was dangerous. Even if Yuuki was in danger, putting yourselves in danger wouldn't help anything.

"Hesitation is dangerous, too," Joshua interjects. "Like at the Ninao office – Dad would've…would've been successfully kidnapped if I had kept hesitating. Along with Yuuki, he…"

Marina nods. "Yes, you're right – hesitation can be just as dangerous as taking action too soon can be. However, in saying that, going inadequately prepared can cause more harm that taking the necessary time *to prepare*. You and your father could've called me before you took action and at least waited for me to get an armed team dispatched. That's what you ought to have done. But I can understand why you didn't wait – as you've both already expressed, you didn't wait out of concern that Yuuki might've expired or have been transported elsewhere by the time anyone got there, depending on how long it took to mobilise a crew.

"In the end, you and Timothy knew the risks, Yuuki has been recovered, and no harm came to anyone – the mission was a success, and not at the expense of anyone's wellbeing. But in the future," Marina says firmly, "should anything arise in follow up of this case, I want to ask that you call me on the matter first."

Joshua musters a grim smile.

"And regarding your concern that yours and your father's initiating and filming a rescue might be interpreted as – don't stress too much. It won't get that far," Marina reassures him. "We're not here to falsely identify someone. That isn't going to help solve anything for this case. You and Timothy have no justifiable reason for having organised something like this to happen to Yuuki. Your Dad being a lawyer and judge – in other words, with knowledge of how case evidence and investigation procedures work – means that you're not about to get pinned as suspicious for having thought of filming their reactions.

"Maybe in some other case, we might consider it otherwise suspicious. But we're not about to label it as such without any real supporting evidence suggesting that it could be. We'll still have to have the images and video files analysed as part of procedure – for authenticity of files and of your own reactions depicted in them. But don't worry too much about that. I have minimal concerns regarding it.

"And don't forget, we'll be collecting a statement from Yuuki, too. Unless he has something to say against you, I believe you should have nothing to worry about."

A statement from Yuuki. Yuuki, who they feared might be gone for good, giving a statement. *Why is it harder to imagine him injured and dead than sitting up awake in some hospital bed giving a statement?*

For the first time, Joshua feels something inside of himself break. It's a psychobiological shattering, snaking up a tempered glass wall. He hasn't been apart from his family members too much in these last few days, and now that he's finally alone...*alone*...and Yuuki is no longer *missing*...

A tear slips out of one eye. His mouth wobbles. He hastily raises one clammy hand to swipe at the tear. He misses, and as he drags the back of his hand across his face, succeeding this time, more tears fall. The silence is thick around him. Deafening. Choking. Waiting.

Marina stops the recording, and Joshua is overcome by the crushing emotional weight of what's happened now settling down around him.

Joshua has no more words.

Yuuki has been found – that's the only clear thought he can manage.

Outside the ambulance van, streetlights start glowing. The cloudy sky loses daylight. By the time they reach the hospital in A'o, it's dusk and night has essentially fallen. Timothy watches the last of the daylight fade with a muted sense of reprieve and the reassurance to be had in knowing that this night will be different from last night and the day before.

This won't be another night that Yuuki spends in that shed.

They arrive at A'o hospital at 5.51pm. Timothy only knows the exact time because he receives a text message from Susan as the van doors open. He checks it after he gets out of the ambulance. Timothy stands in the ever-cooling air. The sky is dark. The lights are bright. There's noise from the city, and from beside him as the Yuuki is unloaded from the ambulance.

The screen brightness on his phone is blinding. *"I'm on my way,"* the text reads.

Timothy can't pick a phrase to respond with. In his indecision, he lets the screen dim and go black. He leaves Susan's message unreplied to. She'll be here soon enough anyways.

Yuuki is taken inside on the gurney. Yuuki's eyes stay closed above the mask. The ambulance crew are communicating with the hospital staff as they run him in, speaking in terms that Timothy doesn't understand but that Susan would. It's a clear reminder that this isn't Timothy's area of expertise, and that he has no say in anything like he might in a court. The trundling sound of the wheels of the gurney with Yuuki on it head for the automatic doors.

"Go wait inside," the paramedic tells him. "Someone will update you on his condition as soon as they're able."

Timothy nods. He watches Yuuki and the medical team with him disappear behind the doors. He's feeling strange. Feeling like everything's surreal. The ambulance that drove them here drives off, leaving Timothy standing where he is by himself. He numbly follows Yuuki inside. Though he knows he'll only go as far as the foyer, and then a waiting room or wherever he'll be allowed to be...

181

The hallway is quiet. But Timothy's head is loud. The walls around him serve as like a blank whiteboard, and all the voices and imagery and sensations of the last hour rush to fill it up.

Yuuki lying on the grass outside the shed. Joshua looking away.

The ambulance arriving.

Marina.

Co-ordinates, and the tense debate as to whether or not they should follow it. Whether or not they're stupid enough to throw themselves into a dangerous unknown like that.

Of all the fragments that stay with him, it's the voices of the ambulance crew that are the loudest, most frequently replaying. But as for the most vivid, visually...Timothy can't get it out of his head, how awful the pallor of Yuuki's skin is. It almost appears *grey*. Pale is one thing, but that greyish tinge accompanying it is...

...far too real a sign that death might've only been a day or two away.

Whatever happened to Yuuki these past three days, they won't know until Yuuki's recovered enough to tell them. Is it something that Yuuki will want to speak about, though? Timothy isn't even sure how much *he wants* to ask to know. He's still having trouble processing it all, and trying to figure out how to feel about finding Yuuki in the condition he was in. It's hard to call it a relief he wasn't hurt more when Timothy and Joshua found him in the state they did. It's a confusing sort of self-contradicting...*something:* Yuuki wasn't hurt, but he was; he was in a bad condition, but not as bad as some of the renderings in Timothy's anxious imagination.

If Yuuki had died, it would have been first because of severe dehydration. Primarily that, but maybe also because a respiratory infection, and lack of sustenance, and *stress* –

"And because we didn't – couldn't – get to him sooner."

Those words leave Timothy's lips, unbidden. He covers his mouth with his hand. His voice wasn't loud just now, but it was loud to him. Some blood leaves his face. *Yuuki could've survived another few days, though, right? If we hadn't found him yet…? He'd have been able to hold on until then, right?*

But Timothy doesn't know – cannot know, at least until the medical examination report comes back and Yuuki is coherent enough to offer his own opinion. The reality is though…it had already been 72 hours. 76 hours 40 minutes, to be exact. Maybe another five or ten minutes, because Timothy doesn't remember looking at his phone for the time after they locked and left the car. It had been 5.04pm then.

Regardless of the precise timing, Yuuki had been missing for more than the 72 hour golden time window. For every hour further that he wasn't found, his chances of survival would decrease at a much higher rate. And besides, no one knows what could have become of Yuuki in the hours to follow. The medicine and electrolyte fluid they gave Yuuki in the van on the way here, via IV, were probably far more vital in the immediate circumstances than Timothy can handle realising.

It's hard to tell how long Yuuki might've lasted in there. Yuuki might not have survived through till morning, given the stress, and if he'd been drugged, and if he'd been cold throughout each night. If the bad guys eventually came back for him and decided to dispose of him rather than trying to keep a now-on-the-way-to-dying person alive. Or otherwise, Yuuki would've been left there, left to live until his energy drained and his organs stopped functioning properly and his breathing grew weak and painfully thin…until however many long hours it took for the last of his life to leave him.

Timothy feels this knowledge sink in like teeth, like harsh blindingly bright LED lights on a vehicle on the road, like…

-…*seat, need to…get to seat….*

He manages to reach the row of seats on the side of the corridor before he gets too overwhelmed. His limbs feel fuzzy. His realisation of reality feels…weird. Timothy knows what's happening. He knows who he is. There isn't that much to process: only that Yuuki was kidnapped, and Timothy and Joshua nearly were too, and Yuuki apparently has been locked up, tied up, in a shed for the past three days without food or water, and Yuuki – this young friend of his who cared…*cares*…enough about the wellbeing of the youth he works with to start a trust fund for their rehabilitation – came tauntingly close to organ failure and subsequent death.

Yuuki is in the emergency room. It's an emergency because of the dehydration, and because he's been missing for three days after being kidnapped, and they don't know what the hell might be wrong with him. *He'll be okay.*

The guys who did this to him…to all three of them, if counting Timothy and Joshua in the equation…they might be back. Timothy frowns hard and puts his elbows on his knees, his cold sweaty palms to his forehead.

Then what do we do to prevent that from happening?

Timothy feels like he's negotiating some kind of emotional settlement

184

with himself.

Susan finds him like that, ten minutes later. Timothy recognises her footsteps, and hears the way they slow, then resumes pace. She speaks no words as she settles into the seat next to him on his left. Her clothing rustles, and her arms wrap around his chest and shoulders from where she is.

Timothy lowers his left hand and finds hers. He goes to hold her hand. But she instead covers his with hers. She intertwines their fingers, and holds him. Her palm is lukewarm over the back of his hand, a shield, a grounding point. Going by the tension in her fingers, she's nervous-stressed. When hasn't she had a reason to be, over the last few days in particular? Timothy should offer her comfort, but what words come to mind sound fake and he can't bring himself to try to speak them.

"I'm here," Susan murmurs. "You're safe. Yuuki's been rescued now." Her voice isn't steady. Timothy can't judge – he knows that were he to speak, neither would his be.

In the consoling silence, Timothy desperately wants to ask, *Yuuki will be okay, right? We all will be – right?*

But he knows Susan doesn't have the answers to those questions either.

When eventually Yuuki is brought out, changed into hospital clothing and being transferred to a ward to recover, Timothy and Susan stand. One of the doctor's meets them, distracts them, while they move Yuuki. Timothy genuinely tries to pay attention to the doctor's words, but he can't focus on them. He can't focus on anything but how pale, exhausted and unresponsive Yuuki looks on that bed. Drained. Hair settled across his forehead in a way it never usually is.

The doctor finishes speaking sooner than Timothy expected.

The last glimpse of Yuuki's black hair disappears behind the walls outside the elevator.

Susan's hands has never left his. She gives Timothy's hand a reassuring squeeze. Timothy barely reacts.

"It's okay," she says quietly. She releases his hand, and draws him into an embrace.

Timothy can detect the uncertainly in her voice.

"We're okay. Yuuki will be okay."

Like a mantra, she repeats those phrases under her breath. Those words echo in Timothy's head, but he isn't sure how much he dares believe them.

It's by those words that Timothy realises that Susan wants to ask the same questions he does – that those statements she's saying are moreso questions. And that they both already know the best answer any of them can give: there's really no way of knowing.

20

Andy is extra-vigilant when he walks into work that evening for his shift. News of Yuuki Takahashi's rescue has been broadcasted across the main news channels. It'll be in the paper tomorrow. And it'll be keeping him on his toes until he's absolutely certain that the anonymous email he sent to Timothy Harrison earlier in the day remains anonymous.

Which it had better.

In the meantime, Yuuki's location is now a hospital instead of a shed. Andy hopes, for Yuuki's sake, that no one else tries anything. No one else being the people he *knows* are behind it. It's not just Jeff involved it. If something else happens again, there's not a high probability that Andy will be able to do something again to intervene. And that's assuming he doesn't get found out in the first place.

He's anticipating backlash as he enters the office. If not that, he's expecting to walk in hearing a second kidnapping mission being organised. Instead, however, all he hears is swearing.

Andy raises one eyebrow at Jeff as he enters the room. He acts normal. "What's with the upset?"

A curse, aimed at the ceiling. Jeff whirls around. "Have you not seen the news?"

"Weren't you were just going to leave him in that shed for whatever?"

Jeff's neck is red with frustration. "The point is he was not meant *to get found*."

Andy sets his back down on his desk. He sighs, somewhat forcefully. "Well, it is what it is now. You were busy with something else, anyways. Did you get any more info on that lead, at least?"

Jeff scoffs at himself. "I wish."

"So, none?"

"Save your comments."

Andy isn't sure how to interpret that. The tone could mean several things: plain frustration, vented; a hissed retaliation at an obvious mess-up being pointed out; or a warning that Jeff knows that Andy had a part to play in Yuuki's rescue. He's sincerely hoping it's the first.

He takes his laptop out of his bag. Opens the screen and turns it on. He considers his words and phrasing for a minute while he waits for the laptop to start up.

"How'd they find him, anyways?" Andy asks. His voice comes out flat. The words are delivered well.

Jeff takes a moment to answer. "It got leaked."

Andy turns around. He raises both eyebrows. "Leaked?"

"From my phone – the coordinates. It must've happened when I had my phone in my pocket. It rained earlier. Rain messes with the touch screen. I had my emails open, and the note with the co-ordinates open. I don't know. But that location somehow ended up in Harrison's email inbox and now there goes the entire operation."

Jeff blames himself for the leak. He'd written the coordinates down in

188

a note on his phone and now he thinks he must've accidentally sent it to Timothy's email address.

"Oh well. The acquisition part of the operation failed anyways – it didn't go the way we wanted since we failed to get Harrison. We've screwed up our best chances of a successful pre-emptive attack now. So let's just...*fricking forget about it.*"

Patches of nervous sweat gradually soak Andy's shirt. He's glad he has his jacket to hide it.

Jeff doesn't suspect him. No one suspects him. But Andy doesn't dare believe it to be entirely true because perhaps the moment he does believe it, it'll turn out that he is mistaken, and that he was a fool to think that he could get away with this so easily.

...but so long as Jeff thinks it was his own doing, his own mess-up that no one else but himself should be held accountable for, then I'm is safe.

It's the inner circle – this team that Andy's commanding officer is a part of – who he is the most wary of. It's fortunate that Andy is able to use Jeff as a scapegoat. Andy's just lucky that Jeff's misplacing of his phone and accidentally calling people is a common enough occurrence that is also plays well into framing him. To the inner circle, it will seem as though the leak was nothing more Jeff's own unfortunate stupid mistake.

So Andy doesn't doubt Jeff's words as a false pretence, or a faking that he doesn't know what's going on with Andy's little game of betrayal. Given the cyber security measures that this inner circle has in place, too, it's unlikely that anyone will be able to trace the anonymous leak back to Andy, let alone this very building. The inner circle will guess that it had to have been one of them, but since Jeff's already taken responsibility for it,

Andy is less at risk of his anonymity being screwed up.

If everything goes well, no one will find out that the sender of the email was Andy – not unless *he* tells them first.

Andy contemplates that, in the back of his mind. When gets up and excuses himself from listening to Jeff's frustrated mutters, he's thinking about it. Coffee only further aids in the contemplative mood. Even in his nervous sweat-soaked shirt, hiding in plain sight, right under the noses of those he just outright betrayed – he considers it: outing this group.

But doing that would be dangerous. For everyone involved. Now is not the time nor place, and he can't risk telling anyone without putting both himself and whoever else in danger. It would be foolish to do anything without gathering evidence of the inner circle's operations, anyway. And even if Andy did… he's not sure the exposing would do any good. The inner circle is powerful.

In the quiet of the tea break room, Andy considers. He watches the steam rising from the coffee. *For now…it's safer not to do or say anything more than I already have,* he decides. Timothy Harrison is smart – he could potentially figure it out on his own. But Timothy Harrison doesn't yet seem to know the danger lurking in the PF ranks. That might be a good thing, because knowing would put him in danger again – this time tenfold.

So long as he doesn't go snooping in anything, he should be okay.

It's better not to put Timothy Harrison and his family, and by extension Yuuki Takahashi, in any more danger than they already are. If Andy decides to intervene again at a later time, it should only be in the event things start to escalate. Too much damage will be done without sufficient enough success to call it worth it if Andy decides to act prematurely. And if Andy does decide to act… next time he might consider not doing it alone.

Officer Marina Tu'u of the Internal Intelligence and Surveillance division. From what Andy knows, she isn't in allegiance with the corruption. Not like Jeff. Not like other people he knows. The way she handled responding to Timothy's pursuing the leaked coordinates makes Andy wonder if she, too, senses something up with some of the cases in the recent several years. Whether she's glimpsed *something* for certain or not, she doesn't seem to be involved in the quiet misconducts taking place among the ranks.

There might come a time when Andy will need to contact Marina Tu'u about this matter of under-the-radar PF misconduct personally. But for now, it's safer for both of *them* to stay under the radar.

The reason: it's hard to blow such a whistle quietly.

21

Yuuki's hospital room is quiet. Sombre. There's a couple of Peace Force officers standing outside. Otherwise, it's just the Harrisons, left to process their numb relief at having Yuuki back – alive. Inside, there's Timothy and Susan. And Yuuki – Yuuki who's heartbeat is echoed with beeps of the vital signs monitor standing by his bed. It's consistent, and a minor annoyance, but for now it's a good thing. Just as the continuous, yet barely visible, rise and fall of Yuuki's chest beneath the hospital clothing and blanket pulled up to his waist is.

These things are perhaps the only confirmation that the sight of Yuuki lying there in that bed is real. That the young man dressed in hospital clothing, a bandage on his cheek, wires shooting out from the hospital shirt and a mingling of IV line and oxygen therapy tubing connecting him to various medical equipment...that it's the Yuuki Takahashi they were missing, and have been searching for, and *found*.

Yuuki usually suits blue clothing, Timothy muses, *but not this blue – no, this blue only makes the contrasting sick hue of his skin tone appear worse.*

Nurses come and check on him sometimes. The checks most often involve the same things: respiration, heart rate, blood pressure, the IV, oxygen levels and how Yuuki's hydration is progressing. The hospital wants to monitor him overnight, to make sure his condition doesn't get any worse. They also want to minimise any developing complications that may hinder his recovery were he conscious and stressed. For that latter reason, Yuuki's been put under mild sedation.

Many hours pass like that.

"When are you going to wake up, Yuuki?" Timothy wants to ask. But he knows that Yuuki needs rest. He needs sleep. He needs time to recover. There's nothing stopping him from being roused, but that would be unfair. And for Yuuki, it would be far too draining of what little energy they're needing to help him slowly regain.

For now, they let Yuuki sleep. For now, they wait and watch over him.

"They're coming back now," Susan says into the air.

Timothy doesn't reply.

Joshua and Sam both arrived not too long after Yuuki was moved in here, and have left to go for a walk to get hot drinks. They're taking they're time. Timothy can understand why. When they finally return, they hand out coffee and hot chocolate and both sag against the wall.

"There's reporters downstairs," Joshua mumbles. He finishes his hot chocolate in seconds.

Timothy hums. "I figured there might be."

"They didn't bother you?" Susan asks.

Joshua shakes his head. "Marina's still here. Think she's been keeping them preoccupied."

Sam takes off the lid of her cup. Her lack of response is a silent agreement.

For security reasons, Yuuki's been placed in a small two-bed room of his own, almost directly across the hall from the reception desk on this wing of the hospital. Timothy is grateful for that – for the extra eyes keeping watch, and the greater space they have for themselves and for Yuuki while they get a grip on things. Being up a few floors means that it's harder for reporters to slip in to question the Harrison family without prior permission. It means that Yuuki's exhausted self can be left alone to rest.

Timothy sits down, exhausted, defeated. He can't be sure how much time has passed. There's a clock on the wall, and a clock on his cell phone, but it's like his brain is in doubt that there's any true time to be read at all. Beside him, Susan stands eerily still. Restless, on guard. Joshua's gaze has an uncharacteristic blankness to it. Sam finds the atmosphere too much and excuses herself from the room. No one bothers her.

Timothy thinks about yesterday, counting the hours up and up from the minute of Yuuki's disappearance. And then, only this afternoon, how keenly aware of time he was just trying to get to Yuuki before it became too late. It's like they can't be sure they have Yuuki back at all. Blink, and he could be gone again.

What if the people who took him come to take him again?

Did we just make the situation worse?

They should go home. Try to get some rest. Try to stop overthinking. But it's impossible to get rest when they've been confronted with circumstance such as these. If they did go home, Timothy knows he would be too on edge thinking about his family getting attacked during

194

the night. On top of that, the distance between themselves and Yuuki, left alone at the hospital, would only play on all their anxious minds all night and keep them up.

The heart monitor beeps, steady. Yuuki breathes, a little weak but also steady. The IV drips.

"He'll be okay, right?" Timothy asks into the air, to no one.

Susan only hums.

They don't know, that's the thing. They don't know if Yuuki will be alright. He's just been rescued from being trapped in a shed for three days. They have no idea if he was there the whole time, or if something else had been done to him, or what his psychological state is going to be when he wakes. That's the primary reason why he's been sedated, after all – they don't want Yuuki's recovery to be compromised by whatever stress he'll face when he wakes up. At least, not while Yuuki's in this condition. The stress will challenge it anyway.

"When he wakes up," Susan says thinly, "just remember that he's not going to be the Yuuki we recognise. He'll be confused. Disorientated. He might not want to talk to us or even see us at all while he comes to terms with things."

"It's not going to be easy on him. On any of us, but least of all Yuuki. He's going to have doctors and PFOs in his face asking him questions for a few days. We need to be there to support him, if possible.

Susan turns to Joshua and Sam. "I'm not expecting you two to stay around, though. Or you, Tim. And I'm not suggesting we neglect our own wellbeing. I just think…"

"We get it, Mum," Sam says bluntly. She blinks. She opens her mouth

195

as though to attempt to revoice the words in a tone they were meant in, but she gives up.

It's an unspoken agreement between all of them: *none of us want to see Yuuki disappear or struggle to cope in the aftermath.*

Timothy feels awful that Yuuki went through this. Guilty, even. Survivor's guilt, Susan had named it for him. It doesn't make him feel any better. Not when Yuuki's the one in the hospital bed, and Timothy's sitting here relatively fine.

It's not Timothy's fault. In fact, if anything, he and Joshua pulled Yuuki out of a worse off fate.

Why does it feel like our efforts are falling short, then?

Because it's not the last three days Timothy's thinking about – it's the coming days and weeks ahead of them that's on his mind. There's only so much they'll be able to do for Yuuki in the aftermath, and that's an important thing to recognise. But who knows what toll that ordeal in the shed really had on Yuuki? The realisation that the ordeal didn't end with the rescue from that shed is what scares Timothy.

Susan's right. During recovery, Yuuki isn't likely to be himself, and maybe not for a while after that – just as Susan says. Realistically, that's to be expected. Even Timothy isn't feeling like himself. He knows that none of them standing here are. But it's scary not knowing what this will look like in Yuuki. Over the past few days, Timothy's seen how the four of them who make up the Harrison family have reacted and responded and *coped* with what's happened. He could anticipate early on what to expect. But he has no idea what might become of Yuuki in all of this.

To add to that, the experience that each of the Harrisons had over the last three days is not the experience that Yuuki had. They don't know what kind of an experience Yuuki had, not exactly, but they do know that it entailed being tied up, locked in an old dusty shed with a cobweb-screened window, and gagged for some time – given that damp cloth that Timothy and Joshua found on the floor…

He wonders if even his family would have any idea how Yuuki might outwardly behave in the wake of all that.

Timothy looks up. "Was his family coming over?"

"The hospital made contact with them when he came in," Susan says. "Apparently his sister is coming. I'm not sure about the rest. It sounds like it might just be her."

"Yumiko?" Joshua asks. "The one we met who came over during the *sakura* festival last year?"

"Yeah."

"It's probably good it's just her," Timothy murmurs. "He just might not like having people around while he…"

"…while he comes to terms with things." Susan finishes.

Timothy nods.

Sam raises an eyebrow. "…doesn't that include us, then?"

There's a moment of silence.

"I think," Susan says carefully, "it might. And we should be prepared for if that ends up being the case. If it does, let's not take it too personally if he doesn't want us here, or if he'd prefer to have some space and time to himself. And also…"

The length of her hesitation is unsettling. Joshua fidgets.

The breath she lets out is heavy. "Yuuki was alone in that shed for three days, presumably. Even if he *wasn't* – alone, that is – he might not be aware of what happened with you two after the point in time he got taken. To have been in isolation, then be suddenly surrounded by people and finding you two here okay... it might be a bit overwhelming."

"But we were with him, there," Timothy starts. "When we found him, he..."

Except we don't know exactly how much of that Yuuki actually was conscious of. And if anything, he was conscious of made any sense to him. If he did register our presence, he might've thought it was simply delirium...

Susan reads his thoughts on his face and doesn't speak any further.

Joshua blinks. "Do you think we should we tell his sister...?"

"What?" Susan asks.

"Not to come? Or... no, that's not what I meant..."

"She's already on her way," Susan says. "But I think it'll be okay. From what we've heard from Yuuki, they're close – him and his sister. Seeing as it's just her coming, and not their parents as well, I think there's less chance of it becoming too much straight away. And I believe she'll be aware that Yuuki might be a bit... uncomfortable with having people see him. She, of all people, is probably most aware of that."

"How come it's just Yumiko?" Timothy wonders aloud. "I would've thought their parents would come too."

"They're probably too busy with work at the moment. I think their father's a high school teacher, and their mother works... at an office job or something? Somewhere they can't afford to just ditch it all and leave."

"It would cost a lot, too," Timothy remarks, "having all three of them fly over just for a few nights."

Susan nods. "Yeah. So that, their work, and the fact that they too don't want to overwhelm Yuuki – and themselves – if they all do come… is probably why it's just his sister coming."

Timothy hums.

"And we're around, anyways. I think the hospital may have told them as much, to reassure them that Yuuki's not on his own before Yumiko has a chance to get here."

Timothy notices how nothing they're saying now is really adding to their conversation. They're just reiterating what's already been said. 'Blabbing', as Samantha calls it. And Susan's 'doing all the talking', but in the sense that she's the one holding the conversation – holding the Harrison family – together.

Their time moves through the night like that.

It's a distraction, is what it is. A sort of distraction from the reality of what's happened, and the state of their friend lying in the hospital bed in front of them. A distraction from the hard truth no one wants to even think about – that Yuuki might've been only hours away from dying.

Timothy diverts his attention away from the spoken conversation, even though it's mostly ended now. He looks at Yuuki's slack, colour-drained face. *Can you hear us, Yuuki? Do you know we're here, and that your sister is coming? You're not alone, Yuuki. We won't let them take you again, not if we can help it. We… and we understand if it's too much for you, though, us being here, so… just tell us if you want us to go, if we're us being here is too much.*

In his peripheral, Susan is watching him out of the corner of her eye. There's a heavy sadness in her expression, a weighted grief.

Just be okay, Yuuki. Please.

22

An exhausted Yumiko Takahashi arrives in the early morning at 10am. She caught the soonest flight she could, and came straight from the airport. Fortunately, there's only a two-hour time difference between Japan and Arkala at this time of year, so in spite of the eleven hour plane flight, Yumiko is spared from significant jetlag.

That doesn't exempt her from the stress and worry of the past three days, though. Judging by the shadows beneath her eyes, she hasn't slept well. Timothy can empathise: none of them have.

"Yumiko," Timothy greets her in the hallway. "Did you have a good flight?"

Yuuki's sister inclines her head forward. "The flight was good, yes. Thank you"

"I'm sorry I didn't come down to meet you at the entrance."

"Don't worry about it. It was better that you didn't – I think you may have been… interviewed. There were a few journalist-looking people down there."

Timothy leads the way down the hallway to their destination.

"Precisely the reason why I thought it might be better to wait for you to come up to the right floor first." He tiredly grins. "You didn't get cornered yourself, did you?"

"No." Yumiko lets out a forced laugh. "Thankfully not. Thankfully no one was aware that someone from our family was coming over so soon – no one who we didn't want to know, anyways. I don't think they recognised any similarity between mine and Yuuki's appearance, either."

"I'm glad."

There's an elephant in the hallway: Yuuki's condition. But since the real unspoken of 'topic' is awaiting them in the room up ahead, Timothy decides not to speak of it. They get there soon enough. Timothy figures that Yumiko would rather get a chance to see her brother first before Timothy fills her in on any details she wishes to know.

They arrive at the room. Yuuki is still sleeping. His breathing is less shallow. There's a vaporiser steaming gently next to the bed. The additional humidity, and the oxygen therapy delivered through nasal cannula, seems to be helping. Hydration and electrolytes keep him steadily recovering, improving... surviving. The nurses are no longer monitoring his heart rate through a vital signs monitor, but they're still monitoring his pulse and oxygen saturation through the pulse oximeter clamped lightly onto of his fingers.

"Is he unconscious?" Yumiko asks in a whisper.

"Asleep," Timothy corrects.

Yumiko nods.

Timothy reiterates what the hospital staff told them last night, about him being sedated for the initial recovery. "The heavier sedative will be wearing off soon," he adds, "but according to the nurses Yuuki is likely going to require sleeping longer."

Yumiko nods again. "I see."

There's the couple of chairs sitting vacant at Yuuki's bedside. Last night, they'd been occupied by Timothy and Susan. Earlier this morning, Susan took herself, Sam and Joshua home so that all of them could get some rest. Now, Timothy extends his hand towards the chairs.

Yumiko gratefully accepts the invitation and sits. She stares blankly across the room, out the window for a moment before her gaze lowers and fixes on Yuuki's face. She curls her fingers into fists on her knees.

"...are you alright?" Timothy asks. "Would you like me to give you some time?"

Yumiko swallows. "No, it's alright. It...is just strange, seeing him like this. I was expecting to find him looking worse, if I'm honest. So I'm relieved that it's not like that. But... it's still..."

"Yeah."

"And I know him. You know him, too. Yuuki...wouldn't have, um, experienced that experience well. *Handled* it well."

"I don't think anyone would've."

Yumiko nods. She hastily wipes a tear from the corner of her eye and sniffs. "Yeah, you're right. But...I don't know." She spies the tissue box on the bed side table. It's loaded with tissues. She takes one. "It's just so unfair, you know? What did he do wrong? Who did he get in the way of?"

Timothy's stomach churns.

"He's been so invested in doing something to help the youth here. Even if it's just being able to be a bit of a kinder warden at the detention centre than some of the other officers who end up working there. I don't know if it seems so to you, but Yuuki's been far more enthusiastic...no, *driven*, to set up this Youth Rehabilitation Trust than he ever was about his graduating as a security officer. This is far more of an achievement to him than getting that qualification was. And now what? It's like he's being punished for caring. Not just Yuuki, either – you as well, Timothy. All you wanted was just to help a bit, and then he get this? You guys get this?"

That's something that even Timothy has had a hard time emotionally dealing with.

"It's unfair. He was just trying to do the right thing." Yumiko glances at Timothy. "Both of you were. He didn't...you didn't deserve this to happen to you."

To that, Timothy cannot answer.

Yumiko turns and leans forward. "Yah, Yuuki." She reaches out and ever so gently lays her hands on Yuuki's arm, one on either side of the IV insert site. She's careful she doesn't shake him. "You better come around soon, okay? You better be okay."

Yuuki doesn't react.

Yumiko releases her younger brother's arm. Her attention lingers on the bandages wrapped around his wrists. She wrinkles her nose. After a moment, her shoulders tremble. She snatches up another tissue and uses it.

Timothy thinks about exiting the room to give her space, but as soon as he takes one step, Yumiko abruptly stands.

"Urgh. I'm such a mess of an appearance right now." She stares at

Yuuki a moment longer before turning. "I booked a hotel room nearby. I think it's only about a ten minute bus ride from here. Anyways, I think I'll go have a sleep for the rest of day, then come back tonight."

"Okay. Good idea. We'll be here. If we're not, we come and go sometimes but are here for the most part. At least some of us. Susan might be back later. I'm not sure what Joshua and Samantha will decide to do. How long are you in Arkala for?"

"Two nights. I'll leave on the third night – there's a late night flight that I'll be catching. I would have stayed longer, but it's the most I can afford to stay away from work for. And accommodation costs, et cetera."

Timothy's mouth quirks. "Kinda chews through the savings pretty quickly, huh."

"Yeah."

Yumiko turns her gaze into the hospital room. Her brow creases, like a frown. She seems to zone out for a moment before clearing her throat. "I feel like I should stay longer, but…"

There's ambiguity in whether she means right now or if she means the duration of her stay in Arkala. Either way, Timothy's response would be the same.

"It's okay," Timothy murmurs. "We're here."

Yumiko hums. "It really doesn't feel right… making you…"

Timothy shifts his stance. "No one's making us. We're here because we want to be."

Yumiko nods. She offers a smile and a brief bow in gratitude. "Thank you."

"It's no problem."

"I'll be back later on then," Yumiko excuses herself.

Susan arrives at the room a few seconds after Yumiko exits. They exchange words of greeting, but it's brief. Yumiko continues walking, and Susan doesn't hinder her.

"She didn't stay long," Timothy comments.

Susan watches her move down the hallway. "She's probably needing some private time alone to process some of this." She has two takeaway cups of coffee in her hands. She sighs, and offers one of the coffees to Timothy. "I don't know about you, but I think it's hitting us all now."

"Now that it's over?"

"Now that Yuuki's safe. I don't know how confidently we can say that it's over. But at least the result-less searching for him is." Susan's eyes are distant. She takes a sip of coffee. "And the wondering whether or not we'll see him back alive…"

The warmth of the coffee seeps through the cup. Timothy cradles it in both hands. A heater in his palms. The heat eventually disappears, as did the comfort that it offered.

Yuuki, lying asleep on the bed before them, does not disappear.

23

Yuuki is exhausted. Disoriented, with no sense of time passing. That much is recognisable. He feels it in every bone and muscle in his body.

Not knowing or having the energy to react to where he is, it's like space and time have ceased to exist for Yuuki. Lurking just beneath the surface of where it does, of where this… void… meets 'reality', are all just nauseating sensations he doesn't want to know about. Thinking about trying to move away from it conjures up the feeling of being sick. It only makes the aching muscles ache more and the pull of hunger and dehydration at his skin and face and stomach worse.

No, it's better not to try to move. He hasn't been able to move in the past… however long anyways. Not much, anyways. Never enough to get away.

But, when he concentrates to the farthest extent he can, there's one thing that seems different from when he was last aware: the ground beneath him doesn't feel hard anymore. Although his body still aches, it's not a perpetual ache now but one born from resting after stress.

So… then, in that case, he must've gone numb… again.

Shed. He's in that shed still. There's still bindings around his wrists he can feel, and pain, so where else would he be? He feels sick, too tired to feel dread. Time will slowly work his body's energy reserves down the drain until there's not enough left to sustain his organs functioning, and his blood moving, and…

It's better not to try to be too conscious for it.

He goes back to sleep thinking he's still in the shed.

It's better not to be awake.

He'll use energy, and suffer distress, and hallucinate more if he's awake.

Yuuki wakes again to hearing Timothy and Susan's voices talking lowly. It's a lulling volume and tone.

As Yuuki listens to it, words blurring into meaningless sentences in his head, he becomes more aware of some different things. Sensations – new ones, different ones. A different kind of atmosphere built around it. Something is set in his nose, across his face, resting on his upper lip, his cheeks, behind his ears. It's uncomfortable, especially when he concentrates on it. He wonders if it's some kind of vine brushing against his face, or maybe a bit of his clothing somehow managed to get positioned that way. He's too tired to think what else. His fingers twitch, and the thing clipped on his finger won't be nudged off. It annoys him, but he's tired, so he leaves that too.

These things weren't present the last time he was fully aware. The pull of pain in the back of his hand hurts, and there's other pains. But most of the pains have changed in feeling somehow – the tightness around his wrists is less bruising, and though his wrists still feel sore there's also a sort of soothing cooling kind of something penetrating that pain.

Something has...changed. That realisation is followed by a brief rush of alertness. He mentally forces his eyes open. It takes a little while before his facial muscles respond to follow that action physically.

The room is white. Yuuki's disoriented. He wonders why it isn't dark and black and brown. The lighting is dim, but it's a soft restful kind of dim, not a shadow-shrouded suffocating dim. The air isn't dusty, and there's a humidifier steaming into the air beside him.

There are no more bindings on his wrists. From what he can see, in a glance the marks on his skin could be mistaken for some, but no...that's just abrasions and bruising. The length of plastic tube connected to his hand, and the one across his face that joins beneath his chin...they're pieces of medical equipment, and are not bindings either. They're not restraining him.

Nothing is restraining him.

He's lying on his back, arms by his side. Free. Floating, almost. But too heavy to really be so. He's too tired to feel any energy in his muscles to test the theory he could get up and walk out of the room if he wanted to.

He groans. Timothy and Susan's talking peters out, stills. Timothy's voice sounds close to him, hovering over him.

"Yuuki, what are you feeling?" Timothy repeats.

Yuuki turns his head a little and stares up at him, unsure. His neck hurts with the lingering ache of a cramp. He's confused, not sure what's real. Because this can't be real, right? Not when the shed is so inescapable, and he has no idea where it is or if anyone can possibly find him.

…when? How did I get…here?

As it is, Yuuki just stares blankly, at Timothy and Susan's blurry figure behind him, eyes not quite wanting to adjust to the shapes and shadows around him. He blinks slowly, and glances at the person beside him – Susan. Glances back.

There are tears slipping down Timothy's blurry face.

Maybe they are real…

Timothy cries. Yuuki's never imagined Timothy crying before. Susan is standing beside him. They reassure him they're here. That he's safe. That he's been rescued from that shed.

Rescued? Yuuki doesn't remember any rescue. Not really. It seems to pull at his memory, but he's too tired to try recall it. His mind's too fuzzy. He thinks he remembers seeing the door open, but it's all vague and foggy, and he's not sure he trusts his perception of things anymore. All of this… it could just be some sick kind of delusional dream or hallucination that his mind's given him to send him off into the depths of an irrecoverable state.

He realises his eyes have slipped shut again, but this time he makes no effort to try open them again. If this is a hallucination or a dream, at least it's not a bad one.

And if it's real?

Yuuki will give that some thought next time he wakes, if there is indeed a next time. Right now, he's not exactly willing to remember or think about anything. He just wants to… *not* have to experience distress.

He's so tired.

Sleep tugs at him. He lets himself go. Timothy and Susan's voices remain, filtering through his mind as he drifts and sinks.

It would be nice if they were real.

24

Yumiko arrives again at the hospital, bleary eyed. She knows how she must look. Wearing a mask up to the room hides her frown, but doesn't help hide the dark circles beneath her eyes. She washed her face several times in cold water before she left the hotel, but the skin beneath her eyes still looks puffy.

Goddamnit, Yuuki.

Having slowly found her way back up to Yuuki's hospital room, she finds that Timothy and Susan Harrison look just about the same as she feels. Timothy has bags under his eyes and Susan has bruise-like shadows that almost seem to cut into her skin. In fact, many people visiting and tending to other people seem to varying degrees and colours of tired. Yumiko doesn't have try to be an exception.

This is a hospital, she reminds herself. *People aren't exactly expected to be looking all held together and cheery.* She'd rather pretend to be held together, though, if she can. She's grateful for the hotel room – it has decent space for her to stay in and have private cry and emotional vent time.

"Hi," Timothy greets her.

211

Susan musters as best a friendly expression as she can, and leaves it at that. Yumiko returns the greeting in a similar way: she doesn't trust her own tone to come out friendly sounding and grounded as she'd like.

Timothy forces an exhausted smile. "Did you manage to sleep much?"

In spite of the long last twenty-four hours, Yumiko barely slept. An eleven hour plane flight from Japan to Arkala at the end of a full day of work has tired her out. That, with what little sleep she achieved in the couple of days prior – in the time between learning of Yuuki's kidnapping and learning of his rescue – should have exhausted her emotionally enough to be able to sleep more.

But it didn't happen, and that's just that. Maybe she's just too keyed up.

"Nah," Yumiko eventually replies. The answer feels far too casual. "But it's fine. I'll try sleep again later. For now, I think I'm too worried about Yuuki to sleep."

Susan nods. "We're much the same."

Inside the hospital room, Yuuki appears to be the same as she last saw him. From the doorway, she can't tell if he looks any better or not. There doesn't seem to be much change from last night, at least not visually. Perhaps if the lighting were the same dim warmth of last night, she might be able to see some colour returned to Yuuki's complexion, even in the slightest. But as it is, the white daylight coming in through the half shaded windows only makes his face look ashen still, and his overall skin tone retains its washed out appearance.

"No change?" she asks. She hears her voice like it's automated.

Susan gives a small shake of her head. "No, though that is a good thing. 'No change' as in, nothing significant or anything of concern. We already know it'll be a slow-ish recovery. Rest. He needs rest, and…time for his body to recover after…" As Susan's voice loses its volume, Timothy raises his hand and offers a consoling hand to rub her back. "The dehydration, stress…, hunger…" she finishes. "That sort of thing."

Yumiko nods. She stares across the room, at Yuuki lying there in that hospital bed, unwell. He will be unwell for days or weeks still. She imagines what that recovery might look like in the days ahead: tiredness, blank expressions, irritability, dismissals of opportunities to try to talk about what is troubling him…

But what do they do if Yuuki is suffering from the trauma of this incident and cannot speak of it, for lack of words or understandable lack of will to remember?

It's strange – this kind of thing happening to someone close. This version of Yuuki is still her younger brother Yuuki. But Yumiko is struggling to fully process that. The lack of more visible, alarming superficial wounds, as well as the absence of need for great use of various medical equipment, offsets the emotional shock a little. But on the contrary, the lack of concerning visual stimuli only makes the severity of the situation harder to gauge, and harder to believe. Especially when Yumiko didn't experience the Ninao Kidnapping first-hand like the Harrisons did. She only heard of it second-hand, through Arkala Peace Force officer and A'o District Hospital staff voices.

Timothy offers belatedly, "He woke up, earlier. Briefly; not for long."

At the glint of hopefulness probably showing in Yumiko's expression, Susan nods and lets out a small sigh. "Sorry, I should've said about that first."

"On his own?" Yumiko asks.

It takes a moment for Timothy to collect her meaning. "Yeah. He woke up on his own. I'm not sure he was all that lucid, though." A pause. "I'm not sure he really knew where he was...or rather, that he was here...and not...*there* still."

"We can't know for sure," Susan murmurs. "At least, not until we see how he is over the next few days. Yuuki might be aware – might *recognise* – that this place is a hospital. But whether or not he emotionally knows that..."

"It might take some catching up," Yumiko finishes.

Susan grimaces. "Hmm."

Yumiko looks at Yuuki and wonders. "I don't know how easy it will be to recognise that, though, to be honest."

"What do you mean?"

"I mean, how easy it will be for us to tell if he's okay or not. If he truly realises... feels like he's not in the sh-... not in that garden shed anymore. I know he doesn't like to let anyone know when he's struggling. He prefers to work out his troubles by himself."

There's a silence between the three of them. It's a weighty silence. The anticipation and dread it bears is heavy.

Yumiko's mouth twitches. It's hidden by her mask. "Yuuki is always so good at coping. He's always been resilient, even when he's struggled adapting to this or that. Because of that, it's hard to tell if something is affecting him. It's hard to tell if it's got to him until he's visibly showing signs of cracking under the stress of it."

"Do you think," Timothy says quietly, "that we might think the same thing here? It sounds like you're speaking from experience."

Susan blinks slowly.

"I can't speak for him," Yumiko says after a while. "But I noticed back when we moved overseas, he doesn't always talk openly about stuff. It's not his way of processing things. Especially when it's something that would only be answered with by someone telling him it's just the way things are and that he's just got to find a way to deal with it. That he's got to change something about himself or his perspective, because the world around isn't kind enough to mind how he feels. So he prefers to wrestle with the thoughts and emotions he has in his own mind first. That's what I've seen, anyways.

"I suppose... that such a coping method may appear as resilience sometimes, but..."

But other times... what is it, Yuuki, if not suffering in silence?

"We'll have to wait and see," Susan says tightly. "Even if it might not be easy to see. In a situation such as this, there's no telling how Yuuki might react coming out of it. Everyone reacts to trauma differently. We might be able to predict what kind of behaviour or coping mechanisms we might see from him, but we can't know for sure." She sighs. "I don't even anticipate half my own ways of coping, half the time. You think it's going to be one thing, and then it turns out to be something different. It's hard to know what to prepare for when this doesn't exactly happen every day in Arkala."

Yumiko grunts. "I would really hope it doesn't. I sure wouldn't want to have to experience or re-experience these emotions often."

Susan locks eyes with her a moment. She seems like she's going to say something, or warn of something, but whatever it is that is on her mind doesn't get spoken aloud.

Timothy makes a small prompting noise, seeing this. But Susan dismisses the open opportunity with a shake of her head.

"It's nothing," Susan says. "Nothing we need to be thinking about right this instant."

It's something to do with re-experiencing emotions of trauma, isn't it? That much Yumiko can gather. She's not able to string together a comprehensible enough question to ask about it further, though. What exactly Susan was going to say, Yumiko doesn't know, but she feels that now is not the time and place for that conversation. It's too early. It's too soon.

For now, such a thing is best left for the days ahead.

With Yumiko intending on staying at the hospital for some hours, Susan and Timothy take the opportunity to go home to sleep for a few hours, wash, do laundry and eat. Have some down time, away from the atmosphere and environment of the hospital.

Yumiko sees them off as far as the first floor. A nurse comes in to attend to Yuuki's oral health care, so Yumiko feels better about leaving the room. It also means she's able to give Yuuki some privacy, some respect, some dignity. She stays by the elevators and flights of stairs while they walk out, not wanting to get caught by any lurking journalists. *Better head back up.* There's a café down the corridor. Yumiko considers following the Harrisons' path toward it to get something from there. *I really don't want to be asked questions, though.*

In the end, since Timothy and Susan leave unbothered, Yumi decides to slip into the café. Ordering coffee for just herself is lonely. *It's Yuuki who likes coffee most, not me. If I should be getting any for anyone, it would be for Yuuki.* When Yuuki has recovered enough to be allowed some again, Yumiko vows to shout him some.

It might have to be in form of some gift voucher instead, though. The idea is good. The only thing is that she won't be able to stay here in Arkala for however long it'll be before that happens.

Given the sort of experience Yuuki just had, and the physical condition he's currently in, it's probably advised he doesn't have caffeine for a while. But who knows? Maybe it would help more than it would hinder recovery. That sort of thing isn't dependent on the majority, but on the individual. Yuuki might be one of some people who don't receive the same handful of negative impacts that the majority of people otherwise would.

Nevertheless, it's not a theory to be tested right now. It's not worth the risk.

Once she's acquired her coffee, Yumiko returns upstairs. When she gets back, she finds Yuuki's bed has been moved to beside the window, replacing the vacant bed. The vacant bed is shifted over to where he previously was instead. A passing nurse ducks into the room to inform her in words about the decision – but they needn't really explain it; Yumiko can see a good reason why: it'll be reassuring for him to wake up in natural daylight, and able to see *outside*.

The nurse adds, "His oxygen saturation levels are back above 92% now, so we've taken him off oxygen therapy. Let us know if there's any issues. A nurse will come by in a few hours to insert a feeding tube. If you have any questions, feel free to ask."

Yumiko nods. She holds her coffee cup a little tighter. "Is it...alright if I stay in here when you do that?" She had a friend who spent some time in hospital after surgery and couldn't eat. The inserting, replacing and removing of a feeding tube always made her friend uncomfortable.

"Yes, of course. That's fine."

"I see. Thank you."

The nurse offers a tired smile and leaves.

In the daylight washing over him, Yuuki seems to be in a more restful state. Enclosed in curtains might be good for privacy and photophobia concerns, but it is also very reminiscent of the walls of a shed. In fact, the spacing available when the curtains are drawn around the bed is about the same as what space that garden shed gave.

Yumiko heard the approximate measurements of the shed from the PF officer who called her. She'll never look at garden sheds the same again.

There's a bench by the window. Yumiko sits on it. She drinks her coffee. Yuuki continues sleeping, oblivious to everything. In a different situation, Yumiko might consider him to be sleeping deeply, but no, there's a notable...weakness – a stress-drained emptiness – to the way he sleeps. He's unwell. What he experienced in that shed, and in the kidnapping in general was trauma.

Yumiko settles back into the seat. She turns her gaze out the window. "What happened to you out there, huh? What did you miss while setting up your Youth Rehabilitation Trust?"

218

The PFO had told her that the Youth Rehabilitation was only a speculated cause, not a confirmed one. But Yumiko, like most other people, can see no other reason why the kidnapping would've happened – and why it would have happened on the day of official establishment, at the place of establishment, to the two people primarily involved in establishing it.

The Youth Rehabilitation Trust was permitted, wasn't it?

Taularh's administration said it was okay, already, didn't they?

"So then…why? Why did this kind of thing happen? Was it really because someone didn't like the YRT? Or was it for some other reason we don't know?"

Yumiko finishes her coffee. She has the feeling that those questions won't be adequately answered for a long while.

A few hours later, Yumiko has finished two games of chess on her phone, and Yuuki hasn't stirred. Nurses have come by to insert the feeding tube. Yumiko's glad Yuuki wasn't awake for it. It would've stressed him, she knows. She can't imagine what being awake for having *that* inserted would feel like for him, especially right after a kidnapping.

Especially right after a kidnapping where anyone could've done anything to him.

In the dying light of the afternoon, Yumiko video calls her parents. Hers and Yuuki's – *their* parents. Although she's messaged them as frequently as needed to update them on Yuuki's condition, she's preparing herself for repeating a lot of things.

No surprises, the first question that is asked after the general round of greetings and weather-and-flight-over small talk is exactly about it. Their mother holding the phone. She asks, *"How is his health?"*

Their father is standing in the background. *"You said in your messages, he's still not awake?"*

They talk in a mix of English and Japanese, though mostly English so as to maintain the family's English language proficiency when they're not as in contact with it anymore since leaving Arkala. The only one in constant contact with it now is Yuuki.

Yumiko choses her words. "...it's not as bad as you're imagining it. He's fine. He's just going to need a lot of rest."

Their mother frowns. *"It seemed like Yuuki is in a bad condition. It must be bad if he's not awake."*

"The hospital gave him stuff to help him rest. Rest for Yuuki includes sleeping. It's not a bad thing. Look..."

She debates the ethics of showing them Yuuki, but at the end of the day, they're family too, and they'd be here too if they could. *If they can see for themselves that Yuuki isn't beaten or roughed up beyond recognition, they might also minimise their frequent asking after Yuuki's health.* It'll help them stop worrying and being vocal about it if they know Yuuki looks relatively okay. They need reassurance. They need confirmation – through more than just words. They need to hear it in tone of voice, and see it in body language and facial expressions.

Moreover, they need to see Yuuki's current condition for themselves.

So Yumiko turns in her seat, and angles herself and the camera so that the front facing camera includes Yuuki in the selfie.

There's a mix of silence and vocal expressions of concern.

"He woke up earlier for a bit," Yumiko adds. "Timothy said he was here when he did. He and Susan were here when he came to before."

Their father nods. *"Ohh, Timothy and Susan Harrison?"*

"Yeah. The whole Harrison family have been here."

"Are there right now?" their mother asks. *"We should say hello."*

"No, they went home. They hadn't really been home much since... since Yuuki was rescued."

"Oh, I see."

Their father clears his throat. *"While you're there, ask Yuuki if he wants to come home. When he's awake. That is, if he wants to come home to have some distance from Arkala for a while."*

Yumiko gives a dubious hum. "I don't know if he'll want to."

"It would be better for him if he did," their mother agrees. *"Yuuki should get away from there for a bit. It's no doubt going to be upsetting for him to stay in Arkala after that's happened."*

"Yeah, I don't know."

"We do think it would be best for him."

"It's easy to think that, but Yuuki might not think that way. His life is here. His home is technically here now. It might just displace him more to come back home while he's dealing with the trauma from this."

Their father hums in consideration.

"I'll talk to him about it, 'kay? Once he's had sufficient rest."

"Okay. But make sure you do," their mother persists. *"It's probably best if you can find time to talk to him about it while you're there, so you can talk in person."* A heavy sigh. *"Oh well, there's little we can do if he decides not to, like you say."*

"Yeah."

"Anyways. It's about time I start preparing dinner. I need to go shopping for the

things. Your father has a softball match to watch soon as well. We better let you go, too. Save your mobile data."

Yumiko grunts. "Alright. What you having tonight?"

"Unagi-don." Eel rice bowl. A pause. *"Yuuki's favourite."*

It's a shame, Yumiko thinks, that Yuuki lying beside her doesn't get a chance to taste it.

"You'll call again before you go?"

"Yeah. I'll message you when he wakes up again, too."

"Let us know if there's any other updates. And if he's safe."

"Yeah. Will do."

"Alright, then. Talk to you again soon, Yumiko. Stay safe."

Yumiko hums. "Yeah. Okay…bye."

"Bye."

The other end of the line cuts, and Yumiko lowers her phone and sighs. She looks at her younger brother, sleeping in the hospital bed. The hospital clothes make the unhealthy pale yellow tinge to his skin even more noticeable. Dehydration and hunger. Apparently he's looking a bit better since first came in – since Timothy and Joshua found him – but it's still a stark contrast to the radiant healthy skin tone she's used to seeing Yuuki with. Yuuki's complexion is paler than the rest of the family, something inherited from their Arkalan European grandfather that neither their mother or Yumiko got. But it's never looked as…sick as this.

Knowing what she knows about the kidnapping, and not wanting to know about what details she's heard of Yuuki's speculated experience in the shed…this is expected – that Yuuki would be looking like this. It's unsettling to try to take in. Still…she's relieved that he hasn't been seriously injured. The dehydration might've killed him if he'd been in that shed a few more days, but other than that there's no major injuries. There's no cuts or bleeding. Bruising and chafed skin around his wrist, she can see. The bruised, slightly swollen skin on his temple marking the fact he's also been concussed, yes.

She leans forward in her seat. With some hesitation, she reaches out and uncertainly lays her hand on his shoulder.

But...

It almost feels wrong, to be minimising Yuuki's injuries like this. He was kidnapped and locked in a shed for three days, during which he'd been left tied up and gagged. That's...

For all the signs of physical health deterioration she can see, Yumiko feels like there's something missing. Something important, but she's not sure what it is. While she's grateful Yuuki wasn't hurt further, it still feels like this isn't all – this isn't all of his injuries accounted for.

Well, she thinks, *I guess we'll just have to wait and see.*

25

9th June, 12-Tau – evening

The Harrisons gather at the hospital again that night. They share dinner with Yumiko there. Joshua and Samantha play card games sitting cross-legged on the vacant bed. Yumiko joins in, and then the game expands to incorporate all of them. Joshua even puts a card pile in for Yuuki. Each of them take turns managing it.

Yuuki sleeps. Given his condition and the experience he just went through, that's not a bad thing. There's the beginning signs of an upper respiratory infection that the nurses have seen to treating. Fortunately, the symptoms don't worsen. Without stress to aggravate it, the infection doesn't get a chance to fully take hold. To support Yuuki's recovery, with both the URI and his overall condition of health, the mild sedation is continued. It's not enough to keep him asleep, and it's not supposed to be – they don't need to be enough to hold him under in such a way, anyway. Now, the only thing keeping him from waking up should be his own exhaustion.

But for now, Yuuki sleeps.

During the game of cards, Timothy finds himself distracted from this distraction. All he can think about is the kidnapping, and wonder what happens now. Should they continue with the YRT, or give it up? What if they go ahead with it and something like this happens again? Is it really worth risking putting Yuuki – putting all of them, in fact – through all this again?

Timothy's turn to play cards arrives. He's not really thinking when he puts one down. He just wants the attention and the waiting off of himself. The main goal of his is just to pass the turn on to someone else since he's not exactly concentrating. He just wants to clear the responsibility of needing to make a decision right here and now.

What does Marina think of it, I wonder. What does she think we should do about the Trust? Perhaps I ought to ask her for her opinion.

"Dad, that's a 'play again' card," Sam says.

Timothy blinks.

"Are you going?"

"Oh, I forgot you guys play with that rule." He didn't forget; it's an excuse.

Timothy plays another card, this time a 'pick-up' card for the person next in turn. Yumiko, who happens to next in the clockwise rotation, yawns and reaches forward to collect five cards from the deck.

"After this round," Susan says, "shall we call it a night?"

Yumiko finishes her turn, picks up Yuuki's lot of cards and makes Sam draw fifteen. Sam shoots her a friendly, tired glare, and picks up fifteen cards. Yumiko mouths an apology.

"Yeah," Sam agrees with her mother flatly. "Sure thing."

Timothy glances past the card game and the rest of its participants.

On the other bed, Yuuki shows no signs of wanting to be awake.

"I thinking I'll back to the hotel to rest," Yumiko says. "Are you all alright if I come back tomorrow morning?"

"Do you want a ride back there now?" Susan offers. "Or here, tomorrow?"

"No, it's alright. Thank you."

"We don't mind, if you change your mind."

Yumiko inclines her head. "I appreciate the offer. But really, I'll be fine. It's only a short distance away, anyways."

Timothy's mind is consumed by imagining figures concealed in the darkness, clothed in inconspicuous clothing. Waiting. Knowing of Yumiko's relationship to Yuuki, selecting her as a target because of it and dragging her into this whole Ninao kidnapping mess. "I'll walk you to the entrance. Make sure you get out safety."

Joshua glances at Sam. "Wouldn't it draw more attention to her if you went with her? People will be looking out for you, not for her."

"Actually, there's… something I wanted to ask her." Timothy looks at Yumiko. "About Yuuki, if that's alright."

It's an excuse to cover Timothy's anxiety. Joshua's right: it would only draw more attention to her, and Yumiko's perfectly capable of looking after herself. *But so was Yuuki, as a trained security officer. And I thought I should have been able to protect myself alright, too.* But there is actually something that Timothy has had in the back of his mind. He's just never thought to ask it.

Yumiko raises her eyebrows. "Yeah, that's fine."

"Why don't you just ask it here?" Joshua asks. "We're fine with hearing it. Even if it's a long, complicated topic, we won't judge."

Timothy hesitates. "I think it's more that I don't know if it's a good idea to ask it around other people. More specifically, around Yuuki." He lowers his voice. "I don't trust my wording… phrasing… *framing* of what I'm wanting to ask."

Susan gives him a supportive nudge. "Well, beating around the bush sure isn't going to express it very well."

Timothy grimaces.

"Ask it here," Sam murmurs. "If we think it's better we don't hear it, we can leave the room for a bit."

Joshua murmurs his agreement. "How sensitive is the question, anyways? Are you going to ask Yumiko if he likes guys, or something?"

Yumiko lets out an abrupt laugh.

"What?"

"I don't even know if he has any preference."

"Oh, he's bi?"

"No, as in – he likes no one. At least, as far as I'm aware, he's not interested in any dating relationship stuff. And before it is asked, no, it's not about not having found the right person yet. Yuuki's just Yuuki. He's not interested. That's how he is. That's that."

Joshua nods, taking in the information seriously. "Huh."

Sam plays her cards and sends the order of rotation in reverse.

"Hey, I had the perfect set up ready," Joshua protests.

"You mean in your hand of cards, or some dating set up for Yuuki?"

"The *cards,* stupid. Leave Yuuki out of it."

"Good. And oops, but I had to get rid of some of my fifteen plus cards somehow. I'm sure your perfect set up will still be there when your turn comes around again."

"Hnnn, hopefully."

Susan looks at Timothy. She waits until he returns the look, then raises one eyebrow. When it takes too long for Timothy to reply in any way, she gestures at Yumiko.

Oh. Right, I keep delaying asking.

"Let's just talk on the way down," Yumiko says. Her voice warps at the end as another yawn overtakes her. "This is my last card anyways."

That last card goes as soon as her turn hits.

"I'll take over Yuuki's cards, if you want," Sam offers.

Joshua raises an eyebrow at the number of cards in the fan of cards she's holding. "With that many still in your own hand to manage?"

Susan exchanges a glance with Timothy. "How about we just call it here, eh? Unless you want to finish it between yourselves."

Joshua and Sam give the thumbs up signs.

Handing her lot of cards over for them to divide between themselves, Susan stands up with a sigh. She looks at Timothy again. "I'll walk down with you."

Timothy doesn't get the opportunity to say he's fine going by himself. Susan's already decided – she's coming with to see Yumiko off, and the more Timothy thinks about it, the safer he feels thinking about the walk back up to this room afterwards. He'd be alone walking back, without her. Normally there would be nothing wrong with that. But he was also kidnapped alongside Yuuki only a few days or so ago. He didn't end up the same as how Yuuki, lying in that hospital bed, did, but he that doesn't mean he's any safer than Yuuki is.

"So what did you want to ask me?" Yumiko asks once the three of them are out in the hallway.

Timothy automatically scans the hallways, the corners, the shadows. He hesitates. "This might sound like an odd question," he murmurs, "and I'm not sure what the right wording is to ask it."

"Just ask it," Susan interjects.

Timothy's mouth quirks. "Okay... what was Yuuki's reason for coming back here? To Arkala? It wasn't the Arkala youth he grew up around, after all. It was the youth in your home overseas. So why not the Japanese youth? Could he not have become a warden there?"

Yumiko sneezes instead of answering. She grabs a tissue from her pocket, turns to the side to blow her nose. She keeps her gaze downcast as she screws up the tissue and returns it to her pocket, and snatches out a recently bought pocket hand sanitiser from a local supermarket. A bottle of hospital hand sanitiser catches her. She puts her own one back in her pocket and trots over to use the hospital one instead.

"That's a good question," Yumiko says, rubbing her hands together. "I've wondered that myself."

"I don't mean to imply that we don't want him here in Arkala," Timothy says. "That's the reason I didn't feel comfortable asking this in front of Yuuki. We do want him here, like him being here. He's a good warden. A good friend. This is as much his home as Japan is."

Yumiko hums in agreement. "Because it's Arkala where his heart is. This country has always been home for him. More than Japan ever could be."

A nurse passes by. The three fall silent until they reach the elevator.

By unspoken agreement, they walk past and instead take the stairs.

"And I don't think he'd want to go back, even after this," Yumiko says. "So don't worry. The reason he'll likely stay is the reason why he left: he couldn't get used to Japanese culture. Or… couldn't fit in. It's not that he wasn't able to adapt, it just… doesn't suit him. He could live and work there if he had to, but given the choice between returning to Arkala and staying, I think it was a much better idea for him to return here to Arkala. He can be himself more, without having to force himself to… *be Japanese* in the way that everyone around him expects of him, especially since we both *look* Japanese. Yeah, we're three-quarters, so that makes us mostly Japanese, I guess. But I suppose you could say we were Arkalan Japanese – before we were ever Japanese kids who were born in Arkala. Arkalahn English was our first language. Arkala was our first home, too. 'Arkalan' was our first real nationality, not 'Japanese'.

"There's also the social…" Yumiko trails off. Her eyes flick to the ceiling as she tries to recall a word. " – *stigma* surrounding people who are half another nationality. You get treated a little differently – though how much differently would depend on how much you appear to be half, how much you fit in with the norms of the culture and what your peers are like in the area where you live. I was fortunate not to have to really experience any different treatment, perhaps because I don't look half and because I was already functionally fluent in the language when we moved over there. But Yuuki… I was bilingual by the time we moved, while Yuuki had only started learning basic Japanese about a year before we moved."

Yumiko takes a deep breath. She lets it out slowly, almost like a sigh. Her expression is distant. She continues, "So I could blend in with society, so I wasn't notably different. But Yuuki...his lighter complexion made him look different, and he spoke and behaved differently to everyone around him. He wanted to be himself, and himself was firmly Arkalan. He had the Japanese language proficiency of a foreigner just learning the language for the first time. While I was able to cover for myself sufficiently enough, Yuuki was... different, and people couldn't ignore that."

They reach the bottom of the stairwell leading to the ground floor. Yumiko strides ahead to open the door and hold it open Susan and Timothy.

"But you and Yuuki aren't even half," Susan says, passing through. "Thanks, by the way."

Timothy murmurs a thanks on his way also.

"Exact percentage doesn't matter. It's how we appear to people. Once our nationally and or ethnicity is known, and they can see some kind of characteristic in us that is not what they'd expect to be 'normal'... that's all there needs to be for some people to judge in default."

"And that's why he didn't want to stay?" Susan asks.

Yumiko nods. "Growing up in the education system over there exposed some insight, I suppose, into the work culture and social dynamics that awaited him had he stayed. If my wording makes sense. Personally, I found it fine, and I still don't mind it. But it didn't suit Yuuki, especially not as much as the prospect of moving back to Arkala to live and work did.

"In his final year of high school, studying so hard with peers aiming to pass university entrance exams and trying to find a way to succeed in a competitive work culture… it wasn't the future that Yuuki wanted. While they were focused on how many hours of study they were achieving, Yuuki was studying the bare minimum he could without letting his grades slip. Instead of considering degree programs or work opportunities in the country, he was spending his time researching scholarships to Arkala universities instead.

"It ended up being Arkala Police College that he applied for first, since they were recruiting. You likely have heard the rest of the story from there – why he took the security officer route instead of the police officer one: because he became aware of the situation the Arkala youth were in under Taularh's rule and it concerned him and he cared about it. Since he already had committed to the decision of returning to Arkala – and staying – it became a sort of… career goal for him."

"Why a prison warden, though?" Timothy asks. "I get preferring security officer study route to police officer study route. But why couldn't he work in a youth counselling programme or something instead as a *career goal destination objective thing?* Why a detention centre, of all places?"

Why this career path that ended up treating him like this – taking his care and concern, then chewing him up and spitting him back out right after he tries to establish a means to help people?

The way Susan glances at him, Timothy can tell that she can read where these questions are coming from.

Yumiko continues on, oblivious or otherwise choosing to let it be. "Because Yuuki's been like in places like them: he's had a taste of social isolation, social rejection, cultural identity issues, personal identity issues, upheavals to ways of living and the frustration of having to live according

232

to someone's 'norms' or 'rules' that only make you feel trapped and like you don't want to belong. He might not have turned to criminal activities or reckless behaviours, or the sorts that might get him into trouble like the youth he works with have done, but he has experienced enough to understand and or empathise with the emotional and or psychological circumstances behind those actions.

"And so he sees them not as wrong-doers and rebels, but as frustrated or socially displaced youth – he sees them as people who have made a mistake and might not have been given a *decent chance* to work through whatever it is that might have compelled them to commit whatever crime they ended up in custody for."

Timothy listens silently, his thoughts blanked out. These things about Yuuki, sure…he already knew or realised some of them to some degree. But somehow, hearing it from Yumiko adds a different tone to it, like realising it all over again, in another light.

And Timothy thinks he gets it now – another reason why Yuuki wanted to create something like the Youth Rehabilitation Trust, and why he wanted to be youth prison warden as a career of all things he could've wanted to be. Yuuki cares. He even went to the effort of creating a trust to help kids get themselves back on their feet. It had seemed like such a good thing, until –

Until this.

Until this happened.

Was it really necessary to attack them? Because of the Youth Rehabilitation Trust? Yuuki didn't deserve this – he doesn't deserve this. He wasn't doing any harm. It's not like he's starting an actual rebellion or something.

But maybe Taularh saw it that way. Or whoever it was who kidnapped them did. It was solely for the purpose of encouraging a healthier society. But if Taularh, or whoever was behind this whole thing, had a different opinion, and they didn't like the fact that Yuuki cared so much in the first place, then...

"Do you think he'll still want to stay?" Timothy asks quietly.

The thought is a jump from his previous line of thoughts. But it's a result of all that that they have to think about.

Yumiko shrugs. "I can't speak for him. But I don't think he'll want to come back to Japan. A kidnapping isn't enough to drive him out of the country. It just... might take him a while to get over it."

"There is a chance," Susan says slowly, "that he won't 'get over it'."

The silence is solemn between them.

At the entrance, Susan presses the after-hours button to open the doors. The three of them walk out into the night. The air is chilly. The breeze is brisk, and stirs in the trees in the carpark. A few stars are out, barely visible beyond the city lights.

"So the question is," Timothy murmurs, "where is going to provide the best environment for him to recover? Where will he have the better resources available for him to cope in the way he needs to?"

The question is one that, no matter how it's worded, they can't answer for sure. *Arkala,* is most likely going to be the answer. That's the one they're expecting. But as for what Yuuki's recovery is going to look like – what it's going to need to incorporate, and what the aftermath has in store for him – they don't know. They still have yet to even find out all that happened to Yuuki during his three days' absence.

Timothy shivers.

Yumiko readjusts her jacket around herself. "I'll head to the hotel now. Thanks for walking with me."

Susan replies with as much a smile as she can manage in spite of the cold air on her face and the exhaustion tugging at them all.

"We'll see you tomorrow some time, then?" Timothy asks.

Yumiko nods. "Let me know if anything changes."

Timothy and Susan nod.

"And thank you for being here for him."

Timothy's throat closes up.

Yumiko sniffs, straightens up and clears her throat. She gives an overly cheerful wave and then turns to continue on her way to the hotel. Timothy and Susan remain at the entrance of the hotel, outside, standing there watching her go. They stay until Yumiko's crossed the road and her figure can't be seen any more on the other side.

A hand settles in the middle of Timothy's back. Timothy looks at Susan, who then drops her arm to hold his hand in hers.

"Come on," she murmurs. "Let's head back up."

26

The light is daylight white. Bright. It takes some time for Yuuki's eyes to adjust, but when they do, he finds that it isn't that bright at all. Outside, it's raining. The curtains are pulled back to give a view of it. It's nice. Yuuki usually likes the rain. It's usually soothing.

But right now, the rain unearths a ghostly sense of dread. If it rains, and the ceiling leaks, and water drips…drips…drips…

It won't. It won't do that here. Here is a hospital. The roof is not immediately above this room that he is in. The sound of the rain is muted, and the building well-constructed. There won't be any persistent dripping to destabilise his grip on…nothingness. There's no beeping of machines in this room to mimic it and taunt him of his fears, either.

Yuuki breathes through the shadow of anxiety.

He distracts himself by studying the person sitting on the window-side bench. His sister, but he doesn't know why Yumiko is here, but she is. She's got one arm propped up on the window sill, head resting there with her chin on her hand. Simply staring blankly out the window.

She looks tired.

236

It occurs to Yuuki then that the setting around him has changed. The window that his sister is sitting by... he doesn't remember there being the window there on his right. Maybe there were just curtain over it then, the last time he woke, but...

No, his bed's been moved. Things have changed with other things too, since he last woke up. There's less medical equipment around him, and connected to him. There's no longer the tubing of nasal cannula running across his face. Instead, the tube that's there only touches one side of his face. A nasogastric tube. It's uncomfortable, being able to feel it running through his nostril, his nasal passage and down through his throat. If he doesn't concentrate on it, perhaps he can ignore it. At least the annoying clippy thing on his finger is gone. And whatever was wrapped around his wrists are gone. And the room feels less frequently monitored – quieter.

Yuuki lies there, trying to take it in. He's exhausted, and doesn't feel good. But at least his body doesn't feel so drained. It doesn't feel like it's started to eat itself or atrophy. *The stomach cramps aren't digging into his abdomen anymore, either*, he realises dully. Nowhere near as viscously, anyways. That horrible muscle pain that spread through his shoulders and legs has eased. The parched sensation in his mouth and throat, and the aching of his head have relented. If he moves, or thinks, that might change, though. It's better not to be too aware of anything just yet.

He'd rather not be aware of anything at all.

It scares him. He doesn't want to try to come to terms with what's happened yet. He doesn't want to let his thoughts start up and gain any momentum. For all he knows, this could all be a lie he's perceiving. If he lets enough time pass, maybe he'll fall back asleep and wake up still in that shed again – and this…seeing Yumiko and Timothy and Susan and hospital ceilings, and sensations of medical equipment, will turn out to be nothing more than a psychologically messed up dream…

…and he'll find out that he never left the shed in the first place.

Yumiko lets out a sigh. It yanks Yuuki out of the thought spiral. His sister yawns and makes an attempt to cover with her hand. She stretches, unfurls from her side lean, and blinks back focus in her gaze.

And turns. She sits rigidly, then, staring. "Yuuki… you're awake."

Yuuki blinks slowly.

"How are you – … Are you feeling okay?"

Again, Yuuki doesn't reply. He doesn't know what to say to that. It takes a considerable amount of energy just to form a string of words in his mind. Summoning the energy to speak them out loud is too much for him right now. Even if he could communicate in sign language, he wouldn't have the energy to form the signs.

"Yuuki?"

It's like part of brain is telling him there's no point in wasting energy trying, anyway – he won't be able to articulate the sounds. He's aware of the taste of sleep in his mouth. He clenches his jaw. There's nothing blocking his mouth, and yet it feels like it's full of cotton.

Yuuki doesn't think it's a good idea to trace that thought.

Beside him, his sister moves to the stool sitting nearer the bed. She has a concerned look on her face. She reaches out to touch him. The moment her hands breach the threshold of the side of the bed, Yuuki tenses.

Adrenaline jolts through him when her hand lights on his arm.

238

Yumiko reactively withdraws her hands, eyes wide. "Sorry. Sorry, I…I should've asked."

Forcing himself to not hold his breath, Yuuki lets his body go slowly lax again.

It's okay, he tells her in his mind. *It's okay,* he tells himself.

… but what's okay?

Yuuki just stares off to the side of the room blankly. He feels like he's viewing someone else's experience. It would be a truer state of reality if he were to close his eyes and open them to the surroundings of the shed again. It's like he almost wants that happen, if just to be sure of where he is and what's happening.

"Are you feeling alright?" Yumiko asks. "Do you want me to get a nurse, or someone? The Harrisons went home for some rest, but they'll be coming back soon."

The Harrisons. What she's saying doesn't fully register in Yuuki's head. He understands the words, and who they're referring to, but their meaning is barely processed. Their meaning doesn't make sense to him – because there's no way the Harrisons could have gone home to rest and then come here so casually. They were caught up in the kidnapping too. So the words Yumiko is speaking don't really make sense.

He forgets that he saw them, or hallucinated them, the last time he came to. Timothy and Susan, at least.

If I stay awake, will I see them again?

He doesn't want to be awake. He doesn't want to be conscious. Yuuki doesn't want to wake up to reality only to find that, all along, this was all just some scene he conjured up in his own delirious mind, then got lost in.

That Yumiko was never here. And Timothy and Susan were never here before, because Timothy got kidnapped when Yuuki did and that's the last he saw or heard of him. He vaguely remembers hearing Timothy's voice a lot since the scenery of the shed changed. But he's too scared to give in to the hope that it's true. He's too psychologically and emotionally exhausted to be able to risk finding out later that it was all a lie.

Clearing her throat, Yumiko shifts. "So…I'll be here another two days. If there's anything you need, just ask. Otherwise…"

She never finishes.

Yuuki closes his eyes while waiting for the next set of words, but they never come. Before any more do, his awareness shuts down and he falls asleep again.

When Yuuki wakes up again, Yumiko isn't there anymore.

Instead, Timothy is back – Timothy who looks like he's just woken up from a ten hour nap. His whole aura reads exhausted. He looks real.

The curtains are drawn. The lights are on. It must be night.

"Hey," Timothy murmurs.

As like before, Yuuki doesn't have the energy to respond with anything but a blink. After blinking, Timothy is still there. Real.

Not a hallucination… or a hopeful daydream…

"Your sister said you were awake for a bit earlier. How are you feeling?"

Again with that question. Yuuki doesn't know. He doesn't want to have to try to put words to it. He doesn't know what words are adequate or appropriate, and he doesn't want to concentrate enough to find out.

Timothy attempts a smile. There is genuine relief to be found in it, but it looks strained. Worried. Unsure.

You ask me if I'm okay, Yuuki thinks, *but what about you?*

"Susan's out getting dinner with Joshua and Sam. Are you okay if we have it in here with you? If you do, let us know, somehow, okay? If it upsets or stresses you in anyway."

Yuuki can't even fully picture the whole Harrison family being in a hospital room with him. He doesn't get why they'd want to be here. It's a hospital room. Yuuki's current state isn't exactly something to want to be around. For their sake, they ought to go elsewhere to have their meal.

An empty room versus the stifling pressure of people making themselves stay when they might not want to. Yuuki would prefer an empty room.

The dusty, shadowy shed.

Empty room.

Yuuki's breathing hitches. He closes his eyes against the image. The image stays, becomes more vivid. Yuuki opens his eyes again.

"Once you're eventually feeling up to eating," Timothy continues, oblivious, "and if the hospital approves, we'll get you some too, if you like."

The prospect of eating isn't a thought that Yuuki wants to entertain. He's tired. Too tired. He doesn't want to talk about food. He can't think about it without nausea creeping into his stomach.

The topic ends there. Timothy sits quietly, glancing here and there and at his hands for a bit. He pulls out his phone and checks through things in his usual manner. Checking his work emails, probably, judging by the serious contemplate frown that befalls his face.

It's almost too normal. Normal, as in like Timothy himself didn't get kidnapped.

You were attacked too, weren't you?

Timothy *did* get kidnapped, too, didn't he? Yuuki saw –

But no, he didn't see. The last he *actually* saw was Timothy getting attacked, and knocked out, and then…

And then Yuuki was knocked out too, and remembers nothing clearly in between then and waking up in the shed. Only voices. And chemically tainted air. And nauseating pain.

So what happened to you then, Timothy?

Why are you here? How are you safe?

…what happened to you?

Timothy notices Yuuki staring at him. He holds Yuuki's gaze, as though weighing up whether or not to tell him something.

Yuuki tries to express – as much as he can with a tired, non-expressive facial expression – to just say it.

"There's going to be someone from the PF coming tomorrow," Timothy informs him. "They're aware of your condition. They're hoping to be able to investigate further into what happened to you. And maybe find some leads on who attacked us."

…attacked 'us'. So you were attacked.

But no one knows anything.

Then how did you find me?

"It's okay if you're not feeling up to it, though. They do need your statement as the primary victim in all this –"

'*Victim*'.

"– but we get that you might not be ready to speak about it. We don't want you to push yourself too far when you're meant to be resting."

If they need answers, they'll expect me to answer regardless of my condition.

"Don't pressure yourself to answer their questions if you're not feeling okay. Of course, they'll need your statement, at some point – and sooner rather than later, for the sake of the case investigation."

'*Case investigation*'.

"But your health is important. And you need to recover fr- from…from this near death experience of yours first."

… '*near death experience*'.

How is Yuuki's experience in that shed best described? It sounds so easy to call it a 'case' and to call Yuuki a 'victim'. But the terms feel washed-out in comparison to the chaotic bone-deep overwhelming stress-ridden nauseatingly sickening…

An involuntary noise squeaks in Yuuki's throat. It makes his throat hurt. It brings him shame, for how much it sounds like a whimper.

Timothy watches him, concerned. "Is it too soon? I believed it might be, but…"

Yuuki grimaces and looks away. His head feels heavy when he turns it. When he clenches his jaw to suppress the shame of the noise he just made, it reminds him of clenching his jaw around the gag, around the pressure that had filled his mouth and –

How am I supposed to speak about all this? What am I even supposed to tell any one? If they found me in that shed, they know the situation I was in. There's nothing I can tell them that they don't already know.

The only thing that Yuuki could give them is a vague attempt at describing what the experience was like to live through. But, at the end of the day, they're not looking to hear how Yuuki felt during those three days. They won't be asking about his emotional and psychological condition. Anyone who does will likely be considering whether or not to introduce him to a counsellor, and Yuuki doesn't want that. He's his own counsellor, and always has been. He doesn't want to have to describe his terrible internal experience to someone who doesn't truly want to hear it for the sake of genuinely caring about him.

Besides that, how on earth is he supposed to be able to find words to adequately describe something he's barely managed to process?

"When they come," Timothy says quietly, but firmly, "one of us will be here with you. Probably me. I'm guessing that it will be Marina who will come to talk with you. She's good. She and her partner are the ones who rescued me and Joshua."

...and Joshua? So Joshua did get in trouble, too. They were both kidnapped – nearly kidnapped, because they were rescued.

They were rescued, unlike Yuuki.

It's a bittersweet realisation. One full of muted grief. Relief. Pain.

At least they didn't have to experience what I did. Or anything similar, or anything worse. At least nothing bad happened to Timothy – that is, nothing of the kind that plagued my imagination during all my free time in that shed.

"I'll fill you in later on what happened to us," Timothy says, reading Yuuki's expression. "But for now, just know that we've been safe. We were rescued on route to wherever they were taking us. The PFO who will likely be coming tomorrow, Marina, she's been helping keep us safe and informed and updated on the…on the case. She was there when we rescued you, too." Timothy's voice sounds unsteady. "It's okay if you don't remember it, though. I'm not sure you were aware enough to remember."

Yuuki feels his exhaustion settle down on him again. *No, I don't remember. I don't want to remember – any of it.* He struggles to keep his eyes open. They burn a little, like his eyes are also dehydrated.

A warm pressure settles on his shoulder. Timothy's hand. Yuuki barely reacts to it. He doesn't know why he doesn't. Why, when his sister reached out to touch him he reacted the way he did, yet when Timothy and Susan do the same, he doesn't react at all and in fact finds it reassuring, grounding.

If he were awake more, he'd consider it more. But he's too tired to think. Too tired to stay awake. His head hurts from being awake, from *thinking*, from *recalling*.

More sleep. Just…sleep.

Yuuki falls asleep with Timothy's hand anchoring him to a faint sense of safety.

27

11th June, 12-Tau – late morning

As per Timothy's words yesterday, a PF officer arrives to ask after Yuuki's testimony. Both Timothy and Susan are there, but Susan has to leave for work in less than an hour.

Yuuki realises that he doesn't even know what day it is, nor what day of the week it is. Presumable a weekday, if Susan has work. Sam is likely at school. Joshua said he was on break at university. Timothy probably took a break from work, since he was a victim of the kidnapping, too.

For whatever reason, Yuuki own absence from work doesn't even cross his mind as he's thinking about the Harrisons. It's like his work life doesn't exist. It's like *he* doesn't exist anymore.

Yuuki Takahashi stopped existing in that garden shed.

Yuuki doesn't delve into thinking about it too much. It's probably just an emotional shock thing. Once he's recovered a bit, he might start feeling more like himself again – whatever 'himself' should feel like. He'll stop feeling so detached from himself when things go back to normal.

The door slides open. Some part of Yuuki's brain associates the sound with the rattle of the classroom doors of the schools he went to in Japan.

246

Particularly his third year home room class in high school. It rattled just like that.

For a moment, Yuuki could imagine himself back there.

A careful yet serious face pokes in. "Yuuki Takahashi?"

Yuuki stares at the person, tired. He doesn't invite them in. He also doesn't shoo them out – can't, really, as the person is wearing an Arkala Peace Force uniform, and he's far too lacking in energy to try.

An inspector, he decides on seeing the respective ranking on the person's shoulders. Officers of that rank don't usually dress in uniform, but Yuuki supposes that it's for the purpose of police presence. A security measure – both a warning to the unidentified perpetrators of the kidnapping and a reassurance to the people they're protecting.

Yuuki glances at Timothy hovering in the doorway. *Is this the Marina you mentioned?* But Timothy's attention is hyper-focused on something on his phone. His phone screen lights up, he swipes the screen and disappears out of the room to answer the call.

Susan rises from her seat. "Come in," she says to the PFO. She keeps her voice deliberately low, likely to indicate what level of volume ought to be sustained – or rather, what Yuuki can tolerate.

With an acknowledging smile, the inspector steps into the room. Taking the cue from Susan, they moderate their voice accordingly. "I am Kia Ihsayu. I'm an inspector from the Ninao District branch, affiliated with the Internal Security and Surveillance division."

Not Marina, then.

Whatever they say next is lost to Yuuki's detached daydreaming. The door's rattle as it closes takes Yuuki back to his last year in a school uniform. Afternoon light. There's a piece of paper sitting on his desk. Every one of his classmates had the same paper handed out to them. His home room teacher's voice overlaps with the inspector's. Drowns out the latter's words.

"Please write down what plans or ideas you have for your future," the teacher had asked.

Yuuki had known his answer, more or less: *Arkala.*

He'd wanted to go back – back here. Arkala Police College were offering scholarships to accept prospective students from overseas – they still do. The study options had been appealing, well-structured... guaranteeing of a job. For someone who only knew they wanted to make their living in Arkala after graduating high school, it was an open door.

And then...

And then Yuuki had gone there. Studied. Met Timothy Harrison. Graduated four years later as a security officer. Found a job as a warden at A'o Youth Detention Centre. Proposed, with Timothy, a trust fund that would help the kids caught up in the pitfall traps of the Arkala justice system to get back on their feet once they left –

And then it lead to this kidnapping happening.

Yuuki blinks. In a roundabout way, he's returned to the place he doesn't want to be right now – aware, in the now: questioned about what happened, about an event...a...a *thing*...that Yuuki doesn't want to be made to recall.

He doesn't want to remember.

The helplessness.

The door that wouldn't open.

The questions that couldn't be answered.

The bindings, the dehydration, the exhaustion and the messed up mentality slowly getting to him...

Susan hovers by his side. Her brow is creased.

The inspector clears their throat. "I know that this is difficult for you, but your statement is important and it will help us in our investigation of this case."

Yuuki swallows. His mouth feels...weightless, in terms of words and voice. He doesn't have the energy to say anything. He doesn't have the will to try to somehow explain things that he doesn't know... that he doesn't... understand.

"Perhaps it might be better to come back another time," Susan says firmly.

"Has he been struggling to talk?" the inspector asks quietly on their way out.

Susan gives a small nod. "Hasn't spoken a word since..."

"To anyone?"

"To anyone."

The inspector grimaces. "I see. I apologise, then – for not have given him more time to recover. Takahashi's experience must've been quite traumatic for him." A hum. "May I ask how long you think he'll need before he's ready to give us a statement?"

Susan leans against the doorframe. She tilts her head. "...not sure how long it'll take."

Kia Ihsayu turns back to Yuuki. "Takahashi. I understand that this is difficult for you, but we do need to find who was behind this. Your statement is a critical and necessary part in ironing out some uncertainties. Please, when you're able to, contact me or one of the primary officers investigating the case. I believe the Harrison family are well acquainted with Marina Tu'u. If you would feel more comfortable talking with her and her partner Conrad Johnson about the incident, then you are welcome to do so."

There's another officer – Timothy has been conversing with them out in the hallway, it seems. The rehearsed tone of a nurse interjects and argues something.

Yuuki hears him say that he's likely still coming to terms with the fact that this is all real and he's not imagining it. He was locked in that shed for three days, assumedly. That kind of experience plays tricks on the mind. Yuuki's likely still out of it. They're also worried that his being drugged made his dehydration worse, and this would also have affected his state of mind. With or without that being a factor, he's bound to be in shock.

Yuuki notes, as the people *finally* take their leave, that the word 'trauma' seems to be floating around a lot. He doesn't really connect with the word 'trauma'. Maybe, he thinks, it's because of the shock they just talked about.

Yuuki is upset and wishes they'd all just leave him alone.

Seeing Yuuki's frustration and stress, Susan ushers everyone out away from outside the room to give him some time to himself to rest.

Tired and frustrated, his eyes land on the door to the small bathroom in the far corner of the room. *Water.* He ponders walking over there, if just to splash some cold water on his face and have a little privacy for a few moments. If he can make it over there at all. He hasn't left the bed since he woke up the first time. He hasn't got up and *walked* since…

… since before the kidnapping.

Yuuki decides he doesn't care. He'll make himself manage on his own. He's too stubborn and ashamed and *overwhelmed* to ask for help with it.

He sits up, forces his legs out of bed. He feels weak, stiff. When he stands, his muscles feel like they have little strength in them. The action feels *too much*. The blood rushes from his head, drains from his face. He reaches for the IV stand as grey blotchy static fills his vision, but his hand slips and he falls.

The impact with the floor hurts. He gasps.

Why am I so stupid?

Susan comes in, finds him. Her shadow falls over him. Her presence is a shelter between himself and the door. "Do you want me to call a nurse?"

Yuuki sucks in a breath. He closes his eyes and gives a small shake of his head. He then looks towards the bathroom, re-evaluating the distance, and wondering how much he actually needs to go in.

"I'll help you up, okay?"

Yuuki considers a moment before giving a resigned nod.

Susan kneels down, slips her arms beneath his and around his back, and hauls him up to his feet. She helps him grab the IV stand, then walks him over to the bathroom. She keeps him steady while he splashes the water on his face, then stands there exhausted, hands braced on either side of the sink, head bowed. He doesn't let himself linger on the thought that he can move his hands freely, without rope binding them together behind his back.

While standing, he goes to the bathroom, too. It's humiliating, and he doesn't need to pee much anyways. But somehow it's less humiliating and awkward than with a stranger who works here. It also means he doesn't have to wear a catheter down there anymore. That latter part involves negotiation between Susan and a nearby nurse, but they deal with the matter swift and clinically and Yuuki is spared from facing too much shame and loss of dignity and privacy.

In fact, if he thinks about it, he's almost glad he isn't left alone in this room. Given another few seconds of thought, and Yuuki might've realised just how small that room was. How much those walls could've so easily taunted him – about how the room is even smaller than the shed.

Yuuki's shaking as he walks with support away from the small bathroom. His nervous system realises it even if his mind's not fully caught up.

He's glad he doesn't realise it.

Susan helps him back to bed, which Yuuki almost collapses in, his legs are dragging and he's barely holding up his own weight. Susan helps position his limbs so he's comfortable, then pulls the covers up over him. Yuuki closes his eyes, spent and head spinning. Faint, feeling like gravity is dragging both his body and his mind down past ground.

Why do I feel like this?

It's a question he already knows the general answer to. The technical details he couldn't care less about right now.

He feels a hand on his head, smoothing his hair down. Normally, Yuuki would've batted the hand aside, but he's not feeling like himself at the moment as it is, and the action is somewhat consoling.

"Take your time recovering," Susan says quietly. "It may take a little while before you're feeling okay again. That's okay. Take your time. We're not going to judge you badly or shame you if you're having a hard time. Or if everything's just simply confusing and you don't want to talk about anything."

Yuuki opens his eyes a fraction, then gives in to letting himself sink. A wave of sudden exhaustion slams into him, and he gets taken under quickly by it.

"Just let yourself rest. We want to help you feel okay again."

If he were alert enough, he might've heard the way Susan's voice wavered.

Yuuki is off the IV when he wakes. While the catheter needle is still in his arm, there's nothing connected to it. It both alarms him and has him feeling grateful that he wasn't aware when all of this was happening. He doesn't like realising that people have been doing things to him without his knowledge of it happening. But at the same time, it means he didn't have to worry about being conscious during it and thus reacting to it.

"Yuuki," says Yumiko quietly.

He turns his head slowly. Yumiko's expression isn't masked, but it's difficult to read.

"The nurse came in about an hour earlier to take you off the IV," she explains. "They said they can put you back on it if necessary, but it's better for your recovery if you try to have some food and water yourself. They'll take the needle out soon, otherwise. Do you think you can manage some now? Food, I mean. They left some here for you."

Yuuki glances to the bedside drawers where Yumiko is pointing. They have left some, and it looks like soft solid food. Yuuki doesn't know if he'll be able to tolerate food and water. Water, maybe. But food…

The nurse is right, as is Yumiko. He should try… even if all it does is prove he's not up to it yet.

But it's distressing, the thought of putting something into his mouth that he doesn't want. The thought of having something solid sitting in his mouth again leaves him shaken. It causes a distress in him he's not expecting. It causes violent emotional reaction that leaves Yuuki shaken. His mouth is dry, too dry to salivate, but he feels a sudden nausea like he might throw up. It must show in his face, because Yumiko doesn't press after that.

Yumiko hands him a glass of water, but he can't even accept that. With a shaky hand and a high focus on the *emptiness* in his mouth besides what is there as a part of him, he pushes the offered glass and the offering hand away.

"Hey, what's wrong?" Yumiko asks. "What's up?"

Yuuki shakes. He shakes his head. *There's no way I can explain to her…* *this.*

All he can think about is that chemical-soaked cloth. Had the chemicals not worn off enough, his mouth could've been damaged more. A few ulcers, a sore throat, a respiratory infection of some kind – he got off lightly. But he can't just get over how much effort it took and *stress* he went through in trying to get that cloth *out of his mouth*. Somehow, forcing himself to accept food is like asking to have he someone shove cloth between his teeth and then seal his mouth shut with tape all over again.

That's not how it is. Yuuki rationally knows, that's not how it is. But it doesn't matter, because the resemblance in sensation and action has enough similarity, and that similarity is all that matters. Yuuki might not remember physically being gagged – he only woke up in that state. But he's not sure what's better; he doesn't know what would be worse: being awake during that, or waking up already gagged like he had done so in the shed.

Yuuki barely suppresses the whimper that rises in his throat. Neither. The answer is neither. They both are 'worse'.

Yumiko has left her seat to go talk with the nurse. They stand in the doorway, the two of them, talking. Yuuki doesn't have to look at their faces to guess the sorts of perplexed looks they might be giving him. He tries to ignore them. Instead, the bruised and scathed skin around his wrists shouts at him. It yells, that these marks are healing, and they don't even hurt too much. There used to be a bandage on his face where his skin got scratched while he dug and tore the tape off his mouth. There's no bandage anymore.

He's not needing oxygen therapy, and they want to lessen the non-natural intervention supplied to him for nutrition and medication and hydration. There's still a feeding tube through his nose and down his throat. There's still a needle in the back of his hand, ready if he needs it for hydration and or medication. But overall, it's an indication that he should be feeling somewhat better, right? Yuuki shouldn't feel so upset about other things that are fading – should be fading now. If he doesn't want to stay in this hospital room any longer than he has to, then he needs to demonstrate to the others and to himself that he's getting better, that *that shed stuff* is behind him, and that he's fine, he's recovering.

It unravels him, unexpectedly – this. Yuuki's not sure what this is. He's not sure where it comes from, only what triggered it. *Triggered it.* Another word that is rightly associated with trauma.

He can only hope that this is only temporary, because it's awful. He's not in that shed anymore. He's gone from there, and just as he's gone, Yuuki just wants the whole shed-kidnapping ordeal to be over with.

They start with a gentle intake of liquid-based nutrition. Yuuki's first reintroduction to food is a hot drink of lemon, ginger and honey. Freshly prepared. Yumiko had brought some along with her in a thermos, for Yuuki to have if he could. There's a note from Susan, reading, "*Homemade. I put a lot of honey it – let me know if it's too sweet.*" Yuuki wonders how much sleep she's getting, that she took time to make this for him.

Yuuki holds the cup in both hands. Feels its warmth seeping through ceramic walls. It occurs to him that this is the first thing he's had to eat or drink since before the kidnapping. Since before Yuuki walked into Timothy's office in Ninao on June 5th to officiate the Youth Rehabilitation Trust.

And just like that, his thoughts are unfocused and flitting all over the place – trying to distract him from the seemingly stupid emotional psychological dilemma of the task in front of him. It shouldn't stress him so much, but it does.

Yuuki slams a mental dam down on the thoughts.

He breathes in and out slowly, focusing instead on the discomfort tickling the inside of his chest when he breathes.

It helps to think of this as being a natural health drink that will benefit his recovery from the respiratory infection, as opposed to a thing being used as a stepping stone to getting him to try eating again. The latter only conjures up an unnerving psychological thought process including, but not limited to, the idea of the food and drink contents replacing the sensation of the cloth gag for him.

With that, he manages to get himself to drink even just a sip.

The liquid is hot, and soothing, and the taste destroys the memory of saliva-soaked cotton filling his mouth.

It's good, Yuuki wants to say, but when he opens his mouth, nothing comes out. Whether it's a reaction caused by the anxiety of hearing and feeling the vibrations of voice through whatever substance or lack thereof might be filling his mouth, or simply his not feeling well because of the sore throat he has, it stops him. Yumiko notices him attempting to say something and raises eyebrows expectantly, waiting.

Instead of speaking, Yuuki glances at the cup, awkwardly gestures with it and inclines his head in a bow. His lips twitch in the best attempt at an appreciative smile or even grimace.

Yumiko returns the small smile without judgement.

Later, Yumiko is joined by the full Harrison family.

A nurse brings in soup. Yuuki looks at her uncertainly.

"Hey, would it help if there's less of us in the room?" Susan asks. Her words give something else for Yuuki to focus on. "Maybe just Yumiko, or...?"

257

I don't know. Yuuki grips the sheets tightly. *I don't know, I just want...don't want...*

The nurse leaves to give them an opportunity for space.

Joshua and Sam come in. Timothy talks with them, and their conversation and familiar presence in the background helps distract Yuuki enough for him to try eating.

It's not pleasant, but he manages a few mouthfuls. Swallowing is forced. The meal isn't big anyways, since Yuuki's stomach needs to adjust again. But it feels big. After a break, Yuuki is able to finish the majority of it. He feels defeated not having finished it all, but the nurse seems happy when she comes back to collect the tray.

Susan briefly rubs Yuuki's shoulder. The touch is grounding, but he's flinchy and he reactively shrugs away from it.

In the middle of listening to Joshua, Sam, Yumiko, Timothy and Susan talking, Yuuki sips lemon water. He listens to each of their voices. Blanking out his mind to add something to the statement of the PF looking for clues about the perpetrators...

He figures he should try say something.

Yuuki whispers, "No one came back."

His voice is croaky, rough from disuse. It's fractured and the words are hard to distinguish. But it quietens the room all the same. Yuuki stares at the reflection of the lights on the water in the cup he's holding. It takes a moment before anyone says anything.

Timothy clears his throat. "What was it you said?"

Yuuki blinks. It takes some mental effort to get himself to get the words out. "Nothing happened. No one... came back."

It's the first series of words that Yuuki has spoken since his rescue. Since his hauntingly pathetic desperate cries for help, after he finally got the cloth out of his mouth that prevented him from being able to say anything at all…

"You mean at the shed?" Yumiko asks hesitantly.

Yuuki nods. "Hmmm."

"So you… you *were* in there the whole three days?" Joshua asks, also tentative.

Three days. He's already heard that it was that long. He'd counted the nights, so he knows he was in there that long. But it felt like longer. In terms of endurance, at least.

In words, three days doesn't sound like much. It could've been longer.

No, it was long enough. Too long. Too long altogether.

Yuuki realises they're waiting for him to answer again. His hands go limp. He nearly lets the cup tip over. "There," he murmurs, intending on saying '*yeah*' and something along the lines of '*was there the three days*'. He tries again. "I was just there."

There's a period of silence as the Harrisons process that information.

Tired, Yuuki puts the cup down on the tray beside the bed and lies back. The Harrisons try to keep their expressions neutral, but there's a mix of various emotions passing between that Yuuki can't help but notice.

A release of tension, hearing that nothing *else* happened to Yuuki in the three days he was gone. The uncertainty of what impact that 'nothing' had in its own right. A forced acceptance, of information they thought could have been what had happened, but still doubt. Grief.

Yuuki doesn't want to read into it anymore. He turns his gaze away.

Averts the conversation too.

"What'd they work with - ... they, what'd they do with work?" he asks. The words come out terribly slurred. The meaning is lost. Yuuki closes his eyes, takes a moment to breath and then tries again. "My work shifts. What'd…what did they do with them?"

Timothy shifts in his seat. "Do you mean while you were…?"

Yuuki's too tired to try amend the potentially confusing meaning of the question. Fortunately, the meaning isn't entirely lost.

"Don't worry about work right now," Susan says. "They'll have sorted something out."

In truth, Yuuki isn't worried about it. He isn't even actually actively concerned about it right now – it was just a vague wondering he's had in the back of his mind. He knows that there's nothing he can do about the shifts he missed – is *missing*. He doesn't have the will to care right now, either.

Susan shifts. "And I'm not intending to try say that you're replaceable. All I mean is that, in your absence – both in the three days you were missing and while you're here recovering, they'll have found a way to manage somehow. So just focus on recovering."

"I guess so."

Yuuki's words are the last of that conversation. The Harrisons don't leave that night, but there's a few minutes where the family are talking outside the ward and give Yuuki some peace from their discussion. Yuuki is left alone, and in that quiet the silence rings loud in his ears. There are words, too many words in his mind. Too many little things to think about. And somehow, he's supposed to sort through all of that.

But the hardest thing of all to face is the knowledge that he's expected to describe his experience of the kidnapping to people. Timothy has already covered the initial attack, presumably.

Yuuki realises then that he still doesn't know what happened to Timothy after they'd both been knocked out. Yuuki feels sick. His friend looks unharmed, but Yuuki doesn't know if he can handle finding out more right now. He doesn't want to be horrified if it was bad, and he doesn't want to have to process the internal screaming at himself '*why?!*' if it turns out that Yuuki was the only one subjected to such a pointless experience of being tied up and gagged and locked in a shed in the middle of nowhere for who knows what reason.

His throat closes up. It's an effort to breathe slowly. The Harrisons will come back in any moment now. Yuuki can't let them see him losing his calm, no matter how artificial it is. He can't let them see him break down so soon.

I'll get over it. I'll get passed it. Then we can all move on with our lives and they won't have to worry about a kidnapping that happened to me because of me, because of a stupid idealistic idea that I had that I thought might be good. They've been caught up in this enough already.

Yumiko watches him sadly. She reaches out to hug him, then hesitates. She reconsiders, and hugs him carefully. This time Yuuki doesn't flinch. He tenses when she hugs him.

His sister holds him carefully for a minute or two.

He lets her.

28

12th June, 12-Tau

Yumiko stayed over instead of the Harrisons since it's her last night in Arkala before she's due to go back. The Harrisons went back home to rest. According to Yumiko, Timothy and Susan will be back soon. One benefit of having been able to consume *something* in the ways of nutrition is that the nasogastric tube gets removed. It's unpleasant. His nose feels sore and dry, but it's much nicer not having to wear it.

But just as Yuuki's proven he can consume without intervention, he's also demonstrated he can now verbally communicate again. The downside of being more lucid and able to speak is that it's harder to suppress and ignore discomfort. Questions. The nurses report that Yuuki is able to speak now, and the PFOs come right away. It's not without checking in with Yuuki first, but in the end Yuuki gives them the go ahead.

Once it's done, it's done. *If I just give them my statement now,* he reasons, *the PF won't keep metaphorically and literally knocking on the door asking for it.* Yuuki might not be able to offer them much in the way of leads. But in the very least, he can let them know that. They might come back with follow up questions to ask, but the longer Yuuki delays this, the longer he's going to have to put up with their insisting he speak to them about the incident.

They need Yuuki's testimony, his statement. He gets it.

But he's just so damn tired and wants people to leave him alone.

Not in-the-shed kind of 'alone', but... at least with some more adequate time to rest. Some personal space to introvert. Some quiet, non-intrusive time to process things.

Is that not the same as the shed, though?

There's a difference, however: Yuuki's choice to leave. The shed didn't give him that option, and the hospital and its eventful people visits doesn't either yet. Perhaps the hospital environment wouldn't be so bad if he was given more time to realise what's happened, and to recover. If he had time to process how he feels without the social pressure to express that coping out loud. Yuuki wants to think about things and recover in his own time, at his own pace.

Unfortunately, he's not going to be allowed that in the short while.

Before the PF have indicated they'll come, a psychiatrist is booked to check up on him. Yuuki isn't looking forward to either visit.

Susan arrives with Timothy at the hospital an hour before the psychiatrist is due to come, while Yumiko heads back to the hotel to check out. Susan leaves with Yumiko briefly to drive her back to the hotel.

Timothy works away at his laptop. Beside him on the seat, Susan has a collection of papers to mark from assignments of students she lectures at the nearby tertiary institute.

They wait.

"Timothy?"

They typing pauses. "Hmm?"

"...what day even is it?"

Timothy has to check himself. "The twelfth," he says, peering at the corner of his laptop screen.

Yuuki nods. His perception of time passing is skewed, so he can't tell if that's the date he was expecting or not.

"How come?"

"No reason," Yuuki mumbles. He's interrupted by an incoming cough. He groans afterwards, then manages, "I just realised I didn't know what day it was."

Yuuki has nothing to check the date with. His phone is still with the PF as potential evidence. No one's mentioned what day it is around him, and the only clues he's had is his own faulty gauge of time passing, and Samantha, if she's here or not during otherwise normal school hours.

Timothy doesn't comment further.

Susan returns. Seeing Yuuki sitting there, zoned out and anxiously fidgeting with his hands, Susan offers him her spare tablet that's not in use. After checking with the nurses, Susan determines that Yuuki's allowed to use electronic devices. Yuuki accepts. There's enough wait time that he might as well do *something*, especially something that might help distract his wandering mind.

In the end he finds a webnovel to read. It's hard to really concentrate on what he's reading, though. There's too much static noise in his head. The anticipation of people coming, and the expectation placed on him to speak about *those things he doesn't want to talk about* but has to be prepared to talk about, is keeping his nervous system hyper-alert and ready. He's far too on edge to read. It's like his brain doesn't even want to give the chance.

The hour passes.

Closer to the time that the psychiatrist is to arrive, Timothy gets a phone call and excuses himself. Judging by the way he doesn't hastily answer the phone, and leaves the room with a tired look on his face, it's going to be a long work-related call.

While they're waiting, Susan waits with him. After Timothy leaves, she asks seemingly out of nowhere, "Do you feel like you might be getting a cold?"

Yuuki raises an eyebrow. As if on cue, one of those small coughs clouds his chest. He coughs, and the irritation lingers. He swallows.

"You've been sounding like you have a bit of a chesty cough," Susan murmurs. "Like that."

Yuuki takes a slow and careful breath. "Kinda, I guess."

"Where's it feeling like?"

"… kinda…" Yuuki considers. "I don't know, the… the throat scathing… chest-hurts-to-breathe kinda a little feeling." He grunts. "I'm not making much sense, am I?"

Susan offers him an understanding smile. "I got what you meant."

Yuuki nods. "I don't usually have the latter with the cold. When I get a cold, I mean. So I'm not sure if I'd call it a cold or not."

"Okay. Well, we've been suspecting you might have a respiratory infection, or could come down with one. They've been giving you medicines, which have probably been keeping things at bay, but we'll want to watch out for if you're showing signs of coming down with anything. Depending on whether it's a viral or a bacterial infection, the ways of treating it will differ."

Yuuki is grateful she doesn't state where he might've gotten the infection from. He already knows. He can still taste the chemical residue of the chloroform, and the mouth-drying cotton of the cloth that was used as a gag on him. That's not even to mention how dusty that shed was...

Susan clears her throat. She has an uncertain gleam in her eye, like she's noticed Yuuki's mind wandering and is nervous about it. "Is it stressing you? This constant attention?"

Yuuki blinks. He doesn't have enough energy to shrug.

"You know why they're monitoring you so much, right?"

"'Cause I'm a hospital patient, was in a bad condition, et cetera…"

"Yes, and because we don't want you getting worse and having to stay a hospital patient longer. Or end up in some other variant of critical condition if you develop something from something that got missed and gets left unseen."

"Like what?"

"Like pneumonia."

Yuuki stares tiredly at the overlocked edge of the hospital blanket.

"That's why they're monitoring you so much. We don't want this, or some other kind of illness or impacting your recovery if it can be prevented."

"I know. I get it."

Susan doesn't immediately reprimand or lecture him like he expects. Instead, she is quiet. Listening. Waiting.

Yuuki looks at her. "You're thinking of whether it's likely or not I'll end up with something, aren't you?"

Susan meets his gaze. Hers is intense, containing a solemn acknowledgement of something that Yuuki is yet to be able to comprehend. "Something in particular, possibly. But it's not something that can be prevented with antibiotics or anything, really. Not once it's already set in."

"What then?"

"…aftermath of trauma."

Yuuki shuts his mouth. He clenches his jaw at the word.

"It was trauma, Yuuki," Susan murmurs. "You might be in denial of it, or of the full impact of it, which is fine right now. But it'll hit you later at some point. To what degree, and for how long, and in what ways…"

"I'll be fine." *I don't really want to think about any of that.*

"You might be. Or you might not be. You might not get much conscious choice in the matter."

Yuuki narrows his eyes. *If I get any say in the matter, I won't be letting that happen. If I succumb to such a thing, won't it be just the same as letting the perpetrators of this whole kidnapping attack thing at Timothy's office…win? They got what they wanted by leaving me in that shed, if their objective was some horrid psychological mind warping.*

I won't let them mess with my mind any further.

"In the meantime," Susan says. She doesn't miss Yuuki's changing expressions and Yuuki knows it. "In the meantime, just focus on recovery day by day as they come. Whatever happens...just know, we'll be here for you. We're not about to leave you to endure the recovery of this alone."

Although a retort is the first thing that comes to mind, Yuuki doesn't voice it. If it were anyone else who said it, perhaps he might've let it slip off his tongue.

But those words coming from Susan...

"Whatever happens... we're not about to leave you to endure the recovery of this alone."

Yuuki thinks he can believe her.

The psychiatrist visits. Yuuki deliberately blanks out as much as possible. He barely answers their questions to the full extent he could.

They don't even press too much, but still, Yuuki doesn't want to give them an incentive to. He doesn't want to hear how they perceive his mental condition. He doesn't want to be made to interrogate his own emotional psychological state all over again, and have to relive and re-experience all the chaotic spinning whirling of thoughts that he's already been through in the shed and in this hospital room.

It doesn't sit well with him – someone else trying to describe his experience before he's had a chance to. Their words depend on their interpretation of his experience. Their interpretation depends on what information they've been given by the hospital reports, the PF, the Harrisons and or Yumiko, and Yuuki himself.

And for Yuuki to give an adequate enough account for the psychiatrist to be able to interpret his mental wellbeing means having to recall *details* of his experience and force those recollections of indescribable emotional experience into words.

He's going to have to do it all again when the PF officers come to question him again. He'd rather reserve what limited capacity he has for trying for them.

Yuuki is handed a questionnaire. Adrenaline flows through him. If it weren't for the psychiatrist sitting there evaluating him, and for Susan sitting nearby almost like a mediator, Yuuki might've torn that page up right then and there.

"I'm not comfortable doing this," he wants to say. He can't say it. He can't say anything in case he damns himself.

Yuuki should answer honestly. But he's irritated – in the nervous, stressed and exhausted way. He doesn't want to have to talk about this. Or write about it. He doesn't want to have to remember details like this right now.

After a half hour session of getting nowhere, the psychiatrist exchanges a *look* with Susan, grimaces, and gets up. She bids him farewell.

In his hands, Yuuki is left tentatively holding the page. He clenches his jaw. Feels a white hot confusion-laced rage course through him. His hands are clammy. He's shaking. With tears pricking his eyes, he shreds that paper up into the shreddiest shreds he can manage.

Yumiko is standing in the doorway.

"What's wrong?" Yumiko asks. "Is something up, Yuuki? Why weren't you able to answer their questions?"

Yuuki fumbles with the torn up paper shreds on the blanket. He inwardly shrugs, then inwardly sighs with the acknowledging thought that neither reaction suffices as an answer.

"Are you not feeling well?"

"I'm *fine*," Yuuki forces out. It's a slurred murmur of a thing, like if audio could be mud. "You don't need to get anyone."

Yumiko slows her steps. "I wasn't... going to."

"..."

Susan re-enters. She obviously sees the once whole sheet of paper now reduced to tatters in his lap. She doesn't comment. "They said that they'll only come back if needed," she says instead of the psychiatrist. "I advised her that it's probably best we come to them first, or approach someone first on our own terms when you're ready, if you want to and f you need to, rather than them coming to us. On *your* terms, I ought to say."

Yuuki's hands are clammier.

"It's okay to be upset at them. I should've realised you weren't having a good time listening to all that."

"It was her tone, more than anything."

"Hmm."

"And I didn't ask for it."

"It's part of the hospital procedure for trauma victims."

Yuuki turns his head to the side. His lip curls. "*Trauma victims.*"

"People who have been admitted to the hospital after or in relation to a traumatic experience."

Yuuki glares at the clouds and the patch of clear sky outside.

"I'm going to go get coffee," Yumiko whispers, and slips out of the room. Yuuki watchers her leave in the faint reflection in the window.

The silence is tense.

"I'm sorry," Yuuki forces out. "I didn't mean to snap."

"It's okay."

"It's not."

"I know you hate the word right now, but it's also a part of trauma. I'm not saying this because I'm implying you should seek therapy at any sign of it. Therapy isn't for everyone, even if those who would like there to be something suitable for them."

"Then what are you saying?"

Susan rounds the bed. She sits down by his feet and squints at the clouds with him. She releases a slow, pent up sigh. "I'm saying it's something human that happens. And that traumatic stuff is confusing. We expect we'll deal with it one way, then our reaction to ends up being something entirely unexpected and different. We do stuff we don't want. We don't do stuff we do want."

Yuuki is reminded that what the Harrison family as a whole have been experiencing during Yuuki's absence must've been touching on the 'traumatic experience' possibility.

"I think it was too soon to have a psychiatrist come. I had been thinking that, but I didn't say anything. I'm sorry I didn't think to ask you how you felt about it sooner. I could've talked to the hospital staff about delaying it."

Or we could've just not had them come at all. Part of the procedure or not.

"The idea of the meeting today was to get some idea of what the next few weeks might look like for you. And to start looking out for things that might impact you worse that others, or be more bewildering than others."

"I'd rather just think about all that on my own," Yuuki says flatly.

Susan nods. "I would too. Think about it on my own."

Yuuki expects her to follow up with a "*but*", however she doesn't add anything on to that statement. The tension in Yuuki's shoulders loosen slightly.

"Can I ask," Susan murmurs, "is there any reason why you find it harder to respond to the nurses' questions or the psychiatrist's more than mine, or any of the rest of our families'?"

"It's not just theirs."

Susan waits.

"I'm not sure I can talk much to the PFOs either."

"Are you feeling like there's any particular reason why?"

Yuuki works his jaw. The connection between his jaw and skull clicks, feels strained.

"It's okay if there isn't. I just want to know if I can help in setting boundaries for you – for them."

Boundaries. Yuuki supposes that the health professionals he's encountered tend to breach those boundaries first. In the case of the nurses and doctors though, he can't be too mad at them. In fact, he finds he has more tolerance for their intrusiveness than what he has for the interrogative questions stabbed at his ~~unstable~~ stable mind from the PF and from the psychiatrist.

He also feels a lot more *judged.*

Is it out of nervousness? Stress because of the circumstances implied by their visits? Yet he's not being incriminated, and it's not like he's being unfairly judged. Financially, too, he's not expected to cover the psychiatrist fee since that and the hospital fees are assumedly covered under Arkala National Accident Compensation. Given that Yuuki's a security officer and therefore technically an auxiliary PFO, he should be able to get full coverage, too.

Nothing bad is coming out of either of their visits, but both the prospect of dealing with investigating PFOs and investigating psychiatrists drains what little mental energy he has. It ruffles his feathers. Yuuki wishes neither party would come. They need to, for each their own reasons – and for his sake, too.

But he's tired. So tired.

Yuuki relays as much as he can of this Susan. Susan listens. At the end of him saying all that he can say, she only continues to sit there staring at the clouds with him. There's no denying how he feels, or minimising the stress that he speaks of. She doesn't tell him how he should be feeling, or how he should be acting.

She just listens, and takes it in. Tries to understand – for his sake.

And for once during this hospital stay, Yuuki feels *heard*.

Kia Ihsayu arrives. Yuuki does his best to answer the PFOs questions. Timothy stays beside him during the questioning. Susan has left to help Yumiko with her bags for the airport.

Yuuki is tired and doesn't have much information to offer anyways.

He tells them everything he can.

Anything he can that they might need to know.

But it's so much more limited that what they're hoping to have heard from him.

They kept me in a shed for three days. That's all they did to me. They never came back. I never saw them again.

Kia tries to work with Yuuki's limited interaction with them to find as much information as she can. "Did they drug you with anything at the start?"

Yuuki shakes his head. "Only the…" The image of the saliva-soaked cloth in front of him slams into his mind. "Th-the cloth. Ku-chlorofrom… chloroform. I think they used it to knock me out… keep me knocked out… 'till they go me to the shed."

Kia takes notes. She frowns hard. "You say they used it to keep you knocked out for a period of time. Were you knocked out before?"

Yuuki hums.

"How did they knock you out?"

"I don't know," Yuuki says dryly, "with a fist?"

Kia grimaces.

She continues, "Between both times they knocked you out, did you happen to come to at all?"

"…not really."

"Not really?"

Yuuki winces. "I can't remember anything clearly."

"Is there any additional details you are able to recall? Even if it's vague and you're not a hundred percent sure?"

"…"

Yuuki's head hurts. Everything about that is foggy and shadowy, and overridden by the commencing three day ordeal in that shed. What happened in between the office and the shed isn't something they wanted him to be awake for – at least, they didn't want him to be awake enough to be alert enough to put up a fight during.

"The car. I think I woke up in the car. That's where the chloroform was. Or... no, I think they had it ready – on the cloth, already ready. Ready in case they needed to use it."

"And I'm guessing they felt the need to use it then."

Yuuki feels sick. He didn't even put up a fight. He didn't get the chance to once they'd knocked him out. *They didn't want me putting up a fight, that's the point.*

Kia hums. "Okay, the only other thing I wanted to ask today is if you remember any specific details about them that could help us identify them? We have surveillance footage of the attack, and we've received statements from both your friends Timothy and Joshua who saw them. However, it is possible that you saw something that could help identify them that we can't see from the footage. Do you remember any distinctive features about them, or any details of their clothing?"

Yuuki tries to think – he earnestly does, but the most he can remember of the attack is what he felt. The alarm, the adrenaline, the exponentially increasing fear before –

Before he was knocked out, drugged, and everything became a blur until he came to in the shed.

Vaguely, he remembers the sound of their voices. But he can't remember it clearly enough to put words to it to describe it. He might even be imagining it, or have heard the wrong thing. He'd been dealing with a concussion and then chloroform, after all. If he were to try to put it to words, he'd have to hear those voices again.

They're not exactly something that Yuuki wants to reencounter anytime soon, though.

"I can't remember anything clearly enough," Yuuki murmurs in the end. "Not without running into them again. Sorry."

"Not anything?"

Yuuki blinks. He gives a small shake of his head. "I... it's too questionable in my own head. I can't articulate anything that could be useful for you, not without risking altering details in an attempt to give them clarity." He sighs. His chest feels heavy, yet hollow. Yuuki's throat catches, strained from all the speaking and stress, and he coughs weakly. How his brain manages to come up with big words when he's feeling like this, he's not sure.

"It's okay," Kia says. "Thanks for considering that, by the way – about the possibility of false memories."

"I wouldn't necessarily call it false memories. Just... misinterpretations It's like when you're out on a walk and you think you see a dog, but when you get closer you see that, actually, it's just a log. I don't want to tell you I saw a dog when there was no dog."

Kia's mouth quirks. "Better we chase a dog and find out it was a log, than have not know about the potential of there being a dog in the first place."

Timothy, having returned from whatever long string of work phone calls he had to make, suppresses a small laugh from the doorway. He tries to mask it with a sound like clearing his throat.

Were he feeling more like himself, Yuuki might've laughed along with him.

*

Yumiko leaves Arkala that night.

Yuuki's starting to realise that it's real here.

"My flight is at 9pm," Yumiko says. "I'll need to leave for the airport soon. International flight, so I gotta be there a few hours before."

"Okay," is the only thing Yuuki can offer.

Yumiko tries to persuade Yuuki to come back home for some recovery. Yuuki doesn't say anything. It's not that he's one hundred percent against the idea, it's just he doesn't have the mental energy to seriously consider it.

In the brief thought he does give it, thinking about whether going back to Japan for a bit would be a good idea for some sort of recovery or not, he realises that he feels uncomfortable with the idea. Not even just uncomfortable, but doubtful. Would it really make that much of a difference? Trying to recover from this ordeal in Japan versus staying as he is in Arkala and trying to recover here?

Because, ultimately, it's not Arkala that is dangerous for him. Even if he were in Japan, something could happen to him. And if he were to go back, he would have nothing to preoccupy himself with. He needs to work. He wants to work.

At the end of the day, his life – and work – is in Arkala.

"You're not so keen on the idea, eh?" Yumiko says.

Yuuki meets her gaze. At least, out of all their family, Yumiko understands his feelings and perspectives the most. In other words, she won't try to press her persuasion when she can clearly see what his answer is.

"If you decide you want to," his sister says, "we'll be there for you. At any time."

For whatever reason, Yuuki feels reluctant to believe that.

They would care, he knows. But they wouldn't be able to fully grasp the emotional psychological horror that he went through in that shed. Nothing happened to him, really – he was kidnapped, and stuck in a shed. But that's it. That's all they'd really be able to grasp.

Yuuki doesn't know how to express that the most terrifying part was having all that time to feel his body deteriorate and his mind be warped and shredded and pulled and tugged and burned...

He doesn't think they'd understand that. Or understand why it's shaken him up so badly, or why he doesn't want to talk or even think about it, let alone even consider seeking therapy for it at this stage.

It's too soon.

Yuuki just wants to... not exist for a while until he can start to come to terms with it. "Sorry," he murmurs. "I don't think I can."

Yumiko gives an acknowledging nod. "That's okay. You know what Mum and the others, will say, but I'll try have a talk to them about it before they ask you again."

Yuuki blinks. "Thanks."

"Okay," Yumiko says, glancing at her phone. "I had better get leaving for the airport. You'll be okay?"

"Hmm."

"If you need someone to talk to, or if your friends aren't around, feel free to message me, yeah?"

Friends? What friends? Oh...she's probably meaning Timothy and Susan and

278

them…"Okay."

Yuuki's flatmate Lee is also a 'friend', but Yuuki's gut tells him that he can't expect to receive any post-trauma support from him. That's not exactly in Lee's personality, offering genuine sympathy and or comfort.

Yumiko gets up. She looks at Yuuki, evaluating his condition, his body language. Then she offers a small parting, sad smile. With a wave, she says bye in Japanese and then heads out of the hospital room.

The space around Yuuki dims and dulls, and the light coming through the window seems to brighten in a cool comfortless way. He takes as deep a breath as he can emotionally manage, and then lets it out quickly before it feels like it'll suffocate him. In the buzzing quiet, he can't decide whether he feels better with no one with him – where it means there's not interpersonal pressure to mask his emotions or absence of emotions, or if the buzzing is from a nervousness echoing in his head that tempts to fear that this rescue is all a short-lived dream he'll soon wake up from.

No, Timothy and Joshua found me. They rescued me. I'm not in that shed anymore. I'm not…I'm not going back there.

Yuuki raises his knees towards his chest. His muscles ache. The action leaves him feeling weak and so keenly aware of he's become so utterly emotionally defeated. Left alone, without social pressure to mask the confusing detached chaos of half emotions inside him, he curls up with his arms around his knees, hugging them to his chest. He lets his head drop. He hides his face against them. The IV needle bruise pulls at his skin. He shifts, but it doesn't alleviate the problem much. In fact, it doesn't alleviate anything.

Least of all the bone-deep fear…or plea…of that he really hopes he's not going back to the shed interior that won't leave from the front or back of his mind.

"Also… I'm probably not going to be able to come visit in spring. It might have to wait till next October. Gotta let the savings get saved up good again. I could otherwise come visit sooner, but I guess we'll see how we go."

Yuuki nods. *Next October.* Even this October feels so far away. Who knows if he'll still be all in one piece by the time next year's one eventually comes.

So as not to prolong the farewell any longer, Yumiko waves. She doesn't impose a hug on him, and Yuuki is grateful. He's not sure how he feels about touch right now; it's something he's conflicted about.

"Take care, Yuuki," she says.

Yuuki hums without any attempt at a smile. "You too."

And with that, Yuuki's sister leaves the hospital.

29

12th June, 12-Tau – evening

Timothy sits with Yuuki in the warm light of the room. With the PF statement giving over with, the concerned family aspect of this all dealt with and now less medical equipment attached to him, it feels quieter.

In that quiet, Yuuki finally feels some sense of reprieve.

Outside, it's raining a little. It's a little too far away from the airport to hear planes taking off, but he imagines he'd be able to hear Yumiko's flight taking off if they were closer.

I'm glad she was able to come – and just her, and not the rest of the family. Yuuki wishes she could've come at a better time, though. For better circumstances, such as visiting for them both to enjoy Southern Hemisphere *hanami* sakura flower viewing together. That would've been nicer, instead of her abruptly using up her flight money savings to visit him after a kidnapping.

Yuuki leans a little further back into the raised back of the bed. He stares past the tablet he's holding. He thumbs the page of text up and down, interested in continuing reading the webnovel he'd been reading earlier but too lacking in mental concentration to get his brain to read it.

I'm a stink little brother, aren't I? Making Yumiko come out like that.

He misses her already. He feels bitter about it – about how he could barely even appreciate her presence here as much as should've, or otherwise would have. Yuuki tries not to hold himself to too much blame, given the fact that he's dealing with the immediate aftermath of a kidnapping and the overwhelm of having to figure out how to feel about surviving that apparent 'approaching death' situation. There's been too many people around and he's been stressed. It's hard to enjoy someone's company properly when all that's going on.

Perhaps this bitterness he feels at himself is more a sense of guilt than anything – guilt that she had to see him in whatever state he's been in for the past few days. It makes Yuuki feels angry at himself, and defeated. He could've been better. Couldn't have he?

It's strange, though, when he thinks about it. He doesn't quiet feel so much guilt with the Harrisons. Perhaps that's since they've been involuntarily a part of these circumstances since the moment the incident happened in Timothy's law office in Ninao. And because they're still here, they're still around. They're coping in these circumstances *with* him. They're also dealing with similar feelings to what he is, and similar stress.

Yuuki realises then, that he hasn't spoken openly about the incident with any of the Harrisons yet. Aside from they've already told him, and what Yuuki told them the other night, they haven't talked about it.

What is there to talk about, though?

They know what happened. Why, most likely, it happened. They don't know *who* exactly, but they can guess: quite possibly a pro-Taularh group, maybe one organised by Taularh himself if they're that unlucky. Yuuki knows that's bound to have crossed Timothy's mind as well. Other details are for the PF to figure out for them, but at this stage, it's more confirmation as opposed to open ended answers that they're looking for.

They just need confirmation that it did or didn't happen because of the Youth Rehabilitation Trust.

"What d'we do about it?" Yuuki murmurs aloud.

Timothy, working on emails and reports on his laptop, frowns. "Sorry, what was that?"

"About the…" *About the Trust.* Yuuki catches himself. Judging by the frequency in tapping, it sounds like Timothy's in the middle of typing like some long paragraph. "Sorry, if you're busy, it can wait."

"You're fine," Timothy says. He eventually finishes off the section he's typing and the insistent typing ceases. "What was it you said?"

Yuuki weighs up his wording. For some reason, he's not sure he can get his mouth to utter the word '*Trust*'. He tries anyway. "What do we do 'bout… about the…the Trust?"

Timothy's expression falls. He considers the question solemnly, all while holding Yuuki's gaze. "How do you feel about it?"

The volleyed question holds no judgement.

"I don't know," Yuuki mutters. "I don't know anymore."

"Because of what happened?"

"I'm not the only one feeling conflicted about it, am I?"

Timothy grimaces.

Yuuki fidgets with the volume buttons on the tablet.

"Do you feel like you want to keep going with it?" Timothy asks.

"Can we even?"

"Hmm. I sent them the files we were meant to send them. The ones I was… getting ready to do… y'know, on the day."

Yuuki grunts. "And they accepted?"

"The confirmation of establishment got accepted, yes."

"In the middle of the kidnapping…"

Timothy nods. "Hmm. I'm sorry, I wanted to wait until you said what you wanted to do with it, but…"

"But I was tied up in a shed in the middle of nowhere."

"…yeah. So it seems."

"…"

"We don't have to go ahead with it if you don't want to."

"I do want to," Yuuki says. His voice is scratchy. "I want to continue it. We didn't go to all this effort for nothing. It's not like we did anything wrong establishing it. I just… I'm not sure I have it in me to manage it like I said I would. At least, not right now. And probably not in the *near* near future. If I'm honest, I don't know if I have the heart to. It's not that I don't have the motivation, it's just…"

"After the incident, it's kind of hard to tell how to feel about it. What to do with it."

Yuuki nods. He sighs.

Timothy hums. "Just so you know, it's okay if you decide you would rather *not* continue it. I know we don't know if the Trust was the reason for why this all happened. But even if we find out that it wasn't, and it was for some other reason we haven't thought of yet – it's okay if you don't want to continue with the Trust. It's okay if it's too much for you."

Yuuki is silent. He puts the tablet down beside him. He reaches over to get the cup of lemon water sitting on the bench.

After a moment, Yuuki asks, "What do you think we should do?"

"It's your decision," Timothy says. "You're the official establisher of the Trust; it's up to you. I'm not going to be disappointed if you decide you're not up to continuing it."

"I don't want to give up the Trust," Yuuki says. "You're technically a co-establisher, too. You don't want to terminate it either, do you?"

Timothy shakes his head. "Not unless we absolutely need to. There's nothing wrong about it. The intention behind it is sound and *good*." He pauses, then adds, "There's no reason it should've sparked such a thing as what happened to us in Ninao."

Yuuki considers. "Then what if there were someone else who might be willing to continue it?"

Timothy raises an eyebrow, but the look on his face says he's already considered that an option.

Out in the hallway, Timothy contemplates the email he has open on his phone. It's from the first donors for the Youth Rehabilitation Trust – Jié and Xiùyīng Chén. They are asking how the Trust will continue from here, and if they are able to help in any way in the wake of the kidnapping and Yuuki's rescue.

Timothy messages them back, after a long considering how best to reply.

He thinks of Yuuki inside the room, now sleeping. Timothy thinks of that utterly exhausted and defeated body language that has taken over him. The way the life has been drained out of him, and that bright passion he had for the Trust only a week ago now replaced by a hollow enthusiasm.

After doing a background check and interview with them, it seems like they are legitimately able to handle helping with administrative and management work of the Trust, especially since the Trust is so newly established and there's not much workload they need to worry about – workload that is more than Timothy, and most especially Yuuki, are able to handle right now.

But are the Chens aware of what they might be getting themselves into?

Timothy's concerned about what their involvement may mean. The Youth Rehabilitation Trust might be under his and Yuuki's names, but anyone else directly involved could be subjected a similar kind of warning if they're not careful. That could mean the others in the Harrison family, or Yumiko, were she to have stayed in the country longer. Surely the Chens must be aware of the risk. Surely they wouldn't intentionally add themselves to the list of potential casualties without thinking it through.

Timothy can feel another tension headache growing. Maybe the Chens know something the rest of them here don't. Who knows? Whatever it is, Timothy hopes they're at least aware of the risks that might be involved for them with their participating in the Trust's management.

He doesn't want anyone else to end up like Yuuki has.

He's already afraid enough that the perpetrators might try something else. That his family might be in imminent danger. That they might try to take Timothy himself again, since they failed the first time, and snatch Yuuki back while they're at it.

Timothy returns to sitting inside the room. Right now, he's keenly aware that it's only himself and Yuuki in the room. Someone could reattempt a kidnapping now, if they were organised enough. If that happened, they might be successful. Yuuki's incapacitated, exhausted and drained as he is. Timothy doesn't have it in him to hold off any attempted kidnapping or attack. If anyone comes back for them both…

It hits him then. Timothy can't protect Yuuki.

He can't protect any of his family from this.

Usually, Timothy wouldn't consider himself an emotional man – at least, not outwardly expressively so. But here he is, silently bowing forward, elbows on his knees and head now in his hands, taken over by crying. He's like this when Susan comes in. He thinks he hears other footsteps, other voices – Joshua and Samantha's – but those presences slip away upon seeing him.

Susan says nothing. She only lets the atmosphere settle again after she's entered, and then lays a hand to rest in the middle of Timothy's back. She rubs slow circles, meant to be consoling, but Timothy finds little comfort in it. And Susan can read that.

She extends her arms around him, enfolding him in a hug, and just hugs him. Leans a little of her weight against him so she can stay there longer, and so her presence reaches Timothy more.

There's no *"It's okay."*

There's no *"Yuuki will be okay. We'll be okay."*

Timothy doesn't need either of those. He'd prefer not to hear them really. Because they don't know, for sure, if they can really say either of those things. There's only so much they can do, and so little they can do to protect each other – from whatever the future may hold for any of them.

30

13th June, 12-Tau – morning

In spite of the recent developments, the Youth Rehabilitation Trust is geared to continue. Yuuki is informed by Timothy in the morning that their first donor, Arkala'ana-Chinese couple Jié and Xiùyīng Chén, have offered to help keep it functioning. They can help handle management of the Trust, with Timothy coordinating things, until Yuuki can get back on his feet again.

Yuuki accepts this information with a mixture of relief and a fermented bitterness carried through from yesterday. He keeps this mix of emotions to himself. Timothy, too, it seems, is feeling emotionally conflicted. Yuuki is unable to get a good read of his friend's feelings to really determine anything, but whatever stress Timothy is experiencing isn't directed at *him* but at the circumstances.

It takes some weight of Yuuki's shoulders, and off his chest and off his mind. Knowing that Timothy doesn't judge him for it. Having the reassurance that he doesn't need to struggle to explain complex and contradicting feelings out loud, because Timothy – all of the Harrisons, really – already get it.

He's still self-conscious of how the Chens will perceive him, however. It makes him nervous that his lack of enthusiasm might discourage them from wanting to get involved in the Trust he and Timothy established.

Regardless of how I feel about it, and how I think they might feel about it, there's still time before the meeting. I should at least make myself look a bit more presentable.

Yuuki has a shower. It's his first shower since the kidnapping. He's not expecting it to make him woozy. It does. The nurses cautioned him about this when he said he wanted to shower, but he insisted on showing alone and he's glad he did. He's glad they let him: he just wants to preserve some shred of dignity.

Turning down the shower water temperature might help, but the heat is therapeutic. Soothing. Calming. It contrasts the lukewarm room temperature of the hospital room in a reprieving way. Even if the enjoyment of the hot water comes at the cost of dizziness, the tangible reassurance of it is something that he doesn't want to give up so easily.

He has to steady himself several times, and even contemplates needing to sit down on the seat provided. But he hasn't stood up in a while. It's been longer since he's been able to stand with his legs able to move, and his feet able to space apart enough to support his weight. The last time he tried to walk, he had to have Susan help because of how lacking in energy he was. The time before that, he can barely call standing because his ankles were tied.

Fortunately, he manages to wash his hair and wash himself and complete a good few minutes of zoning out doing nothing but enjoying the privacy and the nice warmth – all without his body giving way or his head getting too affected by the dizziness and the humidity.

It feels like an accomplishment. It feels like something good.

After towelling himself dry, Yuuki changes into a fresh set of clothes – not hospital ones this time. His own. Susan and Timothy had brought them over sometime in the last couple of days. A comfortable shirt and over-sized sweatshirt, and comfortable pants. Clothing that neither feels like hospital clothing or the kind of closer-fitting work uniform he had been wearing for the three days in that shed. The sweatshirt doesn't have tight close-fitting cuffs on it –Yuuki can hide his hands in the sleeves if he wishes. And the cuffs around the ankles don't mimic the pressure of the rope, either.

He emerges from the bathroom freshly washed and freshly clothed, and feeling like he's regained some sense of dignity and autonomy he's been desperate for. It was taken from him first in the shed, and even in his recovery here at the hospital it's taken what feels like a long time to feel somewhat *better.*

And dare he say, more like *himself.*

The change in appearance does something to relieve some of the stagnant tension in the atmosphere too. The heaviness in Timothy's face doesn't quite seem so heavy. When Joshua comes in, the hesitation with which Joshua would look at him with is slightly less tentative.

Joshua's voice sounds lighter, too. "I brought hot drinks."

Yuuki leaves the towel and used hospital clothing in a folded up pile in the bathroom. He settles back down onto the bed, more than grateful to sink back into its support.

"They'll be here shortly," Timothy says. "The Chens, I mean." To Joshua, he asks, "Are you wanting to stay around for the meeting? You're welcome to."

Joshua hands out coffee for Timothy and keeps one for himself. He passes the other drink he's carrying – home-made hot lemon, honey and ginger drink – to Yuuki.

"I think I'll go out and get some fresh air," Joshua replies. "I'll go up to the rooftop garden for a bit or something."

The three of them drink their hot drinks. The room is quiet. Almost peaceful. But also tired. On June 5th, they were gathered in a room just the three of them, too – the difference now is that the circumstance for them that time was one of success and triumph. Now, the circumstances are nothing but defeat and confusion.

"Wonder when they'll let me have coffee again," Yuuki murmurs, trying to break the silence. Trying to break his own train of thoughts.

Timothy offers a light smile. "You'll probably be fine to have caffeine again soon. As long as it doesn't make you feel *worse*, I'd imagine it should be all good."

Yuuki hums. He's not sure, and right now he doesn't care to find out. Caffeine or no caffeine, he's anticipating being stressed and feeling weird for a while. *Though if coffee were to help me cope with all that, that'd be great if I could have it sooner rather than later.*

He drinks the hot drink he's been made. For now, at least, this is helping settle and overcome the respiratory infection. And slowly, but surely, minimise the lingering physical reminders of his experience in that shed.

The Chens arrive five minutes early. After talking to them out in the hallway, Timothy brings in Jié and Xiùyīng to meet with Yuuki and himself. Joshua takes his leave and disappears up to the rooftop.

"Hello, I'm Chén Xiùyīng," the woman introduces herself. "This is my husband, Chén Jié."

Jié inclines his head.

Yuuki inclines his head in turn. "Takahashi Yuuki," he says, following their pattern on last names first. It's been a while since he last did that, but he got used to it in Japan that it flows off the tongue easily enough.

As part of introductions, Jié extends his hands to pass on his and Xiùyīng's business cards. Their primary contact information in on there. Yuuki glances at them both. Both of them appear to be involve in legal and accountancy consultation sectors.

Another thing catches Yuuki's eye: the characters written above Xiùyīng's name appear to spell 'Chén Xiùyīng', but the characters above Jié's name spell something different.

"*Li* Jié?" Yuuki asks. The tone comes out a lot sharper than he'd like. He clears his throat and amends, "Your name is written differently here?"

"Ah, yeah, I'm half Arkala'ana, half Chinese," Jié says. "When we decided to marry, we chose to follow Arkala'ana marriage customs of the male taking on his wife's family name. I took Xiùyīng's surname, in other words. We wanted to honour my Arkala'ana heritage as a minority culture between us. Hence why both our names are Chén, in spite of shared surnames not being the usual occurrence in Chinese cultures. Formally, on paper, I'm Li Jié."

Yuuki nods, understanding.

Timothy leads the conversation for Yuuki's sake. The four of them go over paperwork and arrangements, terms and conditions, agreements regarding delegation of responsibilities during Yuuki's temporary stepping away for the sake of his health. They agree between them that Jié and Xiùyīng will help Timothy manage the Trust while Yuuki is recovering, and Yuuki has no issue with that. But the repetition of words indicating Yuuki's 'temporary absence' used in conversation and on paper between them feel shallow. Yuuki feels like regaining control of managing the Trust means walking across a makeshift rickety old haphazard bridge that's been put together and shoved over a canyon. A few steps in and he'd surely just go plummeting down to rock bottom. This bridge isn't made to hold his weight. Yuuki doesn't think he'll be able to scramble together sturdy enough materials in time to build a better bridge.

Ashamedly, Yuuki finds himself zoning out during the meeting. It's like, contrary to his earlier words about wanting to continue the Trust, he's lost interest in pursuing actively continuing it himself. This is an important meeting. He should be listening. He's essentially handing over *months'* worth of hard-earned accomplishment to people who he's only ever been barely acquainted with before.

But right now, Yuuki simply doesn't have the energy to think about things. He trusts Timothy and his judgement.

Timothy glances at him every so often. It's an effort to keep Yuuki feeling engaged in the conversation and in the decision making, even if he doesn't have the energy to participate in it much. It's checking in, silently, passively, with how Yuuki is feeling about this whole thing. Thankfully, he notices that Yuuki doesn't want to be prompted to offer his opinion on things unless it's necessary. He continues to lead the conversation, and does so without making Yuuki feel like he's not included in it still. Yuuki wonders how he manages to do it so calmly, so composed, when Timothy must also be feeling tired and stressed with this dealing-with-the-incident-associated stuff.

Grief and guilt rage just beneath the surface of Yuuki's skin. Yuuki preoccupies himself with sipping through the hot drink in his hands. He tries not to let the emotions show on his face, or in his body language or demeanour. It's not something he wants other people to see or know about. This grief isn't something he's prepared to process, and the guilt just stabs and stabs at him in all different places. It skewers him in the centre of his chest – in some place in his solar plexus. Perhaps it isn't guilt, however, but a stress-sharpened blade of *shame*.

The Youth Rehabilitation Trust was something he'd been so *driven* to establish, so motivated to create. He'd been stressed and tired trying to work through the legalities of it with Timothy, but he'd believed it worth it. And he'd been so excited to have it finally see the light of day – and for the beneficiaries, the youth who are in need of it most, to finally begin to receive something from this idea.

And now, after being kidnapped for it, Yuuki is giving up on it.

Isn't that what it seems?

Yuuki wonders about Jié and Xiùyīng. *What if I'm committing them to the same fate as me? What if they're good intentions are stifled in chloroform and yanked back to the ground by rope?* If something were to happen to them, or if they get dangerously questioned for picking up the Trust and helping Timothy and Yuuki with it, do they seem like the sort of people who could cope? Would they be able to handle the risk that might follow – or is this all a big mistake?

Considering, Yuuki weighs up his current perception of them. Jié's presence is warm and gentle, but grounded, strong. Xiùyīng carries a sharp-minded confidence about her, an alertness, an assertiveness. Yet neither Jié nor Xiùyīng's calm appears to solely superficial; their confidence appears to be firm and unlikely to be easily shaken.

Yuuki pauses mid-sip of his drink at that. *Why are they so calm about it?*

The more Yuuki considers, the more it seems like they don't seem worried that they might end up in a similar situation to what Yuuki and Timothy did. It is unsettling, and Yuuki doesn't like the way his thoughts start to lean toward suspecting them of *knowing something*.

So he asks, directly, "If you're aware of the risk, why is it that you don't seem all that concerned about it?"

Jié, Xiùyīng and Timothy look at him with varying expressions on their faces. Between them, Jié and Xiùyīng share a look – it's not a guarded or secretive look, but a care-taking one.

"We are concerned," Xiùyīng answers carefully. "But we have given this great consideration. I have a close friend who is a prosecutor, and she had a look at the details of the Youth Rehabilitation Trust with us. She doesn't believe there is any material in it to warrant or incite any *events*."

Yuuki retorts, "And yet it did."

"Well, we don't know for sure that this kidnapping that you and Timothy were victims of *was* indeed caused by the Trust. It is unsettling, for sure – the timing of the establishment and the timing of the incident. However, we believe there is much good in the Trust's purpose and the preparations of it have been done so thoroughly. We don't want your efforts to go to waste."

Yuuki doesn't know what to say to that.

"We don't believe we'll be in immediate danger," Jié reiterates, "however, don't worry – we are nonetheless aware of the risk and of what happened to you both, and so we will be careful."

Yuuki notes that they are careful and precise with their wording, like they've thought it through. Like they've been in such a position before.

"Do you know something?" Yuuki asks.

Jié presses his lips together. Xiùyīng's expression is masked.

"It's a long story," Xiùyīng says after a moment. "And a personal one, at that. I can only say that we're letting those experiences inform our decisions."

Yuuki is tempted to ask, but that's none of his business. The Chens don't have to disclose personal details to justify their perspective on this. Timothy seems worried, too, but also recognises what is theirs to ask and what should be left not pried into. At the end of the day, Jié and Xiùyīng seem to be taking it seriously and they know the risks. And, like they say, Yuuki and Timothy can't say for sure that the Ninao kidnapping happened because of the Trust.

They sign the agreement between them. Four names now are involved with the Youth Rehabilitation Trust: Chén Xiùyīng and Li Jié.

Yuuki can only hope that the Ninao Kidnapping stays as a one-off incident – for all their sakes.

As Jié stands up, his phone pings. After reading a text, he murmurs to Xiùyīng, "Minharh's prescription is ready."

"The doctor hasn't called me yet?"

"Oh, no, it's the one – for the burn scars."

"Oh."

Yuuki wonders about this mention, and its connection with the personal circumstances Xiùyīng mentioned. He doesn't ask about, though. Such prying isn't necessary, appropriate, polite or welcome. Given the lowered voices in which Jié and Xiùyīng speak, they don't want to be asked about it either.

Jié looks at Yuuki and Timothy. He gives a respectful bow of his head to each of them. "We'll contact you again. In the meantime, I hope you recover well."

Xiùyīng expresses her own farewell.

Jié and Xiùyīng don't linger. They take their leave.

Yuuki tries to offer a response of some kind, but there's only a twitch of his cheek. Sitting on this hospital bed, watching them go, he's not sure how he's supposed to feel about the Trust at all anymore. He's only sure that the drive he once felt for setting up the Youth Rehabilitation Trust is now replaced by an aching emptiness.

Like a fire reduced to an ember that won't ever come alive again.

After they've left, Timothy regards Yuuki carefully. The earlier release of tension is overridden by nervousness and uncertainty again. Yuuki looks conflicted, exhausted. Timothy's mind is blank for words for how he feels about this all himself.

"Do you think it's the right thing?" Yuuki asks slowly. "Handing over the Trust management to them?"

Timothy takes a long drink of his now-cold coffee. He considers the question honestly. "I trust them with their ability and I believe their motives to be genuine."

"No, not that."

"…?"

"We're putting them in danger. They seem so sure in themselves, but what if it's misplaced?"

Timothy lowers the cup of coffee. "It's like they said, they wouldn't have suggested helping us like this if they believed they'd be risking the same fate as us. Even if they happen to believe otherwise for whatever reason, it's not like they're unaware of the risks. They know what they're getting into."

"Do you think they'll get attacked, too?"

"We're the ones responsible for setting up the Trust – if the attackers decide to have another go at anyone, it'll be us they come for first, not the Chens."

Yuuki stares at him blankly. He looks miserable.

"We also don't have any evidence," Timothy reminds him, and reminds himself, "besides circumstantial evidence to infer a reason for the kidnapping from. It's highly likely, in our opinion, that this whole thing happened because of the Trust, but it could also otherwise just be an ill-timed coincidence."

"The Trust is the only thing that makes sense."

"I know. But because it's only circumstantial evidence so far, we can't determine the real risk involved with handling the Trust. It could be dangerous, *or* the attack could have been in light of a completely unrelated cause."

Yuuki gives him a look. "Which would be?"

Timothy wishes he had some good answer to give.

Timothy stays a while. Fatigued, Yuuki lies back down on the bed and pulls the blanket over himself. Susan and Sam won't be back around at the hospital until later this evening. Yuuki should probably rest so that he doesn't accidentally snap at them later, too. He doesn't want them to have to be confronted with this ravaging stress that's slowly but surely taking a hold of him.

Before long, and without warning, that stress sinks its claws in.

"I should go see where Joshua's at," Timothy murmurs. "I'll leave you in peace for a bit to get some rest. I'll still be here, okay? I'll just be outside."

Yuuki nods.

But as Timothy gets up, Yuuki tenses.

Timothy leaves, and Yuuki's suddenly terrified that he's going to be left alone again – *abandoned* left alone. Dumped. That he'll blink and find himself back in the shed, alone, all of this naught but a sick hallucination.

Yuuki abruptly sits up. He flings aside the blanket, disturbed. Adrenaline courses through his system. He's scared. Nauseous. *Panicking*.

And he's not sure entirely why, but...

A stressed out state of emotion overtakes him. He strides forward on unsteady legs and hastily reaches out. He grabs Timothy's sleeve just as Timothy passes through the doorway. Timothy stops, and Yuuki shouldn't keep holding onto his sleeve like this. But Yuuki can't get himself to release the handful of Timothy's sleeve he has. His grasp is weak, and his fingers cling to the material tighter – it's all that's keeping his arm from dropping. It feels like if he lets go, he'll collapse. Or be taken. Or like the ground he's standing on will give way.

Working up the courage, Yuuki raises his head.

Timothy's eyes are wide, just like Yuuki's. "What's wrong? Is there…?" He trails off at the stress and anxiety he sees held in Yuuki's.

He doesn't know how to answer that fear.

Yuuki doesn't know to describe it.

"Do you want me to get someone?"

"Actually, ca' you…" Yuuki swallows. Clears his throat. Something akin to a whimper sounds from his throat. "Can you get me out of here? Please?"

Timothy doesn't move. "I…"

Those aren't the words Yuuki is intending. He's not sure what he was intending to say in way of an explanation, but it wasn't that. Nevertheless, it is something that Yuuki is desperate for – he's just been trying to ignore it, deny it, and *cope*. Because *there's no getting out of the shed. There's no escaping the situation. No one's coming. That door isn't opening.*

Yuuki can't put words to it fast enough.

Fortunately, Timothy is able to make the connection between Yuuki's feeling trapped here and Yuuki's traumatic experience being trapped in the shed. One situation with no people at all, and darkness, and this situation here with too many people, and too much light. Both placing stress on his body and mind while he tries to cope.

Gently, Timothy removes the hand gripping his sleeve and lowers it by Yuuki's side. "I'll go talk to them. Wait here."

Yuuki waits. He folds his arms across his chest. Grips his elbows. A short time later, Timothy returns. Yuuki's anxiety lessens slightly. His hands are shaky, his palms clammy.

The nurse who walks in beside Timothy looks at Yuuki with thinly masked pity. "Sorry, we can't discharge you yet. We want to make sure there's no complications with your recovery. Specifically, we're concerned about the risk of your upper respiratory infection. There's a risk it could turn into a case of viral pneumonia. Can you wait a few more days?"

Wait... a few more days...?

It's the wrong thing to say.

But she doesn't know that. Timothy, on the other hand, registers it a moment before Yuuki's flung back into traumatic stress land.

A few more... days?

Can you be quiet and endure a few more days of suffering, Yuuki?

Can you pull together yourself, last a little longer?

Can you survive that long? asks the shed walls.

Yuuki's throat itches. He resists clawing at the non-existent bindings around his wrists.

I won't survive that long.

Something in Yuuki has snapped. He wants to leave, but he can't. He has to stay, even if it distresses him. He has to cope, he has to endure it, just like the shed, just like the shed, just like the shed.

Nurses checking over his condition just frequently enough to fray his nerves. Yuuki doesn't know exactly why it gets to him so much. But all the attention is stressing. He could go up the hospital roof garden, but he's not sure how his anxiety will do being around a lot of unfamiliar

302

people in a place he's unfamiliar with when he's feeling like this.

He wants to leave.

He *needs* to be able to leave.

"What's wrong?" Joshua's voice sounds from outside in the hall.

Timothy's reply is too quiet to distinguish.

"Oh…well…can't he come home with us? I'll be going back to uni tomorrow. He could have my room?"

"…are you okay with that?"

"Yeah?"

"Okay."

Yuuki presses one hand over his mouth. It's a mistake, the way it reminds him of the tape. The way it silences him. It only makes the panic worse, and the stress louder.

Gentle, protective arms embrace him. They shield him.

Yuuki hugs himself, and Timothy hugs him.

"We'll take you home with us, then. If you're okay with it? So you're not alone if something happens and you're not feeling well."

Yuuki shakes. Manages a nod.

He doesn't know why everything is so stressful, so overwhelming all of a sudden, but it is. The stress of everything is more than he can bear, and the more awake and interrogated he is here at the hospital, the more this situation is feeling like an extension of his time in the shed.

Yuuki expects Timothy to let go, to step away to start getting things organised. But he doesn't. He holds onto Yuuki until the panic subsides. Until the Yuuki's mind stops splintering and whirling, and he feels like the ground beneath his feet isn't about to give way.

It's like Timothy rescuing him from the shed all over again.

31

A few hours later, Yuuki leaves the hospital.

Outside, the daylight is bright. It's sunny, and the sunshine is warm, but the wind is cold. Yuuki wraps his coat he's wearing around himself a little more. In spite of the temperature, though, the fresh air is relieving.

Down in the hospital carpark, people move about between cars and on the walkways. Yuuki tries to keep an eye out for all of them. He senses Timothy watching him in the corner of his eye, but also keeping a look around as Yuuki is doing.

Yuuki feels exposed in the open space. The open space and all the movement around is a little overwhelming. It's better than walking through the hospital corridors, and having to choose between the narrow spaces of stairwells or elevators. It's a relief, knowing that doesn't have to feel trapped inside four walls anymore. But this is the first time he's actually really been outside since the kidnapping – the first time he's gone outside on his own, at least, and while *conscious*. A lot has happened since he last walked free.

He glances at the tote bag that Timothy is carrying. Yuuki's jacket, the

305

rest of his uniform clothing he'd been wearing during the three days of the kidnapping... are in there. *It was then, wasn't it? The last time I went for a walk, went outside, was able to go for a walk, when –* ...

Words don't string together well in his head, but the scene he's imagining is clear: the last time he went out like this was when he left his house to go meet Timothy at his law office in Ninao on June 5th.

Yuuki takes a deep breath and forces himself to try to let it out slowly. It half works.

Timothy leads the way through the carpark. Yuuki fixes his eyes on him and tries not to think. *Do any of these people recognise me?* Yuuki wonders. For good or for bad, Yuuki doesn't want to be *seen* right now. He wants to hide from all the faces he doesn't know. He also wants to hide because he doesn't know if any of these people happen to be one of the four that stormed into Timothy's office.

They still haven't been caught, those four perpetrators. Not one of them. Not the two who kidnapped Timothy and Joshua, and not the two who kidnapped and locked Yuuki in that shed. They could be lurking anywhere. What will they do, now that they know that Yuuki didn't end up dying in that shed?

...will they try again? O-or are they satisfied, now that they've given us a fair enough warning not try too hard to save people?

At least, if they were to try again now, it would only be Yuuki and Timothy who get caught up in it – not Joshua as well this time, because Joshua already went ahead to go back to the Harrison's house. Susan picked him up during her work break so they both can go ahead and get Joshua's room ready for Yuuki to stay in.

It doesn't necessarily make him feel any better, though – the fact that there's only the two of them. Two instead of three makes them more vulnerable. Less eyes to keep a lookout. Less defence if something were to happen.

"It's just over here," Timothy says.

Yuuki's vision is too full of vivid colour.

Also, out of the three of them, Joshua is the one who would have a better chance at identifying them. He wasn't knocked out like Timothy and Yuuki were, and he had enough time to at least get *some* kind of vague idea of what kinds of people might be *them* and what kinds of people might not be.

They could be anywhere, anyone here…

"Yuuki?"

Yuuki stops abruptly, hugging himself against the cold.

He looks at Timothy, standing in front of a black car. Something about the prospect of getting in that car – or any vehicle, in general – right then makes him nervous. It takes a moment for Yuuki to realise he recognises the car. Timothy's expression is concerned watching him. Yuuki grimaces, lowers his head and crosses the last remaining distance to the car.

"You okay?" Timothy asks gently.

Yuuki nods, and reaches for the car door.

The car is already unlocked, so Timothy gets in. Yuuki does a sweeping, darting scan of the surrounding people and cars first before getting in himself.

Timothy drives. The car is filled with hollow silence. Pulling out of the carpark and leaving the hospital behind is a relief that Yuuki's too numb to properly feel. He doesn't know how he feels. He wants to talk with Timothy, if just to try get all this built up trauma stuff out on the table and dealt with right away. But Susan would tell him that's not how it works. Yuuki himself knows that it's not going happen that way.

"It'll take time," she said.

"You hear what the doctor was saying earlier? Regarding the early discharge?"

At least he knows for certain now that Timothy's voice is real. *Even if there's this shaken up aftermath to deal with, surely it has to be a little more bearable than being stuck tied up in that shed was, right?*

Timothy waits, his previous question hanging in the air unanswered.

"Yeah," Yuuki murmurs. "A little."

Between Timothy and Susan, they'll take Yuuki to a couple of check-ups in the following week, one which includes another appointment with a psychologist that Yuuki isn't looking forward to. But it's all necessary to satisfy the doctors, and it may come in helpful in the event that Yuuki finds he needs an extended leave from work.

"If at any time you're feeling unwell," Timothy says, "and you want us to take you to the doctor or see someone, just let us know, okay? We're happy to help if you need it. If you'd prefer private transport as opposed to taking a train or bus as you usually would, to give yourself some privacy and breathing space before and after, we're happy to try help if we can."

"Thanks," Yuuki murmurs.

Both he and Timothy know that that's not going to happen though. It would have to be absolutely necessary circumstances before Yuuki would ever go out and see someone. He'd much prefer to cope on his own without seeing any doctors if he can.

Yuuki tugs at the seatbelt so it's not sitting *quite so restraining* feeling across his body. He makes a face at the road going by. Whether he accepts what happened as traumatic or not, it's not going to change anything. That's what Yuuki would like to believe, anyway. The kidnapping and the shed ordeal happened the way it did and it's affected him the way it has, and that's just the way it is. He's just going to have to deal with it as it needs to be dealt with, and…

Yuuki pretends he hasn't noticed Timothy noticing how over alert and weird he's being.

It's trauma, Yuuki understands that. But he wishes he didn't. Because, in understanding it, accepting it – even to the slightest, it's acknowledging that what happened to him in that shed… it actually happened and it's affected him more than he thought.

Yuuki's afraid of what that means for him.

They stop by a petrol station on the way. Timothy drives by the fuel pumps and parks in the normal car parks.

"You want coffee?"

It takes Yuuki a moment to realise Timothy's talking to him. "Hmm?"

"Coffee? I was actually going to get you one the other day, when Xiùyīng and Jié came to meet us, but I wasn't sure how that would go down with the doctors."

Yuuki grunts, but no sound comes out. "Probably not well."

"Yeah. I thought it could've helped you feel a bit better going into it, but anyways."

"Maybe." In fact, it probably would have.

"So, how about now. I'll pay."

Yuuki looks at him, and then reaches for his pocket. "I should…"

Oh, right. I've been in hospital. I don't have my stuff with me. At least, not in my pockets. Do I even still have my wallet with me?

Checking his pockets anyway, he finds nothing.

"Oh, if you're looking for your wallet," Timothy says, "it's in that tote bag. Your phone and keys and everything are in there too. They're in the clear plastic bag just under your jacket."

Yuuki murmurs a thanks.

"But don't worry about it now, I'll pay," Timothy says. "What do you want?"

There's something that sounds like guilt in Timothy's voice – an apology, an attempt to remediate something. Yuuki can't decipher it. He only knows that there's nothing Timothy should have to feel guilty about that he feels he needs to make it up to Yuuki by buying him coffee. It's out of the kindness of his own heart, too, of course. Timothy's always been like that, and Yuuki being younger than him, much newer to the judiciary field of work, and near to the age of his eldest son, means that it's not out of the ordinary for Timothy to be offering. And Yuuki would usually gratefully accept.

But Yuuki only feels shame, only feels like he's burdening Timothy further. The guilt lacing Timothy's tone sharpens that feeling. "Are you sure it's okay?"

310

"Yeah." Timothy's smile is genuine, but it seems forced. "Let me shout you. Please."

"But what about me having caffeine? Did the hospital say anything about it?"

"The nurses didn't say anything about caffeine. Of course, they'd more likely than not advise against it, but see how you feel. Susan reckoned to just make sure to pay attention to how it makes you feel afterward – like if it makes you feel more anxious, nervous and alert or something, particularly while the trauma is still fresh. If it makes you feel *worse,* in other words. But see how you go."

Yuuki nods. He's distracted watching their surroundings for any suspicious movements or signs of people recognising them. As for coffee…

"So…?"

"Yeah, then. If that's okay."

Timothy seems relieved. "So, what would you like?"

"Black coffee, then, please."

Ten minutes later, they're back on the road and headed home. To the Harrison's home. With coffee. Yuuki cradles the coffee in his hands the whole car ride. He forget to ask for cold water with it. Fortunately, it's winter, so he only has to wait a brief period of time before it cools enough to safely drink. The warmth is a distraction for him in the meantime.

It's good, when finally does get to drink it. The bitterness is balanced, deep. It washes away all other tastes, and recent memories of taste

311

sensations he'd rather forget – the cloth, the tape, the dusty shed air, the sterile hospital air. It's warming for his body and soothing on his mind. Yuuki's thoughts narrow, in a good way. His emotions hone. The sensation of the caffeine on his brain feels like reprieve.

"It's good?" Timothy asks.

Yuuki lets himself slump in the seat a little. He nods a little.

He feels the tension of the muscles in his forehead ease. It feels like the hot water of a bath washing over him. He's pretty sure coffee isn't supposed to have this affect, but it does.

When they arrive at the Harrisons, Yuuki is ready for a nap. Joshua's room isn't quite ready yet, what with piles of clothes, textbooks, notebooks and sci-fi books everywhere to organise, and sheets to change to a nicer fresh set. But seeing Yuuki's fatigue setting in fast again, Timothy invites him to lie down on the couch and rest for a bit.

Yuuki accepts. He continues drinking the coffee, sip by sip until it all disappears and his mind is humming with relaxation and *stress relief*. The Harrison's dog, Ginger, comes in to greet him and stays for pats. She then moves to her bed to snooze. Yuuki, unintentionally, follows suit.

He doesn't mean to doze off on the couch when does. But the house is warm and friendly. Timothy disappears down the hallway to answer a phone call, leaving Yuuki to having some breathing space for moment. In the quiet, Yuuki lets himself sink back into the couch.

He lies down, settling into the cushions of the back of the couch and the arm. This house feels safe, and quiet, and calming. And right now, Yuuki's nerves are quiet too. The caffeine takes some of the pressure of Yuuki's nervous system to stay awake, alert. He closes his eyes and stays like that.

Without the energy to try to stay awake any longer, Yuuki gives in to the need for sleep and lets his awareness slip away from him.

Later, Timothy finds him, half sideways on the couch, arms wrapped around himself and legs extended out front to the floor. It looks uncomfortable, but Yuuki's shoulders are lax. His hands, where they are tucked beneath his armpits as if for warmth, slacken and one of them slips out of its hold.

Timothy gently takes the empty coffee cup from where it's tucked in between Yuuki's arm and torso. Yuuki doesn't stir. Timothy's gut churns. There's a truckload of grief waiting to be realised. For Yuuki, and for himself. For now, for Timothy, it sits in his chest, lurking. Looking at Yuuki, it nudges him anew.

Inwardly, Timothy vows to do whatever he can to help his friend recovery – to get better, to feel better.

However long it takes.

32

Yuuki stays with the Harrisons a few days to rest some more.

The first morning, Yuuki wakes up with a cold. He feels too warm but he shivers like he's cold. A bad headache and congestion, and a cough that causes a pain in his chest that won't abate. No matter how much he tries to cough it up into wads of tissue paper, the pain only gets worse and the discomfort in his chest won't dislodge.

Crap.

When he tries to get up to get more water, light-headedness has him woozy. He's disoriented, waking up in Joshua's room. The house isn't unfamiliar, but he's never slept here before. He's napped here before, but that's only ever been on the couch, like yesterday, or on the floor. *The floor.* Lying down on the floor sounds wonderful right now. The Harrisons have nice fluffy carpet in the living room.

Yuuki stumbles down the stairs. Wooden stairs are not his friend. He's not even wearing socks, but he slips on the last step, and only just manages to catch himself against the railing and the wall before he face-plants down into the landing. Susan is coming out of the kitchen when it happens.

Susan notices right then and there that something is up. Because of that, there's little Yuuki can do to pass this ill feeling off as simple tiredness. Or rather, there's little he can to do avoid the suggestion of a doctor's appointment. When he fails to consume any more liquid than a few sips all morning, and turns down any offer of food, Susan makes the decision for him.

Out of concern for viral pneumonia, Susan takes him back to the hospital for a check-up. There's an outpatient clinic they're able to visit on the first floor. They're not staying any longer than necessary for the check-up, which is a reassurance, but still. Walking back into the hospital, Yuuki feels his face drain of colour. He doesn't want to be back here. There's too many people. Too many people with various health ailments and various stresses and textures of tiredness. And then there's Yuuki, who doesn't want to acknowledge any of his health complications right now. Acknowledging it means acknowledging the kidnapping, and Yuuki is trying his best to get it over it, to put it behind him, to not let it affect him.

Others would call it denial. Yuuki pretends he doesn't care.

Unfortunately, since they have no booked appointments, they have to wait some time before Yuuki's able to see anyone. Susan promises coffee on the way home, if he's feeling up to it – given the way it helped him calm down and rest yesterday. It's the only thing Yuuki is looking forward to about this outing.

It's a necessary outing, though, if I want to not be feeling like this for ages. If it is viral pneumonia like Susan suspects, then it's not something that they want to let get worse. If it did, then there might need to be another hospital stay.

There's signs at the clinic administration desk requesting mask wearing for ill patients. For some reason it strikes a sharp nervousness in Yuuki's gut. He can't pinpoint why. He realises, full-well, that he should be wearing a mask. Why he didn't think of it earlier, he's not sure. He's standing here with an obvious cough, shivering and overheating, chest hurting and fatigue tugging at his muscles. He's sick. He ought to protect others from potentially getting sick and feeling something like this too. But even when the doctors give him a look that says they've realised this too, Yuuki isn't pressed.

When they move to the waiting area, Yuuki tries to brush off the stab of anxiety and panic. It's not until Susan speaks of it after they sit down that he understands where it's coming from.

"They've been informed about the incident in Ninao," Susan murmurs quietly while they're waiting. She doesn't say the word 'kidnapping' out loud for Yuuki's sake, so as not to draw unnecessary attention to him.

Yuuki tries to keep his face turned away from Susan, but he looks at her with a questioning look out of the corner of his eye.

Behind the mask she's wearing, Susan smiles grimly. "You don't need to worry about explaining all that stuff to them again if you don't want to. They already know."

Oh. They know about what happened to Yuuki in that shed. They know that he was gagged. That means, they're also aware that he'll need to be exempt from health and safety request of mask-wearing for patients and accompanying people where contagious infections may be present. In Yuuki's case, whatever virus in messing with his lungs. If this were another time, he would wear a mask. But here, right now – if there's anything strapped or even simply *sitting* over his mouth right now, Yuuki is undoubtedly going to panic – and panic badly.

No wonder Susan never mentioned it.

After they've finally finished with a chest x-ray, bloods tests and blood pressure testing, it's confirmed that the cough that started out as an upper respiratory infection in the hospital has now turned itself into viral pneumonia after all. The pain in Yuuki's chest isn't just because of coughing, it's because of inflammation.

"I don't have to stay in the hospital again, do I?" Yuuki asks. His voice is rough, weak. Croaky.

The doctor shakes their head. "That would likely only make your condition worse. The hospital environment tends to put patients at greater risk of developing respiratory illnesses such as your own, and..." They pause, and contemplate their words. They clasp their hands together. "...and in your case, I'm sure being admitted again would only place you under unnecessary stress. That would only aggravate the illness, and possibly hinder your recovery – from both this and your other present health concerns. It's better you stay home and rest."

Yuuki nods, relieved.

"We will need to give you treatment. However, your friend here is a qualified field doctor, so we'll hand over administering of treatment to her. You're both alright with that arrangement?"

It's a much more preferable option to an extended hospital stay.

Yuuki mouths an inaudible thanks.

Susan nods.

The doctor nods too, satisfied. "Well, then. That's all for you today, then, Takahashi. I'd advise lots of rest, and continue medication until you're feeling better. If symptoms persist, and you're feeling unwell for more than a few weeks without change, or if you're feeling worse, it's best you come in for another appointment. Though here's to hoping you won't have to."

Yuuki would rather not visit again if he doesn't have to, either.

The doctor hums. "Also, have you support at home, may I ask? Or another person who may be able to keep an eye out for a decline in health and bring you back here?"

"He's staying with us in the meanwhile," Susan answers. "My family will be looking out for him. Either my husband or I will be able to bring Yuuki in again. We'll get in contact if there's anything comes up that's out my areas of knowledge."

Again, Yuuki feels guilt creeping up on him. He's the one who dragged the Harrisons into this kidnapping incident, and yet here they are insisting on sticking with him and supporting him in the aftermath of it. It bothers Yuuki that he's putting such pressure on them. Sapping their energy, rather, in worrying about him when they could be worrying about their own recovery and coping.

But then again, maybe it's exactly that – maybe their actively searching for ways to help in my recovering is a way that they are coping. If it reassures them that I'm okay, and if they can feel more in control of the situation by being able to do something…

Yuuki can't finish those thoughts, but it helps alleviate some of his guilt. He can't do much to eliminate what stress they've experienced in the Ninao incident because of him. If letting them help him recovery is some way of remediating that stress, then Yuuki will accept it until he's well again.

With the testing and doctor's appointment finally over, Yuuki and Susan are able to go. They collect the prescription medication from the pharmacy, and Susan acquires IV equipment from the hospital before they leave. The IV equipment is borrowed under her name as a trained and qualified field doctor.

For the first time, Yuuki is grateful that Arkala has such a qualification. He's glad that Susan happens to have it, especially in these sorts of times. Nevertheless, he hopes that her training doesn't have to become of too high of an importance from here on in, however; he hopes it doesn't become a critical thing for Yuuki's and the Harrison family's livelihoods and well-being in the future.

Walking out of the hospital, the impacts of the Ninao incident felt heavy upon each of them, Yuuki realises that the circumstances they've entered suggest that it already might be.

Since Yuuki isn't feeling well enough to drink much, he almost has to forego the coffee. In the end, Susan suggests to get just the coffee shot in the form of a short black. Yuuki decides to go with that. It feels disappointingly minimal, the coffee. But at least it's a quantity of liquid he is able to drink. Because of that, he's still able to have the stress-relief of the caffeine that comes over him – and without making himself feel sicker drinking more liquid than he can handle.

By the time they get home, Yuuki's energy is drained, and he coffee cup is well and truly drained, too. Yuuki stumbles inside, eyes bleary. Timothy and Joshua are home. Samantha is home, too. She comes down the stairs in her school uniform with her drink bottle and a pile of workbooks.

"How'd it go?" Timothy asks. "What did they say?"

Susan comes in behind Yuuki then, carrying in the IV equipment.

The Harrisons are quiet.

"It did turn into pneumonia," Susan answers.

Yuuki stands where he is awkwardly, trying to think of something to say.

"Go rest, Yuuki."

Joshua slept on a roll-out mattress in the lounge. He looks tired.

"I'm sorry for taking your room," Yuuki murmurs. He hesitates before starting the climb up the stairs. "Um, I can sleep down here tonight, if you want your bed back? If everyone was okay with that?"

"No, it's all goods!" Joshua says. "Like I said, I'm going back over to West Coast next week anyways."

"I don't want to contaminate your room."

Joshua lets out an unexpected laugh.

Yuuki's mouth twitches in a smile, but the heaviness sinking into his soul from the recent experiences prevents it from fully materialising.

"Would you prefer that, Yuuki?" Susan asks.

"Sorry?"

"Would you prefer sleeping out here? It might take some extra stress off you with going up and down the stairs while you're not feeling well."

320

Oh yeah, the stairs…

"You'll be closer the bathroom if you need it, too. The only thing is that it might be a little noisier down here, and less private space for you."

Yuuki considers. "I don't want to bother any of you, though. Or make anyone else sick. Actually, maybe I'll just… I'll just go back upstairs."

"If it's contamination you're worried about," Sam says sarcastically, "I'm pretty sure you've already covered the whole entire house anyway."

Joshua splutters. "Sam!"

"And we were with you in the hospital often," Sam continues. "So don't worry about it. It's not like we didn't chose to expose ourselves."

Yuuki appreciates their sense of humour.

"Additionally," Susan says, "I would say that our immune systems are functioning fine enough to fend it off alright. Yours, on the other hand…" She pauses to read the instructions on one of the prescription bottles. "…your immune system, on the other hand, is not doing so great and is having to work extra hard to keep things moving." She glances at Yuuki. "Really, it's you who should be wary of us. Both in terms of us presenting you with germs and us disturbing what rest you're able to get. At any rate, it's up to you where you feel most comfortable being."

Timothy glances around at the others. "Yeah, I'm pretty sure none of us mind if you wanna just stay down here with us. If you want some company. I can't guarantee we won't disturb your peace and quiet, but…"

Yuuki grunts. "My mind isn't giving me much peace and quiet, anyways." He hesitates, then says quietly, "And I think I wouldn't mind the company, to be honest."

There's some unspoken feeling that settles into the atmosphere.

There's no words that anyone speaks in attempt to express it, and it might not be so obvious from their expressions. But Yuuki can almost hear it, and sense it's sad undertone in the wake of a scare of what could've been:

"And we wouldn't mind yours."

That atmosphere continues throughout the rest of the day. It's carried by a fragile sense of relief that feels like it could give way at a moment's notice. It's held taut by something – something solemn, something full of grief. Yuuki struggles to figure out an adequate way to explain.

In the evening, lying down on the couch in the evening, Yuuki thinks of this. Resting, and letting his body absorb the antiviral medication through the IV. Somehow the sting of the needle is less stress than having to continuously uptake fluids orally while he's feeling like this. He'd rather another IV needle bruise than having to consume so much energy just for drinking water and taking medicine.

The background noise of the Harrison's activity is lulling. Distracting, in a good way. Yuuki's consciousness feels like it's moving in water, pulled under and rocked with the waves. He realises slowly, as he submerges and rises in and out of those waves, what the atmosphere in the Harrison's house is: it's the feeling of realising that they all could've lost this – this being together, the Harrison family and Yuuki.

After being kidnapped from Timothy's law office in Ninao, Yuuki might not have ever seen them again, and they might not have ever seen Yuuki again, either – alive, that is. The reality that it so easily could've ended in parting ways for good is hard to process. Yuuki's still coming to grips with not being in the shed anymore. He can't imagine how things must be on the Harrisons' end of things right now, but he guesses that for them, they might be still processing that Yuuki's back with them again, relatively safe and relatively sound.

It's hard finding ways to remind themselves that that ordeal is over. It's especially hard when they have no more answers than what they've already guessed or been given. The case, as it is, still remains unsolved in that they don't know who exactly kidnapped them and *why*. They can guess the latter, but it hasn't been confirmed with hard evidence.

In the lingering uncertainty, keeping each other company in the immediate aftermath is one of the few ways they're all able to cope. For now, it's enough to know that they're all safe; in each other's company, they're reassured of each other's present safety, and their own.

To the Harrisons, Yuuki's physical presence is a reminder that Yuuki isn't missing anymore. And for Yuuki, it means he's not in the shed and that the Harrisons are safe.

Exhausted and ill, but surrounded in this sense of relative safety and company, Yuuki finally regains some sense of rest.

33

Five days later
16ᵗʰ June, 12-Tau

Another week of June passes by.

Yuuki slowly starts feeling better. He's coughing less, and the discomfort in his chest is much less apparent. Fatigue still has him unable to do much at all, but it's not unexpected, considering the fact that viral pneumonia isn't the only thing that Yuuki is recovering from at present.

Nobody talks about traumatic stress. No one talks about this aftermath too often. Susan occasionally mentions it in passing, but it's a topic no one likes to linger on –as though not to jinx it. As though, if they were to bring the topic into conversation too much, they might find themselves dealing with the post-traumatic stress they were so wary of.

There's also the threat of another kidnapping that they don't want to speak into existence.

Nothing has happened, in follow-up to the Ninao kidnapping. There's been no signs of anything being due to happen, though there hadn't been with at the Ninao law office either. The atmosphere at the Harrisons is artificial calm in light of this. It's like their holding their breath, waiting for something to happen. Not wanting to let themselves calm down too much in case they aren't as mentally prepared for the next time something happens.

If there is a next time. At this point in time, there's no way of knowing for sure whether there will be or there won't be.

Joshua left for West Coast, as planned. Samantha continues going to school. Timothy works from home, more often than not – the exception being when he's got to be in court for case trials and other discussions. On those days, Susan stays home from work at those times and delivers her university lectures through an online video meeting as opposed to in person.

In that way, it's ensured that Yuuki isn't left absolutely alone.

Or, alone in terms of other humans.

Ginger, their dog, remains oblivious to the dangerous happenings, but reads their stress and tries to comfort them nonetheless. While Joshua's there, she mostly follows him around. After Joshua is gone, Ginger takes to accompanying Yuuki in his recovery zone in the lounge.

It dawns on Yuuki that he, too, will have to leave here soon. Back to the real place he actually lives, on the other side of Two Lakes district, in a flat with his friend and his friend's girlfriend. With that thought, he starts to mentally prepare himself for going back to that house, back to the flat. He's not sure what it's going to feel like, returning there, and how he's going to go about managing himself in his post-incident and post-hospital coping. It makes him somewhat nervous.

But Yuuki will cross that bridge when he comes to it.

*

Two weeks on from the Ninao kidnapping
19th June, 12-Tau

One Thursday morning, Officers Marina Tu'u and Conrad Johnson, as well as inspector Kia Ihsayu, visit the Harrison house. It's Yuuki's first time meeting Marina and Conrad. There's something weird about meeting them knowing that they technically have met him before, at the shed when he was rescued.

Marina comments, "You're looking a fair bit better than when we last saw you."

Conrad nods in agreement.

Yuuki doesn't know how to respond to that.

The three PFOs give Timothy and Yuuki a rundown of the situation, and illustrate precautions. For the most part, Conrad doesn't seem to be much of a social person so opts to simply manage the note-taking instead of carrying the conversation.

Marina says she's been busy with the investigation, and with another case she's been monitoring with her partner. But as for this case, she has to report that they've found nothing. Kia, also, regrets to inform them that she and her team have found nothing, either.

Kia asks during the updating, "Yuuki, do you happen to have any further recollection of the incident that you're able to share?"

"I haven't been wanting to give it much thought," Yuuki mutters.

Joshua is the only one who could really give any helpful information, he wants to say. But he's exhausted from his recovering from the shed experience and from the viral pneumonia, both which are still lingering in their impacts on his mind and body. He's not been well enough to think. Regardless, Yuuki can't remember anything clearly. He knows that Timothy didn't get any more of an idea of characteristics of the four people than what the CCTV footage could have given – if the security cameras had been working at the time, that is. He knows that it would be helpful, beneficial to the case investigation and to the overall safety of the Harrison family and Yuuki himself.

But Yuuki can't remember anything but fuzzy, blurry, trampled upon recollections. The point is, Yuuki doesn't want to remember any more than he does.

Kia asks Timothy is there's any cases he's been currently working on that might be any possible link. But Timothy isn't sure, in regard to his current cases. Moreover, none of his cases, neither past nor present, involve Yuuki.

The Youth Rehabilitation Trust is the only cause they can think of.

Yuuki almost wonders why he's not asked if there could be any link between the kidnapping and his own work –But then again, he can't think of any. He can't imagine any of the youth he's encountered at the A'o Youth Detention Centre to be that deeply involved with an organised crime group, anyways. He also can't think of anyone who might hold a grudge against him after meeting him there.

But the four people who attacked Timothy and himself were older – how much older, he's not sure, but they were definitely adults, at least Yuuki's age or older. No one he would've met who might've been in detention since he started working, in other words.

There's no reason why such a group couldn't recruit youth as well, though. It's something Yuuki might have to keep in mind, but right now, it doesn't seem relevant to the Ninao kidnapping case at hand.

"What about the email?" Timothy asks. "The email sent to me from that anonymous source."

Marina frowns. "We haven't been able to trace it. I suspect that it was sent by someone on the inside of the group who organised the kidnapping – a whistle-blower, I mean, and one who couldn't afford to have their identity known. But that's just a guess. I have no evidence to prove that."

"Anything other than that," Kia says, "we're not sure."

Yuuki's feelings about it strangely complicated. Someone on the inside cared enough to expose his location like that. Yuuki has no idea what the group planned to do with him, or if they planned to do anything more with him but leave him there to die. But whoever that anonymity is, they spared him from that fate. They saved his life, too.

It makes Yuuki wonder though – did it really have to come to that? Why did it take someone on the inside to risk exposing themselves and putting themselves in danger? Was it really that impossible for the PF and the Arkala Search and Rescue team to find him, or did they simply not bother to look hard enough?"

This plays on Yuuki's mind.

Kia, Marina and Conrad bid them farewell. Marina says she'll be in contact with them to update them when she can. After they leave, Yuuki lies back down on the couch again, neck and back propped up by pillows to help him breathe easier. The chest pain isn't seem so bad anymore, but the discomfort still lingers in his lungs.

The bitterness he's been experiencing since becoming more lucid in the hospital tugs and gnaws at his consciousness. After some wrestling with it,, Yuuki forces the question out into the open air:

"Did they even search for me?"

Timothy doesn't answer him at first. He's busy getting stuck into doing more catch-up work on his laptop. He doesn't reply and Yuuki considers not bothering to ask the question again. But after several long moments, he asks, "What was that, sorry?"

A faint squeak leaves Yuuki's throat. Yuuki coughs a few times, then reattempts speaking. "The PF. Did they even actually search for me?"

Timothy's typing halts. In the silence, a clock ticks. "I believe they did."

Yuuki glances at him, disbelieving.

"They did, to some extent. I'm sure."

"If they were honest about their searching, then why didn't the anonymous person send *them* the email with the coordinates? I don't want to discredit those who searched, but it…"

Timothy grimaces. "I have wondered about it, too. And it was a question I also asked myself – whether I should've handed over the email to the PF to let them handle the situation. But I think the conclusion that I came to was that the anonymous source who gave me the coordinates to the shed knew a lot more about the situation than we did. And I think they had already decided that it wasn't safe to give those coordinates to the PF directly – for the sake of their own safety, primarily. That email was likely sent by someone affiliated to or acquainted with the perpetrators, after all.

"But maybe it was also for the sake of yours, too – for the sake of your safety."

Yuuki is starting to grasp what Timothy's suggesting, but it's not something he's ready to consider. "What are you saying?"

"It could very well be me overthinking," Timothy says, "and I'm just considering possibilities, but I have wondered if the anonymous source might even be someone in the Peace Forces. For them to contact me directly and not give the coordinates to the PF instead. At the time, it very much looked like a summoning to a hostage situation, or a trap. But…"

"So you're saying that the person thought that the PF might be dangerous to give the coordinates to?"

"Maybe not the entire PF, but some people within. And if that were the case and this is true, then…well, there could have been someone inside the PF manipulating direction of the search for you."

Yuuki stares at the light on the ceiling.

"If the perpetrators had links to someone in the PF, or they themselves are part of the PF, then they could have been directing the search away from or around where you were. They could've been deliberately searching in places where they *wouldn't* find you."

"That's just a hunch, though, right?" Yuuki asks hoarsely.

Timothy says, "Yeah, it's just a hunch. Or a gut-feeling, whatever you might call it. But this is why I – why Joshua and I – foolishly rushed into going after you on our own. It's not that we didn't trust Marina, but we felt something was being implied by the anonymous nature of the leak. It could've been a trap, we knew that, but…"

Yuuki lets out a hysterical-edged laugh. "It's almost like – " He coughs. "It's almost like you're the only ones who tried to look for me."

Judging by the look on Timothy's face, Timothy can't pretend like he didn't feel that way, either. "I'm saying all these things, and they may or may not be true. But Yuuki… please understand that, no matter how hard people could've searched, there were no other traces leading to you except for those coordinates. They left nothing, those who did this to you. Marina was earnest about hunting any information about your whereabouts, and I really do believe she was serious about trying to find you. But there was nothing left to hint at your location even from the vehicle me and Joshua were taken in. Nothing. If not for those coordinates, it would have been impossible to find you."

Yuuki's eyes glaze over.

"I'm sorry," Timothy murmurs.

"I know it must've been extremely hard for you…experiencing that. In that shed. That waiting, with no one coming. While you were…"

Timothy can't finish. Timothy doesn't need to finish.

"…"

"…"

Yuuki feels numb. "…thank you for deciding to come for me. Thanks for finding me."

Timothy takes a mouthful of coffee. Yuuki doesn't have the heart to look at his face to see his expression. "Thank you for holding on until we did."

Yuuki looks away, and glares at the edge of the couch, even as his eyes burn and his throat constricts. The first painful, hot tear spills out.

34

Yuuki stays at the Harrisons one more night.

The pneumonia will take another week or two to recover from, maybe a little while more, but it's not something Yuuki can't manage with rest. He's able to eat and drink again like normal, and he's not experiencing the same depth of exhaustion that's been overwhelming him since he woke up in hospital. He's still unwell, though. He'll have to take an extended leave from work to make sure he gets better. Fortunately, since this health issue is in relation to the kidnapping, he's able to be paid reparations to sustain him for another two weeks until he can return to work.

It takes Yuuki's mind off the stress of wondering how he's going to be able to afford to get himself groceries and pay rent at the end of the month.

In the early afternoon, Susan drops him off home with a small bagful of groceries and the last of the antiviral medication. There's also a bag of plunger coffee put in with the clothing he'd worn on the day of the incident – a parting gift from Yumiko. A note from his sister is stuck to it with sticky notes: '*Stay safe, get better soon! – Yumiko*'

Yuuki gathers these in his arms, bids Susan farewell, and unlocks the door to the house.

When he enters, the house doesn't feel too different from when he was last here.

Yuuki dumps his stuff by the hallway, then wanders numbly over the windows. He opens them. It's a little windy outside still, and it catches the curtains and flings them aside.

His flatmates Lee and Rachel must be out. The house is quiet, though somewhat in a lonely way. But for all the warmth and company he enjoyed at the Harrisons, Yuuki is more than relieved to have his own space back again. He doesn't have to impose on the Harrisons anymore, either.

He sighs. There's washing to put away, still hanging on the clothes horse how he left it. The washed and folded clothes in the bag he's carrying, he doesn't even want to look at right now.

Yuuki plugs in his phone. He's about to flick on the switch at the power point when he realises the battery isn't low like he was anticipating. The Harrisons must've charged it for him, because the battery is full.

He double takes. He checks the date on his phone again, still trying to get a grip on reality. On time.

It's 19th June. *And...Timothy and I were going to officially establish the Youth Rehabilitation Trust on June 5, so...*

I've been gone two whole weeks.

Yuuki has to recalculate a few times to get it through his head. June 5 was the day he was kidnapped. He was in the shed for three days. In the hospital for... five. At the Harrisons for another six or seven.

So it's been more than two weeks.

Now he's back. It's Friday now. Yuuki left here more than two

Fridays ago. The information makes sense, but it only makes Yuuki's sense of reality feel distorted. When he left here on June 5th, he'd been intending on returning home after work late that night.

I never thought I'd be gone that long.

Yuuki opens the door to his room. His stomach hollows and the abyss in it twists. The shed is superimposed over the room. *This isn't the shed. This is my room, not the shed.* He enters, slowly. Step by step. Heart beating a little faster, and shakiness coming over him quickly. Yuuki all but yanks the curtains to the side and shoves the window open. He stands there, hands gripping the window sill, looking at the outside space he could climb out into and *breathes.*

Maybe it'll be better if I come back in here a bit later.

While the house is empty, Yuuki decides to nap on the couch for a while. He closes his eyes. As soon as he does, scenes of shed walls and the hospital room flash into his mind. Other scenes come unbidden too – the attack at Timothy's office, the insistent voices of nurses and PFOs, and even the Harrisons and Yumiko filter into his mind. Yuuki turns, rearranging his napping position to lie on his side. It's reminiscent enough of how he lay defeated on the shed floor, dying –

The scenes follow.

Vivid. Too vivid. Muted, but loud.

Exhausted, he gives up the attempt at napping before the scenes get to him any further. He sits up. The room spins. He leans his elbows into his knees and buries his face in his hands.

It occurs to Yuuki that this is the first time he's been in a place alone since he left for Timothy's office that morning. That is, of course, excluding those three days of forced isolation in the shed. It's making him antsy, nervous, anxious – this being alone all of a sudden. Left vulnerable to another attack were one to come. Left to remember what it felt like to have to try to cope with all his overwhelming feelings in that shed.

He realises then that the shed experience isn't over as soon as he'd thought it would be. Sure, he's back – physically. But psychologically, emotionally, mentally… Yuuki still hasn't completely left that shed.

With a sharp exhale, Yuuki gets up and makes coffee.

Lee and Rachel come home later that evening. They come in seemingly light on their feet. When they see Yuuki sitting on the couch, the whole atmosphere turns awkward, uncertain. Yuuki feels like he just crashed a party.

"You're back," Lee says.

Yuuki replies thinly, "Yeah. I'm back."

Rachel offers a grimace of a welcome back smile.

Oops, I forgot to tell them I'd be back today, didn't I?

Almost simultaneously, Rachel and Lee's eyes flick over Yuuki like they're searching for some visible mark or injury that he might have returned with. Some souvenir from the kidnapping, or something. But if she's looking for some concerning to note, she must find none. Yuuki knows she won't find any: there's no obvious sign of how chafed and bruised the skin on his wrists had been, and the graze on his cheek has already healed over beyond easy visibility. Those were the only physical impressions left on his skin. Even the bruises from the IV have faded.

The only thing Yuuki has returned with is stress and a cold.

"Well, you seem to have come back in one piece," Rachel comments. "That's good."

"I, uh, I'm a bit sick at the moment," Yuuki confesses. He tries to ignore the way Rachel's remark stings. *I don't feel like I've come back in one piece, all put together.* "It's getting better, though. I've got medicine for it."

A lie. This all feels like a lie.

"So do we just… carry on as normal around here, then?"

Yuuki nods. "Yeah, I guess."

Rachel seems satisfied – slightly relieved, even. Lee only looks uncertain.

As the atmosphere in the room grows steadily more awkward, Rachel breaks away and heads down the hallway to get ready for bed. In her wake, Lee remains in the living room, standing stiffly.

Lee clears his throat. "So…are you really okay?"

Yuuki's mind blanks. *No. Yes.* "Hmm…"

"But you were…"

"I know."

If it were the Harrisons, they'd not need to ask that question. They already know that he's not okay. Lee and Rachel, on the other hand… they don't want to acknowledge that. They don't know *how* to acknowledge that.

"Okay," Lee murmurs. "Let us know if there's anything we can do to help."

Yuuki replies almost automatically, "Thanks."

Standing in his room later that night, he finds the silence swirling around him like thick fog. He finds himself repeating Rachel's words in his mind, involuntarily.

"So do we just… carry on as normal around here, then?"

The question somehow feels heavy, like it carries a weight of expectation – an expectation that Yuuki has to shove aside any stress that he might be experiencing due to the recent events, for the sake of some sense of normality. It's like another request for him to fake he's okay if he's not feeling okay – just as he had to do when adapting to living a new life in Japan from when he was seven years old.

Yuuki distracts himself with unpacking his clothes. He puts the prescription medication on his bed to remind himself to take it. *It's funny how they're wanting to act like everything's fine and carry on like nothing ever happened.*

As if in uncanny timing, Yuuki's phone pings. The screen lights up, showing that Yuuki has a text message from Timothy. Yuuki slowly steps over to it, and picks it up. He reads the message.

Just checking in, making sure everything's relatively okay.
'How are you flatmates around you?'

Yuuki stares at the screen, a feeling of dark sadness and shame welling up inside his chest. He suppresses it firmly before the muscles in his throat have a chance to constrict.

'Fine, thanks,' he replies. Thinking that might be too curt a response, he adds, *'Thanks for letting me stay with you all. I appreciate it.'*

338

Timothy says that they're here if he needs help with anything, or wants to stay somewhere different one night if things get overwhelming. It echoes what they've already said, and it's the same sort of thing that Lee tries to say as well. But whereas Timothy's and Susan's words hold full-intentioned meaning, Yuuki's not so sure about Lee and Rachel.

I'm fine, Yuuki tells himself. *I'm okay.*

It's a lie. He knows it. Still, he'll continue to lie to himself if it helps him feel better. Until he turns off the lights and the room is plunged into darkness and he is plunged back into the shed as it was at night. Until lying down alone in a room invokes memories he'd rather forget. And until what calm, what *collectedness* and *coping* he's faking unravels and his efforts to be okay all come undone.

Surely, as things gradually settling back into a familiar routine of doing things, Yuuki's shaken up emotional state will settle too. For now, however… he'll be probably drinking a fair amount of coffee and leaving the light on in his room at night when he sleeps. He'll be learning how to cope until things stop feeling so confusing and stressful.

And what if it never stops?

Yuuki certainly hopes that it does, but if it doesn't, then he'll have to learn to cope in a whole new kind of aftermath.

35

Timothy reads the text from Yuuki. He hasn't been able to formulate a response.

'Fine, thanks for letting me stay with you all. I appreciate it.'

You're not fine, Yuuki. You don't need to pretend to us that you are.

He is worried – about things he doesn't know. About the trauma Susan keeps bringing up, and implications of that word for them. Most specifically for Yuuki, but also for himself and his family.

But what gets to Timothy the most is that he doesn't know what to do. He doesn't know how to help Yuuki in this aftermath. Yuuki went through something horrible, something that Timothy feels guilty to have been spared from.

We rescued him. But why does it feel like we found him too late? What if we'd managed to find him sooner? Could we have prevented him from experiencing worse in the aftermath?

It's a miracle they were able to find him at all, though. Yuuki so easily could have been left him in that shed to die. If it weren't for that anonymous email – and if it weren't for Timothy and Joshua deciding to act in response to that email – then…

It won't help anything. This overthinking. They did what they could, and they managed to get Yuuki back to them, safe and alive. No matter how much Timothy wishes it, they couldn't have found him sooner than they did. They couldn't have rescued him sooner.

Even now, they can only do what they can to help Yuuki recover. Timothy wants to commit to it though – to helping Yuuki recover. He's afraid, because he doesn't know what recovery from this sort of thing may look like. He doesn't know what to look for, and how to recognise the difference between adequately coping and not coping in Yuuki. But Yuuki's sister's insights have given them something, And Timothy is willing to *try to learn,* to *try to understand.*

So long as Timothy has the capacity too, and Yuuki allows it, he wants to at least try to protect Yuuki from at least some of the aftermath that might come to play.

That aftermath isn't going to pleasant for any of them.

Especially for Yuuki.

Yuuki is only twenty-four. Timothy's own eldest kid is only a few years younger. And Yuuki – the young man with a heart for kids facing the snares and emotional neglect of the justice system, who was motivated to try do something about it… what will become of him? How long will it be before he can smile easily again? It's only been some several days, but…

Susan's right, isn't she? Timothy recalls the conversation they all had as a family, gathered outside Yuuki's hospital room a few hours after his rescue. *Yuuki may no longer be able to be the same Yuuki who we used to know.*

341

12-Tau Ninao Kidnapping:

The Aftermath

36

Early July, 12-Tau

First day back at work. It is Yuuki's first time back out in public, too. First 'real' time, anyways, going out by himself into people-frequented places. It's been a good month since he went out like this.

Initially, Yuuki had thought that wearing his uniform again might trigger some unwelcome memories from the kidnapping, but fortunately it doesn't. He's probably so accustomed to wearing it that it doesn't feel particularly associated with that day... those three days. It also helps that – besides Timothy, Joshua, the PFO commander named Marina Tu'u, and the ambulance and hospital staff – no one knows that Yuuki had been wearing this, ready for work later that afternoon. It means that he's able to walk and take the train to work without his clothes participating in identifying him as '*the kidnapped person from the Ninao Kidnapping that was talked about on the news*'.

Of course, Yuuki's expression and body language might give it away, though. If no one recognises him by his face alone, they might come to the realisation if they consider his flightiness long enough.

Catching the train didn't use to unnerve him this much.

He's fidgeting, thumbing the edge of his cell-phone case off and on, off and on his phone repeatedly, over and over until the muscles in his hand start feeling strained. The closer the train gets to Ninao, the more Yuuki's vigilance rises. He's not going as far as where he got off for Ninao Law Office on June 5th, but it's close enough to make him nervous.

He's looking around too much, but he needs to.

He's cornering himself into the end of a carriage, just so that he doesn't have to watch his back.

Yuuki can fake being composed, but he's fairly certain his flightiness betrays him. No matter how discrete about his nervousness he tries to be, the anxious feeling gripping his body only gets worse.

This doesn't feel like how Yuuki perceives 'security officer Yuuki Takahashi' should be acting, should be feeling.

It's hypocritical, isn't it? Dressed in his work uniform, Yuuki probably looks like a security officer who knows what he's doing. At least, that's the composed appearance he *should* be giving off. Inside, he feels like a seven-year old kid scared of a thunderstorm. He feels like a bird who knows how to fly, but is staring out at the wide open space in front of him too scared to throw himself off a ledge out into the air out of fear of plummeting down into the trees below. Or perhaps a bird of prey would swoop down and snatch him up, and carry him off in its talons to who knows where, if it's not a crash-landing that would get to him first.

Is this just because this is the first time I've really been out among people in a while? But Yuuki's sure it's not that simple. He's been on walks in the last two weeks, even if those were on quieter paths. He's been back to the doctor's for a general post-release check-up. Sure, that was with Susan –

so maybe he'd had some sort of emotional anchor point to focus on.

But this...?

Yuuki can't help but wonder how Timothy feels, and if he feels anything similar to this. Part of hopes he does, if just so that Yuuki can know he's not overreacting. The greater part of him doesn't. Timothy's still been having to go into Ninao Law Office for the court cases he has to judge and prepare for. They might be letting him work from home a bit more for the time being, when it's work he doesn't have to be at the office for, but he still has to go into that exact same building and room that they got attacked in.

The very thought of having to do that himself sets Yuuki's nerves on fire. He's not sure if he could do it. Even now, simply standing in a train heading that way, Yuuki feels like he's walking directly back into a zone of danger. Sure, he's not going to Ninao Law office, he's going to A'o Youth Detention Centre. But there's only a few train stops' difference or a half hour walk in between those two places.

It's near enough to that place matter.

Getting off the train, he's even more alert than usual. The train ride isn't long, but it's long enough to stop his thoughts from whirling all over the place. From thinking, about all the parallels or similarities of today to June 5th. From quietly fearing that any one of these people around might have the intent to kidnap him.

Yuuki can image what kind of stress Timothy must be under, if Yuuki's feeling this and he's not even having to be physically present at Ninao Law Office on a regular basis. He's not sure how Timothy manages to keep enough steadiness about himself.

How do you know how to function? Yuuki wants to ask him. *Do we just pretend nothing's happened, and carry on like we were never attacked, and like we never tried to start the Youth Rehabilitation Trust in the first place? Even if technically speaking, we didn't give up the Trust, at least not yet...*

Yuuki doesn't know how to act. He should just be himself, but it's hard to do that. He feels like he's having to put on an act. That he's pretending to be himself – pretending to be the Yuuki Takahashi who took the train out to Ninao on the morning of June 5th, dressed in these very clothes. A Yuuki who hadn't been kidnapped, and who never knew what the interior of that particular garden looked like.

But the lingering ache and tinge in his chest, however, and this exaggerated nervousness prickling his skin, confirm: no matter how much he acts, those things happened. And he's affected by it.

At least he can still sort of pretend.

A'o Youth Detention Centre feels more familiar than Yuuki himself does. Walking in, using the card with his name and ID photo on it, feels disjointed. Yuuki doesn't have to think when he puts in his key code for the back door of the staff room. It's muscle memory. But cognitively, he feels like an imposter.

Before he's finished signing in, footsteps sound. Yuuki recognises them, but his newfound anxiety swells nonetheless.

"Yuuki. Welcome back."

Yuuki looks up from the sign-in sheet. He nods politely. "Mitchell."

His boss, senior security officer Mitchell, greets him grimly. "It's good to have you back."

Yuuki tries to find decent words to respond with, but none come out. He returns the grim smile.

"Are you doing okay?"

"Yeah. I'm fine now, thanks."

Mitchell weighs up his expression with doubt.

Yuuki tries to appear steady.

"So," Mitchell pauses and glances out at the foyer. "I wasn't sure how you'd be feeling today, so I'll just have you work in admin today. That okay?"

With clammy hands, Yuuki scribbles the last few letters of his name, sets the pen down and straightens up. The date is left blank. Yuuki doesn't even know what day it is, and he can't get a grip of himself to guess.

"Yeah," Yuuki replies. "That's fine, thanks. That'd be good."

Mitchell nods. "You can let me know if you are feeling up to working with the kids, but I figured you might find it better to ease yourself back into it."

"I appreciate it."

"...okay. So... let me fill you in with updates on our current intake. Not many changes. The kid who was supposed to leave late last month is still here – something came up in their home situation, so we're looking for another placement for them. They're still in our care in the meantime. Otherwise..."

Yuuki nods along like he's listening, but his mind's adrift. He can't keep his attention focused on Mitchell – on anything, really. His mind's only focused on one thing: *distract, distract, distract.* An artefact from the enduring of the stretched out time in the shed, maybe. It's an excuse, perhaps, but it's the best Yuuki can make sense of it.

"What happened with my shifts?" Yuuki asks, once Mitchell's finished this part of his update and there's a pause.

Mitchell gives a shake of his head. "You don't need to worry about your shifts. I had someone cover them."

He'd already guessed that much, but it felt polite to say something to demonstrate he'd sort of been listening.

"I've employed another staff member," Mitchell informs. "Part-time, on call. I understand that your capacity to work may be limited for the brief while, so we've got someone else to help if need be."

Disappointment – in himself – sinks into Yuuki's stomach.

Seeing his expression, Mitchell adds, "They're not here to replace you. They're hired on the understanding that they're covering for you. It means they're here to give us back up if need be. And also give *you* the certainty that if you're not feeling well, and you need to leave early or have someone cover parts of your shift, we have someone who can take over. You don't need to push yourself, in other words."

Yuuki nods. "It's okay, I understand. Thank you."

"We had been getting close to needing another staff member, anyways. So don't worry; there's still plenty of work to go around. It just means the workload will be distributed a little more reasonably now."

There's no reason to argue. It's a good thing. Nevertheless, Yuuki feels ashamed of his absence, and guilty. He wants to apologise to his senior officer for his insufficient health, and he wants to make amends by working all the newcomer's shifts himself if just to compensate for the inconveniences he's caused himself.

He wants to prove that he's still capable – not only to Mitchell, but also to himself, and to Timothy and Susan and his family…

The Yuuki of the morning of June 5th and the Yuuki of this morning in July are the same person. What happened in between can be forgotten – *needs* to be forgotten. It's a tripping hazard, and Yuuki has no intention of holding onto it. He'll let go of it, if he hasn't already. He'll move on. He can assimilate these experiences back into the *normal* or more *familiar* version of himself; he'll get over this anxiety and return to being the Yuuki Takahashi everyone expects him to be.

What Yuuki doesn't understand yet, though, is that it doesn't matter if he lets go of it or not – traumatic stress doesn't work like that. No, moving on from it depends on how vicious its claws are and whether or not it's ready to let go of *you*. Once it's sunken its teeth in, the damage is done. Moving on from it means healing from the wounds it leaves.

And for Yuuki, that means there's no going back to the Yuuki Takahashi who he wants to go back to. He can only be this emotionally ravaged version of himself. Maybe he can regain some sense of his familiar self, but the self that he's trying to mimic has changed. It got hurt. It got damaged.

This is a reality that he has to learn how to accept.

After all, that self he once knew got left behind in that shed.

Fortunately, being on surveillance in the admin, Yuuki is able to work without being bothered or asked too many questions. He's also able to get by with less risk of being *triggered*.

There's no one in the isolation units at the moment, either, fortunately; the rooms in the solitary confinement wing are empty. But those rooms still call out to Yuuki like rooms in a haunted house. It's all too quick a happening for him to visualise himself in there, imagine himself experiencing that enclosed environment... and just how similar an oppressive feeling those inescapable four walls have. It's not like he hasn't considered how those isolation cells might feel to the youth before – it's part of the reason why he wanted to establish the Youth Rehabilitation Trust in the first place. But it's a different story thinking about it before and thinking about it now.

Now, Yuuki can't help but notice how similar that solitary confinement environment is to Yuuki's ordeal in that shed. Or how much it holds the potential to be. Sure, they don't get left in restraints when in there. But it's not that part of the shed experience that was the most overwhelming: it's what the endless entrapment in nothing happening did to his mind; it's what he had to endure emotionally, psychologically, while in there.

Mitchell sees it, too. He makes an effort not to treat him any differently, but Yuuki notices the way Mitchell doesn't order him around as sharply as he used to. He notices how he occasionally gets a few extra looks his way, and not just from his boss either – the other staff he's working with do it too. It bothers Yuuki somewhat – irritates him, burns some kind of prickly self-consciousness beneath his skin.

Some time into his shift, a couple of his colleagues come up and ask him how he's doing. One awkwardly mentions that they saw the news. Yuuki sits there and listens to how they reportedly felt while watching it.

Yuuki has to clench his jaw hard and fix his eyes firmly on the monitor screen in front of him. *Let me tell you how stressed and bewildered and* shocked *I was feeling, lying in some dusty garden shed, tied up, eating cloth, while you were in your home watching that on your device.* He bears through the shallow sympathies and *welcome backs.* When he's left on his own, he has to resist the urge to lash out at something.

Don't vent. Now is not the time and place to vent. Regardless of time and place, Yuuki would prefer not to vent at all. He'd rather ignore it, minimise it. Not let it get to him so much for it to *need* to be vented.

But there's only so much good that will do. There's only so much denying of what he's *really feeling* – the anxiety, the uncertainty, the unprocessed stress – before something makes what little, fragile composure he has snap.

37

Six weeks on from the kidnapping, and then on the eighth week, Yuuki has his last couple of check-ups.

Lee offers to take Yuuki to the second to last one of his check-up appointments. Yuuki wishes he hadn't had to go at all. The appointment is straight after his work shift finishes – he'd have gone himself, but there's no way he'd get there on time. Susan is busy with a tutorial evening at the university she teaches at, and Timothy has a trial he needs to prepare for. Yuuki is not in a good mental state to take the train alone at rush hour. Even if the appointment weren't crossing through Ninao, the amount of people he'd be surrounded by and have to stay vigilant of – in case any of them happened to be one of his kidnappers – would be far too much anxious stress for hm.

It's fortunate that Lee works at a tertiary institute in northern A'o. It's near enough to A'o Youth Detention Centre that Yuuki is able to walk there in fifteen minutes. It doesn't take him even that. He sees Lee talking to a caretaker – a middle aged man who gives Yuuki a weird vibe. Then again. Everyone has been giving him a weird vibe, so it's probably just in

353

his head. When Lee sees Yuuki, he bids the caretaker farewell. The caretaker resumes carrying garden supplies to the garden shed visible just beyond a lot of trees.

Yuuki's eyes lock onto the shed. He fixates on it, and automatically compares it to the shed he was locked in. It seems bigger than the one he was in. He watches the caretaker friend of Lee's put the equipment away. *Yeah, that one is bigger.*

The garden tools are allowed more space that he was.

Lee approaches and distracts him with a wave of his hand. "Hey?"

Yuuki blinks, and forces himself to refocus. In the near distance, he can hear the garden shed doors closing, and being locked.

"You all good?"

Yuuki nods. "What did he want?" he says abruptly. It's a means of distracting himself, but the words come out blunt, almost accusingly. Yuuki tries to correct his tone in adding, "The guy you were talking with?"

"Oh." Lee turns, and starts them walking off in the direction of the carpark. "That's the caretaker. We sorta became friends, mates, after striking up conversation here and there."

"Ah, I see."

Friend.

Somehow the friendship dynamic between them seems almost similar to Yuuki himself with Timothy. It sparks an odd sense of jealous in Yuuki to see it happen before him with someone close. Yet it's not envy that pricks him, but rather a kind of loneliness, longing, yearning... shame.

Shame. Guilt. Angst. *Fear.* A deep-seated anxiety that *'friendship'* is something that Yuuki and Timothy no longer have, at least not to the same degree. That what connection they had got destroyed when the kidnapping happened, when Yuuki dragged Timothy's whole family into a stressful, dangerous situation – all because Yuuki had a vision and Timothy is kind and serious enough of a person to have wanted to help him turn that vision into a reality.

Do I even deserve to have the Harrisons care and concern for me? Is it even okay for me to still call myself their friend?

The doctor reassures Yuuki that the pneumonia has been resolved. Satisfied that Yuuki isn't presenting any further complications arising from the kidnapping itself, the remainder of the appointment is devoted to informing and enquiring about the physical and mental symptoms of general stress and anxiety.

It's funny, though. What they talk about is mostly stuff Yuuki has already come to terms with and figured out on his own. His homesickness for Arkala when he moved to Japan taught him as much. His social isolation he experienced at high school taught him to deal with his stress on his own.

What he would benefit from learning from these appointment… is minimal. Yuuki leaves, frustrated.

It's not until he's had some time to cool his emotions down that he's able to pinpoint the reason why nothing they say is helpful in the way he needs it to be: they're talking about general stress, and generalised anxiety; what Yuuki needs more information on is *post-traumatic* stress. But he's not ready for talks about managing post-traumatic stress, and he's not wanting to hear about the possibilities of this developing into something long-term. It's much too early in the piece to determine the latter, anyways.

Maybe it's something he'll have to ask Susan about someday, if he's ever feeling brave enough to.

Yuuki talks with Yumiko face-to-face for this first time since his hospitalisation. Thankfully it's just his sister. He's not sure he's feeling up to showing his face to their parents just yet.

"You had those doctor visits to go to after leaving the hospital, eh?"

Yuuki hums.

"How did they go?"

"Alright."

"And how are you feeling?"

That I can't even answer honestly myself. He shrugs.

"Or," Yumiko says, "how have you *been* feeling?"

"I don't know. Not so great, I guess. But better now. The pneumonia is cleared now, at least."

"Pneumonia? Wait, were you sick?"

"…did I not tell you that?"

"You said you got weren't well for a while, but you didn't go into any details."

"Ah…"

"I didn't realise it…" she clears her throat. "I didn't realise your condition got worse like that."

That's not even the half of it. "I'm fine now, anyways. Sorry I didn't mention it, if you wanted to know. I just… I've had a lot on my mind."

Yumiko's brow creases. "That's alright. I'm not mad or anything. But… it must've been serious, getting sick like that."

Yuuki grunts. "It wasn't fun. But it was anticipated, and Susan helped me with the medication side of things. But like I said, I'm better now. So you don't need to worry."

"Did you have any other doctor visits?"

"Just check-ups. There's supposed to be one more, but I cancelled the last appointment."

"How come?"

Because they'll probably only be talking about trauma and coping methods that don't work for me, and talking in superficially sympathetic tones that make me feel even more stressed. "I'm not going to find it useful."

"Was it about psychological stuff?"

Yuuki's mouth twitches.

Yumiko smirks. "Correct, aren't I?"

"*Yes.* And you know what I'm like with those."

"Still, I think it might a good idea to –"

"If I feel I need to see someone, then I'll see someone. But there's no point in taking up mine or someone else's time if I'm not going to get anything out of it."

To that, Yumiko doesn't argue. Yuuki's nerves are jittery, nonetheless. It feels like ruffled feathers, like irritation. How much of this is conveyed through his body language and reflected off the screen to his sister, he's not sure. But Yumiko must pick up on it, for she changes the topic of conversation.

Yumiko asks, "How are the Harrison family?"

Yuuki hesitates before answering. "I... I haven't talked with them much," he answers honestly. He realises that he's been unintentionally avoiding them. He feels too guilty, and too much like he's imposing on their mental health. He's already burdened them enough with the matters of the Trust and now this *trauma*. He'd rather not encroach on their personal space for the time being; the Harrisons need breathing space, and emotional space to recover as family.

Yuuki asks aloud, abruptly, "Do you think we should've been more careful?"

Yumiko takes a moment to decipher and process Yuuki's question. She thinks, then says, "What care could've been taken? You were careful. It might just be that the case is a little more confusing and complex than you're all able to reason on your own right now. But it's not yours or Timothy's job to figure it out. The PF are the ones in charge of the investigation. All you need to do is stay safe, and try to recover from the experience you've just had."

Gloomily, Yuuki nods.

"It's not your fault what happened them," Yumiko says firmly. "Even if the kidnapping happened because of the Trust, it's not your fault. You're not the one who instigated the kidnapping. You didn't deliberately put the Harrisons in harm's way. Even you didn't know it would happen. You're a victim of this attack, Yuuki, not a culprit of it."

Then why do I feel so ashamed and so guilty?

"...I asked this in the hospital," Yumiko murmurs, "and I understand if your answer is still 'no', but... do you want to come home for a bit? It might help to just… I don't know, distance yourself from… all of *that* for a bit."

"The house with the nameplate reading 'Takahashi' out the front is not 'home' for me," Yuuki retorts. "Besides, running away from Arkala isn't going to help anything."

It's bordering on snapping at her, his tone. It's an uncalled for outburst, and he instantly feels guilty for it. More guilt. It's like he's feeling constantly at fault. He apologises, and can't help but wonder if he's needing someone to blame for this whole incident, and the designated person for that is himself. *Maybe if the perpetrators had been caught already, and there were names and faces and a clear, dang objective to find closure with, I wouldn't be so insistent on pinning some kind of blame on myself.*

And then Yumiko asks him something isn't expecting in response: "Are you okay?"

Yuuki looks directly at the screen, trying to think of good response. Instead, tears well up in his eyes unexpectedly. He ducks his head to hide his face behind his hair. With a grunt, he shakes his head. "I don't think so."

After a few moments, and an extended shared silence with Yumiko, Yuuki raises his head, sniffs, and deftly wipes the tears off his cheeks. "I don't know," Yuuki says thickly. "But I'll be okay."

"Maybe." Yumiko's voice softens. "But in the meantime, we could put together enough money to see you here – to Japan – and back, and help you during your stay."

"No, I need to work. I need the distraction. Plus, there's rent to think about. I need to be able to afford that."

Yuuki's aware of how much it sounds like he's giving any excuse he can come up with to provide a reason not to go. To say he's better off staying. Maybe it's premature thinking, insisting he doesn't want to go even though the rest of his family genuinely have his wellbeing in mind. However, for Yuuki, the underlying reason he doesn't want to fly over to stay with them is the same reason he left: the stark social isolation he experienced while living there during his childhood and teenage years isn't something he wants to re-experience.

The situation might've changed. Yuuki is older, now, too, and he's not in high school anymore; maybe he'll find he'll be treated differently by people who he crosses paths with – maybe, now that he's able to be identified as working in a distinguished role in Arkala society as a security officer, he'll be able to be treated better, even. But it's a lot to risk, especially when seeking psychological and emotional rest is the primary objective. Yuuki would have nothing to do over there, and having to put in effort to try fit it with the social expectations of that part of his cultural identity would be far too much of a strain for him right now. That's not even mentioning any culture shock he might have to deal with going there, or coming back.

Since he can remember, Arkala has always been his home country, and Arkalahn English his native language. This is his default. In other words, he'll better able to cope with the emotional side effects of living through a three-day 'tied up, locked in a shed' kidnapping if he stays here in the place he recognises as 'home'.

Yumiko, at least, seems to acknowledge this. "Okay. Well, I'm just a call away if you need me. We all are."

Yuuki hums uncertainly.

Yumiko tries to smile as best she can.

38

Late winter, early spring

Things don't get better like Yuuki thought they would.

He loses sleep. A lot of sleep.

One night, he doesn't sleep at all. One night becomes another a few days of two hours sleep later. Weeks pass like that. 'Insomnia' starts to register as appropriate word in his brain. Nothing cures it. He doesn't have enough money to afford to try different things, and he doesn't want to see a doctor for prescription medicine that's chemically crafted. That costs money, too, anyways.

The only thing that has any decent effect is coffee. It does wonders at helping alleviate the pre-existing frustration levels, too. But soon enough Lee calls him out on what Lee proposes is a caffeine addiction, and that Yuuki's fluctuations in stress and frustration, as well as his inability to sleep, is all caused by five cups of coffee he's been having each day.

Eventually, Yuuki gets too stressed by Lee's remarks that he just stops.

The frustration doesn't go away.

The insomnia doesn't go away.

All the goes away is Yuuki's having something to help him through the waves of stress that won't leave him alone.

He cries, but he only lets himself do so when he has emotional privacy. If Lee or Rachel are around, that means silent crying. Sure, he's an emotional person as it is. But this is a shameful crying. It's a helpless, stressed and *ugly* crying.

It'll pass right? This will all pass? They say it will – everyone who speaks optimistic stuff to me says it will. They say it'll get better. They say I'll get it over it?

Yuuki feels a gut-wrenching *something* sink into his belly – *but what if I don't? What if I don't get better? Or get better in some ways, but horrendously worse in others?*

All that he knows for now is that he has no way of knowing. Time will tell. Yuuki really wishes it wouldn't.

Yuuki feels that Lee's behaviour is strange and he knows it's because of him. Rachel, on the other hand, doesn't seem to give a damn – and as Yuuki's finding out, that's so much worse.

She slams doors, drops cutlery back in the drawer without a care for the crashing noise. It's too much for Yuuki's post-trauma hypersensitivity. It has him flinching, has adrenaline shooting through his system and his muscles tensing up. He'll be trying to calm himself down, taking a nap or distracting himself from thinking about the shed and the what-ifs and the what-will-happen-nows, when sharp bangs and clashes and thuds erupt in the atmosphere and ricochet off the walls. He tries to bring it up, if just to politely ask if she could perhaps be a little quieter – *careful* – with these things while he's recovering. Rachel gives him a condescending look and says that his request is 'a little over the top'.

Yuuki has a bad breakdown that day. He can't remember if Rachel offers any words of apology or not. Lee comes home to tense atmosphere resembling the aftermath of a fight. Yuuki hears them talking about it – about *him*, and about his *trauma*. He doesn't answer when Lee knocks on the door to check in on him. He's too ashamed. Yuuki's shut himself in a room and sent himself reeling at the resemblance to the shed as a result, but he still can't bring himself to go open that door. Not when it's the only barricade to himself and his wreck of a mental health condition and them.

He considers, an hour later, lying on his side while a fresh wave of tears slip down his cheeks and over the bridge of his nose, if he should leave. Move – to another place, another house. But where would he go? If he left, he'd only be bringing his issues with him. If he left, it would be seen as running away from a situation he should be able to deal with and sort out with the other people he's living with.

In the end, it's not Yuuki who leaves but Rachel. Fortunately, he's not at home when she makes that call. It happens after a fight, according to Lee. A breakup. She slams the door in her usual way, leaving Lee to live with a traumatised Yuuki without her, and a note saying she'll cover the next two weeks of her portion of hers and Lee's shared room rent as per their agreement. When Yuuki returns home to receive the news, the first thought in his mind as he looks at Lee is *'How long until you do the same?'*

But for now, *for now,* Lee reassures him that he's not going anywhere.

Yuuki doesn't feel much reassurance, but it's enough. Enough to numb the impact of the realisation that he is directly or indirectly responsible for making the lives of the people around him more difficult, and that he's the reason why Rachel left.

"I'm sorry," Yuuki says quietly.

Lee lets out a mirthless laugh. "Don't be. I saw it coming, anyways. Rachel and I have been together long enough to know that no matter how much we want it to work out between us, it just… wasn't working how we wanted."

Oh, he thinks I'm just offering condolences for their breakup.

Yuuki doesn't have the heart to correct his interpretation.

Yuuki gets a text message from Timothy that night:

Hi Yuuki, would you like to meet for coffee and catch up some time next week? Let me know if there's a day and time that suits.

Yuuki sarcastically responds, 'Anything but June 5th, 12.30pm.'

He back-spaces every letter in that sentence before he presses send. Timothy doesn't need to have his cynical-tinged dark humour. That thought develops, progresses – Timothy doesn't need to have his *issues.*

The text reply almost results in declination. Yuuki considers his own state of mind, and Timothy's wellbeing, and the devilish voice inside his head says that Timothy will soon have had enough of him, and leave, just like Rachel. Not meeting with Timothy might prolong the time until Yuuki has to face the crumbling of their friendship.

However, in the end, perhaps out of desperation for someone, a friend – *an understanding friend* – to talk with… Yuuki gives in and accepts.

365

39

Late October, 12-Tau

Yuuki meets with Timothy the following Monday, one of his days off.

"Coffee?" Timothy asks as they approach the counter. "I'm paying."

Yuuki pauses.

"It's okay. I'm happy to pay." That guilt – that expression of '*I need to repay you somehow*' – has crept back into Timothy's tone.

"No, it…" Yuuki wonders how best to say it. "I actually…"

"Have you gone off coffee?"

"…just trying to avoid caffeine. Trying to see if it helps things."

"Oh, right. Okay, well, I think they do good decaf here, if you wanted?"

"It costs extra, though."

Timothy's mouth quirks. "So does the triple shot that I'm about to order. Don't worry; get what you want, I'll still pay." He lower his voice respectfully. "Save your money for things to help you recover from…from the incident."

Glancing around, it looks like nobody picked up on Timothy's words and identified either him or Yuuki. Yuuki lets out a breath.

"Is that alright?" Timothy asks.

Yuuki nods. He notes the action unintentionally nearly resembles a Japanese bow. "I appreciate it, thanks."

Timothy offers a half smile. "So what will it be?"

Yuuki considers just asking for tea, but tea can have small amounts of caffeine in it too. In any case, the only tea Yuuki feels like having right now – *sencha* green tea – gave him a stabbing headache in the centre of his brain last he had it. That's new, that side-effect; he never used to get headaches from tea like that before the Ninao kidnapping.

"Yeah, okay," Yuuki murmurs distractedly, "Decaf sounds good, then. Thanks."

Having to deny himself an opportunity to have something that *would* make him feel better, he can't help but feel his recently developing depression deepen.

"It's probably caffeine addiction," a voice in his head remarks. The voice sounds suspiciously like Lee's. Realising that, Yuuki's emotions turn even bitterer. No, Lee wouldn't stop there; he'd take it a step further and argue that having any kind of coffee won't help with staying away from his supposed potential 'caffeine addiction'. In other words, decaf or not, he'd recommend Yuuki stay away from coffee altogether.

Yuuki is almost too tired to care. There's enough coping to do in his life right now. He will take the guilt, and carry the shame silently. Lee doesn't have to know. They're not dating, he's not his mother, and he sure as hell isn't someone Yuuki considers a therapist. *Heck, maybe Lee's wrong about this whole caffeine situation to begin with.* It grates Yuuki's emotions, considering that. Caffeine helped him. It did. But now he's doubting himself and his own perceptions so much that he's not sure who's right – Yuuki's emotional stress-inflicted self, of his friend Lee who has a strong opinion on how caffeine affects the majority of people.

Yuuki tries to hide his disappointment when one of the café staff arrive at their table with a decaffeinated coffee in one hand and a triple shot coffee in the other. Both coffees are placed on the edge of the table, then the caffeine-less one is directed toward Yuuki and the normal one given to Timothy. Yuuki can't manage vocalising a 'thanks'. Whether Timothy notices his disappointment or not, Yuuki can't tell.

"How is your work?" Yuuki asks abruptly. A distraction.

Timothy lets out a sigh. "It's... going."

"Are you having trouble too?"

The way Timothy looks at him, it's like he's weighing up Yuuki's expression and intended meaning.

"In terms of with this whole *aftermath* thing."

"After the incident?" Timothy clarifies.

Yuuki hums. Without meaning to, he vents about his frustrations with his *incapacities* and shortcomings at work. About the interference of his sleeplessness, and of his unrelenting emotional stress. Timothy receives the information and prompts him to add more detail, without judgement. Something about the way Timothy ponders what Yuuki's saying – the way he doesn't look directly at Yuuki's face as someone might if they were learning new information entirely – makes it seem like Yuuki's not alone in having difficulty in the aftermath.

He's proven right; when Yuuki redirects the question back at Timothy, Timothy averts his gaze and lets out a heavy sigh. "I guess I can't honestly say 'no, I'm not having trouble'. It's been a bit hard to concentrate lately, but..."

Timothy tells him: how, in the wake of the stress caused by the Ninao incident, Timothy's capacity for work has decreased too. Yuuki learns that he works from home more when he can, and that he didn't return to the Ninao office for a while. "And when I did," Timothy says about the latter, "it was only to pack up my stuff and shift."

"You've moved office?" Yuuki asks.

Timothy nods. "I'm still based in Ninao, in the same building. Just moved a couple of corridors down to a different office. It's smaller, but it's less... immediately accessible from the main doors. Feels a bit safer, from a security point of view, too."

Yuuki feels relieved and nervous for him at the same time. He imagines their kidnappers attempting a second kidnapping, not minding the extra process to get to Timothy's office. Snatching up Timothy again, and then coming for Yuuki again next, if not before.

"I've given up on my revisiting of the A'o Fire case, too. The one I was wanting to inquire about before *this whole thing* happened."

Yuuki's thoughts snap back to present. "The A'o Fire? The one you thought might be arson?"

Timothy goes to take a drink of his coffee, but it must be still too hot for him to drink, because he lowers the cup again without taking a sip. "Yeah. I just... I have my hands full with a ton of other work already. That's not even mentioning taking into account this decreased capacity for working in general. I'm sure it'll improve, this... state of things, for us – at least, I hope it will – but in the meantime, for me, I just don't have

369

the capacity to pursue the A'o Fire case. It's a suspicion I simply can't prove, and I don't have the energy to find proof for."

Yuuki nods in understanding. "You couldn't delegate that work to someone else? Not just the A'o Fire case revisit, but some of the stuff?"

Timothy tilts his head. "I don't think anyone has the spare capacity to help. Things are already delayed and piling up because I had to take leave." The sentence finishes there, in an almost interrupted way. But Timothy says no more, and his silence since speaks of a grim, bleak present lot of circumstances for both of them.

Around them, the café hums with people catching up. It's lively. The music is jazzy and chill. Timothy and Yuuki's table in contrast is dull and drained of energy. Yuuki decides to drink his decaffeinated coffee in one go in an attempt to ignore it. And, of course, in an attempt to ignore his disappointment that there won't be any caffeinated emotional pick up following the coffee. Things aren't going well for them. It wouldn't surprise Yuuki if Timothy requested to move his office to a different district. But then again, Timothy might have a better grip on his emotions than Yuuki does. Maybe he does feel nervous, similarly to how Yuuki feels right now heading into his own workplace, but he might be able to push past that without letting it affect him this much. He might be able to stay in the Ninao Law building, even when Yuuki can't handle the thought of stepping foot inside the property grounds boundary line.

Yuuki doesn't know, though. For Timothy's sake, he hopes that Timothy is more okay than he is. But he can't presume. And even if Timothy is able to walk into that Ninao office without panicking, that doesn't mean he's not having issues emotionally and psychologically, too.

He might show a coping façade on the surface, and it might seem like he's managing, but that doesn't necessarily mean he really is.

It doesn't mean that Timothy is okay.

"How's your flat?" Timothy asks, finishing his own coffee quickly.

Yuuki is broken out of his contemplating. Shame washes over him.

Timothy waits.

"Well, Rachel left."

"Oh? Did something happen?"

"She had a fight with Lee, broke up with him and moved out before the month was over. Happened in July. She couldn't deal with it anymore – her words."

"Deal with… what?"

The ambiguity in those words is something she never clarifies: whether it be about him, or about her and Lee, or about both of them. But Yuuki suspects it's half because of him – because of the pressure he's put on the people around him to 'beware the traumatised person'.

Judging by how Lee regards him, Yuuki doesn't think he's all that wrong.

"Me," Yuuki eventually answers. "Most probably."

"Because of…?" Timothy prompts, but his tone conveys that he's already guessed the answer.

"Because of how I've been since I got home after Ninao, and after the hospital and stuff."

Timothy is quiet for several moments. "I'm sorry that happened."

"Don't be. It probably would've happened eventually."

The words echo Lee's. But coming from Yuuki's mouth, those words bring something ominous to the table: the plausibility that Yuuki won't be getting over the Ninao kidnapping any time soon. Perhaps Timothy senses that too, for he doesn't say anything.

Yuuki changes the topic. "You haven't heard any more from Marina, have you? It was 'Marina', wasn't it? The name of the officer who was keeping you updated during my...?" *Shed ordeal. Kidnapping. Disappearance.*

Timothy hums. "Yeah. But, no, I haven't heard anything back from her."

"Ah, I see."

"To be honest, I'm not sure we'll see an update. Not unless something else happens to us, at any rate."

Yuuki frowns. "What's wrong with the case investigation?" He says it like it's someone else's case, not his Timothy's very own case that they were victims of, or in.

"Insufficient evidence," Timothy says. He sits back, takes a deep breath and lets it out slowly. The expression on his face says he's pondering words. "It tells us this much: the perpetrators are skilled. I mean, we saw that. It's not exactly as though the PF aren't doing any sort of investigation at all. I'd say it's more an issue with the fact that we're dealing with some kind of organised group of individuals here. Whoever came at us knew what they were doing, and seeing as they're keeping hidden now and have left us alone since, they did what they came for."

Yuuki clenches his jaw. *I didn't die there in the shed, though.*

"I'm not saying I believe it's over – I know we don't know for sure what's going to happen. But... if there was needing to be a follow-up, they would have done it already. Waiting longer would be disadvantageous to them; it would allow us more time to anticipate or prepare for them launching another attempt at getting to us. I think they fulfilled their main objectives to the best as they could on the first go; it seems like the Ninao incident was as fulfilling as the perpetrators wanted it to be." Timothy's expression is drawn. "That's my gut feeling, anyways."

Yuuki lets out a laugh. "What more could they want to do, anyway?" He lowers his voice and his tone drops to a mutter. "They did plenty. Can we really say they're finished, though?"

Timothy grimaces.

"Maybe you're right, though – that there's nothing more to it. Maybe they already got what they wanted: warning you and catching a hold of me, and locking me up to die a slow death somewhere. What an ironic joke. They had to have known the Youth Rehabilitation Trust was my idea. It's like they wanted me to die like the prisoners the Trust was meant for, f-for those imprisoned, but…"

"We don't know for sure it was about the Trust," Timothy says gently.

"You and I both know it's the only plausible thing."

"There could be something we don't know about, that we're not aware of."

"Like what?" Yuuki snaps.

Timothy's brow is furrowed.

"Why else would they do what they did to us?"

"I don't know."

"What other reason do they –?"

"I don't know what other reason."

Yuuki closes his eyes and exhales slowly. "I'm sorry, I don't mean to… whatever this is."

"It's okay," Timothy murmurs.

Yuuki grimaces. His face heats up, ashamed. *It's not, though, is it?*

"I mean it," Timothy says. Kindly, certain. "I know it's not the same, what we went through – us Harrison family, I mean – compared to your experience, but even we've been each acting and reacting differently than usual. We've been short with each other. We've been tired, and frustrated, more easily than we'd normally be. That's why I'm saying this. It's okay not to be okay. And I get it. I'm not going to judge you personally for it. You're not okay, Yuuki, and it's not fair to expect you *to be* after… after what you went through in that shed."

There's something about Timothy's wording that stabs Yuuki in the gut – that it wasn't the experience of being kidnapped that so traumatised him, but rather, the experience he had being tied up and lost to his mind for three days as he slowly and surely deteriorated towards dying, without knowing if anyone – friend or foe – would come for him.

Colour drained from his face, Yuuki swallows hard. "Thanks."

"Is there…" Timothy begins tentatively. "Is there a reason why you might *want* it to be about the Trust? Why the Ninao incident happened?"

Yuuki's throat constricts. "Then we have someone to blame for it." *Me.* "And…" Tears prick his eyes, painful and hot. He doesn't let them fall. "I don't know? Because I'd already spent so much energy and emotional torment trying to figure out a *why*, and asking the shed walls if they knew the answer."

The look Timothy gives him could be mistaken for pity. But the

374

javelin of pain spearing Yuuki in the gut tells him that it's not pity but *grief*. Sorrow, even, in learning this additional detail about the kind of emotionally psychologically tormenting experience Yuuki had in the shed during those three days.

On the way out, they stop and stand outside the entrance. They'll part ways here – Timothy to work, Yuuki to… wherever. It's Yuuki's day off, and he had nothing else planned but this catch up with Timothy. He expects the older man to leave without delay, but for some reason, Timothy lingers.

Expecting bad news, or a final good-bye, Yuuki tenses.

"So…" Timothy begins awkwardly. He clears his throat to be audible above the noise of the traffic going by on the road. "Yuuki, I know things are hard for you. And sure, I'm going through stuff myself. But if anything comes up and you want to talk, or go for a walk together – with or without venting about, whatever you need – … I'm here, okay?"

Yuuki stands stiffly. His mind is blank for words or a decent reaction to respond with.

"Regardless of the fact that we're both victims of that darn kidnapping, to varying degrees of impact, I'm still your friend. That's not going to change just because you're going through stuff." Timothy raises a hand, hesitates, and then lightly places his hand on Yuuki's shoulder. "Take care, okay? Call me or flick me a text if you need anything."

For whatever reason, Yuuki finds himself unable to promise he will.

Timothy takes his leave.

Yuuki takes a deep breath, and leaves, too.

Yuuki stands on the train, emotionally strained, feeling a numbness settling over his body. It grips his chest, and spreads from there to his shoulders, his arms, his legs, and then to his mind. It suppresses a pummelling emotion he can't name and doesn't want to know about.

"You're not okay, Yuuki, and it's not fair to expect you to be after…"

…after that.

Timothy's right: I'm not okay.

Scenery flashes by in the windows, and Yuuki drifts away from recognising himself. A few stations pass, and Yuuki's thoughts drift back to mulling over making Lee's girlfriend leave. It *was* because of him, wasn't it? Because of the unrelenting 'trauma issues'? She hadn't been like this before – and neither had Yuuki. So what else could it be? At the start, she'd seemed to be fine with taking it in stride. But in hindsight, that only lasted a short while before her awkward tip-toeing around Yuuki's presence turned into an exasperated 'you know what, I can't take this anymore.'

I could have just removed myself from the situation somehow. But then, where else would he go? If he moved, he'd only be placing himself and his stresses in someone else's environment. He'd only be taking himself elsewhere to bother someone else. If he could afford to live alone, he would. But right now, that option is out of the question.

Yuuki has been wondering about asking the Harrisons for help, if things went further south, but they already have a full family and Yuuki doesn't want to impose on them. Joshua might be away at university, but Yuuki would feel bad if he didn't have his room to come back to if Yuuki were to ask to move in there. Moreover... Yuuki is afraid that he'll drive a wedge in between his and Timothy's friendship, and fracture what connection he built up with the Harrison family. He's already wondering if, or when, it might be Lee's turn to leave. What of the Harrisons, what of Timothy?

Yuuki keeps losing things. The interpersonal connections around him, his ability to work,... *himself.* He needs to be better in order to stop that from happening. He'll deny the 'trauma' as much as he needs to, if it keeps him going. He'll pretend he's fine, just like how he got through those first few years living in Japan after his family moved. If that is what it takes, then he'll just have to deal with it.

It's hard enough to find friends as it is. If Lee goes, and or if I lose this friendship with the Harrison family – with Timothy, in particular – then...

Pain pricks his eyes. Grief wells up inside of him, tightening his throat. The anxiety roiling in his stomach is unsettling, and all over the fear of losing the only few friendships he has. No, it's not just that – it's the fear of not being able to cope, of losing and losing more and more until there's nothing left of 'Yuuki Takahashi' to revive. He's already tired from dealing with the impacts that the kidnapping is having on him. How much more will it take from him before it's over, and he can say he's over it?

Yuuki's energy must be so fried, as a burnt electronic circuit, to be spiralling, catastrophising like this.

So much so that he doesn't sense someone coming right up behind him.

The person appears beside him, materialising out of nowhere. There's no warning of their approach. No sound. Their shoes scuffs the train floor and Yuuki flinches. Adrenaline sparks and washes over him. His vision turns white. He reflexively reacts, shoving himself against the vertical handrail at the end of the row of seats that he's been standing by.

It's too late to react if it's someone dangerous, he knows that. But –

But the person who spooked him is a non-threatening quiet teen. After a moment's reassessment of the situation, Yuuki realises that the person is simply awaiting his exit, standing by the doors waiting for the train to stop.

The teen looks at him, eyebrows raised beneath their fringe of shaggy dark brown hair. Non-judgingly, surprisingly. Instead, the expression holds a tired kind of wariness not unlike Yuuki's own. They turn back around to face outside, shifting the weight on their feet as the train slows, and waiting the moment the train will stop as it pulls into the station.

Yuuki looks away, ashamed, and fixes his eyes on the passing scenery outside the window. His nervous system is antsy, shot with adrenaline. Anxiety. His ears burn in shame. He's glad he doesn't startle too badly.

The teen gets off at a stop near a cemetery. As the doors open, and the person walks out, Yuuki notices for the first time that he has flowers with him. Hand-picked wild flowers, probably taken from some empty park field somewhere. He cradles them against himself, protecting them from the wind that blows. By the time the train door shut, the person with the flowers has disappeared into the cemetery.

Kyle Kindall gets off the train.

At the cemetery, he follows the path leading through the site. It's not something he usually would do – visiting graves on anniversary. But Kyle is having a bad time and the grief of Sa'a Kindall's absence hits him hard. This year, he decides to make a day of it.

He stops by where his father's name is written first. It's not even the anniversary of his father's death. Instead, it's his mother's grave he's here to visit. His mother has a grave, at least. His father was burned until they couldn't salvage anything left of him to bury. All that's given for his Dad is a collective monument for the firefighters who perished in the A'o Fire of 8-Tau.

Standing before the monument, Kyle holds tightly onto the wild flowers in his hands. He puts some of them down in a small crack in the tiles of the monument, and finds a stone to keep them from blowing away in the wind. It feels like a pathetically small gesture.

"I still miss you," he murmurs aloud. There's a whole crew of firefighters' names listed here, but Kyle's only speaking to one of them. "I wish you were still around." He clenches his jaw. His throat tightens. He waits until the stress passes before adding, brokenly, "You're the only friend I ever had. And you're the only one who cared."

His seventeenth birthday just passed and his foster family got him nothing. He didn't expect anything, and he doesn't need or necessarily *want* anything. But it's like they didn't even care to remember it was his birthday – didn't care about *him*. They don't particularly want him, he knows; they're only doing it out of pity that he has nowhere else to go. The feeling is mutual: Kyle doesn't want to stay at that house or with them any longer than he legally has to.

After that...

After that, then...

Kyle wishes his father at least were still alive.

The grief of losing both of them hard – one full of guilt and the other full of loneliness. If he had friends he could talk with, perhaps it wouldn't be so bad. But he's an introverted social isolate, half-Arkala'ana and a social outcast.

The wind rustles the trees, and leaves skitter by on the pavement. Kyle breathes. "I know it's been four years already. But I…"

He thinks of his classmate Sam and her family. Apparently the victim of the June Ninao Kidnapping was a family friend of theirs. Yuuki Takahashi. For whatever reason, Kyle still remembers that name from all the times he'd heard or seen it in news updates. He hasn't heard of that name since, though. He wonders how that person is doing in the aftermath of the Ninao incident. He wonders, briefly, how they're all doing. There's been no news on the Ninao kidnapping and why it happened. Nothing has happened to Sam, so that's a good thing. And Sam seems to be coping, at least from what he's seen of her at school. It's good he's not alone – he's got the support of Sam's family, and whoever else, right?

In contrast, Kyle feels alone. So utterly alone.

"How do you even live in the aftermath of something like that?" Kyle murmurs.

I suppose it helps having a support system.

With or without a 'support system', Kyle vows to pull through just one more year. Then he'll be able to leave the foster family scene behind and support and live for himself. As long as nothing happens to him in the meantime – nothing out of the blue like what happened to Sam's family, he should be able to do it.

Kyle visits his mother's grave – an earthly residence for someone he never knew. It's partially his own fault: she passed away only a couple of days after giving birth to him. With his thoughts in a whirl, and turning against himself, he doesn't linger. He sets down the remaining flowers, secures them with a rock as he did with the first lot, then gets up from the grave, and reluctantly starts the journey home.

This grief and loneliness... he doesn't realise he's echoing the same tone of grief of the stranger he met on the train. Kyle also doesn't realise that, in between half a year and a year's time, the lives of himself and that stranger will become more intertwined than either of them are prepared for.

He doesn't realise that that stranger was Yuuki Takahashi.

Yuuki walks back home, taking a long way home through Two Lakes. Avoiding Lee. Avoiding that house. Distracting himself.

The cherry blossoms lining the driveway of one of the lakeside parks are in bloom. It's a pretty sight. Beneath some of the trees, some people are taking pictures and selfies. Not quite *hanami* like culturally done in Japan, but '*hanami*' enough. Usually, at this time of year, Yumiko would have flown down to spend time in Arkala with Yuuki, and to enjoy the blossoms. But her savings for such a trip got used up visiting him in the A'o District Hospital in June instead.

Maybe next year, if the weather is good – and if no physical or metaphorical storms come sweeping by to snatch away the opportunity for a decent *hanami*.

A year feels like such a lengthy stretch of time from here. Yuuki doesn't want to think about what might happen in that time, and what he might lose by the time the next year's sakura flowers have lost all their petals again.

That feeling lingers with him the rest of the way home.

40

Weeks go by, and then another month passes, and the date of the Ninao Kidnapping falls further and further into "the past".

Yuuki tries to return to normality, but can't.

The seasons change, but for Yuuki, it's still winter. Yuuki has no choice but to respond to it, but psychologically he's still processing what happened during those mid-winter days in the start of June. Around him, the days are slowly warming up, and the weather is constantly changing. Normal spring weather, albeit with some influence of climate change. The weather is telling him that time is moving, and that life is moving on from what the winter brought. Yuuki is stuck, however, tethered down against his will, as though the seasons never began to change for him in the first place.

Yuuki stares at the worksheet in front of him, mind blank. He needs to fill it in. Preferably before his shift's over – which is in fifteen minutes from now – but he's barely managed to write anything. He should've had all the notes written by now. Or, at least, be writing the last details down.

The vertical line blinks. Yuuki still can't call forth any of the words he needs. So far, all that's on the page is the general information of his work shift and ID, and a half formed sentence sitting in the 'comments' box.

He puts his elbows up on the desk and buries his face in his hands. *Why is it so hard to do this?*

"Yuuki?"

Yuuki jolts. Adrenaline spikes in his blood as he resumes an 'at-work, yes I'm working on this' position. "Yes?"

Mitchell is standing in the doorway with a coffee and a tired expression. A frown creases his brow.

Oh no, I'm in trouble.

"Are you okay?"

Yuuki fixes his expression to mask as much stress as he's able. He nods. "Fine, thanks. Sorry, I'll get this to you real soon."

Mitchell takes a sip of his coffee. He regards Yuuki – no, *the computer screen* – a moment longer before his eyes flick to Yuuki's face once more, then he continues on his way without entering the room.

Sitting there in the silence, Yuuki can only wonder what Mitchell is thinking.

Yuuki's not up to the same work ethic as he should be. He knows that. Mitchell knows that. In fact, Mitchell probably sees it far more than Yuuki would like him to. As of yet, Yuuki hasn't told him about these concentration difficulties, or about how his body tenses up when he's having to check on the youth, or how he startles at sudden sounds and movements so easily. But it won't be long before Mitchell notices these things anyways. If he hasn't already.

Yuuki sighs, and turns back to the document. In the end, what's on the screen is all he submits – albeit with a few extra words to make that half written sentence a more complete sounding one.

The next day there is someone in the isolation unit wing. Mitchell, his senior officer, asks him to get the kid. "Yuuki, can you go escort the kid on time out back to their cell?"

Time out – aka sent to the temporary isolation unit for an hour to get one's emotions back in check.

Yuuki doesn't think anything of it. He really should have.

Yuuki only opens the door and the panic sets it almost instantly. It grips his body like claws. Violently, it digs into his chest like a sharpened spade. A sharpened rusty spade, the rust which sends adrenaline flooding through his veins like an infection.

Yuuki braces a hand against the doorway. There's no one in this cell. He must have the wrong number. Maybe that's fortunate, because Yuuki can't shake this feeling that's come over him. He can't get enough air in his lungs.

Yuuki lets out a strangled gasp. *Stupid situational awareness security training on overdrive. There's nothing out there! There's no one about to harm you!* But it seriously feels like there is. Yuuki can't convince his nervous system that there's not. It drives that nervousness further, because he can't tell whether the threat is truly real or not.

What if he ignores a gut feeling, and it lands him back in a similar situation to the shed? Does he really think he can afford to risk subjecting himself to that kind of experience all over again? Does he really think he'd be able to endure, let alone recover from that?

His workmate on shift with him comes by five minutes later. Her footsteps slow as she approaches.

"Yuuki? Is something the matter?"

Yuuki, leaning shakily against the doorway, hands gripping it like he'll crumble if he so much as releases a finger... he's obviously not okay. It's shameful. He's hyperventilating, whilst staring at nothing nonetheless.

He steels himself. Swallows. Internalises the panic and does his best to ignore the way his blood pressure drops as he straightens himself.

"I'm fine," he says, voice thin. *Yeah, like that was convincing.*

His workmate merely raises her eyebrows. She blinks, as though she's not sure what to do with acting-really-weirdly Yuuki. "I came to get the kid," she says. "I thought Mitchell sent you to get him, but..."

Yuuki nods. "He did. Sorry, I-I..."

She waves her hand dismissively and sighs. "Don't worry, I'll do it. Go step out for some air or something if you need it."

Her sigh is laden with tiredness, exasperation... annoyance. It taints her tone so much that it's clear she hasn't the energy to try to mask it, let alone the care to.

She leaves, and Yuuki is left to figure out what triggered him so badly.

It's the temporary isolation cells, isn't it?

It's separate from the solitary confinement units, which are located on the other side of admin. But it's similar an environment enough to cause Yuuki to reel – similar enough to the confining space of the shed, in which he was left to experience a deteriorating state of mind and body, and in which he was left to die in. The chaos in his mind was the worst part of it.

Looking at the cells, even just taking a glimpse of the inside of them, is enough to remind Yuuki *vividly* of that experience all over again.

Frustrated with himself, Yuuki goes for a hard run after he gets home. He's tired, he's exhausted, but he's angry and desperate to try burn through some of his stress. His energy flags faster than it used to, but he ignores it. He'll go for as long run as he needs to in order to cool off, if necessary.

If I run longer, and faster, I won't have the energy to think…

Usually, that would be how it would be. But Yuuki's brain doesn't allow him such reprieve. Instead, it amplifies the voices in his head so that Yuuki can hear Mitchell's tone just as clearly. The zoned out white noise of running isn't loud enough – isn't enough of a silencer – to drown it out. And beyond that, he can still see the kid, his colleague and his senior officer's perplexed, disappointed expressions.

Lol, what's up with you?

Leave your issues at home – you're at work.

Go home, Yuuki. You're not any good to us here like this.

Yuuki finds a steep hill to run up. He puts all his strength into angrily pushing his legs up it. Twists. Swings his arms from side to side. Digs his elbows into the air and his fingers into his hands. His shoes slam into the road. At the top of the hill, he's running on breathlessness and lactic acid. Shortage of sugar in the blood. He feels sick now, and still angry. He pants in a failed effort to regain control of his breathing. Each exhale is rough and he hates the way each inhale has an edge of desperation to their final notes.

What am I even desperate for? Desperate for what? Sleep — dreamless sleep? Energy? For my brain to let me live and get on with my life without interfering with all this stupid kidnapping aftermath stress stuff?

When he gets home, he's feeling like his body is leaning towards the ground. The scenery around him is warped. He skips the cool down. His legs are too wobbly. He's shaking. Hands fumbling for the house key he can't even grip properly.

He hopes the neighbours aren't seeing this.

Finally, Yuuki gets the door unlocked and stumbles inside. The dim light is soothing. The house is warmer than outside. Usually Yuuki wouldn't mind it, since it's a nice neutral warmth. But right now Yuuki is frustrated and nauseous, and the warm air doesn't help quell that nausea.

He gets inside and stumbles for the tap. *Glass, I need a glass.* But he stops, hand braced against the edge of the bench, when his spatial awareness warps again. Swirls. Yuuki can feel the loss of colour to his face.

There's an energy drink of vitamin water in the pantry. Yuuki would prefer cold water, but looking at the less-risk-during-accessing bottle of recovery fluid there…

Yuuki blanks out his mind. He focuses his attention and energy on retrieving that bottle of water, not falling over, ignoring how his knee buckles on the way back to the bench, and his nausea. After a weak attempt to take the cap lid off, he puts an excessive amount of effort into getting into it. The cap flies off and his hand follows it across the bench. Yuuki breathes out carefully, props himself back up again and drinks.

Half the bottle vanishes in one go. Yuuki's head feels somewhat better. The shakiness in his body doesn't. On legs that feel like they'll give way at any second, he moves over to the couch. Despite the sweat still clinging to his clothes, Yuuki sits. He puts the drink bottle down on the table, gripping it like he's trying to stake it there.

Unbidden, Timothy's words replay in his head. *"You're not okay, Yuuki."*

Rest. He just needs to rest for a moment.

It's not long before it happens – that Yuuki's issues become hazardous: one day makes a mistake, and someone gets hurt because of it.

It happens outside work, at work. Yuuki's coming back from dropping paperwork off at the law administration building across the carpark when he sees there's a girl at the admin with a PF officer. She's upset, if raised voice is anything to go by. Based on what Yuuki hears as he's approaching the building, she's wanting to visit her friend who's in the detention centre, but the officer barring her way isn't letting her.

The girl swears. "...okay, whatever, but why the hell is it so difficult to get?"

"Like I've already told you," the PF officer says, casting a glance in Yuuki's direction. "Your friend has expressed that she doesn't *want* to see you."

"Yeah, right."

"So please take that into consideration, and respect her wishes."

"She can tell me that herself!"

Yuuki clears his throat. "What's going on here?"

The girl seizes the opportunity. "This piece of birdshit right here won't let me visit my friend who got sent here."

Language, Yuuki thinks, but he doesn't say it.

"Her friend was incarcerated for drug abuse," the PFO explains. "This young lady here also was charged with the same thing, but let off with a lighter sentence."

"Are you on probation?" Yuuki asks the girl.

"Rehab," the girl mutters. "But at least I'm frickin' allowed to have rehab. Why can't my friend be allowed to have the same?""

The PFO sighs. "Because your friend had other charges to her name." *They sounds like they're repeating themself,* Yuuki wonders.

"She stole money because she wanted therapy, goddammit! I didn't even want therapy, and they gave it to me when they could've given it to her, or at least both of us."

"They gave 'it' to you?"

"The Youth Rehabilitation Trust."

Yuuki's blood runs cold.

"And the judge wouldn't even let her apply! Said she was at too high a risk of reoffending and deserved detention first."

Yuuki forces himself not to think about the YRT. About who created it. About the implications of it. About how the people standing in front of him seem so oblivious to the connection between it, and Yuuki, and the kidnapping incident that occurred in Ninao on June 5th.

He manages, "How long's your friend in detention for?"

"Twelve weeks. It's only the second."

The PFO exchanges a look with Yuuki. "I apologise for the trouble, but it is really not a good idea to have them meet."

The girl's hands curl into fists. "I already told you –"

"They might pose a risk to each other. I'll escort her away – I'm in charge of supervising her while she's on probation. Good day to you, sir."

"Hang on." Yuuki stops them.

The officer raises an eyebrow.

Yuuki asks, "Would be alright to at least take her in for five minutes? They can meet in the meeting room. Five minutes. If the situation isn't... favourable, as you say, then she can leave."

The PF officer looks dubious, but a quick look at the body language of the girl they're supervising tells them all he needs to know: the girl will not be leaving on her own will unless she at least is allowed some chance to see her friend.

"Five minutes, then," the PFO says. "On the condition that you will leave when that five minutes is up, and that you will leave without raising an issue. Understood?"

The girl's shoulders are stiff, but the sharp spark of anger in her eyes seems to have died down a little.

"Understood?"

"...whatever."

Yuuki offers a grimace of a smile. "Okay. What's your friend's name?"

"Vienna. Tell her Rose came to visit."

"Rose is your name?"

"Well, duh."

"Okay, Rose. I'll go in and see her. I'll bring her out to meet you in the meeting room if she agrees to meet you, but you do need to be aware that if she does not wish to meet you as the officer here says, then that's something you'll need to accept. That all good?"

The girl, Rose, agrees.

Once in, Yuuki goes and fetches the friend. The rows of cells unsettle him. He makes a beeline for the group cell number 'Vienna' is recorded to be in. One of the three girls in the cell respond at the call of the name, and comes forward.

"Your friend wants to see you."

"Friend?"

Yuuki can't read her expression. "Rose. She's outside wanting to meet you."

The girl grunts. "I thought we weren't allowed to see each other."

That's not a detail that was mentioned. "Five minutes. We can allow five minutes."

"I don't really want to see her…"

Yuuki waits.

"…actually, okay. Five minutes. I'll have a talk with her, make her not come back."

There's a red flag present in her tone that Yuuki fails to recognise.

As per protocol, he ought to place her in handcuffs. But it's always made Yuuki uncomfortable, and the recent experience of being restrained in that shed for three days makes him sick to the stomach just thinking about it. He can't compel himself to follow through with what he should be doing for safety measures. He doesn't handcuff her, on the rationale that it will only be five minutes. That, and also the fact that both he and the PF officer will be supervising them both and can intervene if necessary.

So Yuuki goes against protocol. It's the first time he's done so, and it's a mistake. Allowing this interference of personal trauma is a bad mistake.

Once out, the friend acts calmly, albeit a little too calmly. When she comes to meet Rose, however, she launches herself out of Yuuki's grip and starts attacking Rose, yelling that it's her fault for ratting them both out and being too honest for her own good. Moreover, she's upset that she got sent to prison instead of receiving rehab like Rose, like she actually *wanted* – she wants to try therapy, she doesn't want to be like this. Rose, on the other hand, apparently didn't care for therapy anywhere near what her friend did.

Yuuki hears this, struggling to process it. He feels like he's hearing it from another person's point of view, and he's struggling to process this feeling of separation from himself, too. But right now, there's more urgent matters to deal with, namely separating the two. Even with the PFO assisting, Yuuki struggles to part them, and gets kicked at. The PF officer also gets kicked at, and yelled at by Vienna's accompanying scream of "Stop touching me!"

In the end, Mitchell has to come and help.

And Yuuki, who didn't see him coming, reflexively lashes out and hits Mitchell hard in the face.

In the moment of stunned silence that follows, Mitchell seizes the opportunity to grab the girl, pull her into a restraint as appropriate, and escort her back to a temporary isolation area for calming down.

As they leave, Mitchell tells Yuuki to escort Rose out. The PF officer accompanies Mitchell.

Yuuki, meanwhile, is still reeling from the fact that he hit Mitchell. He hit his boss. After failing to adhere to protocol and causing an incident like this in which Mitchell had to come and intervene. Shaking the thought, or rather – dismissing it for later, Yuuki escorts an upset and startled Rose out.

Outside, Rose protests. "This is all because she got shoved in there! It's unfair! Why'd we have to get different sentences? Why isn't she allowed rehab instead, like me?"

Yuuki pushes aside the shakiness in his hands. Somehow his voice manages to be steady. "The imprisonment time is to remove her from the environment which caused her or encouraged her to do the things she did. It's supposed to be so that she has time away from that environment, and so that we can try to organise for her to be in a healthier place if necessary. Who was the judge of the trial?"

"I don't know, some Harris guy or something."

Yuuki pauses. "Harris*on?*"

Rose raises her hands in an exasperated shrug.

"If it was Timothy Harrison who was the judge of your guys' trial, then you both should consider yourselves fortunate that she ended up with the sentence she did. The prosecution can push for worse sentences, you know. And given the current national policies for youth justice, they often do."

That would also explain why Rose was left off with probation and granted help from the Youth Rehabilitation Trust.

"I know twelve weeks seems like a long time. But if you were able to get help from the Youth Rehabilitation Trust, then

Rose blinks. "Oh, you know about that Trust? Nobody seems to know about it. They look at me like I'm making things up. I'm not."

"You're not," Yuuki says stiffly. *I should know, I made it.* "But it's new, and... there were some complications with the coordination and management side of things, so word might take a while to get out there."

"At least that judge knew about it then. And my lawyer."

Yuuki hums. It's welcome news to hear that at least one youth advocate has heard about the Trust, too. *Not that I've been of any help getting it off the ground and spreading awareness of it among the relevant justice sectors. I've just been... what have I been doing?* It occurs to Yuuki that, while he's been dealing with the aftermath of the Ninao kidnapping incident, Timothy must've hauling both his own and Yuuki's weight in the Trust management. Even with the Arkala'ana-Chinese couple helping – Yuuki can't recall their names, since it was in hospital that he met them and everything's been overwhelming since then – Timothy is still supervising. Timothy remains the final authority in decisions when it comes to the Trust.

Thinking about it like this, Yuuki realises how detached from the whole project he feels. It's like the moment he left that shed – another something he doesn't remember – the ties he had willingly knotted between himself and the Youth Rehabilitation Trust were severed. Or maybe it happened earlier, at some point in time during those seventy five hours he was trapped in that shed for. *Seventy five hours.* Compared to the imprisonment times that the kids who come in here get, that seventy five hours is nothing. It was three days, not three months. It wasn't –

But three days of solitary confinement here, even, is different to three days of solitary confinement in a shed via kidnapping, tied up, gagged, abandoned, left without food or water, left without any proper reason why or any indication of where he might be and when he might see that door open...

Yuuki doesn't know if he could handle it, though: learning of anyone sentenced to solitary confinement here. It doesn't happen often. At least, when it does happen, it's normally only temporary, or for some initial period before the person is moved to a shared cell. Still...if it were to happen...

But he saw how he acted when he was sent to retrieve that kid on time out in temporary solitary confinement the other day. If he came to work one day and found out they had someone in isolation for more than three days, he wouldn't be able to keep his personal issues at bay. Yuuki knows personally what the isolation aspect of such a thing can do to the mind, regardless of differences in situation. Even an introverted person would soon feel suffocated and trapped. It would be more bearable if they were given things to preoccupy themselves and their minds, but...

The shed. Dust. Painfully dragging daylight.

Gnawing hunger and muscle pains. Unrelenting aching, draining, stiffness, numbing, exhaustion...

Anguish.

Psychological wrestling with his own voice.

Emotional turmoil, fluctuating – between temporary suppression of feeling and uncontrollable confusion-amplified and stress-fuelled overwhelm.

And the questioning.

And bargaining.

And wondering, why, and who exactly, and when will...

Someone clears their throat.

Yuuki lurches out of the memories.

"Anyway," Rose says, glancing at Yuuki with a raised eyebrow at his weird probably distant expression and sudden silence. "I'll go then."

On autopilot, Yuuki nods.

"Thanks for…for letting me see her."

"That's alright." He tries to reorient himself to the here and now. It half succeeds. "I'm sorry things turned out the way they did."

Rose waves her hand in a dismissing action.

"And about rehab for your friend, I think it's possible for her," Yuuki assures. "There'll be someone come in to talk to her, and if she's serious about being willing to go to rehab after, they can help her apply for funding for therapy from the same Youth Rehabilitation Trust, provided she finishes her sentence here. It might be possible for her to have her time in detention reduced, but – " *given what just happened today, I don't think that's likely, so* – "I wouldn't get your hopes up."

Rose listens.

"Also, it's likely that you won't be able to visit her again while she's here – primarily due to the terms of your own probation terms and of your friend's sentence clashing a little. The outcome of your seeing each other today won't help that case, of course. It'll help her friend's application for therapy funding if you don't meet, in fact, since it'll decrease the 'likely to reoffend' sentiment that may turn her friend's sentence into an extended period."

Rose curses the Arkala justice system, then amends, "At least this Youth Rehabilitation Trust thing exists now. There needs to be more like it."

She doesn't realise, does she, that me and Timothy are the ones who established it? She doesn't realise that she's talking to one of the people who created it… let alone what happened because of it…

Then again, when the kidnapping happened, the media didn't mention the Youth Rehabilitation Trust too much when writing about the incident for public media, did they? It stirs doubt in Yuuki's only mind. Why wouldn't they mention it? Unless it wasn't necessary, or the PF feel that a reason shouldn't be given unless it can be confirmed. Or…do the PF suspect there to be another reason?

Yuuki's mind whirls.

It was a speculation that couldn't be confirmed, that the kidnapping happened because of the YRT, a speculation first drawn by the fact that the timing of both things coincided with each other. It's not a speculation that's been ruled out entirely. Yuuki and Timothy have sure had it going around in their heads and in their own lives like a public broadcast. The Peace Forces are probably following that as one of the only possible leads out there. But it seems like this bit of information – this possible connection – has been kept within the bounds of the PF investigation. There's been no follow-ups from the media. Oddly, both Timothy and Yuuki have been left in relative peace.

Which means that the general public don't know that Yuuki and Timothy had been finalising the Trust at the time of the kidnapping. They don't know that connection, that reason. Yuuki hasn't gone out of his way to read the news to double check, but given how he's not come across it or heard rumours or gossip about it around work, that's apparently how it is.

So then… no one really knows that the reason I was kidnapped was likely because of the Trust…

The thoughts of the Ninao incident linger as Rose takes her leave, and Yuuki's left standing in the carpark feeling detached from the world around him.

"The Trust existing now isn't all a good thing," he murmurs aloud, to no one, to himself. He swallows. His throat tightens. It's helped people – is helping people – just like Yuuki had hoped it would. But it's also damaged people.

Would it be better if it didn't exist at all?

Is it selfish of me if I wish, even a little bit, that I had never pursued setting up the Youth Rehabilitation Trust in the first place?

Without knowing what will become of the Trust in future, let alone what will become of himself, Yuuki doesn't know exactly how he feels about it. He doesn't know what he wishes of it – only that the Trust could've been established peacefully, quietly, and the kidnapping that happened on June 5th never happened.

It happened, though. Yuuki has to find a way to deal with it.

'Deal with it'. If only it were that simply.

He sighs, turns. Straightens his expression, as best as he can. Fixes his composure. Shoves all stray threads of thoughts of that kidnapping and that shed experience to the back of his mind in a muddled, knotting mess.

He broke protocol, because of that mess. Instead of unravelling that mess, it's unravelling him. However, with or without having a say over in, Yuuki still has to take accountability for his actions. It's not something he can, or should, avoid.

I better head back inside, then, he decides, *and face whatever wrath or repercussions Mitchell has for me.*

Mitchell is holding an ice pack against his cheek. When he shifts to adjust it, Yuuki sees the blooming bruise beneath it.

Yuuki winces. He bows his head, then lets his stance fall into a chest-deep bow. This isn't Japan. He doesn't need to do this. But he'd trained himself to express sentiment in this way and now it's become a habit that's stuck. It's also the only form of expression he feels is adequate for the circumstance.

Mitchell signs. "It's okay, Yuuki."

Yuuki raises his head again. He keeps his gaze averted, downward, fixed on the floor beneath their feet. "I know I messed up."

"I'm more concerned about you than I am of the result of the situation."

Yuuki presses his mouth into a line. He clears his throat. He nods.

"What's going on?"

"I broke protocol."

"Yes, you did. But that's not exactly what I'm most concerned about."

Yuuki meets Mitchell's eyes. *Well, at least he's not livid.*

"This," Mitchell says, raising the ice pack in gesture. "You've never reacted like this before."

Oh... "About that, I'm sorry, I..."

"I" what? Over-reacted? Got started? Didn't see you there, oops — my bad?

"Is this a trauma thing?" Mitchell asks.

Yuuki can't decipher the tone his senior officer uses. Is it concern, or disgust, or disappointment, or a mix of all of it?

"Look, your decision to not use handcuffs – I'm dismissing that as a minor error since it wasn't without lack of judgement. I know you don't do things without a reason. You've been diligent in following protocol where it's necessary, and in the occasional time you've chosen to deviate from it, it's been with fair enough judgement and no incident has arisen from it.

"But this...? I'm not scolding you for it. I'm just...based on observations, I'm thinking if it would be wise if you took some more time off."

Yuuki's heart sinks.

"I think you need some time away from this place."

"No, I can work."

"I appreciate your willingness to work, but this sort of thing hasn't happened before with you."

Things don't often get violent in the meeting room. Unless mistakes are made. And misunderstandings happen. And security wardens don't react in the ways they're supposed to.

"You don't usually react to things like you've been doing lately. I think you need more time off."

Yuuki feels frustration prick his skin. "I can work."

"Not effectively."

"I'll do better."

"Yuuki. This isn't about that. I know you're a good warden. I know what your usual work ethic is. But what I'm observing right now is that recent circumstances are having an impact on you and your ability to meet that same level of work ability. You're not over your experience that you had. And from what I can see, this workplace isn't helping."

"It'll pass. I'm sorry, I shouldn't be letting it affect me like this."

Mitchell regards with pity. "If I'm not wrong, it'll keep affecting you unless you acknowledge it for what it is and give yourself the time off that's due. I'll extend your paid leave – we're paid by Taularh's Ministry of Justice officials anyway, as you know, so I can send the application through tonight and it should get processed fairly quickly, given your circumstances. Just…give yourself some more time to get over things…"

'Get over things'. Yuuki clenches his jaw hard. Telling himself that is one thing; hearing it from someone else is another.

"…and when you come back, you'll probably find you're able to handle working again."

Yuuki suppresses his anger. Anger at himself. "Is there anything I can do in the meantime, or before my shift is over today, then?"

Mitchell closes his eyes and shakes his head.

"…then what do you want me to do?"

"Go home, Yuuki," Mitchell tells him, but not in an unkind way.

The fight in him lingers, but Yuuki knows that this stubbornness needs to give way. In this state, he wouldn't be able to carry out his duties properly if another situation arose where he needed to be able to. In this state, he's more a hindrance than a help. Yuuki clearly isn't fine to stay right now.

They'll be finer without him, too.

They had enough staff on to be fine in his absence.

On his way out, Yuuki keeps his eyes downcast. He signs out, his signature a half-hearted scribble that makes it look fake. He grabs his coat, slips it on even though it's warm outside. Disheartened, he leaves.

It feels wrong, leaving before his shift is over. At this time of day.

He feels wrong. Not like himself anymore. Not the Yuuki Takahashi he strived so hard to be, who he wanted to be…who he was, and should be, but isn't.

Standing on the train, he makes a conscious effort to cover up his security officer uniform as much as he can. The teal shirt, at least. He soon gets too warm, as expected. It's not as cold as it was this morning. But the lack of additional clothing would only make him feel exposed. If he wants to hide, then he shouldn't draw attention to himself. Taking his jacket off would only draw attention to himself.

As if standing on a train when there's seats available isn't standing out enough.

It's less about standing out in general, though, and more about standing out because of his uniform. Being seen in uniform means he'll be judged as a security officer. Because of the confidence he ought to be conveying through his body language, but right now likely isn't. He's tired. He's ashamed, and guilty. Failing, falling backwards. Concealing his security officer uniform means he can partially conceal how much he's falling short of how a warden at a youth detention centre should be. Even if no one knows these failures, it feels better to be clothed in a too-warm jacket than to be clothed in a heavy cloak of shame.

The train ride towards home is a silent one. Yuuki's chest feels so empty.

41

After that day he was sent home, it becomes increasingly apparent – Yuuki can't handle work. Can't handle seeing young people being put away in cells the size of the garden shed he was locked in, or seeing the ones who raise a ruckus being handled with restraints.

It's worse with any issue involving the temporary isolation unit, or the solitary confinement cells. There's a reason why Mitchell hasn't put him on any shifts which involve the latter. That's why Mitchell hasn't wanted him on any shifts at all.

Yuuki insists he can work, *wants* to work. He understands Mitchell's reasoning, his caution. And he appreciates being looked out for financially, in that he is able to receive paid leave while he recovers some more. But Yuuki feels useless. Frustrated. Even with the limited amount of A'o Youth Detention Centre paperwork he's given as 'work', it's not enough.

So they compromise, in the end: Yuuki is allowed to work part time in-person at the detention centre, however, what hours he's given will depend on his capacity to work safely. The hours that he's no longer scheduled to be at work for will have to be replaced by someone else.

With the staff already at their maximum workload, and the Christmas and New Year holidays right around the corner, though, this means that they'll be short-staffed.

It seems like Mitchell is already anticipating that things aren't going to improve in the course of two weeks, though. One day that Yuuki has hours on night shift minding surveillance, he sees a business card for a contracted security company on the desk, and a half written job description on the computer that Mitchell likely left and forgot about.

...are they already looking at replacing me?

The disappointment Yuuki experiences is replaced by guilt. By shame. By understanding, and an acceptance that climbs on board like it had been waiting for this train of fate to arrive at his station for a while.

If I want to stay, then I'm just going to have to step up my game. Push past these issues of mine. They're personal issues that I shouldn't be letting get in my way. It's not as if I was tortured in that shed. I should be over it already. Nothing happened to me in that shed. What did happen happened months ago.

Pushing past his issues is a far-fetched ideal. All it leads to is a faster burn-out, and a crashing of health that comes harder and heavier than Yuuki ever thought to consider.

December, 12-Tau

Yuuki's birthday, December 6th. He doesn't celebrate it.

Yuuki carries on.

He continues to work, feeling increasingly gloomy. Or lethargic. Or...

405

some kind of detached out of it state of mind. Not quite depression, but something kindred to it. He feels vague in himself.

It makes him reconsider what Susan once said about the 'trauma' thing.

Late December, 12-Tau

One day he can't get out of bed, he has no energy. He has hours that day. Some staff wanted time off for Christmas – naturally, Yuuki, who isn't spending time with family, was asked to come in. They might be short-staffed, in other words.

Even knowing that, though, Yuuki finds he cannot move.

He should dig deep, and muster up energy through sheer willpower to get himself to work. But the moment he turns his head, everything around him spins. Dizziness washes through him like vertigo and seasickness. Yuuki covers his face with his right arm – the movement sending another disorienting wave of dizziness through him – and takes a few deep breaths. He swallows hard.

I don't think I can go to work like this. Yuuki knows what Mitchell would say of him if he showed up at work in such a state, especially considering how Yuuki has been in recent times. He won't be able to do his job properly like this, let alone make it to the train station without falling over. Yesterday, Yuuki couldn't sit up for longer than 15 mins without feeling dizzy. It's sleep deprivation and insomnia, and stress and fatigue, getting to him.

THE NINAO INCIDENT

With his eyes closed, bracing against the ill feeling, Yuuki reaches out with his other arm and fumbles for his phone.

Yuuki decides he has no choice but to: he calls off work, sick.

When the message reply dings on his phone several minutes later, he half expects Mitchell to ask him to go to the doctor's for a medical certificate. But he doesn't. Mitchell knows what's up, that Yuuki's been having trouble with his health of late. Yuuki swallows back nausea now mixing with shame and guilt and relief.

How long can this last, though?

He's not fired yet, but he wonders how long it will be before he is. Or, at least, before he's no longer fit for the job. He's been mostly just in surveillance lately, or managing paperwork. Anything but the practical – the stuff he's likely to mess up. His frequency of showing up to work in person, at the actual detention centre, is becoming less and less.

Yuuki doesn't want to think about what he'll do if he can't function there anymore – let alone if he can't work as a security officer anymore. He falls asleep before the fear and the grief can carry him any further.

A knock on the door. A voice.

Yuuki stirs with a groan.

The voice comes again, and a woman's voice he recognises but his brain is too foggy to pinpoint.

Was someone meant to be coming? Belatedly, Yuuki checks his phone. It's after 11am, and there's a message from Susan Harrison on the screen. The rest of the words are blurry. Yuuki's eyes won't focus on them.

Another knock on the door. "Yuuki, it's Susan. Are you home?"

Oh.

Yuuki hauls himself off the couch. His vision whirls. He trips over the edge of his blanket, and stumbles the rest of the way over to the door. Eyes bleary, he fumbles to unlock the door and pushes the door open.

Susan is standing outside, a supermarket bag slung over one arm. It's full of lemons. She opens her mouth to speak, but is stopped by her taking in the visual representation of Yuuki's current state of health circumstances.

"Sorry, I didn't answer your message," he mumbles. His voice is thick with exhaustion and sleep. He clears his throat. "I only just woke up. I was napping." *It was the only sleep I could get in the last two days, but that's that.*

The way Susan looks him tells him that she already guessed.

"What's up?"

"Timothy said he heard that you had been taking some time off work," Susan says softly. "I wanted to check in with you, make sure you're alright."

Yuuki attempts a smile. But he's keenly aware of how drained his face must look right now, and how the shadows smudged into his skin beneath his eyes must appear.

"Do you mind if I come in, for a bit?"

"If you want. Sorry if the place is a bit of a mess."

Susan grunts. "You're fine. I'm not a real estate agent here for a room inspection. I did bring lemons, however. If you want some."

Thinking about that, Yuuki can't help but stress. *That's right – there probably will be another one of those coming up soon, won't there? Another room inspection.* With Rachel gone, it's just Lee and Yuuki responsible for tidying things. But Lee's away for a few weeks. That means that the responsibility of ensuring the whole place is clean and tidy falls on Yuuki's shoulders. The last time it was fine, but Yuuki's run out of energy to help with chores lately, and Lee has been out more often than not now.

Yuuki sighs, and shoves that thought to the back of his mind. Another thing to file into the 'deal with later, after resting' pile.

Inside, Susan deposits the bag of lemons on the kitchen counter. Yuuki takes a moment to turn around and yawn, and rub at his eyes that don't seem to want to stop stinging. It doesn't go unnoticed, though.

"Yuuki, have you been sleeping?" Susan asks. Her tone is quiet, as though a volume too loud will be all that it takes to send Yuuki reeling.

Yuuki takes some time to decide how he should answer. "I've slept."

It's the truth. He has slept; it's not like he's gone the extent of several days without any.

"And when you do," Susan says, "do you have nightmares?"

Yuuki's throat tightens. He stares a little harder at the spot on the couch his gaze seems to be fixed on. Snapshots of the recent dreams he's had flick through his mind. They're different scenes from the reality of what happened to him in Timothy's office, and in the shed. But they're still all too vivid in his memory, and his body recalls what it felt like to experience both the imagined and the not imagined reality.

"Judging by your face right now, yes, you have been."

With a sharp exhale, Yuuki focuses his eyes back to the face in front of him. The lines beneath his eyes pull and hurt. His eyes water. He gives a small nod. "Yeah." And then, a moment later he confesses, "Haven't really been wanting to try sleep because of them."

Susan hums. "I see why you wouldn't."

Susan watches him without pity, without any kind of overexpressed sympathy in her eyes. Instead there's a discerning look about her expression, a careful concern, and...

Pain.

Why is she even...? It's similar to Timothy's reactions. *I'm not even family. I wouldn't even call myself a family friend right now. Not when I've brought this trauma into their lives. Sure, Timothy had worked on developing the Youth Rehabilitation Trust with me, but if it hadn't been for me thinking it was such a great idea to go ahead and turn it into something real in the first place...*

It's my fault the kidnapping happened. What's become of me is, by indirect consequence, my own fault. The Harrison family didn't deserve to be dealt that hand in fate...and they sure don't deserve to have to deal with me in the aftermath of it either.

Yuuki bows his head. It's nothing but an act of defeat, of exhaustion. Of apology. If Susan will be able to recognise it, let alone accept it, as such.

He takes a deep breath. "I, uh...I'll be fine. So...you don't need to worry about me. I'll manage. I'm managing."

"You are."

"Yeah, so –"

"You're managing alone, though."

Something sharp strikes Yuuki in the chest. He blinks. The sharpness shifts to churn in his stomach.

"Yuuki," Susan murmurs. She looks away to give him emotional privacy. "Our family has had each other in this. Timothy and I have been looking out for Joshua and Samantha. Joshua's been checking in with me and Sam, particularly when Tim isn't in the right mind to – doesn't have the emotional capacity to, is what I mean. And Sam's been doing a hell of a hard job looking after herself, et cetera. Everyone is looking out for each other, actively."

"I'm fine managing on my own. Honestly."

Susan looks up then. "And that's fine. It's okay to want to try manage it yourself in your own way. But you're also suffering. Alone. And yet you went through a greater ordeal than the rest of us involved in that kidnapping."

Yuuki shifts his feet. *But it's my fault it all happened, so that's to be expected.*

"Can we help, in any way?"

That's what she came over to ask…

"I know, 'it's okay to ask for help'," Yuuki mutters. "That doesn't mean I need to. Not right now."

"Regardless, I'm offering it," Susan says firmly. "*We're* offering it."

"I can't im-…impose on your family." *I've already done so enough.*

"You're not imposing on us, I promise."

Give it a while of your offering to be supportive of me and that might change.

Susan leans back against the edge of the counter, thoughtful. She crosses her arms over her chest and tilts her head. "What are you doing for New Years'?"

"I don't know," Yuuki says. He yawns again. "Working, if I'm able to. Napping, when I'm not. Lee's away until a week after New Years', so I'll probably just flop around and do nothing. What about you?"

His attempt at redirecting the conversation doesn't go unnoticed. Susan takes it in stride, and answers his question rebound, "We're just going to do nothing together. Might go for some walks or whatever, but for us it's kinda just another day. We used to have family friends who lived nearby who were used to go visit and hang out with, but they since moved to New Zealand." She pauses. "Would you like to come over and stay with us for a night or two? While Lee's away."

Yuuki blinks. "Why…?"

"You're alone this weekend, aren't you?"

Yuuki looks at her. His lip twitches involuntarily. Nervously, with how easily she can pick up on things. He instinctively goes to decline, but then hesitates. There's a difference between the solitude and the time to himself that he likes and being alone in a building for a few days involuntarily reminiscing of a trauma involving being stuck in a building by himself for a few days.

I can go out for a walk if I feel trapped, he thinks. But at the end of that walk, he'll just come back here. Or he'll wear himself out avoiding triggers outside and possibly end up fainting out on the street because of exhaustion. Either way, he'll only end up back here, subjected to whatever recollection of trauma his brain and body throws at him.

Finally, Yuuki resigns. "I'll think about it."

Susan nods. She looks relieved. "Alright," she says, standing up straighter. "Well, I'll leave you to napping. Unless you happen to want to come over for a bit even today – if you want some company. You don't have work?"

Yuuki goes to shake his head then thinks better of it, what with the dizziness. "Called off sick," he admits. "Not feeling that well. But I don't want to bother you guys with me being there like this."

"We don't mind, Yuuki. Honestly. You're family to us, too, you know. We like having you around."

"Even when I'm like this?"

"Even when you're like that."

Yuuki is too tired to protest, or make up more excuses. Susan is offering, and Yuuki's at the stage where he could do with some company, even if just for a little while. He weighs up between the prospect of staying at home versus taking Susan up on her offer.

Considering that she came over especially to see if I'm okay, and is offering to have me over in spite of knowing that I'm in such a state like this...

"Okay," Yuuki replies. "If that's alright."

After Yuuki's collected what leaving-the-house items he needs, Susan drives them across Two Lakes district to the Harrisons' house.

On the drive there, Susan asks about work, and Yuuki confesses how Mitchell sent him home the other day after the mistake he made. After he describes it more, Susan glances over at him with a discerning look.

"Sounds like your reaction was an exaggerated startle reflex."

Yuuki blinks. "There's a name for something like that?"

"It happens as a trauma reaction."

Oh. That's why she knows about it. Because of her field first response training.

There's other things, too, which she'd probably class as a trauma reaction if he told her. Yuuki's silence is an indication that there are these other things. Susan asks about them, and so Yuuki tells her: how it's not strange for Yuuki to feel frustrated at things; that he's confused; and he has outbursts of anger.

413

"But the outbursts of anger aren't a usual thing for me." Yuuki fidgets with his phone case sitting in his lap. "I raised my voice at a kid at work the other day – one who likes to starts a fight every so often during visits to the detention centre's library." Yuuki grunts, shame brewing. "I barely restrained my irritation there, and ended up with a headache from clenching his jaw so hard afterwards."

Susan listens.

"I *am* very much aware that I am stressed. And I know it's unfair if I take it out on them. I know that, and that's why I hate it when it happens. I don't want to take it out on them – on anyone."

"Timothy has that happen with him, too," Susan says quietly. "Sam, as well."

"…oh?"

They stop at traffic lights.

Susan taps her finger on the steering wheel. "At first, I did too. Mine were quite explosive. I kept my stress hidden most of the time, and I think that's what the problem was."

The lights turn green. Susan puts the car in gear and takes off.

"Was it bad?" Yuuki asks as they cross the intersection.

"It felt bad. But I think we all understood each other. And that helped us manage it, and recognise when we were getting randomly angry and frustrated out of nowhere. Being around each other all the time while dealing with things got to us a bit.

"But when Timothy and I went back to work regularly, and Joshua went back to West Coast for second semester at university, it kind of… broke things up for us, though – in a good way. It gave us back personal space, switched us all out of Ninao kidnapping incident time and put us back on the rails we could make sense of, I guess. For a lack of better way to explain it right now."

Yuuki understands it well. "It gave a distraction, I guess."

Susan hums.

They reach the last road before the Harrisons' street. Yuuki watches a small park go by, looking past it at the water of Lake Kano glistening far too brightly in the sun. People are out running and walking their dogs, and cycling with their children on the footpaths around the streets. Yuuki has no energy and thereby zero interest in joining them outside.

"The stress side of things has mostly calmed down for us now," Susan finishes with a sigh. "But I can't imagine what it's been like for you."

Yuuki doesn't know how to respond other than with a grimace.

They pull into the driveway, slowly. After they park, it takes most of Yuuki's willpower to make himself move through the dizziness and unsteadiness to get out of the car. He drops his phone on the gravel ground as he does so.

"Would you like some coffee?"

Yuuki picks his phone up. He stands up too quickly, and his ears ring. "No, thank you," he says tightly. "I shouldn't."

Susan glances at her phone clock. "Oh? Too close to bed time? Or...whatever is applicable for you?"

"Pfft. Bed time is whenever the insomnia allows it."

"Caffeine keeping you up? Alongside the nightmare apprehension, I guess?"

Yuuki huffs. "I haven't had any caffeine in months."

Susan falls silent then. She opens the house and they walk inside. She closes the door behind him with a frown. "That long? I thought you used to enjoy coffee."

"I did, but… someone suggested not having it, thinking it might interfering with my sleep pattern. That it was responsible for my insomnia."

"There's more than caffeine that can keep someone from sleeping – including, but not limited to, trauma."

"Yeah, well…"

"Can I ask who thought it would be a good idea to say that in the wake of your ordeal?"

"…Lee."

Susan's expression is like a hawk's.

"He meant well. I just… I mean he's not wrong, in thinking that caffeine could be contributing to it…"

"But it isn't, is it?"

"…no. Apparently not. But he was concerned I was addicted to it. Since I was showing signs of it."

"Like?"

"Anxiety, sleepnessness, frustration… shakiness… depression-like… whatever. In between, when not having any coffee."

Susan stares at him incredulously. "Does he not realise those can also be symptoms of trauma?"

Yuuki shrugs.

"And have those symptoms abated?"

"…no."

"Well, though it's possible for there to be an overlap between caffeine and trauma symptoms, given what I know about you, I'd say that set of symptoms seems to have been... or, seems to *be*... coming from post-traumatic stress."

Yuuki feels his face heat up. He's so tired, and he's only now realising just how much making himself stop having his one favourite drink has been affecting him emotionally. Susan's hearing him out gets to him, and before Yuuki can stop himself, he finds himself crying.

"How long since you've had any?"

"What?"

"Coffee."

"Uh... two and a half months ago. No, *three* – three and a half."

Susan raises an eyebrow. "Then I think it's safe to say that coffee shouldn't have too significant an impact on your ability to sleep, if you decide you want some. You can always monitor how it interacts with you, and make the call again later if it seems like it's not doing you any good."

Yuuki brushes away some tears with the back of his hand. He sniffs. "...then maybe a coffee would be nice. If that's okay?"

Susan offers him a small – *grim* – smile over her shoulder. There's a spark in her eye that says she wants to elaborate, or say something more, but she simply says, "Of course."

He's fighting back tears at the relief he can feel immediately on his brain as he drinks the good coffee. He loses that fight; tears start coming again anyways.

Susan notices too – how the creases in his forehead ease, and how the muscles in his face in general relax. How he loses some tension in his shoulders. The shadows beneath his eyes, though still dark, seem to become less prominent.

While he slowly makes his way through the coffee, slowly, cradling the cup, savouring the coffee like it's the only thing that's brought him any sort of relief in the last several weeks, Susan remembers the towels in the washing machine. She briefly ducks outside to hang them out on the washing line. In the ten minutes she's gone, Yuuki's finishing the coffee and has sunken down off the couch to sit on the floor. She leaves him to finish it in peace, and revisits the laundry to put on another load of washing.

When she returns, the empty cup is on the floor, and Yuuki is lying half-curled up on the floor, one arm crooked beneath his head as a pillow, asleep.

Susan lets out a huff. "Why are you sleeping of the floor, when the couch is right there?"

Yuuki is able to nap after that coffee. He actually sleeps. Susan finds a lightweight blanket for him and lays it out over him, careful not to disturb. Yuuki doesn't stir. Susan's stomach churns with concern, seeing the weight of his exhaustion crashing down on him like this.

It's sometimes easy to forget that Yuuki is only twenty-five. He makes himself out to be older than he is. But he's only a few years older than her oldest son, and Joshua's only just turned twenty-one this year.

And this trauma doesn't seem to be letting go of him.

Susan grieves for how tormented Yuuki's life has become at twenty-five.

42

Yuuki takes up Susan's offer – the Harrisons' offer – to spend time at their house with them for New Years'. Yuuki can't handle the thought of being alone in an empty house while fireworks get set off all around. It doesn't matter if they do or don't mimic the sound of gunfire – something that might be understood as a trigger of trauma for someone else. What matters is that, if something were to happen and someone were to come to kidnap him again, there would be too much noise and activity around to hear it coming. People might not see him vanish, either.

It might simply be that Yuuki is catastrophising, perhaps. But the anxiety is real, all the same. And that anxiety builds up in his system. But at least if he's with people, and not passing time alone at home trying to distract himself, there's less chance he'll have to be anxious that he's leaving himself open for yet another kidnapping.

Yuuki goes over in the late afternoon, after work. It gives him enough time to get home from his last work shift of the year, have a shower, attempt a nap and then walk over.

419

But the nap only makes him feel worse. And maybe walking wasn't such a good idea, in this heat. The sky is overcast and patchy blue in places, and everything feels bright. He doesn't like wearing sunglasses when he doesn't absolutely have to, and he can't make himself without remembering the tape being stuck on his face in that shed in Ninao. His hat doesn't set him off as much, yet it doesn't do much for the bright daylight.

Yuuki squints against the brightness feeling dizzy and nauseous. Perhaps he should've had more water to drink than just that one cup. He should know that after what happened with the Ninao incident. Or perhaps he ought to have taken the train, if just to lessen the time spent out in this. Maybe he should've slept more, or tried to eat something…

He gets to the Harrisons feeling sick. He knows he's neglecting his health, but he can't bring himself to face it for some reason. Too busy keeping up the façade that he's fine, or at least pretending that he is, to let even himself acknowledge fully – and accept – that he can't go on like this.

But if he stops pretending, he's worried he won't be able to get back up again. That he'll stop being able to function entirely.

In the end, it's his body that gives out on him before his will does.

At the Harrisons' that evening, Yuuki faints.

The fuzziness in his ears is the warning. He's barely walked through the door when the effort of pushing down the expression of not feeling well gets to him. He transfers all his energy into the social energy he thinks is needed to face the Harrisons, and into staying upright and appearing fine, and then his blood pressure drops as soon as he walks out of the bright outside and into the relief of the shade indoors.

Yuuki's vision fills with black fuzzy spots. He feels blood drain from his face and his sense of balance tilt. He braces himself against the wall. He should call out to whoever's home, let them know he's here. But...

Water, I should get water...

He lets his bag of overnight stay belongings drop to the floor. He tries to make it to the kitchen, shakes his head in an effort to keep himself upright. The last thing he manages is his hand reaching for the benchtop in the kitchen, a futile attempt to steady himself, before exhaustion gets the better of him.

Timothy must walk in to find Yuuki collapsed. When Yuuki comes to, Timothy is crouched beside him, deep concern in his voice as he calls his name. Yuuki is lying on the floor. He doesn't remember dropping. He doesn't recall the impact of hitting the floor.

"Yuuki?"

There's a moment where he cannot react, then Yuuki shifts. Yuuki's fingers twitch, and he raises his hand to his head with a groan.

"Yuuki," Timothy repeats. "Are you alright?"

The answer is obviously a "no". Yuuki moves his head and peers over his shoulder to look up at Timothy. He watches Timothy approach without saying anything.

Timothy kneels down and tentatively places a hand on Yuuki's shoulder. "What's wrong?"

Yuuki turns his head and averts his gaze. He grimaces, and tries to pick himself up. His arms tremble, and his balance is off. Uncoordinated, his tilts, falls sideways against Timothy's leg and drops to the floor again.

His ears burn in embarrassment. He tries again, pushing himself up onto his elbows. His arms shake, he feels faint and...

Yuuki sags his weight between his shoulders. He hangs his head in shame. Tries to breathe.

"Hey, easy..." Timothy murmurs. "You're still not feeling all that well?"

"I don't know what's wrong with me," Yuuki whispers hoarsely. He doesn't intend to say those words, but they come out anyways. "I should be doing better by now... not worse..."

"There's no time frame," Timothy says. "Here, I'll help you up. Can you tell me what's wrong?"

Timothy lays on hand on Yuuki's shoulder again, arm extended across his back. He loops his other arm around Yuuki's side, hand ready and braced against his shoulder and chest. Yuuki plants one hand and locks his elbow, this time. His right hand resorts to using Timothy's upper arm as a support. Yuuki is unsteady, and it seems as though his strength will give out at any moment. But slowly, they're able to find some sense of balance. Yuuki gathers his legs beneath himself and, relying heavily on Timothy's steadiness for support, stands.

"There you are," Timothy murmurs. He keeps his hands in contact with Yuuki for support, and in case he loses balance and falls. "Are you alright, though? What happened?"

The way Timothy keeps asking isn't intrusive but instead inviting – allowing more than one opportunity to answer, and waiting openly to hear it.

Yuuki screws his eyes shut, and raises a hand again to his head. He inhales, and lets it out in a controlled manner. "...I'm fine. Just...feeling faint."

Timothy's hands support his balance.

"From lack of sleep. And... from trauma that won't go away." The line of his mouth contorts at the last sentence, and he covers his eyes.

"Apparently trauma can be like that. Can take a while to heal."

"Why does it feel like I'm not healing?"

One of Yuuki's legs gives way, and Timothy doesn't have enough of a hold on him to catch him properly before he does. Timothy lowers him to the floor again. After a moment's hesitation while thinking, Timothy settles with sitting on the floor with Yuuki instead.

Yuuki deflates, sitting cross-legged, back bowed, head bowed, elbows on his knees and head in his hands.

"Hurting can be a part of healing," Timothy says gently. "Albeit a rather unpleasant part."

Yuuki grunts. His lip twitches.

"Or, it can mean, in your case, that you had a much rougher experience that you realise. That it had a greater impact."

Susan comes in, sees the two of them sitting on the floor.

Timothy just grimaces.

Yuuki can't find the words to say anything.

After Timothy quietly tells Susan that Yuuki fainted just a minute or two ago, Susan's aura becomes careful. Susan joins them sitting on the floor.

"Your experience in that shed was something awful for you, Yuuki," Timothy says. "You're allowed to be hurting in the wake of all that."

Yuuki threads his fingers through his hair. "It was three days. It's been nearly seven *months*."

"Yeah, and just because spring has passed and summer is here, doesn't mean that you're not still suffering the chills of winter."

Yuuki looks up at him then, one eyebrow raised.

"Sorry. Philosophical metaphorical what-have-you wasn't intended."

Yuuki's mouth curls in a half-amused grin.

Timothy returns a similar expression.

Susan is eerily quiet. Tense, almost. Until: "I think we might need to consider the possibility that this is PTSD you're dealing with."

The quiet turns to stiff silence. The mild amusement vanishes.

"I haven't been in a warzone," Yuuki mutters. "An intranational one, an international one or even a household one."

"Maybe not a physical warzone, but a psychological, mental, emotional and spiritual one."

Yuuki remembers the experience in the shed. He stills.

"It's genuine post-traumatic stress," Susan says, "and it's lasted for, like you say, months. Over six months. What you're experiencing typically should begin to ease – or gradually become less frequent and or intense – after about one or two."

Yuuki frowns hard. "I'll get better."

"You can. But how you get better depends on the nature of what you're going through."

"Just because I was kidnapped, doesn't mean…" He sighs. "I mean, no one hurt me. Nothing happened. I was just…there. Nothing shocking happened. It shouldn't be enough to screw me over like this."

"The whole thing was the traumatic experience. You were trapped in that shed for three days."

"But nothing happened. Aside from the whole being kidnapped thing."

"That's still something."

"Is it?"

"What you suffered in there was still something. Do I need to describe the condition in which Timothy and Joshua found you? Tied up and – "

"I'd rather you don't."

Susan presses her lips together in a tight line. She grits her teeth. "You see," she says tersely, "that wasn't nothing."

Yuuki stares at her, unable to object.

"You nearly died in there. Could have died in there. A near death experience could be considered traumatic in its own right."

To that, Yuuki can't argue with either.

Susan softens her tone. "Is there a reason why you don't want to consider the possibility?"

"Of what?"

"You know what – having PTSD."

Timothy has been quiet this whole time. He clears his throat now. "It's okay, Yuuki. You can be honest with us. We're not going to think of you any less, whatever the reason."

"You can call it denial or whatever you want, I just...I should be better by now."

"It's okay not to be."

"Is it?"

Susan thinks. "When you and your family moved overseas, were you expected to be able to handle everything? As in, to get used to the different cultural environment, and the new way of living, and the way people around you treated you?"

Yuuki's brow furrows.

"You seem to be expecting yourself to be fine already. To have adapted to post-trauma living already. But when someone's been through something truly traumatic, it changes them. That kind of experience has an impact. For some, it's short term. For others, it's long term. For others still, they may spend a longer time even then trying to heal due to the chronic and or repetitive nature of the trauma. I'm not saying you're the latter. But I'm saying that trauma can have a devastating impact on someone's life, and such experiences aren't something you can just 'get over'. They're not just emotional upsets that simply go away over time. Those experiences have impacts on every aspect of your health – not just mental; physical, emotional, psychological, spiritual, social…

"Trauma, in general, can be recovered from with the right coping strategies and healing, but when your system becomes locked in a state of surviving as a result of it… and you're in that constant state of post-traumatic stress even after leaving that experience you survived…that's PTSD. And examples of trauma that can result in PTSD are things that pose a threat to your life or your psychological well-being."

Yuuki drops one arm and digs the fingers of his hand still on his head into his hair. *The shed did both.*

"So you're saying I have this?" Yuuki already knows the answer.

426

"I'm not a proper psychologist or a psychiatrist, though even those people with such job titles can get things wrong – trust me, I've seen it happen, a lot." She sighs. "But I'm trained in Arkala field medicine, and chose to specialise in first responses to trauma. Trauma doesn't always involve or refer to a physical injury, and part of my training involved learning how to recognise the other signs of traumatic aftermath, and at what stage it can be considered that one's post-traumatic stress may in fact be post-traumatic stress disorder. We had to learn what to do – what it encompasses – if we needed to help someone dealing with such a thing."

Yuuki keeps his gaze trained on his hand.

"You don't have to do things like go see a counsellor or a therapist if you don't want to, or if that doesn't suit you. It doesn't suit everybody, even if does benefit a lot of people."

"But having a formal diagnosis might help you with work, and maybe other things too," Timothy adds.

Susan hums. "That aspect of seeing a psychologist would be good, if we can find someone adequately and appropriately informed enough to give a formal diagnosis. But forcing yourself into therapy that doesn't work for you isn't what healing is about. It's about finding healthy ways to manage your stress and alleviate unnecessary suffering in the meantime. If you find therapy and or medication works for you, that's fine. But if it doesn't…that's okay, too. We can figure out something else."

"And we're here for you," Timothy says quietly. "I mean that. And I don't mean that in some kind of 'this is the sort of thing you say' thing. Wow, doing great with words now, aren't I?" He pauses. "Anyways, what

I mean to say is that…we want to try to be there for you in the ways that matters. We know that you're trying your hardest to cope. To get by. To keep going. To –"

Yuuki interrupts. "You shouldn't be."

"What?"

"You shouldn't… be so concerned for me."

"Just because everyone else left you," Susan says sharply, "or gave up on you halfway, doesn't mean we're keen on doing the same."

Yuuki's throat constricts. He clenches his jaw, tries not to let his mind fully picture the myriad of faces of people that flash through his mind. Lee's frustrated expression and Rachel's over-it exasperation. His own family's unwillingness to try to understand why Yuuki hasn't been able to uphold himself to the same standards of responsibility and duty and social interaction like he used to.

None of them are responsible for my getting better, though. They're not obliged to care. Just as Susan and Timothy shouldn't have to feel such a need to make sure I'm somewhat okay.

Perhaps there's some survivor's guilt there, for the Harrisons. For Timothy, especially. Even so, Yuuki does know that they're earnest in their expressions of wanting to be there for him. Still…he doesn't know how to respond to it or what he should make of it – he's not their family, after all. One of the last things Yuuki wants is to make them have a share of his trauma aftermath when *he's* the reason they had to experience the trauma of what happened in Ninao in the first place.

Timothy reaches over and gently places his hand on Yuuki's shoulder again. "We don't want you to have to go through this alone."

When Yuuki doesn't move away from it, Susan leans forward to mirror Timothy's action. Instead, she follows the action through and hugs him. Timothy adjusts how he's sitting to hug him too.

Tired and stressed, and worn out, Yuuki cries.

It's addressed that Yuuki hasn't eaten anything in the past day. He's only had a little water, too, in spite of the heat. He hasn't slept much either, and his body's been stressed. Too stressed. The little water he's able to consume gets thrown up within minutes of drinking it. And when he tries to eat *something*, unwelcome memories slam into him of cloth in his mouth, and any food he'd managed to swallow comes right back up again. Anything he successfully consumes soon only gets purged.

Yuuki's given an IV – Susan manages to negotiate permission with the hospital and is able to get equipment. Susan ducks out to collect it.

"There's an update from Xiùyīng and Jié," Timothy says. "They say that it looks like the Youth Rehabilitation Trust is recovering: they've had their second beneficiary receive financial aid from the Trust – a girl named Vienna."

That name sounds familiar…

Yuuki remarks, "I've met her – Vienna. Her friend was upset that she couldn't also get help from the Trust."

"Also? Then her friend was the first beneficiary? Who was it…someone named Rose?"

"Yeah, I think that was it. Rose said was grateful to have received the Trust sponsorship as an option, though." Yuuki shifts to get comfier. "…and I heard you were the judge of her trial. So… thanks, on behalf of her… for giving her a chance."

Timothy's expression is a humble one. "I'd propose it as an option more frequently if the Trust was more established with greater funds. But I know that there's a limited capacity for what we can currently do, especially with a trust fund not even a year old yet.

"It's building, though," Timothy says. "Xiùyīng mentioned last I spoke to her that, over the last couple of weeks or so now, they've had some new donors pledge contributions."

Yuuki is surprised. After what happened with the Ninao kidnapping, he wouldn't have thought be any people wanting to risk attaching their own names to the Youth Rehabilitation Trust.

Susan arrives back with the IV. She takes a while to set it up, and Yuuki is torn between apologising repeatedly and thanking her – thanking both of them. But they don't seem bothered by him, nor the number of times he apologises. Timothy keeps Yuuki company with idle chatter, and stays with him in the lounge to watch the start of a New Year's concert in central Arkala on TV. Susan joins them, and Yuuki's able to distract himself from the guilt plaguing him about how much it feels like he's already given up on the Trust.

It hurts worse than the IV being inserted.

Later, Sam comes home. Yuuki has been dozing off, but notices that she looks upset. It's not until Joshua comes home, too, alone, that Yuuki realises that the Harrison's old dog is missing. Not in the house, or outside, and she apparently hadn't been out on a walk or with Sam or Joshua visiting friends either.

Oh. She... Susan notices Yuuki noticing and tells him, "Ah, I forgot to tell you. Ginger passed away just before Christmas."

The last time Yuuki was here, he'd thought she'd simply been out for the day with Sam or Joshua, but...

"I'm sorry. I'm... not intruding, am I?"

Susan offers him a small sad smile. "You're fine. You're welcome here. Just rest."

Yuuki doesn't have the strength to argue.

He falls asleep, feeling better with more people around him.

When he wakes up, it's to another blanket over him, the warm light of lamps around him, and Timothy sitting at the table working.

Not alone, Yuuki reminds himself. *I'm not there....*

This house is not the shed in rural Ninao.

Yuuki takes a deep breath. Blinks slowly as he stares out at the Harrisons' living room. Feels the lines beneath his eyes, mildly aching. It's beginning to sink in now, that what is wrong with him is a reality that isn't likely to go away anytime soon. He might, sooner or later, have to accept that this post-traumatic stress isn't going be as temporary as he'd hoped it to be.

Yuuki swallows the rising lump in his throat. Grief burns, but the pressure on his eyes it brings doesn't bring tears to process it with. Just pain.

That night, 12-Tau turns into 13-Tau. The thirteenth calendar year in which Taularh's reign has continued. Yuuki doesn't see an end to

Taularh's reign anytime soon, and neither does he see any change happening in the youth justice system.

Fireworks are let off at midnight. One lot is particularly loud, presumably close by in the neighbourhood. Others can be heard from other parts of the surrounding areas. Yuuki listens to the first series of bangs, then stands by the living room doors to the outside to watch the rest through the window panes. He stares at them, unfeeling. He's heard of war-zone related PTSD being triggered by fireworks. No matter how Yuuki thinks of it, he can hear the reminiscence of gunfire cracking in each '*paat*' of those explosions; he can't unhear it. The fireworks are loud. Fortunately, they're brief.

Yuuki tiredly sips hot coffee. He exhales slowly. He notices his reflection in the window and resolutely redirects his gaze out at the night sky. He solemnly considers the possibility of PTSD attaching itself to his own life, to his soul. He finishes the coffee, and makes himself another. Timothy and Susan had expressed he could help himself. At the same time as gratefully taking up their offer and accepting their generosity, he still can't help but feel selfish.

As the caffeine settles into his stress-addled brain, however, he knows he needs it. Normally, this would be unhealthy – a lot of people would have such an opinion. Lee surely would. Maybe Yuuki is sinning, and he's not thinking straight, thinking of coffee as some sort of homeopathic medicine. That's the only reason why she suggested he have some before she went to bed, in spite of Yuuki having just received IV intervention. The IV needle isn't in his hand anymore, but the stand remains by the couch in case it's needed again.

Yuuki wonders, as he becomes sleepy again while drinking through the second coffee, what 13-Tau will decide to throw at them. He doesn't want to think it through too hard. For now, he's here at the Harrisons', drinking good coffee in a quiet home, and the fireworks, for now, have stopped.

That night, Yuuki sleeps well into the late hours of the morning.

43

Joshua and Sam go for an evening walk one Sunday as the sun sets and the daylight fades. It's past 8pm, but it's daylight savings times in Arkala, so it's still light.

Sam is frustrated at the lack of closure and how it seems like the PF are doing nothing to alleviate Yuuki and her family's stress. Sam can see her father struggling. No matter how much a façade he and or Susan try to put up as parents, she can tell they're not okay on in the inside. She knows that Joshua can sense it too, even with her brother being away at uni for several months in the latter half of last year.

It makes her wonder if the Ninao kidnapping incident is still bothering him too – more specifically, the lack of resolution of it.

"Hey," Sam says. She waits until they pass a person walking before continuing. "Do you ever wonder if there could've been some *other* reason for why the incident happened?"

Joshua looks at her. "What?"

"I know that everyone is thinking that it's because of the Trust. But they're only suspicions. And it doesn't make sense – coming after you because of the Trust, I mean."

"I don't think I'd call them 'suspicions'," Joshua murmurs, "when it's pretty obvious why it happened."

"Is it, though?"

Joshua doesn't answer straight away. "I'm not sure what you're getting at here, about the Ninao incident…but I get the feeling this isn't something you're suggesting lightly. You've been thinking about something, haven't you?"

Sam's expression is one of narrowed-eyed contemplation. "I'm meaning – … the Trust had nothing wrong with it, right? It was for a good cause. So then, what about it made those people so upset that they thought it would be a good comeback to have a go at Dad and Yuuki? What if they weren't even upset about the Trust specifically, but something else?"

"The thing is, though," Joshua says slowly, "think about the timing of the kidnapping and how everything aligns with them establishing the Trust. What else would it be?"

Sam pulls her hands out of her pockets and lets them swing at her sides. "I don't know. But that's the thing – what if we're focusing too much on what's in front us, on just what all the circumstantial evidence loudly speaks of? What if we're spending too much time looking at that and not questioning what else might've been a cause or reason for the incident?"

Joshua stares ahead, quietly considering Sam's words. "What else would've warranted such an attack, though?"

They pass by Village Park. Sam notices a lone figure sitting on one of the swings. They have their hood up against the cooling air of the evening, but their dark hair peeks out beneath it. She doesn't need to see their face to know who it is.

Joshua notices Sam's gaze fixed on this person and asks, "Someone you know?"

"Yeah," she says. "Kyle. A guy from my school. We have classes together sometimes. Just bio this year, I think, though."

Joshua acknowledges with an, "Ah."

"His dad was in that A'o fire that Dad was looking at again."

"Oh…"

They continue on their way.

"So yeah, what's got you like Dad and that A'o Fire case of his? The one he couldn't seem to let go of?"

Sam allows herself a small laugh. She lets it fade and thinks. "It's just… if they had it out for you because of the Trust," she says quietly, "don't you think they'd have hurt us more? Wouldn't they have attempted to kidnap Dad again, or harm someone else in our family – like me or Mum – or do something more to Yuuki?"

"You don't think they did enough to Yuuki as it is?"

Sam frowns. She remembers walking in on New Years' Eve, expecting to see Yuuki. She hadn't been expecting to see him lying on the couch attached to an IV, looking ill and like he'd been crying at some stage. *Joshua's right. What am I saying…?*

"When're you heading back to West Coast?" Sam asks.

"In a couple of weeks."

Sam nods.

"Your last year at high school now, huh. When's that start for you?"

"Tomorrow, actually."

"How're you feeling about it?"

"I don't know. I kind of wish that the whole Ninao thing of last year had been resolved by now, though. I feel like I'd be feeling better about going back to school tomorrow if it was."

Joshua hums. "I do get what you mean."

"Am I just thinking too much?" Sam mutters.

"About what?"

"Ninao. The kidnapping. I've been so caught up in my little conspiracy theory or whatever."

"I mean, our Dad's a judge who revisits cases if his gut instinct tells him something's up. At least one of us is likely to take after him in that sense."

"Is that a good thing? I feel like I'm overanalysing."

"Not analysing enough can be an issue, too."

Sam nods. "True."

"Just don't expect yourself to solve this one. There might not be anything you *can* solve. It's not that you aren't capable of it, it's that you're not in the position to and don't have the expertise. It's not your responsibility to, either – there are trained professional PF officers and investigators out there, and lawyers and judges and prosecutors, whose job it is to look into these things. If you happen to figure something out, that's cool. But I think we should let the PF handle it."

There's no words Sam can think of to argue with. At least her concerns haven't been outright rejected.

On the way back from their walk, they notice Kyle walking away from the park, slowly. Hood down. Head tilted back slightly. Expression blanked out but aware. Like he's not all there, but...he is. He notices Sam and Joshua heading in his direction and corrects his posture, composes his expression to a neutral alert and continues on his way back home.

Joshua doesn't comment, just glances at Sam with a raised eyebrow. He waits until Kyle is out of hearing range before murmuring, "What's up with him?"

Sam just shrugs. "I don't know," she says. "He's a weird guy. Not in a bad way, he's just...different. Quiet. Often stressed, I think. Prefers alone time."

Joshua watches his direction for a while then lets his attention go.

"What?" Sam asks.

Joshua switches hands for carrying his drink bottle. "...nah, I was just... thinking about how Yuuki used to come across a little that way. Quiet. Reserved. Different from other people around." He nods in Kyle's direction. "I mean, I don't know him, so I can't really tell. But..."

"But?"

Joshua puts his free hand in his pocket. He nods in the direction Kyle left in. "The kind of quiet Yuuki has regressed to… seems a little like that, don't you think? I don't know. Yuuki had been so lively and friendly and upbeat lately, you know, before...all this."

"He's still friendly."

"Well, yeah, but...he hasn't exactly been wanting to be around much anymore. And I don't know, but the way your schoolmate-classmate-person was walking just now...maybe I'm reading into things too much, but he seemed to give off the same vibe. Maybe he has something going on in his life."

"What, are you saying I should talk to him?"

"No, I'm actually…wondering if maybe we need to give Yuuki space. For all our trying to get him to come hang out, maybe he needs alone time to process it. It's different for us: we're an unusually close family, and it helps if we're supporting each other. It might be different for Yuuki, though. Either that, or maybe he doesn't yet have someone he can trust to expose his hurt self to yet. If that makes sense."

Sam hums. "Or maybe he needs someone who understands him better, on a deeper level, if he is going to want to be around people while he processes stuff."

Joshua echoes her hum in agreement. "He's probably still feeling like crap after the whole Trust thing. He tried to do something good for people, and ended up…experiencing something traumatic, twice over if you count this post-traumatic stress its given him, instead. Let's give him time."

How much time do we give Yuuki, though? What if we end up giving him too much time, in fear of giving him too little? And through that, he thinks we've all abandoned him – given up on really caring for his wellbeing?

"Look, I know we'll each have to go back to study soon," Joshua says, "but if you wanted, we could compile what we know about the incident and have a look at it together before I leave?"

Sam raises an eyebrow at him.

"I know I'm not seeming all that interested in investigating the case with you. But to be honest, I'm just as frustrated that there's been no resolution to the case as you are. Seeing Yuuki become unwell like this, after surviving that shed ordeal that we ourselves had to go and pull him from...it...it doesn't sit right with me either. And..." he hesitates, then continues, "even though me and Dad knew going to rescue Yuuki on our own was stupid, we still did it anyways, and we were able to find him and get him to safety because of that. Telling you 'no, don't investigate' would be pretty hypocritical of me."

Sam can't stop the wry grin from creeping on her face. It fades. She sighs. "So what do we do then? What can we do?"

"There's not much we can do, Sam. Not without putting ourselves at risk. But... if we compile everything we have or can get access to that we can think of – the photos and video evidence me and Dad took, and copies of photos, records, statements, etc. – that might help us see some kind of pattern, or... something."

"How long would that take to get everything together, though?"

Joshua grins. "I have a little bit of time left before I'll be heading back to uni."

Unfortunately, Timothy soon discovers their endeavours – through conversation with PFO Marina Tu'u. Joshua's barely just gone back to uni in February when hears about. When he finds out they've been attempting to conduct their own kind of investigation, it sends a chill through him like he hasn't felt in a while.

Timothy is nervous about all the uncertainties and asks them stop before Ninao 2.0 happens. He tells them to leave it to the PF. If they interfere, they'll only get themselves in trouble. They should stay quiet, as they and Marina still haven't acquired any further clues.

He gets her frustration – that Yuuki's not doing well and it feels like no one's doing anything to at least bring him some closure so he can maybe get better from it. Timothy's starting to wonder if it's too late for that now anyways, though. Even if they found out who kidnapped them, and or at least had some official confirmation that the kidnapping happened because of their setting up the Youth Rehabilitation Trust, what healing would it bring Yuuki?

The damage is done. It was done in that shed, and Yuuki's not been okay ever since the dust settled and he began to 'recover' from that experience in the shed.

Was this simply their objective from the start? To make debilitate Yuuki like this?

Maybe Yuuki is right: maybe they only wanted to make Yuuki suffer in some sadistic, mocking way over his idealistic idea of helping incarcerated youth build a better life after prison for themselves. But still, they can only assume – based on circumstantial evidence – that the Ninao Kidnapping happened in reaction to the YRT. As for why there hasn't been any follow-up attack, they can only assume that the perpetrators weren't able to organise one without risking exposing themselves.

As a judge, and having been a lawyer, Timothy understands that many cases aren't able to be concluded. Some are left unanswered, with sufficient evidence not found. He's dealt with a lot of those in his line of work. This might be another one of them. And yet, even as he acknowledges that, a part of him clings on to the idea that the YRT was the reason the kidnapping was instigated. Because, without such an idea, there would be no adequate explanation for what happened.

It scares him – the idea that Sam and Joshua have been pursing, that there might be another reason. That would mean that the June 5, 12-Tau Ninao Kidnapping case isn't over. They've struggled to come to grips with the incident last year as it is. Timothy just wants to be able to put all of it behind them so that they can move on.

As they're realising, though, it's not quite that easy.

That night, Timothy gets a call from Yuuki. He saves his work on the laptop. Susan's destressing reading a book in the living room, so Timothy steps out of the room to answer it.

"Hey, Yuuki. What's up?"

"*…are you busy right now?*"

"I am working on something, but it's not *urgent* urgent. We can talk. What's up?"

Hesitation. Yuuki's voice sounds worn out.

"*I want to end the Trust.*"

44

February, 13-Tau

Rather than terminating the Youth Rehabilitation Trust entirely, Yuuki and Timothy come to the decision and agreement that they'll relinquish what authority they've maintained on it and, the Chens be willing, let Jié and Xiùyīng Chén take over. Yuuki confirms, after a long talk with Timothy on the phone, that this is his final decision.

Yuuki wants no part of it anymore. They can have the management, if they want. Otherwise Yuuki says they might just have to ditch the idea, or find someone else to run it if Timothy wants to discontinue it too.

As Yuuki's finding out, he can't handle that workload right now and he's unsure of when he'll be able to.

In the end, they agree to sign over full management. Until now, Yuuki has retained ownership and rights to amendments. From here, Yuuki is signing over the entire Trust to them in full. Really, it's been theirs since that day in the hospital. But now, Yuuki is relinquishing his part in it.

"You're sure about this?"

Yuuki nods.

"We can arrange it so that you can still come back and take up

443

management of it when you're feeling better."

"No, that won't be necessary."

Yuuki feels bitter. He's grateful for the bitter taste of the coffee in front of him. He made it too strong. It feels like it's sympathising with him, though.

He draws in a breath. "I don't know how long I'm going to be like this. And I just... I don't have it in me to continue it. It's not that I want to give up on it..."

"It's okay, Yuuki. We understand."

Yuuki nods. His throat tightens. He drinks the rest of the coffee before the whole situation threatens to make him cry. If he's going to cry, he'll do so later on when Timothy can't hear it so obvious in his voice.

In the next week, Timothy, Yuuki, Jié and Xiùyīng meet at a café to discuss the Trust. Jié and Xiùyīng have been managing it well, and they're seeing it gain traction slowly. They suspect that potential donors may have been wary of having any input in the immediate wake of the "Ninao incident", but concerns appear to be settling down in regard to that now.

They ask about how Timothy and Yuuki are doing with work. Timothy is quiet, and takes a moment to cast a concerned glance over at Yuuki. Yuuki is silent.

Timothy answers for them, "It's going."

Jié and Xiùyīng don't need them to elaborate to know it's not going as well as it could.

The seemingly undisturbed way they regard Timothy and Yuuki has

Yuuki's on edge anxiety flaring. Why aren't they as nervous about taking on the Trust as they should be? Do they know something? Or are they really just not worried about what danger taking on the Trust in full might bring them?

But then he realises they are concerned, they're just expressing it differently. Expressing themselves differently. There's a tense line in their shoulders, and in spite of their calm composure, the air about them is alert. They know the dangers. But the Trust must mean something to them, the same way that it means something to Yuuki and Timothy. The only difference between them is that Yuuki and Timothy have trauma affecting their lives and their ability to manage the Youth Rehabilitation Trust like they would've normally been able to.

Yuuki distracts himself with sipping slowly away at the espresso in front of him. He's keenly aware how much coffee he seems to be drinking, but it's no more than what some other people have, and Timothy doesn't judge him for it.

In fact, Timothy almost looks relieved.

Jié and Xiùyīng comment about the strangeness and eeriness of some of the things that have happened in Arkala that never resolve – they even mention the A'o Fire, and they look a little nervous and keep their voices down when speaking of it.

Timothy expresses his opinion and frustration about it too, and his relief that someone else shares his opinion.

Yuuki picks on some disjointed vibe between Jié and Xiùyīng at this, like they're wanting to say something but don't know if it's wise to say it. In the end they don't say anything. Yuuki can't be sure he interpreted their reaction right anyways.

Jié says, "My brother is a paramedic who attended the scene. He tried to save some of the firefighters who died in the blaze."

Timothy and Yuuki don't need it explained to them what the outcome was - they all know what happened to the firefighting crew. None of them made it home that night. None of them survived.

Timothy expresses his sympathies.

Jié finishes by thanking Timothy for taking his cases and investigations, and justice in general, seriously. "It matters to people, that there's someone who cares. Even if it might be hard to put so much energy into it… it's sure to make a difference in people's lives, such as with the Trust."

With this, he redirects his gaze to Yuuki, and expresses his thanks to Yuuki too. Xiùyīng inclines her head in agreement.

Yuuki can only manage a twitch of his lips and a half-hearted smile.

Timothy and Yuuki stay sitting at the café for a while. Jié and Xiùyīng leave before them, and the atmosphere that settles in their way feels like a good, yet bittersweet, resolution.

But it's clear it's going to take a while for Yuuki to feel better about the decision he made. Timothy can tell just by looking at him how frayed his nerves must be.

Timothy can't help but notice the way Yuuki keeps tabs on all their surroundings as the café grows steadily busier, though, gaze flitting back and forth across the café, keeping track of every person's movements, his posture stiff and body lined with apprehension.

Yuuki clears his throat. "Has there been any update on the case?"

"Which one? Ninao?"

Yuuki nods.

"Nothing I've heard."

"Still none…"

"At any rate, the lack of evidence suggests that the kidnapping was organised and executed by experienced individuals, for there is no trace of them. This means that there could be some syndicate around in Arkala hiding under the radar. But they leave no trace."

Yuuki frowns hard at that thought. "You don't think something will happen to Xiùyīng and Jié, do you?"

"I'd say if something were to happen to them," Timothy murmurs, "it would have happened already. And I think they're aware of that."

"But sir, don't you think –"

'Sir.' There's a heart-sinking silence that settles in between them.

Yuuki must realise it immediately – the formality his tone and words convey. The distance they imply. The separation of status, and defamiliarising of their friendship. Timothy watches Yuuki gather himself, gather his broken up composure, and awkwardly apologise with a bow – yet another distance implying thing. Yuuki never used to bow to him like that, even if it is a habitualised action he adopted from his time growing up in Japan.

This isn't the first time it's happened, but it's like Yuuki's slipping into readopting the formality more frequently.

"Yuuki, is something wrong?" Timothy asks.

He's genuinely concerned.

Yuuki shakes his head slightly, lips pressed together. He swallows visibly, face pale. "...sorry."

"It's okay, Yuuki."

Timothy knows that Yuuki is unsettled and exhausted, even if he's seen the caffeine numb his anxiety. Timothy offers him a ride back home. Yuuki must be having an internal debate as to what he wants to do, since he doesn't answer straight away. But in the end, Yuuki accepts.

The drive is a quiet one. The classical music on the radio attempts to alleviate the heavy silence. When they pull up the driveway to the house, Yuuki thanks Timothy then gets out of the car wordlessly. Yuuki goes inside with a sad smile.

Timothy reverses down the driveway and out onto the street. He spends the drive home processing a sorrow he cannot name, and wondering but not knowing how to make things easier for Yuuki.

45

Coffee becomes a main stress relief for Yuuki. Sometimes it's the only thing that allows him to sleep at night. Lee reprimands him for it and blames Yuuki's insomnia on that. But Yuuki knows it's not the caffeine keeping him awake, but cortisol. Stress. From flashbacks.

He can't sleep with the light off. Sometimes can't sleep at all, because lying down and closing his eyes simulates being tied up and unable to move on the shed floor. He's sick and tired of the shed being in the back of his mind and in front of his eyes all the time – when he's awake and when he tries to sleep. He gets up and plays a video game or watches a movie to distract himself for as long as it takes to become tired enough for his brain to let him sleep. Coffee at 3am at least helps convince him to try to sleep again, even when that sleep takes its merry time.

It's like there's no off switch. He just can't sleep, even if he tries. Insomnia becomes chronic. Stays.

Just like the post-traumatic stress.

Eventually, Yuuki's denial wears thin.

Yuuki has a bad panic attack at work that renders him unable to do anything. Mitchell is bewildered and sends Yuuki home sick – again.

Timothy excuses himself from paperwork to pick Yuuki up.

Timothy has a trial to attend, so has to leave Yuuki. Yuuki goes home feeling sick processing the panic attack on his own.

It's as the onslaught of the panic ebbs, and as the emotional exhaustion hits – slams into him – in the aftermath, that Yuuki realises that this is something he can't go on denying like this. The way he is, the way he's become.

He taps on Susan's contact information. Yuuki hesitates, remembering how his interaction with Timothy went the last time they met. He wonders what Susan will think of her calling her now. What does she think of him after hearing about that? After a minute of doing nothing but delaying, Yuuki grimaces, shoves the thought aside and taps on the green phone button.

Susan picks up after a few rings. "Yuuki, what's up?"

Yuuki listens to the quiet around him. It's a consoling quiet. The dim light is nice too. Unintrusive, and perhaps sharing the same depressive quality about it in its undertone that Yuuki is feeling right now.

He clears his throat. "…are you free at all this week?"

Susan goes along with him to see a psychiatrist. She's done a pre-evaluation as someone trained in field medicine and first response. That means that she's able to communicate to the psychiatrist here all he needs to know, without Yuuki stumbling over words he's still somewhat unfamiliar with.

That means they don't need to be there that long.

"Yuuki Takahashi?"

Yuuki looks up. His palms are clammy. Since he and Susan are the only ones in the waiting room, he can't pretend the name belongs to someone else.

The psychiatrist approaches with a small folder in her arms. "I am Dr. Aylin Sahin."

Yuuki nods his head politely.

Dr. Sahin looks at Susan. "And you are?""

"A family friend of Yuuki's. Susan Harrison."

"Nice to meet you. I take it you will be accompanying Takahashi today?"

"Yes, if that's alright."

"So long as that's fine with you?" Dr. Sahin asks Yuuki.

Yuuki nods. "I asked her to come with me." *I asked her to take me here, actually, since I don't think I'd have managed to get myself to come by myself.*

Dr. Sahin smiles kindly. "That's cool, then. Alright, my office is this way, if you'll come with me."

As they walk, Yuuki tries to ignore how tense he is. His mind searches for something else to distract himself with as they walk the corridors, and it settles with remembering Susan's odd wording just now.

"A family friend of Yuuki's."

"You mean, I'm a friend of your family?" Yuuki retorts aloud.

Susan takes a moment to realise what he's meaning. She snorts and shrugs. "You're a friend of our family, and your family and our family get along friendly, so either wording works fine."

Yuuki grunts. "You're right, I guess."

They arrive at the end of a long corridor. Yuuki's skin prickles with hypervigilance. He glances at the plaque reading '*Dr. Aylin Şahin*'. It stops him thinking too much about the hallways of the Ninao Law building he walked down before arriving at a room from which he was kidnapped.

"Before we get to it," the psychiatrist says as they enter her office. She closes the door behind them and invites them to take a seat with an open-palm gesture towards the chairs. "Thank you the documents you sent through. They were very helpful."

Yuuki and Susan sit.

"I understand that you're here in relation to the 12-Tau Ninao Kidnapping that happened in June last year. It must be affecting you still."

Yuuki's ears burn in shame. He nods.

Susan watches him carefully, knowing.

"I have another evaluation form for you, if you wouldn't mind filling it out. I'll ask a few questions afterwards, just so we can confirm what it is you appear to be dealing with. Please know that everything is confidential, and no information will be disclosed about you unless we deem there to be a risk to your safety. If we would like to discuss your case as a case study to help with other studies in the field, we will ask for your permission first."

Yuuki tries to pretend that the word 'case' doesn't fail to get to him. First the 'Ninao Kidnapping case", and now this – his own post-trauma issues being called a case as well. He looks at the form, and tries to pretend he doesn't get upset at what some of the questions presume or fail to account for.

"Also, bear in mind, the form in front of you isn't entirely representative of conditions and extents of trauma. It merely serves to give a broader idea of what you might currently be experiencing, and how we might be able to respond to that."

Yuuki relaxes slightly. He fills out the form as quickly as possible in the stiff silence of the room, and hands it back to her. Dr. Sahin reads it, and Susan doesn't pry.

"So…I'd like to ask a few more questions, if that's alright. For starters, I would like to ask if you've any history of other potentially traumatic, or otherwise overwhelming or genuinely distressing, experiences. This could include any deaths in the family, or any time you might've felt that your physical or psychological well-being was in danger."

"Before?" Yuuki asks thickly, "What does that have to do with the kidnapping?"

Dr. Sahin sets her folder on the coffee table between them. "Bad experiences can build upon each other. Trauma can become complex if it is repetitive or prolonged."

Yuuki blinks. "…I…I don't know? I've had overwhelming experiences before, but they're not something that I would call traumatic." *Not anything akin to what the shed experience was like, that's for sure.*

Dr. Sahin pauses – choosing her words, weighing up Yuuki's response. "The reason why I ask is because, if it does indeed seem that the post-traumatic stress you have been coping with appears to be PTSD, then we'll need to consider if there's complex trauma involved. There's more than one kind of post-traumatic stress disorder: there's standard PTSD – which may differ in severity – and there's Complex PTSD, which as the name suggests, is more complex in nature and therefore more difficult to heal. The latter may develop of a series of repeated experiences of trauma. And, well… I have observed how easy it is for misdiagnoses to occur if the full complexity of trauma has not been adequately acknowledged. It's easily overlooked and or dismissed, but in my experience and in my general beliefs, acknowledgement of these things is extremely important."

Something about the way she's talking, Yuuki finds himself releasing the tension in his shoulders that he'd been carrying. Dr. Sahin cares about unacknowledged or inadequately acknowledged things that might be impacting clients' lives. It reminds Yuuki of his own care for the Arkala youth he sees imprisoned at the detention centre, and his feeling frustrated at the lack of regard there is for their psychological emotional wellbeing with the current justice laws. It's why Yuuki wanted to do something about it. It's why Yuuki started the Youth Rehabilitation Trust.

It's why the kidnapping happened, and why I'm here like this.

Yuuki drags himself out of that thinking.

"So, I've read the preliminary diagnosis that your friend Susan Harrison sent," the psychiatrist is saying. "And based on that, as well as your own pre-evaluation, I would say that this is PTSD for you."

The words sink in like a heavy rock in his chest. He zoned back in at the wrong time.

"Sorry," Yuuki murmurs – his hands are sweating – "I zoned out there."

It's an excuse. A plain distraction.

"I would say that this is PTSD," Dr. Sahin repeats. "Although I would like to ask just a few more questions just to confirm it."

Yuuki would be happy just to take the near-confirmed version of the diagnosis and go. Especially when the questions become intrusive. He answers them, as best he can. The psychiatrist recognises the intrusive nature of the questions enough to phrase them carefully and considerately. When it gets to answering questions about suicidal ideation and self harm – symptoms that are a normal part of PTSD, as Susan has already helped him understand – he feels like his safety has been compromised. He trusts that Susan won't turn his confession into ammunition, and he has to trust that Dr. Aylin Sahin sitting in front of him won't do the same.

By the end of the time allotted for them, the diagnosis is made.

Yuuki has Post-Traumatic Stress Disorder, developed it as a result of his experience with the Ninao Kidnapping case. It's not like it wasn't expected. The reason the diagnosis could happen in one session was primarily due to Susan's preliminary evaluation of his condition had already determined this to be what Dr. Sahin has also assessed it to be.

Walking out of the office, Yuuki is shaking. It's only noticeable in his hands, and he tries to hide it. But he's been fidgeting with his phone case since the mention of doing therapy and or taking medication, and he just wants to *leave*. Keep leaving. He can't walk calmly out of the building fast enough.

Dr. Sahin tries one last time to talk about therapy options, but Yuuki isn't listening anymore. Yuuki pays for the session. He'll be able to get it covered by Arkala Accident Services later.

Susan respectfully closes the conversation and helps them leave.

Yuuki's sweaty shirt clings to his back. The air conditioning was on inside, by the fresh air and the breeze is so much better. Even with the bright early afternoon sunlight.

So I have developed PTSD, after all...

He suspected as such – denied as much. Susan already suspected as much also.

Susan says casually as they cross the carpark to her car, "If you change your mind about therapy or counselling or prescription medication – "

"I just wanted confirmation," Yuuki interrupts.

Susan nods. She drops the sentence she'd been saying. "As I said before, it's not for everyone. We respect your decision. But just know that there's nothing wrong with if you do – want to try therapy or medication, that is. If you pick it up and decide right after you want to not – that's cool, too. And at the same time, it's okay if you don't want to have any of that."

Yuuki squints in the reflected sunlight bouncing off the cars. "I don't feel comfortable taking chemically made stuff." Especially after he'd been drugged by whoever kidnapped him, and had that same chloroform soaked rag shoved in his mouth. Yuuki's never really liked taking artificial medicines anyways. "And counselling's never been for me. Therapy... "

Susan waits for him to find words for his sentence.

"I'm not sure about therapy. It's too soon. If I were going to try anything, I'd need some time to think about it. And I'd need to make sure I can afford it financially first."

"Whatever you decide, Yuuki, we respect your decision."

Yuuki doesn't know why, but Susan's non-judgement is freeing.

"In the meantime, that was a pretty intense hour and a half. Wanna go get some caffeine?"

The way she says it is so casual and informal sounding, Yuuki lets out a laugh.

Susan gives a small laugh at that too, though it doesn't reach her eyes. "That stuff's heavy to come to terms with," she says seriously. "Psychologist visits, I mean. Not caffeine. Well, depending on the person, I guess, but you get what I mean."

"You don't have anything else on?"

Susan shakes her head. "I don't have any classes to teach at A'o Uni today, and I can finish preparing for the rest of the week's lectures later on." They reach the car. Susan unlocks it. "I told Sam I'd pick her up from school today – she's got her school's athletics day today, and she volunteered with her friends to help with the packing up, but they won't be finished for another couple of hours yet."

Yuuki, with nothing else to distract his mind with, realises that for all the heavy air he feels like he's bringing along, if Susan offered, then maybe it wouldn't be a bad idea.

"Alright," Yuuki says. He tries to smile. "I think that sounds good."

46

Winter, 13-Tau

By the time 5th June comes around again, Yuuki is changed. What happened a year ago haunts him, still. He can't sleep without fearing he'll wake up in the shed on the other side of it. When he closes his eyes, he sees the attackers rushing in to get him. Or without feeling the restraints around his wrists and ankles, and seeing the walls of the shed closing in on him.

Those are real scenes, in his alert mind; he's not dreaming those.

He still wishes there were some greater meaning to the kidnapping to be had – if just to feel some kind of closure. But there's nothing. Yuuki feels like there should be some kind of answer to have, some explanation to give, but there is none. No matter how he looks at it, there's no other reason there could be: this happened because of the Youth Rehabilitation Trust. There's no answers beyond 'it happened because of the Trust'.

They hear nothing back from Marina besides what she's told Timothy: that there's no new information to update. Kia Ihsayu has said the same.

*

458

As days go on, Yuuki's trauma doesn't abate. He's accepting it now.

He learns how to cope with his anxiety attacks and panic attacks, and what trigger them, and what helps to recover from them. With it, he learns his triggers, and his coping mechanisms. He drinks coffee, and shuts off his mind to what Lee thinks about it.

The emotional stress of learning to live with PTSD gets to Yuuki. Coffee helps Yuuki with stress management – in Susan's opinion, for something like PTSD, it's a valid homeopathic remedy, a readily available one at that, and one that Yuuki ought to allow himself. He does allow himself to have it now. It's the only thing that get him through some days. But it's not a fix-it all thing, and even with the reprieve that coffee gives him, Yuuki finds himself slipping back several steps for every step he tries to take forward.

One gradual thing he notices happening is that he finds himself withdrawing into himself more and more. He spends less time with the Harrisons. When they reach out to him, he answers as best he can. But Yuuki feels guilty for the traumatic event he seems to have brought into their lives, and indebted toward the Harrisons for supporting him and looking out for him during his recovery – and for rescuing him from that shed, in the midst of it all.

Yuuki doesn't deserve them.

Healing. Yuuki feels like that word is unattainable at present. It's too soon. He's still reeling in the aftermath, trying to come to terms with the full extent of damage the kidnapping has done to him.

Yuuki adapts as best as he is able.

Mitchell helps him continue working, but Yuuki's still frustrated with his declined ability to work. He becomes somewhat cynical. He avoids triggers. Fights flashbacks – both the background ones that haunt him in the daytime and night, and the ones that jump out at him from unexpected triggers.

Yuuki wonders if these things would be easier, less intense, less *intrusive,* if the Ninao kidnapping had been resolved? If there had been a proper sense of closure? Yuuki would like to think that it would be, but now that he's learning the nature of post-traumatic stress, he's not sure. He's not sure to what extent it would help, and to what extent it would make him feel any better.

Whether the June 5 Ninao Kidnapping of 12-Tau happened because of the Trust or something else, what they know is that it happened and they survived it. Yuuki only knows that the trauma from the Ninao incident has devastated his life, as well as created a messed up scar in the Harrison family's lives. There's still uncertainty as to exactly why the kidnappers did what they did, what they might be up to now and what other things they might do in the future. But there haven't been any subsequent attacks, at least. They can only hope there are no more.

As for how to live in this aftermath... that's a day by day thing for them to figure out.

With or without closure, this is the aftermath they have to live in.

Epilogue

June 27, 13-Tau
Village Park

Epilogue

I

The night of the 13-Tau Village Park homicide
29ᵗʰ June, 13-Tau

Another night of sitting alone at Village Park. Kyle breathes in the night air, not quite relaxed but not uncomfortable either. It's cold outside, but his jacket is just warm enough to keep him from shivering. It's borderline not thick enough, really, but it'll do. It'll have to do, since it's all he has.

Beyond light pollution of the streetlights, he can see the stars. Not tonight though. It's cloudy tonight.

Why he chooses to come outside on a cloudy winter's night and just sit here like this, a lot people don't understand. His foster family even have a fireplace. But Kyle would rather be alone outside, where the emotional space around him is his. It's lonely, he'll admit, but it's a far more bearable aloneness than what he feels when inside the house. After spending most of the day at school only to return 'home' to that house to a room that was never his…

He'd like to not have to do this, but he feels better doing this than the alternative of staying within those walls. It's easier to contend with his thoughts out here, and whatever mess of emotions his too-keen feelings shove at him.

Five more months.

Not even that. He'll be eighteen in less than four months now. Legally, he can leave the foster system then. He can leave this house he's staying at.

Given that his final year high school exams don't finish until the end of November, though, he'll probably have to stick with them for one additional month. Just so he can focus better on graduating high school, and try to get some reasonably good marks in the exams first. Then he can spend all his energy job searching, and he'll finally be able to leave.

That is, of course, if his foster parents allow him to stay, and he doesn't get kicked out the moment he's eighteen. Not that he'd mind. Even if his foster family said good riddance to him, he's already wanting to leave them anyway. Be it four months away in October, five months away in November, or six or seven months if he factors in the time needed to find a job and a place to stay… regardless of how long it takes, he'll be glad to be gone.

He isn't aware that the day he'll be leaving is actually tonight.

It's just past 7pm when it happens. Kyle hears someone enter the park and pays them no mind. But their footsteps veer in his direction, sounding like they're approaching. Kyle looks then, and sees that it's his schoolmate Daniel Wilson.

Something seems off about his body language. It's stilted. Intentive.

Unnatural. Drunk, almost. He's also skirting around the park, keeping close to the tall wooden fences, but Kyle is in his direct line of sight.

Kyle feels warning take a gripping hold on him.

Something about this feels wrong.

And it shrieks "danger".

Daniel keeps approaching. Kyle stands nervously. He watches Daniel warily, brow creased. The expressionless look on Daniel's face is disturbing.

For a terrifying second, Kyle thinks Daniel's going to try sexually assault him. He's disturbed, scared, sickened. Daniel's beat him up a couple of times before in middle school. Kyle thought the grudge was over. Is his schoolmate really the sort of guy who would just…? And this is a public park, and it's not late in the night. But would anyone stop Daniel if they saw? Or would they walk on by quickly, pretending they saw nothing, and leave Kyle to his fate?

Kyle doesn't react in time. Before he can ask Daniel what he's doing, Daniel grabs him as soon as he reached Kyle. Startled, Kyle lets out a yell. With a grunt, Daniel shoves him down onto the playground wooden bunker and pins him there. Straddles his back to keep him there. Resisting, Kyle writhes and shouts and tries to get free. There's a gloved hand grasping the back of his neck holding him in place, and then the other gloved hand seizes Kyle's and plants the handle of a kitchen knife in it.

There's a knife in Kyle's hand. Daniel keeps a firm hold on Kyle's hand, locking his fingers around the knife hilt.

Kyle's heart beats wildly. "What are you doing?!"

Daniel hisses and forces Kyle's hand – the blade of the knife – closer to Kyle's neck. "What was asked of me."

He struggles, almost wrestles his hand free, but Daniel only slams it back down again. He yanks on Kyle's hand, forcing the knife up towards his neck until the blade brushes his skin.

It's clear now: Daniel's intent isn't to sexually violate him – it's to kill him.

But somewhere amidst the struggling, the blade ends up flipped the other way. Kyle wrestles his hand free long enough to twist his wrist so that the knife isn't pointing at his throat. Daniel still won't release him, and still wants to succeed in whatever mission he's brought upon himself. So Kyle struggles, shouting, fighting, until Daniel slips up, Kyle's arm swings free of Daniel's hold, and the blade stabs into something solid.

Daniel exclaims in surprise, and in pain.

The gloved hand grips Kyle's hand. Daniel laughs, then stills, but doesn't let Kyle go. Kyle's hand is still around the knife. He can feel the vibrations of Daniel's laughter travel through the blade of the knife into his fingers. Kyle twists around in horror.

"You'll be dead for this," Daniel grits out.

He lets go of Kyle's neck. He doesn't let go of Kyle's hand. Daniel stares at the blood dampening his shirt. It's almost too dark to see in the thick shadows his jacket casts over it. Daniel grunts. He pulls out the knife then, with Kyle's hand still on it. Only then does he release Kyle's hand. He stands, then, staggers back and double over, clutching his stomach.

Kyle stays crumpled against the playground bunker. Daniel shouldn't have removed the knife. He'll bleed out. What if he bleeds out like this?

Kyle gets up shakily. His legs feel weak. The knife slips out of his hand to lie on the grass. He should call an ambulance, right? But Daniel just tried to kill him. Should he call the Peace Forces as well? But if he calls the PF, won't they blame him for Daniel's wound and thus pin the accountability for the situation on him? Still, he should call an ambulance, for starters. That much he can do.

As for the police...

Before he can get his himself to move to get his phone out, though shock takes a hold of him. And bone-deep fear. He's scared. Too scared, thinking about what the PF will do with him. He knows how his teachers would react if they caught him in a situation like this. His foster family would think the same too – that Kyle is to blame for this.

He hyperventilates. On the ground in front of him, Daniel is in a state of drunkenness and growing shock. There's blood staining the edges of his fingers. An awful cry leaves Kyle's throat. He wants to sob, but the terror won't let him. Disbelief expresses itself in the form of bewilderingly hysterical laughter.

Sirens sound. It doesn't register for another minute – until the street fills with the flashing of blue and red lights – that it's the police who got here first.

Kyle never called the police.

Fear shoots through him, afresh. He never even called the ambulance.

This only adds to Kyle's panic and confusion. If he didn't call them, and Daniel didn't call them, then someone else did.

And who knows what they told the police on the phone, but Kyle knows what it looks like. He knows what it looks like, and –

Tears won't come. Kyle's throat is gripped with helplessness. They say things, warnings, commands, but Kyle can't get himself to move. In a matter of seconds there's a couple of PF officers with their hands clamped down on his shoulders and arms. He's checked him for weapons, and one Peace Force officer stands saying his rights. Kyle doesn't understand, wishes he doesn't understand, but does. It floods him with equal parts horror and anguish when the police officer gets out handcuffs.

A few metres away, Daniel is reportedly unconscious, bleeding out.

Daniel is dying.

No, I didn't… Kyle tries to say it, but the words are stuck. He can't react. He's being arrested. For assault. As a murder suspect.

The police officer grabs his arms and secures his wrists behind his back. *Behind his back.*

…no, not as a suspect – as a murderer. *The* murderer. If it had yet to be determined if Kyle was the perpetrator or not, his hands would have been cuffed in front of him.

The metal is sharp and cold and tight. Unforgiving. Uncaring, of whether Kyle acted in intent or in self-defence.

There's little to suspect, seeing how Daniel's the one lying injured on the ground and Kyle's the one who was seen standing over him, uninjured, with what's likely a wild look on his face and a witness' interpretation of the scene against him. Kyle tries to raise a hand to his neck, to see if Daniel's knife left a mark when it touched his skin. But he can't try to see, because his hands are bound behind his back. The PF officers don't bother checking him over for injuries to tell him either.

But given they say nothing, it's likely there's no evidence of Kyle's

468

near death experience scratched on the skin of his neck.

Whatever hope Kyle might've had to be believed after trying to explain the situation is gone.

As hands plant themselves on his back and wrap around his upper arm, as he's forced to walk in the direction of the PF car waiting for him... it occurs to him that once he gets in that car, he'll be confined to whatever fate the PF and the justice system decide to put him through.

Kyle feels like he's being strangled. "I didn't mean to hurt him," he cries out. "H-he came towards me, and I....I didn't stab him."

But he did, didn't he? His hand was on the knife when the knife blade pierced Daniel's body. No one sees the scratch left by the same knife on the surface of Kyle's skin just under his jaw, and Kyle's too high on adrenaline to feel it.

The PF officer doesn't break stride. He exchanges a glance with another PFO nearby. "Save your pleading for the judge," he says. "And for whoever ends up being your youth advocate."

The PF car door is opened in front of him. The hands on his back and upper arm stay rooted. Kyle throws a glance back at the scene behind him. The ambulance have arrived now, and there's people gathered around Daniel's still body. Trying to keep him alive.

"Get in."

Kyle tears his gaze away and lets himself be manhandled into the vehicle.

He's taken to a local Peace Force station and thus taken into custody. Kyle's only ever walked past the building. He's never had a reason to go in to the Two Lakes PF station, let alone to be walked towards the holding cells. He's released and then caged within them in there. Left there, to reflect on what he's done, what just happened, and wait until someone calls the proceedings for judgement upon him.

His foster family is contacted. They don't come to see him.

Kyle finds out later that Daniel didn't survive. Daniel died.

And the verdict is, as a result of it, that Kyle killed him.

Kyle can still feel the cold sting of the knife against his own neck. His chest grows tight. He can't stop himself from crying when it starts. He's shaken up emotionally, psychologically, and he –

I'm going to be trialled for murder.

They won't believe him, will they?

The most he'll be 'let off' with is manslaughter.

Kyle feels nauseous.

The peace forces ignore him. Disregard him. Even when Kyle shakes and hyperventilates and has a panic attack and throws up and cries in distress and confusion. He knows, with certainty, that no one will listen to him during the trial either. It's Kyle's word against everyone else's.

He wonders what his father would think, if he were still alive. The thought has Kyle breaking down, in grief, in anguish, in pain.

This isn't how he wanted to leave the foster house.

Kyle's going to end up in prison, and there's going to be no one to care if he never gets out.

Epilogue

II

The day of the 13-Tau Village Park homicide case trial
2nd July, 13-Tau

Timothy arrives home from work. Susan is out. Sam is out – probably round at her friends. Joshua is now back at university in West Coast. Nobody is home, leaving Timothy alone to contemplate the ill mistake he's just made.

"I just…what did I just…?" He speaks out loud since no one is around to hear him. "I muted that kid…what the hell is up with me?"

He called for the physical muting of a defendant in youth court today. Muted them. It's a measure of keeping order in court, as well as a means of safety for both parties involved in the case. Today he used the measure to silence a distressed seventeen year old kid – a kid the same year in school as his own daughter Samantha.

Although how can he allow himself to call it a mistake when he was opposed to doing that stuff but did it anyway?

"Kindall is the same year at school as Samantha, for crying out loud. I wouldn't have done that to her if she'd been defending herself."

Besides that, Kindall had a right to speak – had a right to express his distress regarding the jurisdiction weighed against him. So then, why did Timothy feel so compelled to keep him quiet?

He feels detached from himself in disbelief at his own actions.

Something was up with that trial. Timothy knows that in his gut. And it's not just about his guilt regarding how he dealt with Kindall in the court room.

No, this…

Dare Timothy even *think* it, there's something about Kindall's case that gives off the same vibes as the Ninao Kidnapping case did.

Timothy sits at the table. Gets up. Halts.

But what can he do? Just because this case might be linked to Ninao somehow, doesn't mean that Timothy should get involved. *But I just sentenced a kid the same age as my daughter to two months in solitary confinement for something he insistently pleaded not guilty for. What if getting involved does this more harm than good?*

I'm already involved…

So then…should I call for a retrial? I'd have to come up with a logical reason to do so, though, and if something really is fishy about this whole situation then it'll only risk putting myself and Kindall in further danger.

Could I tell the PF about my concerns…? Timothy immediately scratches that thought. The PF aren't bad, per se, but there was that one PFO standing at the back of the court room who looked like he *wanted* Kindall put away, and for reasons that weren't to do with justice for the case at hand.

Going about an investigation is just too risky. At the end of the day, that's that, and Timothy just has to realise that there's nothing he can do about it. Not without making things worse. The only way he could get away with an investigation is if he conducted one privately, but that's far too expensive, and word would get out.

Besides that, he –…

Timothy stops. The realisation hits him like a shock of cold air. It takes a moment for his brain to catch up.

Yuuki.

Yuuki works as a warden at the A'o Youth Detention Centre.

Kyle Kindall is to be sent there.

But Yuuki hasn't been working on site as much lately, due to his health…which is true, but that frees up time…is it worth asking him?

Most likely, but is it worth asking Yuuki, when Timothy already knows that Yuuki is dealing with far too much stress as it is? There's a reason why Yuuki hasn't been able to work very much lately – several reasons actually, one of the major ones being how the prison environment triggers his PTSD.

Timothy raises his hands to his face, folds them over his nose. Rubs the aching sides of the bridge of his nose where his glasses have been resting all day.

Do I ask Yuuki, or don't I?

Yuuki will say yes. Because of course will. Even though he's not doing anything with the Youth Rehabilitation Trust anymore, doesn't mean he won't see the need to help where he can.

But is it right to ask him? Knowing Yuuki, he'll prioritise the investigation over his own health. So is it right to ask him? To tempt him with such…work opportunity, or whatever kind of thing this ought to be called?

And yet…was it right to sentence that kid to two months in isolation? Is subjecting him to solitary confinement – and just leaving him to the detention centre's care – any different from curating for Kindall the same environment of despair that Yuuki suffered in the shed in rural Ninao?

The cost of asking Yuuki to help him quietly investigate Kindall's case may be that Yuuki's health gets screwed with. On the other hand, the cost of *not* asking Yuuki to help means that Timothy is essentially making the choice to abandon Kyle Kindall and leave him to whatever fate becomes of him.

It sounds like too much like making a choice to leave Yuuki in the shed.

Timothy lets out a stressed sigh and rubs his face.

He can't do this alone. If he's going to try help Kindall – if wants to at least try to mitigate what damage he's already set Kindall up for by giving him the sentence he gave – then…

Yuuki will find out eventually – about Kindall. He'll find out through his work. Even if he didn't meet Kindall in person *at work*, since that would involve being around the solitary confinement wing, Yuuki will still learn of Kindall's presence there through whatever paperwork he's given.

The difference between Yuuki finding out sooner or later, though, is what he – and Timothy – might be able to do about it. Kyle Kindall's livelihood might depend on it, especially if it turns out he was pleading the truth when he was pleading not guilty.

Which brings Timothy back to the original core question at hand: what if Kyle Kindall is not guilty of manslaughter?

Timothy will investigate. But first, he'll ask for Yuuki's help in this. He'll tell Yuuki about the case and then let him decide for himself what he wants to do – if he wants to get involved in this case or not. It might not be much, but it's a start.

Timothy makes himself coffee and returns to his seat at the table in front of his laptop. He opens a blank document, and sets it up with a formal letter template from his work.

He types in the date.

If something really is up with this case, then Timothy needs to be proactive about it. And he'll need to do something about it sooner or later.

Epilogue

III

On the day of Kyle Kindall's trial, Yuuki is having a particularly dark day. The suicidal thoughts, though passive, are strong. Rationally, Yuuki knows that this is a part of what PTSD involves – it's not necessarily his own voice conjuring up these thoughts and these words, but the voice of his trauma…or is it?

His mind keeps casting back to the shed. To vaguely, distantly considering ways he could end his life if this falling backwards doesn't end, or if things only worsen. He can't deal with this version of himself, and the fear of how much else of himself will be taken, lost.

Music isn't a comfort to him today. Neither are his favourite films. There's no song or story that can hug his soul right now. Coffee distracts him and keeps a stronger overwhelm at bay, but it doesn't alleviate the heavy air in his lungs.

If he tries to sleep this off, he'll only nightmare or *remember*.

If he tries to ask someone to be there for him…well, who would he ask? The Harrisons, maybe. But what would he even say, and how could he explain how he's feeling without wearing them out? Besides…what would he even ask? What exactly would he be wanting to ask from them?

Yuuki can't ask them for what it is he really wants. What he probably *needs,* actually, if he's going to manage and navigate living like this. In this new reality. But what he wants…is too selfish. And he knows he can live and manage fine without it. But…

A companion. A close friend.

Someone with whom…he'd want to *live.*

If he confessed this to anyone, they'd probably say he should get himself a girlfriend. But he doesn't want a girlfriend. He doesn't want to date, and besides that, he doubts anyone would want him.

Regardless of romantic or platonic relationship, he's got PTSD issues now, and he's become a person with trauma tissues who freaks out over things people might call silly. There's days he gets scared of shadows and flinches when the wind sends a leaf skating across the footpath abruptly behind him.

There's no way Yuuki would want to bother anyone with himself. It stresses him to do so, and it shames him. These are Yuuki's issues to deal with – his trauma, for which he needs to take responsibility to manage.

Yuuki would rather deal with his issues privately, alone.

Yuuki hasn't heard about the manslaughter incident at Village Park. It's mentioned on the news, but Yuuki doesn't see it. He's learnt not to watch the news or read the newspaper.

Nevertheless, Yuuki does, however, hear about a new intake in A'o Youth Detention Centre. It's in the title of one of the unread emails filling up Yuuki's work email inbox. He doesn't read it.

A couple of days later, he receives a letter from Timothy. Yuuki opens that one. He reads the letter.

It's regarding the case of '*Kindall, K.*'

The Case of Kindall, K.

(Kindall K #1)

When seventeen-year-old Kyle Kindall is imprisoned despite pleading not guilty, the judge - suspecting Kyle may have been poorly represented at the trial - assigns a trusted friend to find more evidence that may support Kyle's story.

But Yuuki Takahashi is already dealing with a lot of stress in his life when Timothy, the judge, approaches him. After an incident rendered him with PTSD a year ago, he's at war with himself as to whether or not he should take on Kindall's case.

However, it's not just his health at stake here; it's Kyle freedom as well. Why would anyone still insist they aren't guilty even when everyone and everything else suggests otherwise?

Yuuki can't help but feel that something isn't right and he's determined to find out why.

Second edition (published May 2019)
ISBN-13 (paperback): 978 0 473 47876 6 | ISBN-13 (hardcover): 978 0 473 63051 5 | ISBN-13 (Kindle): 978 0 473 47877 3
ISBN-13 (ePUB): 978 0 473 56213 7

Read on for a preview – Chapter 1

Chapter 1

What am I getting myself into?

He's still plagued by doubt. In a few hours Yuuki will be voicing his final decision, and though the meeting with Timothy is casual, the subject is far from it.

For the twenty-eighth time that morning, he weighs up the consequences of if he says yes and if he says no to looking into Kyle Kindall's case. Again, Yuuki reassures himself that it's okay to say no to the position; Timothy had written that letter the way he did specifically so that Yuuki won't feel guilty about it if he does.

But the weight behind those words 'won't feel guilty' dawn on him and wrench his heart. He'd stayed up all night thinking about it.

And what if this Kindall guy is innocent, like he says he is? What if the trial really was unfair and he's being kept in prison – in isolation *– for something that wasn't even his fault?*

It's why Yuuki's mind is made up to say 'yes.' No matter the doubt. No matter how much self-preservation urges him to reconsider. He can't bear the idea of denying this young guy a second chance all because Yuuki decided he wasn't worth the time and energy. He can't do that to the kid, guilty or not guilty.

There's a knock on the bathroom door. "Yuuki," his flatmate, Lee, calls. "You all good?"

Yuuki runs some water and splashes his face, trying to make the lines beneath his eyes not so conspicuous. It doesn't have much effect. "Yeah," he mutters into the face towel. "I'll be out in a sec."

"I'm sure you've thought about it a hundred times over," Lee says, "but you know you don't *have* to do this. The trial's already been held. Whether you take up this job or not isn't going to change much."

Yuuki frowns. He tosses the towel onto the bathroom vanity and pulls the sliding door open with a little more force than necessary. "It might," he counters.

Lee doesn't step away from the doorway. "You don't know that, though."

"You're right, I don't. But what I do know is that nothing's going to have a chance at changing unless I give it one."

Reluctantly, Lee takes a step backwards, allowing Yuuki to leave the bathroom. Yuuki tries not to express his frustration but he's not sure if it works. He's too tired for this.

"Yuuki."

"No, don't say it."

Lee's brow creases. "I'm going to say it, whether you like it or not. Think about what you're doing. You have enough going on in your life already. Cut yourself some slack."

There's an uncomfortable burning in Yuuki's chest. It's fierce. It's instinctive. Yuuki's health be damned, this could be Kindall's last second chance. He has to do this – for the sake of this kid's freedom.

"Yuuki."

Continuing to ignore his friend, Yuuki grabs a decent t-shirt from the bedroom and shakes it out in front of him. He shoves his head through the shirt and wrestles it on. Giving the hem a quick tug, he sidles past Lee and heads back into the living room to pack his bag.

"Yuuki," his flatmate murmurs, following him. "I'm worried about you."

"I'm fine. Don't be."

"You're not. You haven't been since Ninao."

Ninao. Yuuki grits his teeth against the wave of fresh emotion overwhelming his mind. No, he will not think about that. *Cell phone. House key. Wallet. Timothy's letter. A pen, just in case I need it for whatever reason.* He will not think about it. *Right, and I need a jersey. Back into the bedroom.*

"Do you think you need to see someone?"

Yuuki's getting really sick of this. Lee cares, he gets it, but it's really starting to get on his nerves and he doesn't know why. Maybe it's because Ninao happened a year ago and all Yuuki wants to do with the memory is forget it.

If only that were possible…

"I am seeing someone," he retorts. "His name is Timothy Harrison."

Lee gives up. "Fine. Fine. Just…take care of yourself."

This isn't an argument Lee's able to win and he knows it, but Yuuki feels no triumph in the matter. If anything, his friend's silence only makes the relentless pain in his heart bitterer. Ever since Ninao, their friendship has been strained. Yuuki blames himself for that: if he was able to get a better handle on his PTSD, maybe they wouldn't be fighting so often these days.

Yuuki decides on his thicker jacket since it's only just gone sunrise. He also takes his warden uniform, carefully folding it up and putting it in his satchel. Timothy often decides things spontaneously; so it's better to go prepared.

Neither Lee nor Yuuki say anything for the next half hour. Yuuki eats breakfast and finishes making himself presentable while Lee absent-mindedly reads through teaching material on his tablet. It's close to eight o'clock when Yuuki slips his satchel strap over one shoulder and heads to the door to put on his shoes.

"I'm off to meet Timothy," he says, even though Lee already knows where he's going.

"I'm going to my mate's place tonight. I'll be home late."

Yuuki nods. "'kay. I'll, uh… I'll see you later, then," he says, opening the door.

Lee answers with a wave of his hand and a forced smile. Yuuki ducks in his head in goodbye and shuts the door behind him.

It's an hour's train ride into the city and from there a fifteen minute walk to where he's meeting Timothy. Yuuki gets off a couple of stations early.

The fifteen minute walk turns into one that takes forty minutes. Buying a coffee at a nearby vendor, he spends those forty minutes thinking and attempting to walk off the anxiety swimming in his gut. The air is crisp, but due to the overnight rain they had, it's thankfully not freezing. The warmth seeping through cup is nonetheless comforting.

Yuuki thinks about what Kindall will be like. He wonders if he'll be one of the more difficult ones. He wonders if his PTSD will get in the way of talking to him, maybe even make things worse – for himself, not so much Kindall. Maybe for both of them.

By the time he reaches halfway, he's consumed half the coffee and he's not so stressed, but Yuuki can't shake off the anxiousness. Belatedly, he realises it has more to do with the area in which he's walking than any thoughts regarding his potential involvement in the case: the streets are narrow and the second-story housing throws the pavement in shadow; it's not a dodgy area of the city, but there's lots of corners and shortcuts where dodgy people could be hiding; and then there's the way his footsteps echo in the quiet of a winter's Sunday morning, echoing, echoing and sounding like someone else's footsteps coming up behind him.

Yuuki grimaces and walks a little faster. Being vigilant and situationally aware is one thing; being hypervigilant because you're still on edge about something that happened a year ago is another.

"Do you think you need to see someone?"

Maybe he does, but he doesn't want to. Yuuki's never been good with talking about himself so he has no idea how he'd go about it. He doesn't understand his issues well enough to be able talk about them anyway, so he reasons that even if he did go to see a counsellor or a psychiatrist, he'd have too much trouble trying to describe what he was going through for such sessions to be of any use.

Timothy is the only person he trusts enough to be able to talk about it. Yuuki knows what Timothy's about and Timothy knows what Yuuki's about, all without him having to verbally explain himself. Part of that's because Timothy was directly affected by what happened at Ninao, and involved in more ways than one. Though they haven't been friends for long, they trust each other completely.

It occurs to him that Kindall probably doesn't have anyone like that in his life. If Yuuki's conclusion is correct, then the only person who spoke on Kindall's behalf at the trial was his youth advocate. No one else did. If the kid had any other support, they weren't present. Even his foster family spoke strongly against him.

Something about that doesn't sit right with him. There seems to be a strong bias in the words used to describe Kindall, all giving the connotation that the kid is some sort of hot-headed mess. Who's to say the people describing him are even reliable sources in the first place? Who's to say Kindall's behaviour wasn't misinterpreted or provoked to begin with?

Thinking about that, he understands why Timothy called him up about this case now. Yuuki's no judge, but he's had plenty of experience dealing with misinterpretation issues such as these. He's been a warden long enough – even if what he mostly does now is paperwork – to know it's more than an occasional problem.

It didn't escape Yuuki's attention last night, though, that the word 'isolation' was listed as Kindall's form of imprisonment. Isolation. Solitary confinement. Kept in a locked room, just himself and his shadow. It might be a concerning punishment for someone who might not even deserve it and it might be something that Yuuki hates to think of someone possibly not guilty being subjected to, but he has to be careful how much he lets himself get involved in this investigation.

Yuuki knows what Lee's warning is about. What happened at Ninao still haunts Yuuki, and the setting of an isolation cell might end up being too much. While that's true, where Yuuki had people looking out for him, searching for him and fighting for a way to get him back, Kindall has no one. Not now, not when the incident at the park happened and seemingly not even before.

Yuuki hadn't been alone when he was kidnapped. Timothy had with him, helping him finish setting up the Youth Rehabilitation Trust fund. He was there when Yuuki had been abducted from the Ninao office, and he would've been kidnapped himself had it not been for his son Joshua's quick action.

The unidentified pro-Taularh people had taken Yuuki to a shed and left him there to die.

Of all people to have an idea of how Ninao impacted him, it would be Timothy, and Timothy wouldn't suggest working on reviewing this case with him if he thought that it might prove to be too triggering. Yuuki trusts Timothy's judgement, and that alone is enough for Yuuki to be convinced and assured that Kyle Kindall's case deserves to be looked again.

Timothy and Joshua had rescued Yuuki. If Kindall's innocent like he says he is, then Yuuki hopes that he'll be able for Kindall what Timothy and Joshua had been for him.

Ten o'clock rolls around fast. Yuuki only has to wait five minutes before Timothy's car pulls into the carpark. They order and find a spot in one of the corners where they can talk in relative privacy.

"Alright," Timothy says, hands clasped where they rest on the table. "Before you give me your answer, I want to make sure you know what you're dealing with. You're already a warden, so it's not as though you haven't interacted with any of the kids before, but to Kindall I'm going to need you to be a counsellor and possibly a mentor to him also." He pauses, watching Yuuki's reaction carefully. "Are you prepared for that?"

Yuuki breathes out slowly and leans back in his seat. "If I'm to be honest, I…I'm not sure. I don't know if it's something that can really be prepared for, I guess. But my answer is yes, regardless. I want to give him a chance."

"I figured you'd say 'yes'." Timothy says, mouth quirking. "Just know that you aren't alone in this, okay? If it gets too much, there's no shame in pulling back."

"Thank you. I appreciate it. I just…I feel like this is something I must do, you know? If Kindall really is innocent, then I'd hate to think what two *months* of isolation is going to do to him – on top of being accused of taking someone's life."

"You're kind to a fault, aren't you? But, Yuuki, if things don't work out with Kindall, don't beat yourself up over it, okay? Or at least try not to."

Yuuki smiles. "You know me too well."

They break off conversation when the waitress brings over their coffee. Timothy acknowledges her with a thanks as she steps back and walks away. He takes a moment to sip his coffee and gather his thoughts while Yuuki waits for his own to cool.

"Have you got any questions?" Timothy asks eventually.

"I do. When will I be meeting Kindall?"

"Today."

Yuuki opens his mouth to automatically say he can't but Timothy only grins.

"No need to worry. I sent Mitchell the contract details before I sent you the letter with the case details on it. He said you're all good to start work after you've met with Kindall."

"Good thing I brought my uniform, then," Yuuki murmurs. "Mitchell's not worried about how it's going to affect my hours? I'm surprised he hasn't just replaced me, for all the days I've had to take off."

"He's reworking your schedule." Timothy crosses his arms over his chest. "You probably won't be doing your usual work while working on this, at least not to begin with, but Mitchell still wants you around. I know work's been hard for you since…since Ninao, but you're an invaluable member of the team, Yuuki. Since the change in legislation, there's not many who would be willing to give out second chances. It's going to take every person we have to keep fighting for fair justice."

Since Taularh took over the Arkala kingdom, the rules became stricter and the punishments harsher. One chance is all most people get. If a person is wrongfully convicted, the compensation is minimal. While it isn't anywhere near as bad as medieval penalties were, it's still a far cry from King Fahlu's ideals. There's no way King Fahlu would have allowed a seventeen-year-old to receive a punishment of two months in isolation for something he may not have even done.

Timothy unzips a jersey pocket and pulls out a folded piece of paper.

He puts it down in the centre of the table and smooths it out. It's a photograph.

"Here," Timothy says, sliding the photo closer to Yuuki. "This is Kindall."

Yuuki spends a minute familiarising himself with the teenager's appearance. His features suggest he's of Arkala'ana ethnicity, or at least partly. The contrast between dark brown hair and too pale skin is concerning – that and the purple-tinted shadows in the corners of his eyes. There's no hint of malice in his expression.

In fact, the longer Yuuki looks, there's no hint of anything in his expression. He looks...empty. It's like getting arrested destroyed the last sliver of hope he had left and after that he just...gave up on life.

The coffee's cooled enough for Yuuki to drink. He savours the bitter aftertaste as he mentally prepared himself for the challenge that lies ahead. His heart hurts for a person he's never even met before.

"You personally believe he was telling the truth when he said he wasn't guilty?" he asks Timothy.

Timothy raises an eyebrow. "You know that I'm not allowed to say. What I can say, though, is that I believe he was poorly represented and it basically came down to his word against everyone else's. There was sufficient evidence to suggest he may have been guilty, but none to suggest he wasn't. What I want to know is if there actually *was*, and if so, for what reason it wasn't presented at Kindall's trial."

Yuuki nods. Timothy may not have articulated which side of the fence he's on, but Yuuki can hear it in his tone. It's also clear in his actions of asking for another perspective on the matter.

"I will do my best, sir," Yuuki says firmly.

Finishing the last of his coffee, Timothy smiles and shakes his head. "No need to be formal here, Yuuki. Now, you said you brought your uniform along with you? Finish your coffee, go change and then we'll head over so you can meet the one at the centre of all this."

Since the Ninao incident, Yuuki hasn't been in his warden uniform often. The royal blue seems duller than he remembers, the material lighter, and when he shrugs off his jacket on entering the heat pump warmed building, it makes him feel more vulnerable than it should.

He and Timothy wait in the meeting room as requested, Timothy standing off to the side and Yuuki sitting at a table with a vacant seat opposite him. He's nervous now. Though he studied the photograph in the car on the ride here, Yuuki knows it'll be much different meeting Kindall in person.

Yuuki's anxiousness builds again. He hasn't really been involved in anything outside paperwork for over a year now. What if his interacting skills aren't up to scratch? What if he ruins all of Kindall's chances of a retrial because of his own incompetence? What happens if Kindall says something that triggers Yuuki's PTSD, and though he wants to keep helping Timothy, he can't because his head's such a *mess* –

"Yuuki."

Timothy's watching him stress himself out from where he's leaning against the wall. He's smiling softly, though there's a crease in his brow. He's about to say something when then the door opens.

Yuuki's nervousness dissolves into concern at the sight of the youth.

THE CASE OF KINDALL, K.

Kindall shuffles in, eyes downcast, shoulders slouched. His wrists are hand-cuffed in front of him, secured to a belly chain wrapped around his waist. The orange prison uniform makes him look ill. The shadows beneath his eyes are like bruises. His expression is blank.

"Take a seat," Mitchell orders, guiding him to the chair opposite Yuuki.

Kindall sits. He leans heavily against the back of the chair.

"This is Officer Yuuki Takahashi," Mitchell says gruffly. "He's here to help. All goes well, your time of imprisonment may be reduced a few weeks or you might even be offered a retrial. If that's going to happen though, you're going to have to cooperate. Understood?"

Yuuki hopes the boy will look up so they can make eye contact, but he doesn't. He just…sits. It's like he doesn't have the energy to function properly anymore. Yuuki tries to recall how many days it's been since the trial and his stomach starts churning.

Hasn't it only been a few days?

Unfortunately, Mitchell interprets the behaviour as flat-out disrespecting a warden. He gives him a sharp nudge in the shoulder.

"Answer me, Kindall."

The teen's throat moves as he swallows. He murmurs something, but it's too low to hear.

"Kindall!"

"Yes, sir," Kindall says, louder this time but voice still husky.

Yuuki studies him carefully. Kindall's eyes are void of emotion. His body language is that of someone defeated, of someone who's given up. Someone who's been given up on.

But not by everyone. Yuuki takes a deep breath and asks, "Name's Kyle, right?"

The question is met with silence. Yuuki's afraid Mitchell's going to reprimand him again when Kindall replies with a small nod. Yuuki lets out a relieved breath.

"My name's Yuuki Takahashi," he says. "I'm a warden here…well, off and on, these days. I've read about your trial and I've heard that you may not have had as fair a trial as you should have. I want to help change that."

Kyle's eyes flick to where Timothy stands at the side of the room. He glances up at Yuuki briefly before dropping his gaze to hands. His voice is barely a whisper. "Why?" he asks.

Yuuki opens his mouth to reply but the words catch in his throat. *'Because I want to help'* isn't going to be very convincing to someone who's in his position. He's probably heard it a hundred times over only for the same people who said it to give up on him. Yuuki pauses for a few seconds to think, aware of the silence stretching out longer.

"Because I believe in second chances," he says. "May I ask you something?"

He waits for a response. Kyle shrugs.

"It's recorded that you pleaded not guilty. Do you still stand by that, Kyle?"

Kyle's gaze hardens then. His brow furrows and his frown deepens into a scowl. He closes his eyes, nostrils flaring. "What does it matter?" he mutters. "It doesn't matter what I say. If they say I'm guilty, then fine, I'm guilty."

"But are you?"

Yuuki fights the urge to lean forward. The action might be an inquiring one, but it's also one that'll impose on Kyle's space. Maybe if Mitchell weren't standing at Kyle's back he would because he wants Kyle to look at him.

Kyle does look at him. The intensity of his glare is scolding and painful all at once.

"I'm not asking you to tell me what you think everyone else thinks," Yuuki says. "I'm asking you what you think."

The heat dies in Kyle's eyes, leaving only a deep-seated loneliness and an anger born from injustice. At least, that's what Yuuki makes of that expression. He knows other people see it differently, but Yuuki's not here to see Kyle in the same light as everyone else.

"What do *you* think?" Kyle asks. There's a challenge to those words.

Yuuki shrugs, forcing himself to hold eye contact. "I don't know. The only information I have on your case is generalised, and I'm glad it is because I want to decide for myself what I think. But you're going to have to help me. There's a number of people who I could ask for their opinion on whether you're guilty or not, but I want to hear your side of the story."

"For all you know, I could be lying. What's my word worth?"

Yuuki feels a small smile tugging at his lips as the challenge redirects itself. "And why would you try to succeed in lying if you knew all the evidence was going to be against you anyways?"

The scowl eases back into a frown. Kyle considers Yuuki warily. *He's fighting himself*, Yuuki realises. *I'm giving him hope, but for all he knows that hope isn't going to last. At this stage, it's still his word against everything else.* It occurs to

Yuuki then that even with his added perspective, it still might not be enough. Judging by the way Kyle doesn't seem to be overly excited about the opportunity, he's already realised this.

We've still got to give it a shot, Yuuki thinks resolutely. "So," he says, leaning forward this time. He extends a hand across the table. "Will you let me help you?"

Mitchell's posture changes slightly, as though he's preparing for Kyle to grab Yuuki's hand and yank him over the table. Yuuki ignores him and remains as he is. He keeps his expression neutral. No fake smiles. No trying to convince the kid he's as honest as he is when he says he wants to help. That's all for Kyle to decide.

For a long moment, Kyle just stares at Yuuki's hand as though waiting for him to withdraw it. But Yuuki waits patiently. Kyle grunts, sits up slowly and awkwardly accepts Yuuki's hands in his hand-cuffed ones. There's a drop in tension in the room.

As they both sit back in their respective seats, Kyle remarks, "I suppose I have nothing left to lose."

Yuuki doesn't understand how much weight those words carry.

"Alright," he says, "Officer Mitchell here is going to sort out a schedule for us to meet a few times during the week, starting from...uh..."

"Starting tomorrow," Mitchell supplies. "Half an hour every three or four days to start off with."

Kyle doesn't react.

Yuuki frowns. "Is half an hour long enough?"

Mitchell grunts. "He's lucky to have even that. The terms of isolation mean no contact."

Kyle's eyes have gone dull and lifeless again. *Talking about him as if he's not in the room. Treating him like he's not deserving of healthy social interaction.* Yuuki forces himself to control his anger. Mitchell's not the one who made these rules – Taularh did. Expressing his anger at how much he resents this kind of punishment is not going to change them.

For now, Yuuki agrees to the terms. Kyle has no choice but to do so.

With the purpose of the meeting achieved, Mitchell takes Kyle by the arm - Yuuki doesn't miss how Kyle flinches - and escorts him back to his cell. Yuuki's gaze lingers long after the door shuts, a sense of helplessness overwhelming him. It's Timothy who stirs first.

"Yuuki?" he asks quietly. "Are you okay?"

It's hard to breathe. Anger turns to a sharp pain behind his eyes, and before Yuuki's able to get a grasp on his emotions, he's crying.

He thinks of Kyle being forced back into isolation this very minute and memories of what happened at Ninao flood his mind. The darkness. The hopelessness. Losing his mind. Minutes stretching into hours that felt like days with nobody coming to rescue him. He thinks of Kyle going through that, accused of something he may not have even been entirely responsible for. He thinks of Kyle having to go through what he did.

Timothy's strong arms wrap around him as he begins to hyperventilate.

"It's okay," Timothy murmurs. "You're okay. Just breathe, Yuuki. You're safe. You're not there anymore." The door opens but he ignores it, continuing to rub Yuuki's back. "We're going to do all we can to help Kindall, okay? We'll do all we can to get him out of there."

Yuuki nods, fighting for control of himself.

"He's going to be fine. Okay? We'll see to it that he is."

If Yuuki wasn't a hundred percent on board before, he is now. Taularh's rules or not, he's going to find a way to make sure that Kyle is out of there as soon as possible – guilty or not guilty.

www.ingramcontent.com/pod-product-compliance
Lightning Source LLC
Chambersburg PA
CBHW022235020726
47496CB00004B/908